Karin Baine lives in Northern Ireland with her husband, two sons and her out-of-control notebook collection. Her mother and her grandmother's vast collection of books inspired her love of reading and her dream of becoming a Mills & Boon author. Now she can tell people she has a *proper* job! You can follow Karin on Twitter, @karinbaine1, or visit her website for the latest news—karinbaine.com.

Louisa Heaton lives on Hayling Island, Hampshire, with her husband, four children and a small zoo. She has worked in various roles in the health industry—most recently four years as a Community First Responder, answering 999 calls. When not writing Louisa enjoys other creative pursuits, including reading, quilting and patchwork—usually instead of the things she *ought* to be doing!

Also by Karin Baine

Reunion with His Surgeon Princess
One Night with Her Italian Doc
The Surgeon and the Princes
The Nurse's Christmas Hero

Also by Louisa Heaton

Risking Her Heart on the Trauma Doc
A Baby to Rescue Their Hearts
Twins for the Neurosurgeon
A GP Worth Staying For

WED FOR THEIR ONE NIGHT BABY

KARIN BAINE

THEIR MARRIAGE MEANT TO BE

LOUISA HEATON

MILLS & BOON

First Published in Great Britain 2022
by Mills & Boon, an imprint of HarperCollins*Publishers* Ltd,
1 London Bridge Street, London, SE1 9GF

www.harpercollins.co.uk

HarperCollins*Publishers*
1st Floor, Watermarque Building,
Ringsend Road, Dublin 4, Ireland

ISBN: 978-0-263-30115-1

01/22

This book is produced from independently certified FSC™ paper
to ensure responsible forest management.
For more information visit www.harpercollins.co.uk/green.

Printed and Bound in Spain using 100% Renewable Electricity
at CPI Black Print, Barcelona

WED FOR THEIR ONE NIGHT BABY

KARIN BAINE

MILLS & BOON

For my Maisie Moo xx

CHAPTER ONE

One of these girls is not like the others... The words sing-songed in Emmy's head as the wedding guests focused on her and her sisters, Lorna and Lisa, at the top table. She knew they were studying the three of them and seeing the physical differences.

The need to deflect their stares was as necessary to her as breathing. A defence mechanism developed from childhood to pre-empt any insults thrown her way, having received many over the years. She had never seemed to fit in anywhere. A legacy of being bounced around the care system at a young age, she supposed. Given up by her parents at the tender age of three and moved between foster homes until she was adopted at five, she remembered too much of it.

It was difficult enough being big sister to identical twins who were not related to her by blood, but she could not have looked more different. They were slim with porcelain skin and long blond hair. She was curvy, with caramel-coloured skin and dark corkscrew curls. A product of a mixed-race partnership, which she unfortunately knew nothing about because she had not had any contact with her birth parents since they had given her up. Thankfully, the Jennings family had adopted her, and she was lucky enough to have David as her big brother who treated her just the same as his two biological sisters. Unfortunately, it also meant being part of the bridal party on display today.

'I've known Dave for pretty much my whole life and, Bryony, you couldn't ask for a better husband.' Sam Goodwin's best man's speech drew a chorus of 'Aws,' along with Emmy's attention. Not only had he been sincere and funny in all the right places, but he looked damn hot in his grey, silk morning suit, and baby pink cravat.

Emmy had harboured a crush on her brother's best friend for as long as she could remember. Even when he had not looked this hot. During their teenage years he would frequently turn up on their doorstep splattered with mud, holding a football under his arm, looking for his mate. To her dismay he had treated her like his little sister too. Someone to tease, someone to confide in when needed and someone he looked out for. Unfortunately, that also meant Emmy being rendered invisible where Sam's love life was concerned.

Nothing romantic had ever happened between them but with a never-ending supply of new girlfriends, he never had reason to look at the chubby, frizzy-haired kid with a crush on him. Emmy wondered who was lined up tonight to occupy his bed as he had not brought a plus one with him to the reception.

'I want to take this chance to say thanks to the beautiful bridesmaids who've been taking excellent care of the bride today. To the beautiful bridesmaids,' he said, lifting his glass to encourage the rest of the guests to repeat the toast. Emmy shifted uncomfortably in her seat as all eyes were directed towards her again.

'Hey! Don't forget about me too,' she shouted from the far end of the table, raising the laughs she was aiming for. Except from Sam, who was trying to burn a hole through her with a pointed look. Clearly unamused by the interruption. Too bad. It was his own fault. He should know her well enough to expect her to open her big gob and spoil the moment when she was under pressure.

She stuck her tongue out at him in another fit of pique, so he would get back to the job at hand. Which he did.

'Anyway, we all wish you good health and happiness, Dave and Bryony.' He lifted his glass again. 'To the bride and groom.'

This time Emmy was happy to join in with the toast. However, she did not miss Sam's glance at her or the shake of his head.

'What?' she mouthed in response and shrugged, feigning innocence.

At least now the dinner and speeches were over Emmy could climb down off this stage and fade back into the crowd. Bryony had likely only included her in the bridal party to save her from sitting on her own. Honestly, she could have done without the spotlight. Not to mention the humiliation of the dresses when she was at least double the size of the other bridesmaids. The strapless pink silk ensembles hugged her sisters' slim bodies beautifully, but Emmy had spent the entire day hoisting hers up, trying to avoid flashing her bountiful assets at the congregation.

The wedding pictures had been mortifying, getting shifted around until the photographer had given up trying to hide her curves between the willowy blondes. As usual, she looked completely out of place next to them.

The chunky five-year-old the Jenningses had taken in had not really changed. For the first few years of her new life, she had had her big brother to adore. Just the two of them playing and sharing adventures and bonding together. Then the miracle twins had been born. The biological baby girls her adoptive parents thought they were too old to conceive.

With their hands full looking after two babies, they had left a lot of Emmy-sitting to David, though he was still a child himself. She was no longer the youngest and Emmy supposed it was around that time she had become the joker in the family. Fooling around for laughs and attention from their parents, believing she had become the unwanted houseguest once the twins arrived. The treats and special outings she had revelled in as the latest addition to the Jennings clan had promptly stopped until she felt like more of a nuisance. As though looking after an adopted mixed-race child was more hassle on top of twin babies.

Still, the Jenningses were her family. The only ones willing to put up with her. Her birth parents had not been so inclined…

'Why did you do that?' The sound of Sam's voice startled her into almost spilling her champagne.

The hotel staff were clearing the tables away to get ready for the evening celebrations and Emmy had taken herself to the bar to avoid any more photographs or attention. She was not in the mood to socialise.

'Why did I do what?' she asked, leaning back against the bar. The best way to survive this night was probably to drink enough to forget she was here on her own and not care what people thought about her. As if there was sufficient alcohol in the world to do that. Constantly worrying about being liked and accepted was the permanent hangover she carried from her unstable early years.

Sam ordered himself a whisky before he answered. He was standing so close to her, that woody aftershave of his was doing strange things to her insides. The scent alone an aphrodisiac she did not need when she was probably the only single thirty-something here. Apart from Sam, who had never looked twice at her.

With his gaze fixed on the bartender, Emmy took the opportunity to study him up close. It had been a while since she had last seen him. They only met at these occasional family get-togethers which he was always invited to, but where he was usually occupied with his female companion of the moment. He had clearly made an effort with his appearance for the occasion. Not that he had to work too hard to get female attention. His usually mussed dark brown hair had been clipped short and the scruff of beard around his full lips shorn away. He looked like the boy next door, except with sexy come-to-bed grey-blue eyes and pretty, long dark lashes. More like the naughty neighbour who would pop round for a roll in bed when your parents were out.

Nope. She still was not over her childhood crush.

'Why did you put yourself down like that?' he asked, tossing back the golden liquor handed over to him. A grimace, then he slammed the empty glass back on the counter. Apparently the responsibility of his role today had been stressful for him too.

'Sorry if I ruined your deeply heartfelt platitudes.'

Emmy washed her sarcasm down with a sip of champagne, the bubbles tickling her throat on the way down. Adding to that fizzing sensation already going on inside her.

Sam gave her his trademark half-smile that perfectly displayed the deep dimple in his cheek. 'You know that's not what I'm talking about.'

'No? I thought you were mad at me for interrupting your sensitive best friend act. I assumed you were advertising for a wedding night sex buddy since you came unattached today.' She was attempting the sassy banter she was known for but there was jealousy at play behind the teasing. Sam appeared to have hooked up with every woman who had ever crossed his path. Except her. It was only natural she should wonder what was wrong with her when it was a question she had been asking herself her whole life.

What was wrong with her that her birth parents gave her away after three years of raising her? That her adoptive parents wanted more children even after taking her on? Why didn't her ex-boyfriends see her as a long-term prospect?

'Ouch!' With a hand clutching his chest, Sam staggered backwards. 'So cynical.'

'Uh-huh. I know you, remember? So, who have you got your eye on?' She glanced around the room. 'Is it the redhead wearing the scrap of ice-blue lace or… the mother of the bride? Do you go for the sexy older woman? Do you even have a type?' Whatever it was, it clearly was not her.

'Believe it or not, Emmy-Lou, I am here for your brother's sake, not my libido.'

She raised an eyebrow, waiting for the punchline.

'Besides, if I brought a woman to a wedding, she might get romantic notions I have no intention of being party to.' Sam caught the attention of the barman and shook his empty glass.

'What is your aversion to commitment, Sam Goodwin? One of these days your looks will fade, and you'll be forced to rely on your personality alone to hook women. I'm not sure that's gonna cut it. You could end up a sad, lonely man.' She sucked a breath in through her teeth, not believing it any more than he would. There had been a steady queue of women waiting for his attention since they were teenagers.

Emmy was not even in the queue. Merely on the sidelines watching as he made his way along it.

'I'm married to the job. You know that.' It was true, he was a dedicated consultant paediatrician, popular with staff and patients alike by all accounts. However, she was sure Sam's father being absent for most of his childhood had something to do with his inability to settle down. Sam had spent a lot of time over at the Jennings house and seemed to live independently from his family at a young age. Emmy supposed he had got too used to it.

'Anyway, you can talk, Emmy-Lou Jennings. Shouldn't you be married with a load of kids by now? Your sisters seem keen to get those rings on their fingers.' He nodded towards the twins and their appropriately handsome, financially stable boyfriends. At least they were taken. If Sam had designs on either of them, she did not think she would have made it through the night without breaking down.

'It's not for want of trying,' she muttered, thankful that Sam was too busy getting a whisky refill to hear her. She sounded pathetic. Desperate. She had never managed to hold down a long-term relationship but not through choice. When she had brought up the subject of a future with her last boyfriend, he had literally laughed in her face.

'No offence, Em, but I'm with you for a good time, not a long time.'

Who would not have taken offence at that? Worse than that, most of her exes had gone on to marry and have children so it was not the idea of settling down they had an issue with, just the idea of doing it with her. She was still getting passed around like an unwanted gift, never finding the right fit. Apparently she was okay to sleep with but not wife material. Whatever that was. Not that she was in any rush to get down the aisle whatever the cost, but it would be nice to have someone in her life she could see herself having a future with. Despite her troubled upbringing, or perhaps because of it, she wanted babies of her own. A family she truly belonged to.

'Maybe I'm married to my job too.' It was an attempt to deflect the sad truth of her love life. As a paediatric nurse she worked equally unsociable hours and could therefore use it as an excuse for still living on her own just as he had.

Sam raised his glass in a toast. 'To the job.'

Emmy clinked what was left of her champagne to it.

'You still haven't answered my question though, Emmy-Lou.'

'Emmy. I don't know why you insist on using that name. It makes me sound eight years old.' Emma-Louise was her given name, but David had always shortened it to Emmy-Lou to tease her. When Sam called her that, it made her feel like his kid sister. No woman wanted that from the man she had had a life-long crush on.

'Stop trying to change the subject, *Emmy*. Why did you make that joke? You're always putting yourself down in front of others.' He spoke as though she was someone to be pitied, making her defences spring up twice as fast.

'Cheap laughs? Your speech was getting kinda soppy and I thought it needed lightening up.'

'You don't fool me. We practically grew up together and I know you always make yourself the butt of your own jokes.'

'Well, it is quite a butt.' She fluttered her eyelashes and patted her ample behind to a roll of Sam's grey-blue eyes.

'Just stop it,' he said, so forcefully and with such authority that Emmy immediately stopped fooling around.

'I only say what everyone else is thinking. It's not an insult if I get in there first.' It was unnerving that he had seen right through her jolly façade to the imposter child who was on the verge of tears at being found out.

'There's no need for it,' he said, much softer now. 'Just because you look different to your sisters, it doesn't make you any less beautiful.'

He reached out and let his fingers brush against her cheek.

Emmy momentarily stopped breathing. Was Sam actually showing an interest in her beyond their usual back and forth banter?

There was no time to analyse what was happening

or how intensely Sam was looking at her as the DJ announced the first dance.

'We should, uh, probably go and…' Uncharacteristically flustered by the interaction, Emmy struggled to find any coherent words. The idea that her long-term unrequited love might actually be reciprocated had totally thrown her off form.

'Yes. I suppose we should.' After setting their glasses down, Sam took her hand and led her towards the dance floor.

In all the years she had known Sam he had never once flirted with her, not even in jest. Perhaps now they were both grown up she was considered fair game and they did not come much gamer than her tonight.

Everyone applauded the newlyweds as they twirled around the floor, wrapped up in each other and the beauty of the moment. Emmy had to swallow the ache of emotion welling in her throat to see her big brother so happy. She had always been grateful to David for accepting her as family even when his real sisters came along and loved him unconditionally. To see him smiling as though he had won life's lottery made her truly happy for him.

'Can we have the rest of the bridal party on the floor, please?' the DJ requested, with David and Bryony beckoning to them.

'Looks like we're up,' Sam said, leading Emmy out to meet them. He slid his hands around her waist, Emmy circled her arms around his neck and they swayed together to the slow beat. Oblivious to the crowd watching, or the other couples who joined them. Her inner teenager's heart was full to bursting as Sam held her close.

'This is a first,' she said with a nervous giggle. 'I don't think we've ever danced together.'

'There are a whole lot of things we've never done together.' Sam's voice was low in her ear, full of innuendo and promise. Emmy had no idea what had brought about this sudden change in their usually platonic relationship, but she was enjoying it. It was the perfect balm to soothe the rawness of her recent break-up. To know she might be wanted and by someone she had fancied ever since those first teenage hormones had kicked in.

'Are you coming on to me, Mr Goodwin?' She clutched at the gold 'Bridesmaid' necklace Bryony had presented her with this morning, in fake horror.

Sam chuckled. 'Would that be such a terrible idea?'

'Probably.' The confirmation made her a tad breathless.

'We've always enjoyed one another's company and we're both single…'

'Why now?' Despite the euphoria there was a niggle of doubt refusing to let her get too carried away by the idea he wanted her.

'I don't know. Right time, right place, and I have a feeling you and I would have a really good time together. On our own.'

Emmy's good mood deflated as quickly as a burst balloon. She dropped her arms from around his neck. 'I see. I'm convenient. You won't have to work too hard with me.'

Tears were burning the backs of her eyes as she refused to let them fall. Sam was just another man who saw her as a good-time girl. Someone to kill time with until a better prospect came along. It hurt more from him because he had known her for most of her life. She guessed that did not mean as much to him as it did to her when he was willing to forget their shared past for the sake of a quick hook-up.

'I think you have the wrong girl,' she said quietly before fleeing the room just as the song ended.

Sam could only watch helplessly as Emmy took off. He did not want to cause a scene and draw attention by calling her or running after her when all eyes were still on the bride and groom. A round of applause accompanied the couple as they left the floor and came to join him.

'Where did Emmy disappear to?' Dave asked on his way towards the bar.

'I, er, think she got a bit emotional. Needed some fresh air.' Sam had played it completely wrong with her and stuffed everything up. Emmy had looked so beautiful tonight he could not stop himself from flirting with her. Forgetting she was not someone he could simply walk away from the next day. Not that he would have wanted to, he was sure. He had always had a soft spot for her when she was so easy to talk to. Unlike the spoiled, superficial girls who had chased after him in high school, only interested in being popular and showing off. Emmy was thoughtful, funny and adorable. Unfortunately, she was also his best friend's little sister and Dave would have pulverised him if he had ever made a move on her. He still might.

Perhaps it was the shot of Scottish courage or seeing her again for the first in a long time that had made him act so recklessly. More than likely it was actually having her in his arms, holding her so close, that had prompted his proposition. Usually the rest of the Jennings clan were in attendance, preventing any private time, but tonight they were all otherwise engaged.

'Can I get you a drink?' Dave slapped him on the back.

'I'm fine, thanks. I should be the one buying drinks to celebrate you being a married man.'

'Don't worry, Bryony's dad is paying,' he said, ordering a bottle of lager.

A few more guests appeared to offer their congratulations, and once Dave's attention was diverted elsewhere, Sam took the opportunity to slip away. He needed to find Emmy and apologise for being so crass. She was more sensitive than she pretended to be and he of all people should have remembered that.

When he had frequently used the Jennings house as an escape, Emmy used to join him and Dave to play board games, cards or listen to music. Sometimes, if Dave was out or busy with something else, he and Emmy would have hung out together anyway. As angst-ridden teens they used to confide in each other. Emmy had had her problems with bullying and being made to feel like an outcast, while he had to deal with his father's frequent absences and the difficulties that left at home. Finding that common ground with someone who understood there were more important issues than having the latest fads or not wearing the right clothes let Sam know he was not alone in the world. It made things a little easier when he had someone who understood life on a deeper emotional level to talk to.

On the outside no one would have known he or Emmy was struggling. She played the clown, often making jokes at her own expense, trying to make friends with everyone. Sam used to put on a façade the same way she did. His reputation as a ladies' man might have been deserved but it hid what was really going on inside him. Having a string of girlfriends was an attempt to make him feel good, so he was never on his own. The way he had often felt with his father gone and his mother pushing him away because he reminded her too much of her two-timing husband.

Anyone who entered into a relationship with Sam knew from the outset he would not commit to anything long term.

The truth was he was afraid of causing anyone the same pain his father had inflicted on him and his mother. At least Sam was honest in telling prospective partners he would not be there for them. Unlike his dad, who had constantly disappointed and hurt the ones he was supposed to love.

Sam knew all that self-deprecating humour of Emmy's was a flimsy cover to protect her soft heart. He had simply forgotten in a moment of lust-filled weakness and now he had to make amends or his conscience would plague him for ever.

The lobby of the hotel was filled with guests chatting and drinking but there was no sign of Emmy among them. She tended to stand out in a room because of her huge personality and warmth which drew people towards her. Yet, with a few misjudged words, he had made her disappear. The last thing he had wanted to do was upset Emmy when he had been so looking forward to seeing her again.

She had always seemed to understand him the way no one else ever had. Perhaps because they both had that same sense of abandonment by their parents and were grateful to the Jennings family for welcoming them in. Unlike the younger members of the Jennings siblings, Emmy had made him feel comfortable there. Of course, he and Dave were close, but his best mate would never understand the worry and fear of not belonging or being loved, the way Emmy did.

He had parents who doted on him. Not a father who used to disappear for months on end leaving his family to fend for themselves. Emmy could relate to that kind of loneliness, but it was not always easy to get her on her own to talk to. It became harder once they had all grown up, moved on to college and gone their separate ways. Only meeting up on occasions such as this. Now he had upset her he might never get to see her again. The thought was too depressing to contemplate. He had to make things right.

Sam headed outside. It was dark now, with a nip in the air. Only the hardiest smokers appeared to have ventured beyond the warmth of the hotel, huddled at the main entrance in a cloud of smoke.

Sam squeezed past and walked away from the giddy guests, sure Emmy would have sought privacy elsewhere. There were plenty of places to hide across the vast country estate now that the night was closing in.

He followed the path away from the hotel, past the gazebo and gardens where the wedding photographs were taken earlier. Even then Emmy had joked that it would look like she had eaten the other bridesmaids if she was forced to stand up front and insisted on hiding away at the back of the group. The twins had happily shown off for the cameras while he and Emmy had messed around in the background, pouting like ducks and generally acting the idiots. Having fun together to hide the embarrassment of being in the spotlight. It had felt like old times, when he had escaped to the Jennings house because things were rocky at home. Emmy had always been there with a laugh and a joke to make things better or a listening ear when he needed one. Spending today with her was what he had needed after another stressful break-up.

Despite being honest with Caroline that he did not want anything serious, she had tried to force him into a 'proper' relationship. Her constant hints about moving in together or wanting to introduce him to her parents had signalled the end for Sam. They had not been together long, but telling her he did not want to see her any more had brought more tears and anger from Caroline than he had expected. Apparently dating any woman over thirty was leading her on if he had no intention of getting married or having babies. Dating at his age was beginning to get messy.

Perhaps that was why he had propositioned Emmy tonight. She had reminded him of the old days, when they had been able to be themselves with one another without things getting complicated. The time they had spent together today larking about had revived those old feelings he had had for her, and he had acted on them this time without thinking about the consequences.

Sam spotted a figure down by the river sitting on the white wrought-iron swing seat and instantly knew it was her.

'Emmy? I'm so sorry for upsetting you,' he said quietly as he approached her.

'It's okay.' She did not look at him, continuing to rock the seat back and forward.

He hopped on beside her, took her chin between his thumb and forefinger and forced her to look at him. Seeing her tears glistening in the moonlight almost broke his heart knowing he had caused them.

'I was an insensitive prat.'

'Yes, you were, but what's new?' Emmy stuck her tongue out in her usual playful fashion but the tear running down her cheek belied her real feelings.

Sam caught it on the back of his finger and wiped it away, wishing he could erase the hurt he had caused her so easily.

'I really am sorry. I wouldn't hurt you for the world, Emmy.'

'It's fine. I'm a big girl. I have a hide like a rhinoceros.'

He put his finger to her lips before she could say anything else derogatory about herself.

'Shh!' He was all too aware of her soft full lips against his finger and it was easy to let his mind wander about what it would be like to kiss them. Not for the first time.

Emmy was watching him with those big brown eyes and waiting for him to let her speak. Except he did not want the talking to ruin things again. Instead, he did what he had wanted to do for as long as he could remember and leaned in. Gently replacing his finger with his readied lips, to taste her, to marry his mouth to hers and express everything she meant to him in a passionate kiss.

Emmy was afraid to breathe in case the fantasy ended. Sam was kissing her and definitely not in any chaste fashion which could be open to misinterpretation. It was blowing her mind to find he might actually be romantically interested in her. The way she had always thought of him. Yet here he was, cupping her face in his hands, kissing her slowly and gently teasing her tongue with his.

Everything in her wanted to believe him when he said this was not a matter of convenience. That he wanted her, only her, in this moment. It was not as though she was expecting him to declare his undying devotion to her and get down on one knee to propose. Was it? Perhaps in her more whimsical fantasies, where they married and lived happily ever after with their chubby little babies.

In reality, all she wanted was for Sam to notice her the way he noticed every other woman. Let her believe for a while that she was not completely hideous. She had dreamed of his touch, this kiss, and it seemed as though the next logical step was to let nature take its course. Why deny herself the pleasure of Sam Goodwin and let paranoia win?

Why should she care what had prompted him to make a move tonight if it was making all of her wildest dreams come true? She would be crazy not to enjoy everything he was offering. This could be her only chance. Next time she saw him he was sure to have hooked up with a new leggy beauty. This was her time. She had skipped to the head of the queue and, rather than feel guilty about those she might have pushed past, she decided to party the rest of the night away.

'Do you want to come back to my room?' It was a bold move from someone who had been sobbing only moments ago because no one wanted to be with her for any meaningful kind of relationship. Now Emmy was willing to put the one she did have with Sam on the line for the sake of one night in his bed.

Exactly the type of move he probably made on a regular basis without his conscience bothering him. Emmy decided it was just what she needed after being dumped again. Rebound sex with someone who was well versed in one-night-stand etiquette would give her confidence a much-needed boost.

'Don't you think we'll be missed?' It was not a 'no,' making Emmy all the more determined to see this through.

'Not for a while. We can always come back down later.' Doing things this way could make it less awkward than having to face each other in the morning. There would be no confusion about what this was. A hook-up. Not even a full night together. No reason for either of them to stress over it at a later date. They were two consenting, single adults looking for a little company.

'You're sure about this?' Sam was giving her another chance to back out if she wanted. One look at him, so handsome in his suit, with the moonlight highlighting the sparkle in his eyes and that sexy dimple in his cheek, and she had never been more sure of anything in her life. For one night only, Sam was going to be hers and she was not going to miss another minute of it.

Even the thought of finally sharing a bed with him made her shiver. Goosebumps popped over her skin as she anticipated his touch.

'I'm sure.'

'Let's get you somewhere warm.' He shrugged off

his jacket and draped it around her shoulders as he led her back towards the hotel.

She practically floated back to her room, half convinced she must be dreaming. Until they were alone in her room and the air between them was sparking with sexual awareness.

After this, there would be no going back. They could never look at each other the same way again. A shame when this shared, hungry-for-one-another exchange was so hot.

Instead, they proceeded, wordless and breathless, to take off one another's clothes. This was the point when Emmy usually insisted on turning out the light, sucking in her tummy and trying her best to be someone else in the dark. Here, with Sam, she did not need to do any of that. He knew exactly who he was dealing with and what he was getting. Besides, she had fantasised about this moment long enough that she wished to see Sam in all of his splendour.

He had already loosened his cravat and was in the process of wrenching his shirt off while she was still trying to unzip her dress.

'Turn around.' The gruff demand was an instant turn-on and she did as she was told.

The heat of his hands scorched the bare skin of her back as he unzipped her. When she was about to step out of her dress, his fingers deftly undid her strapless bra. Emmy's pulse quickened at the intimacy, and when he began to kiss the skin at her neck, she almost went into cardiac arrest. She fought to breathe normally despite her release from the restrictions of her bridesmaid's outfit. It, along with her underwear scaffolding, fell to the floor, leaving her standing in nothing but her panties.

Sam remained behind her, kissing his way along her shoulders, and cupping her breasts in his strong hands. He teased her nipples with his thumbs and forefingers until they were aching with need as much as the rest of her body.

Still, Sam continued the torturous exploration of her body with his hands. Slipping one under the lacy fabric of her remaining underwear to stroke her where she needed him most. She was leaning back against him, relying on his support as he let his fingers ease that ache inside her. Filling her, circling her and driving her to distraction.

Emmy turned her head, searching for his mouth, wanting to feel him everywhere at once. Sam took the cue from her and unbuttoned his trousers, dropping them onto the floor along with his boxers. Of course she looked, and she was not disappointed.

Sam kept in shape—she knew that. He jogged, and he played football, and it showed in every taut, lean muscle. Seeing him turned on looking at her naked body simply made her want him all the more. Before she knew it, he was backing her towards the bed, at the same time kissing and squeezing her tight. They fell down onto the mattress smiling and giggling in between the kisses, gasps and moans.

Emmy wanted to believe that this encounter was the culmination of a lifetime of wanting each other but she was not that naïve. This was just about sex and as long as she remembered that, her heart would survive having Sam for one night, before losing him again.

Primped and preened for her role in the wedding,

this was the best she would ever look. Likely the best she would ever feel, with Sam kissing her all over, and not having to pretend to be anyone other than who she was to get him here. The only person she was trying to fool was herself if she thought having him just once could ever be enough.

CHAPTER TWO

Three months later

EMMY HAD FINISHED typing up her patient's details but took a few minutes to enjoy the luxury of sitting down. She had been on her feet all afternoon and no amount of cushioning in her trainers could ease the aching feet which came as part of the job.

She fished the cereal bar out of her pocket, broke a piece off and shoved it into her mouth.

'Hungry?' Shelley, one of her colleagues, joined her at the nurse's station to collect the information on her next patient.

'Always. I think I'm going to burst out of this uniform soon.' Since hitting puberty, Emmy had always struggled with anything fitted, her bust straining the fabric to breaking point. These days she was sure it was only a matter of time before all the stitches in the seams of her tunic gave way and left her in nothing more than her support underwear.

'You need to stop being in denial about this. It's happening. Give in to the inevitable, get a bigger size and try to be as comfortable as possible.'

'I'm not sure I'm ready to accept it yet.'

'Don't you think it's too late for that? When's your first scan?'

'Next week.' When that wriggling jelly bean appeared on the screen there would be no choice but to acknowledge there was a baby on the way. She was going to be a mother and that meant facing up to all the challenges that would bring.

The huge responsibility of another life was something her own parents had not been truly prepared for. Though Emmy intended to do everything in her power to raise a happy, well-adjusted child, there was that ever-present anxiety that she simply would not measure up. She had always wanted to have that chance to raise a family of her own, the right way. With unconditional love. However, her hopes for the relationship she would have with her child did not take away the fear of getting it wrong.

It was impossible to work in a field like paediatrics and not realise your potential as a caring mother figure, but worry had cancelled out her desire of having children and making up for the wrongs done to her in her early life. Even if she had found Mr Right, Emmy might have let her parents' mistakes overrule that maternal instinct she knew was deep inside her. Perhaps it was better things had turned out the way they had now there was no way back. Whatever happened with Sam, she was having this baby. It could be her last chance to be a mum and it was a blessing, despite the complicated circumstances.

Her hang-ups about parenting and her own upbringing were part of the reason she was yet to share the happy news with the father. She needed to get her head around everything before dealing with Sam's misgivings or issues about having his own children. After all, he had not had the greatest childhood either and chances were he was going to have to work through a lot of personal demons too before accepting his new role.

'Who's going with you?' Shelley perched on the edge of the desk, settling in for the interrogation Emmy knew was coming. Despite being a couple of years younger than her, Shelley acted like a concerned parent at times. If she was not worrying about Emmy getting home safely after a late shift, she was fretting over her getting ripped off by every con man in London apparently waiting for 'soft touches' like her. Emmy put it down to Shelley having grown up in the city and considering herself more streetwise than the country bumpkin working alongside her.

If Shelley had been at David's wedding, she would never have let Emmy sleep with Sam and completely turn her life upside down.

Even if Shelley could not have convinced her it was a bad idea, she would probably have reminded her to be safe and use protection. Emmy's current predicament was entirely her own fault. Carried away in the moment her fantasy had come true, the reality of pregnancy had not seemed possible. Until a few weeks later with the shock of a positive test.

'No one. I don't need anyone. I'm going to be doing this on my own anyway. I may as well get used to it.' It had been her decision entirely to keep the baby. Sam had made it clear he did not want anything more than a tumble in bed with her at the time. A baby together was the opposite of no-strings sex. She had got what she wanted and would have to live with the consequences. It did not seem fair to derail his successful career with a responsibility he never asked for. Most of all, Emmy could not bear the thought of her child growing up knowing it was unwanted by one of its parents. She knew the consequences of living with that stigma and would never inflict it on another innocent child.

Shelley folded her arms and tightened her mouth into a disapproving pout. 'I thought you were going to start telling people. They're going to notice soon anyway. You're pregnant, it's nothing to be ashamed about.'

Except she was. When she had imagined having a family of her own she never expected to do it without a partner who loved her sharing the experience. Emmy had always felt alone but at least there were going to be two of them from this moment forward. She rubbed her hand over her belly, which, these days, was a result of more than her sweet tooth.

Up until now she had let everyone believe she had simply put on a few extra pounds. They would not be noticed on a girl like her. Only, in another month or so, it would be obvious this was more than a cake baby.

'I told those who needed to know.'

'Such as?' Shelley raised an eyebrow, not content to let her skimp on the details.

'You…'

'Because I figured it out for myself. One month you're playing bridesmaid at your brother's wedding and the next you've got your head stuck down the toilet bowl every morning.'

At that stage Emmy really had been in denial, convinced it was food poisoning, a virus or a sudden allergy to chocolate making her ill. It did not seem possible that after years of lusting after Sam she was having his baby. Without ever having the luxury of a relationship with him. The result of a wedding hook-up made it sound more sordid than the experience had actually been. Not that either of them had hung around to cuddle afterwards, and had gone back to the evening reception as though the world had not just rocked beneath them.

'I told management and human resources.' Forced to let them know in case she was put in a position which might have jeopardised the pregnancy. It also meant she could have her appointments and scans without having to make up excuses for her absence.

'What about David? Or the rest of your family? The father?'

Emmy shook her head at all three, waiting for a tut after every denial. 'I'm not ready to have those conversations yet.' If ever. It had crossed her mind about never going home again and raising her baby in secret but that was the fear talking. They might not be blood but the Jenningses were still her family and the time would come when she would need their support. She hoped she would get it. At least the twins were not at the stage of starting families of their own or her baby might have had difficulty getting her parents' attention, the way Emmy had. Competing against her sisters was not something she had anticipated after being adopted but that was what had happened when the twins' needs had seemed to come before her own in the household. She wanted her child to have better. To be accepted and loved equally as anyone else in the family. Again, that worry of things that had happened in the past was preventing her from moving forward.

'Well, you've got six months before you drop the baby bombshell on them so maybe you should start working on your speeches. Beginning with the father. Even if he isn't interested, he has a right to know.' Shelley handed her a notebook and pen before she collected her files and went back onto the wards.

Emmy knew she was right, but she could not bring herself to explode Sam's life just yet. The weight of guilt was pressing hard on her shoulders over the fact she had kept this secret from him for three months, without having to see or hear his disappointment too when she did finally tell him. He did not do commitment, she had known that from the start, but he no longer had a choice or a say in the matter. What was a baby other than a permanent, lifetime commitment he never asked for?

Emmy never wanted to upset Sam's life or trap him into being tied to her for the rest of his days. He was going to hate her for this.

'We'll send you for some X-rays and see what's going on with that arm of yours.' Sam smiled, trying to reassure the young patient that there was nothing to be concerned about. At that age he knew what it was to worry about things beyond your control, unsure of the future.

At nine years old, Sam had been aware something was not right at home. His father worked away all the time, yet they never seemed to have any money. The feeling that all was not as it should be had eaten away at him, but he had been powerless to do anything. He could not even have confided his fears to his mother when she was struggling to keep them afloat. To all intents and purposes a single mum, given how much time his father spent away from home. Life became so utterly unbearable for her, and a distance had emerged between Sam and his mother and he had been forced to grow up quickly. Mature beyond his years when it came to financial and emotional matters and not through choice. Neither of his parents had been there during his formative years, and looking after number one had been a necessity to Sam because no one else had been around to do it for him.

Finding out his father had a second family, and that he had ineffectively split his time between both, had come as a shock to his mother but not to Sam. It explained a lot, even if it did not make the consequences any easier to live with.

'Thanks, Doctor.' Marcus's mum was on her feet before Sam had barely finished his consultation.

The boy did not return Sam's smile. He hardly acknowledged he had spoken. Marcus was a sullen sort of child. Understandable when he was in pain after his fall. Yet the behaviour seemed more fitting for a teenager. Something simply did not feel right about this patient and Sam was expert enough in his field to trust his instincts. Usually.

His recent decision-making might be called questionable by some.

'If you could wait here with Marcus, Mrs Moseley, I'll get someone to take you both down to X-ray.'

The woman plopped back down into the chair by her son's bedside with a frown, looking as though she would rather be anywhere else.

Sam understood hospitals were not everyone's favourite place to be but he did come across some family members who did not always think of their child's wants or needs first. He also knew from personal experience. Treating their illness as an inconvenience rather than being sympathetic to their little ones who clearly needed reassurance and comforting for the duration of their hospital stay unfortunately was not a rare occurrence.

It never failed to irk him. Some parents, including his father, were too selfish to have had children. Never putting them first. That was why he had decided a long time ago family life was not for him. He would not inflict the sort of pain he had endured as a child on anyone else. No matter how unintentionally.

That selfishness was already in him when he devoted his time and energy completely into his work, often letting down partners who thought they deserved more of him too. It would be cruel to risk doing the same to an innocent child. This job often showed him how that turned out and it was not a pleasant scenario he wished to partake in from the other side.

'I hope this isn't going to take long?' Mrs Moseley took her phone from her pocket and began scrolling through her social media feed. No doubt one of those who posted their whereabouts to gain sympathy, he thought uncharitably.

He kept the smile pasted on as long as he could. 'I'll come back later to check in on you.'

Sam was determined to get to the bottom of Marcus's problems and was glad he had agreed to take on this short-term contract after all. He had worried about being too hasty in accepting the post soon after the wedding.

At the time he could not get Emmy out of his mind. They had not even had one full night together so he should have been able to get over her. He had always been fond of her and enjoyed her company but the three-year age difference when they were teenagers made so much more difference then, compared to now. Plus, Dave would have kicked his head in for even thinking of his sister in that way.

Seeing her after such a long time reminded him of how close they had been at one time, and she had looked gorgeous. In and out of the dress.

He shuffled through his notes as he walked down the corridor trying to take his mind elsewhere. Impossible. Especially now. If anything, sharing Emmy's bed had simply increased his desire to be with her. To the extent he had accepted a consultancy placement at the London City Hospital where he knew she worked. Something which now seemed impulsive given they had not spoken since the wedding.

In hindsight he could see that he had acted purely based on his desire to bed her again. Giving no thought to the consequences of turning up here out of the blue or considering if she would even want to see him again. Though, to his mind, their time together had been incredible and something worth repeating.

Emmy might be self-conscious around her sisters, but she was confident in bed and rightly so. Her soft skin and womanly curves were imprinted on his mind and body for ever. Yet, somehow, they had managed to rejoin the wedding reception that night without another word to each other.

He should have told her he would be working at the hospital when he accepted the post, but he hadn't. Convinced they would be in contact at some point where he could slip the information into the conversation. Now he was here, and it was only a matter of time before he ran into her. There was no way of knowing how she would react to his sudden appearance, or what he would do if she did not want him here.

Hell, he did not even know what he had hoped to achieve by coming. They were certainly not going to launch into a relationship and he could not expect Emmy to settle for being his sex buddy. She was worth more than that. The only reason he could come up with for accepting this job was that he simply wanted to see her again. He missed her.

With each step he took into her department, his doubts grew that being here was a good idea. He was no longer sure sleeping together had been one of his smarter decisions when it would change the nature of their relationship for ever.

It was too late to change his mind now. He was invested in his new patient and Emmy was at the end of corridor looking at him…

'Hey!' he shouted, watching her face turn ashen. Then she turned and fled in the opposite direction.

'Emmy! Wait!'

She could hear Sam calling her and knew there would be questions asked about why she was running from him but right now she needed space to breathe.

There was a conversation which needed to be had but Emmy had expected to do that on her own terms. Somewhere other than her workplace. Guilt crashed into her at full force now she was faced with the enormity of the secret she had been keeping from Sam. He had deserved to be told he was going to be a father from the moment she found out. To be involved in the decisions she had undertaken by herself and be a part of the process, but she had taken all of that away from him. Now the truth was going to have to come out on terms other than the ones she had planned. This was an ambush, and it was too late to scrabble back out of it.

Her pace gradually slowed when she realised how bizarre it would look to him to see her running away. Sam would have no idea why his sudden appearance here had sent her into such a panic.

'Emmy?' He called her name again, and she was forced to stop and talk to him. She would never outrun him anyway. Even if she got away from him today, he was so deeply embedded into her family life she could not hide the pregnancy from him for ever.

'Sam? What brings you here?' When Emmy finally faced him, it was with fake surprise.

'Didn't you hear me calling you?' He bounded up beside her and she noticed he was in his smart work attire, not the casual wear a passing visitor would have been sporting.

Her stomach lurched at the implications of that and having to lie straight to his face. 'No. I was in a world of my own. Sorry.'

There was a flicker of uncertainty across his forehead before he smiled. 'No problem. As long as you're not trying to avoid me?'

'Why on earth would I want to do that?' Her laugh was much too loud and high-pitched to be believable but she could not tell him the truth just yet. Not here or now.

'Well, uh, after the wedding, you know…'

It was the first time Emmy had ever seen him look remotely coy. The bloom of pink in his cheeks and the way he was shuffling his feet, unable to stand still, was endearing. He had never struck her as anything but a confident ladies' man. At least, not in adulthood.

Unless he was embarrassed by the whole affair and regretting it had ever happened. That would make things even more complicated, or more clear-cut, if he decided he wanted nothing more to do with her. Since he had not called or texted during the intervening months, she assumed she had her answer. They had agreed that their time together would not be anything other than just sex, even though she had always known it would to her. Even more so now.

Regardless of Sam's ignorance of her feelings and current situation, the facts hardened her resolve not to get all mushy around him again. It would not do her any good.

'I'm a big girl. Don't worry, I think I can control myself around you.'

'That's not what I meant. I don't want things to be awkward between us.'

Like this? she thought.

'Why should they? It was a spur-of-the-moment thing. Over and done with.' Each lie that fell from her lips made her want to hold her stomach in a little more.

'You're my best mate's sister.'

This was not about her or her feelings at all. Sam was merely worried that it might affect his relationship with David. If she had been a bitter person she could easily have ended their friendship by confiding in her big brother about what had happened between them. Luckily for Sam, she cared too much about David to upset him by casting his best man in a very unfavourable light. He would not be pleased to learn that Sam had bedded his kid sister on his wedding night, got her pregnant and hoped they could forget it ever happened. If he knew, he would probably try and force them into a shotgun wedding, making Sam do the honourable thing. Not that Sam was aware of the outcome of their passionate tryst but they had not been as careful as they ought to.

'There's no need to get snarky about it, Emmy. We had a good time together, but I don't want to let what happened between us spoil my relationship with any of the family.'

It might be too late for that particular hope but only time would tell.

'Why are you here, Sam?' It certainly was not for her but she was curious and dismayed as to why he appeared to be working on her territory.

'I've taken up a consultant post. I'll be here a couple of days a week.' He seemed pleased with the news, but it was not what Emmy needed to hear. If he was going to be here on a permanent basis he would notice her condition pretty soon.

Bang went her plan to wait until the last minute to tell him he was going to be a father. She could not keep it from him for ever.

'That...that's great.' The words almost choked her.

'I probably should have told you. I know it'll come as a bit of a shock, but we've known each other for a long time. Hopefully we can carry on as we've always done.' His eyes were bright, his grin wide, but Emmy wanted to cry. Sam being here changed everything. She had been counting on the distance between them to help her manage. Now he was right on her doorstep there was no hiding. Not the pregnancy or her feelings about him. How was she going to be able to work here, seeing him around, if he did not want anything to do with her or the baby? It was his right to walk away when he owed her no commitment, but it was going to be more difficult to sever all ties if they were working in the same place.

'Of course. I'm sure I'll see you around.' She ended the conversation and the not-so-happy reunion. There was no point in carrying on this pretence that they had any kind of relationship now after sleeping together.

Deep down she had known it would change everything, but she had wanted him so much she ignored the risks. Sam never promised her anything other than a good time and delivered on it. He would not want this baby and that was primarily why she had delayed telling him. She would be lucky if he was still talking to her once he found out that not only was she carrying his baby, but she had kept it from him all this time.

Neither of them had planned this pregnancy, but now she was going to be a mum, Emmy wanted the best for her baby. To her mind that included stability, and parents who loved unconditionally and completely. By his own admission that was never going to include Sam.

She had let her baby down at the first hurdle.

CHAPTER THREE

SAM CONTINUED HIS rounds with a heavier heart than when he had started. The aim of coming to the city was partly to repair his relationship with Emmy. Perhaps even to pick up where they had left off at the wedding, but she appeared anything but happy to see him again.

It had not occurred to his giant ego that she would not want him in her life in any capacity. Yet she had made that obvious with her reaction after running into him. Emmy could not wait to get away from him. Which was going to make things strained between them at work and family get-togethers. One of which was scheduled for the following weekend.

It was Tom Jennings's seventieth birthday and Sam was not going to miss being part of the celebrations, regardless of whatever regrets Emmy had about their time together.

'It's good to see you again, Marcus.' Sam had taken a look at the X-rays he had requested and there were some concerns about what they had revealed. The calcification on the bone suggested an old fracture which had not healed properly.

Sam suspected it was an injury which had not been treated in hospital and the overriding question for him was why? He had to be careful around the boy, who was withdrawn enough as it was, and he did not want to say or do anything to upset him further.

He perched on the side of the bed. 'Marcus, the X-rays show an old fracture. Do you remember ever hurting your arm before?'

The boy bit his lip and shook his head. Usually, children of this age were chatterboxes or trying to play football down the corridors. Full of character. Marcus seemed broken more than physically. Sam knew the signs from a personal and professional prospective and was not happy sending him home until they got to the bottom of this injury. It had made all the difference to him having Emmy and David in his life when he had gone through problems at home and he would be only too happy if he could make the same difference in another child's life.

'Are you sure? It must have hurt at the time.' A broken bone was not something easily dismissed. Especially if it had not been stabilised properly at the time.

'Doctor? Is everything all right?' Marcus's mother walked into the ward. Another person who did not look particularly pleased to see him. Surprising when it was his job to treat her son and make him better.

Sam got to his feet. 'I was just telling Marcus we found an old fracture on the X-ray which hasn't healed properly. That might be what's causing the problem. Do you remember how that could have happened?'

She shrugged her shoulders. 'He's a clumsy child. Always falling and bumping into things.'

'This would've been more painful than a mere bump.' He could see her hackles rising as he probed for more information, but it was necessary in case they had to inform social services about a possible safeguarding issue with the boy's home life.

'How am I supposed to know? He lies and exaggerates. If you had kids of your own you'd know how difficult it is to figure out when they're genuinely ill and not faking it to get out of going to school.' With her arms folded and standing straighter, she was unsurprisingly defensive at the turn the conversation was taking. She was not to know if he had kids or not, and despite his own experiences and misgivings about being a parent, Sam was sure he would notice if his son had broken his arm.

Sam was about to point out a fracture should have been easier to diagnose than a sore throat but thought better of it. She would only clam up if he pushed any further. If he had suspicions about Marcus's situation at home—and he did—there were procedures to follow. He would have to voice his concerns if there was any sign of a life endangerment issue. Where children were concerned they could not take any chances and rightly so. Getting involved could make all the difference in a child's life if they were having a hard time of it and Sam should know.

'We're going to run a few more tests to make sure there's nothing serious going on, so we'll be keeping Marcus in overnight.' In these circumstances they would have to carry out a full safeguard medical assessment—a full skeletal survey along with a CT and MRI scan—to make sure there were no other injuries.

The 'concerned' parent tutted before taking up residence in the chair by the bed again.

'I'll call back and see how you're doing later, Marcus.' It was a promise, even if his mother was eyeing him warily as though he had just threatened her.

Sam was still wondering what was going on between the pair when he passed Emmy on the stairs, on his way to see another patient.

'Hey.' For a second he thought she was not even going to stop, never mind acknowledge him.

Then she paused halfway down the steps, with her hand on the rail, bracing herself before she spoke to him. It was not any more reassuring than if she had completely blanked him. For the life of him he did not know what he had done to make her hate him so much. He thought their time at the wedding had been amazing. Certainly nothing that should warrant the cold shoulder she appeared to be giving him lately. If she regretted anything, he hoped a civil discussion could have worked things out but he understood this was not the ideal venue to do that. It was better to stick to safer, more relevant topics. Such as the patient he had just left.

'Hey.' Emmy's returned greeting sounded more like resignation that she would have to talk to him. A long way away from the warm hugs and squeals she once gave upon seeing him. He was missing that side of Emmy as much as the passionate woman he had made love to only a few months ago.

'Um, Dave invited me to your father's birthday this weekend. I hope that's not going to be a problem?'

'You're coming, then?' There was no attempt to hide her disappointment at the news. Clearly she did not want him in any part of her life.

It would be a shame to let what had happened spoil things between them and Sam wished they could stay amicable. The bond he had with Emmy was the closest thing to a relationship he'd ever had.

'Yes. You know he was like a second father to me growing up. I'll be there with bells on. Unless you've a good reason for me not to come?' It was a direct challenge to her to tell him what was bothering her. Either she stopped trying to avoid him or explained once and for all why he should not continue to be involved with the family the way he had always been. He wanted to move past this awkwardness and get back to what they used to have together.

Her silence spoke volumes. She did not want him there but was not willing to tell him why.

Eventually she said, 'No. No reason. I suppose I'll see you there.'

If Sam had hoped for a repeat performance of the wedding night, he knew he was out of luck. There was no hint of flirtation or any evidence she liked him at all now. He could not fathom what he had done for her to turn against him after all of this time.

When she went to walk on past him he had to ask, 'Did I do something to upset you, Em?'

Again she hesitated too long for her answer to be true. 'No.'

He had definitely done something. Whatever it was, he was determined to put it right.

'Emmy—'

His plea to set things straight was lost in the sound of someone shouting for help from the children's ward. An emergency took priority over his private life and everything else when a child's life could be at stake.

Emmy continued on down the stairs and he turned back too, both rushing to the source of the commotion.

'Nurse! Help. He's fitting.'

Emmy was at the child's side before Sam got there, checking there was nothing blocking the airways, or anything around which could hurt the boy having the seizure as his mother watched, horrified and helpless.

'Oxygen.' Sam grabbed the mask and placed it over the child's mouth to help him breathe, and Emmy checked her watch.

'This is Liam. Twelve years old. Epileptic,' she said, brushing the hair from the boy's eyes whilst timing the event. If the fit lasted more than five minutes they would have to administer buccal midazolam to try and stop it. Until then all they could do was reassure the boy everything would be fine.

'It's going to be okay, Liam. We'll get you through this one.' There was that calm, soothing tone she used to use on him, when he would come to the Jennings place, upset after another problem at home. No doubt caused by his father. It was no wonder she had gone into nursing when she had always looked after everyone else. Her kindness could not be taught at school. Emmy was a natural carer.

Liam's tremors gradually began to lessen and Sam was glad Emmy had been on hand so they could act quicker. She likely knew more about every child in here than was written in their files. He was sure she brought a smile to the faces of everyone on the ward. At the same time doing everything she could to make them comfortable as possible, while trying to get them back on their feet.

Sam only hoped he had not messed things up for her at work by inserting himself back into her life.

Once Liam was stabilised, and the adrenaline was

no longer pumping so vehemently in his veins, Sam tried again with Emmy.

'Are you ready for a cuppa after that?' he asked as they left the ward.

This time her reply was instant. 'Yes, please.'

Helping Liam get through his latest seizure had taken all of the fight out of Emmy. She got tired quickly these days and she needed her energy to hide her condition from Sam. Right now, she could do with a timeout from having to think and a seat to take the weight off her feet. Something sweet to boost her blood sugar would be welcome too. Sam had caught her in a moment of vulnerability, but she could not avoid him for ever. He would be part of her life in a big way from now on, whether either of them wanted that or not.

However, she was going to wait until after her dad's birthday to break the news. She did not want to bring any drama to the festivities. If she told Sam now about the baby it would come out at home too, and she could do without the derision from her sisters over her current predicament. There was time enough after she had her scan to make sure everything was all right first. Another chance for Emmy to beat herself up about shutting Sam out of the pregnancy, even if she thought it was probably for the best.

'Coffee? Tea?' Sam asked as they joined the queue in the canteen. He knew she was partial to both. What he was unaware of was her decision to go caffeine-free for the duration of the pregnancy.

'A glass of milk, please.'

Her request stunned him momentarily. 'Okay. I'll get the drinks if you want to go and get us a table?'

Under other circumstances she might have protested about paying her way, but her feet hurt. 'Thanks.'

She left him to pay and relaxed as best she could in the hard plastic chair, aware that things would only get harder over the next few months. Maternity leave and when she would be taking it was the first of many decisions she would have to make as a prospective single mum.

'One glass of fresh milk for m'lady.' With the flourish of a wine waiter in a high-class establishment, Sam set the drink in front of her.

He was trying, bless him, and if it was not for the repercussions of their night of fun she would enjoy the company. As it was, he put her on edge, knowing he was going to feel differently around her soon. Being faced with a responsibility he had never asked for was not something he was going to appreciate. Along with being kept in the dark because she did not want to face reality.

'Thank you.'

'Are you okay after that little drama? If you don't mind me saying, you look tired.' He produced a snack pack of biscuits from his pocket and Emmy pounced on it.

'You're a lifesaver. I think my blood sugar's a little low. You know how it is…skipping meals always catches up with you.'

'Exactly why you should be taking care of yourself, Em. It's a demanding job and it takes its toll. Lucky for you, I know you've got a sweet tooth.'

'Yes, Doctor.' It was nice to hear the concern in his voice for her and she wished it was related to the fact she was carrying his baby.

He laughed and shook his head at her. 'Who would ever have thought we'd both end up going into medicine and specialising in paediatrics at that?'

Emmy murmured her agreement, deciding not to tell him she had followed him into medicine because his passion for it had been intoxicating. In listening to Sam's desire to help others, she had believed going into nursing would somehow bring them closer too. That dream of a lovestruck teenager had become the nightmare of an adult who had not made any better life decisions.

'Our troubled childhoods might have played a part. We want to help kids who are having a hard time of it.' That much was true. Her whole reason for being in this department was to try and make life better for the youngsters who had been dealt a rough hand at such a young age.

'I suppose so. I've never thought of it in that way. We might actually have something to thank our feckless parents for after all.' The way he gulped down a mouthful of hot coffee told her he did not believe that any more than she did. They had become essential workers despite their absent parents, who deserved absolutely no credit for the way their children had turned out.

The dull buzz of a pager went off, and as soon as Sam checked it, he was on his feet, taking one last swig of coffee. 'I've got to go but I'll see you on Sunday, yeah?'

'Yes,' she confirmed, as their break came to an end and her mind and body filled with foreboding over their next planned encounter.

Intuition told her it was not going to be as pleasant

and relaxed as the last ten minutes together and could change things between them, and her family, for ever.

For the whole train journey to her parents' house, Emmy had been praying that Sam would have a work emergency or get caught up in traffic. Anything to prevent him attending the celebrations. Being close to the family was great when she was younger and looked forward to his visits. Now, it was an inconvenience at a time when she would rather not see him. It was bad enough they were working together without socialising too. Every meeting raised the possibility of him finding out about their surprise baby and her having to own up to keeping it to herself for three months. It was difficult to know if the unplanned pregnancy or her betrayal would have a bigger impact on Sam. Emmy never wanted to hurt him but knew that was exactly what would happen once he found out about everything.

He had offered to drive her, but she could not bear the thought of a long car journey when they would invariably bring up the subject of David's wedding night. The memory of which she would always treasure but was also a reminder of her uncertain future.

As Emmy made the short journey from the train station to the house on foot, her nerves began to get the better of her. Family occasions always made her fret over what to wear and her appearance when she wanted to make a good impression. The pressure was twofold today, knowing Sam would be here too, oblivious to his impending fatherhood.

In the end she had gone with a sunny yellow, empire-line dress which hugged her bosom and skimmed over her tummy, in an effort to detract from any changes in her body. The addition of a sunflower clip in her hair was projecting a bright countenance she was not feeling.

On the way to the door she took a deep breath and rapped. Whether it was due to good manners or an instilled sense of not completely belonging, she did not simply let herself in, but waited for someone to open the door for her.

'Don't stand on ceremony, Emmy, come in.'

She was glad it was her dad who answered, genuinely happy to see her.

'Happy birthday.' She flung her arms around him and hugged him tight. The squeeze in return made her feel more secure than she had in months.

'Thanks, sweetheart. It's good to see you.'

She handed over the card and present she had chosen so carefully and hung her coat up in the hall.

'So, uh, who's here?' There could have been a hundred people inside but there was only one person's presence she was concerned about.

'Oh, it's just a quiet family dinner. I didn't want a big fuss.' That was her dad, humble and unassuming, but unhelpful when it came to her personal life.

'Hello, stranger. I haven't seen you since the wedding.'

For a heart-stopping moment she thought the strong arm around her shoulders was Sam's until David spoke.

'I was giving you newlyweds some privacy.' She kissed him on the cheek and took advantage at the chance of another hug. Goodness knew how he would react when he found out his best friend had got his little sister pregnant. Especially when Sam would not want the responsibility of the unplanned pregnancy.

'It's been nearly three months, sis. You're welcome to come to our house anytime. There's no need to avoid us, we're family.'

Emmy could tell from his tone and the strength of his embrace he was worried about her feeling pushed out by Bryony. Given that was exactly what had happened when Lorna and Lisa had been born into the family.

Although nothing could have been further from the truth where Bryony was concerned. David's new wife brought him happiness and that was all she could ask for him.

He was right about one thing though: she had been avoiding him and talking about the wedding day, along with his best friend. Although that had proved pointless now Sam was working at her hospital.

'I know. I know. I've just been busy…with stuff.' Hormones, morning sickness, anxiety and sleepless nights worrying about the future or if she should have included Sam in everything earlier.

'Well, today you rest and enjoy. Your mother has been cooking all day.' Her father directed them towards the dining room where the rest of the family was already seated around the table, including Sam.

All the air seemed to escape her lungs at the sight of him sitting there.

'You're just in time, sweetheart,' her mother greeted her from the far end of the table, which was already laden with platters of food.

Despite all the hellos and smiles from her sisters as

well, Emmy could not help but note they had started without her.

As if sensing her disappointment, Sam spoke up. 'I knew your train had just got in so we thought we'd have everything ready for your arrival.'

True or not, the explanation, along with the knowledge he had bothered to check on her train, eased a tiny bit of her trepidation.

'Get stuck in before everything goes cold. Roast beef, and your favourites, Yorkshire puddings. There's a seat beside Sam for you.'

Directed towards the empty chair, Emmy sat down and exchanged an awkward smile with Sam.

'Hey,' he said. Enough to make her blush.

'Hi.' She managed a brief sideways glance before sitting down and helping herself to slices of roast beef before David ate them all.

The room was momentarily filled with the sound of the happy diners' chatter as they passed around the dishes piled high with food, and Emmy longed for it to stay that way.

'I can't remember the last time I had a home-cooked meal. It's usually something quick in between shifts.' Her appetite had not been quite the same lately. Certain strong-smelling foods made her stomach roll and her favourite curries were giving her heartburn too. It was small, simple meals these days, although she was trying to eat the right foods for the baby's sake.

'You've got to look after yourself, Emmy. Doesn't she, Sam?' For some reason her mother looked to him on the matter. Probably because he was a doctor, and in her eyes better qualified and more respected than a lowly nurse.

Emmy had always been proud of the job she did looking after the kids at the hospital, but her parents thought it beneath her. They were a very middle-class family and having money without being seen to labour hard for it seemed more acceptable than working with 'the great unwashed.' Her parents had a snobbish attitude when it came to mixing with the general public because their careers had been very much at the top of the pay scale. Although now retired, her father had been a successful investment banker, her mother a financial advisor, and it had been a long time since either of them had to worry about money. They did not understand why she would undervalue herself so much to work for the health service.

According to them she should have used her brains and gone into an office-based job where she could charge exorbitant rates simply for use of her time, like David the solicitor. Nursing was a poorly paid profession compared to his and the airy-fairy, social media 'influencers' her sisters proclaimed themselves to be. She had no issues with their make-up tutorials or vlogs about their travel adventures. They had not been as book smart as Emmy or David and she admired their ability to make a career from their interests. She simply did not understand why their paths were more acceptable than hers. Especially when Lorna and Lisa had borrowed money to set up their venture into the world of social media until they had sufficient paying subscribers and sponsors to fund their lifestyle. Emmy had never asked for a handout, nor had one been offered. Her sisters had asked for financial help from their parents to start their online business but Emmy had been aware from the moment she had professed an interest in nursing that they thought it a poor career choice with no prospects for significant financial gain. Money seemed to be their marker for stability in life and so Emmy did not want to further their concerns for her by getting into debt from the off.

Instead, she had worked where she could to get her through her nursing course and stood on her own two feet financially from the day she finished high school. Just one more example of the different standards separating her from her sisters.

Still, at least her mother was showing some concern for her welfare, even if the delivery stung.

'Yes. Yes, she does.' Sam smiled and went to pour her some wine. Emmy quickly covered the glass with her hand.

'Not for me, thanks. I'll stick with water.' She poured herself some from the jug in the centre of the table, ignoring the bemused looks around the table. Anyone would think she had a reputation when it came to alcohol simply because she had turned down one glass of wine.

'That's a beautiful dress. It's a lovely colour on you,' Bryony commented, oblivious to the sniggering going on around the table at Emmy refusing a drink. If everyone found it so unbelievable, she was going to have to look at her drinking habits when the baby was born. Unless this was merely another example of her family taking the opportunity to make fun of her.

'Thanks.' It was nice to have another woman onside when her sisters' compliments often hid a thinly veiled barb.

'Hmm. Not sure it's your style though,' Lorna piped

up on cue, ready to spoil Emmy's mood as she nibbled a piece of a carrot.

'Yeah. It does nothing for your figure. Have you put on weight?' Lisa was as direct as expected.

'Now, girls, it's not Emmy's fault she hasn't inherited my good metabolism. You should think yourself lucky.' Her mother did not even realise how incredibly insensitive she too was being, pointing out yet again that Emmy was not biologically one of the family. It was entirely possible she had passed on more than the ability to stay slim to the twins when their acerbic tongues sounded suspiciously like their parents' at times.

Emmy should be used to the comments by now and, usually, she did not react, but her hormones were making her more sensitive at the moment. Tears were already blurring her vision at the fact she was not allowed to enjoy a birthday meal without criticism.

Their parents would never dare criticise the wonder twins and that was part of the problem. They had always been allowed to say or do whatever they pleased without retribution and had grown from spoiled children into mean-spirited adults who got their kicks putting others down. Emmy in particular.

'I think you look lovely, Emmy.' Sam reached out and squeezed her hand in solidarity, but it only furthered her regret about coming here at all.

'Hang on, no wine…extra weight…you're not pregnant, are you?' Lorna snorted at the idea and set her sibling off too. Either the notion of Emmy becoming a mother, or that someone had slept with her, apparently was hysterically funny.

Heat rose in Emmy's cheeks and she could not find

the strength to deny the possibility with a blatant lie. Her delay in spouting a witty comeback told a tale.

The collective sound of gasps, dropped cutlery and astonished laughter was almost deafening. She did not dare look any of them in the eye. Especially Sam, who she was sure was currently glaring a hole into the side of her head.

'Emmy? Is this true?' Her father's stern voice broke through the humiliation of her worst nightmare come true. His vocal disapproval made her feel as though she had besmirched the family name like some unmarried teen mum from the fifties when such a thing was considered a scandal. These days, her situation was not unusual, and better accepted. In other circles, apparently.

No, this was not how she wanted anyone to find out, overshadowing what should have been a joyous occasion, but Emmy knew there was never going to be a good time.

She could already feel her parents' disappointment emanating in waves.

Emmy lowered her head and gave a small nod. Her mother cried out. She was a grown woman but still their daughter, pregnant and without a partner. It was natural they should have concerns but it was not the end of the world for any of them. She only wished they could skip the shock factor and move straight to the acceptance stage.

David cleared his throat. 'Congratulations, sis. I mean, I thought we'd be the ones having the first grandkids but I know you'll make a great mum.' Her brother's attempt to make her feel better was undone when her father spoke.

'Who's the father?' At least he hadn't asked if she

knew who the father was, which was something the twins would likely have come up with.

They were unusually quiet. Probably realising they did not need to say or do anything when she had caused maximum damage already.

'I didn't mean to spoil your birthday,' she said, quietly.

An uneasy quiet descended around the table as they waited for the big reveal like some awful TV talent show, delaying the name in order to increase the drama. Only in this case they could do with dialling down the drama. No one was coming out of this a winner.

All of a sudden Sam scraped his chair back and stood up. 'I'm the father and we're getting married.'

Her 'Pardon me?' was drowned out by the loud squeals of delight from all around.

Before Emmy knew what was happening, everyone was congratulating them and shaking hands across the table. Meanwhile, Sam was grinning like an idiot and she was left bewildered by what was happening.

'When did this happen?'

'I'm so happy for the two of you.'

'You kept that quiet.'

'Our first grandchild...'

The effusive congratulations were a stark contrast to the previous feeling she was about to be disowned, and the only difference had been Sam's apparent involvement. It made her wonder if he was considered more of a son than she was their daughter, or if she was somehow more acceptable as part of a couple with him. Albeit a complete fabrication.

Emmy had no idea what Sam was playing at but was at a loss to do anything other than sit there and pretend with him. It seemed better to go along with it for now than to call it out for the lie it was and spoil the day again. They could talk it over later and she would put him straight on a few matters. Number one being that he was under no obligation to her or the baby. Despite what her family might think.

CHAPTER FOUR

SAM SLUMPED BACK in his chair in a daze. What on earth had he just done? He looked at Emmy, who was staring at him, mouth and eyes wide open, silently asking him the same question. All he could offer was a pitiful shrug.

Everything seemed to have happened at once, giving him no time to think about what he was doing before he had got up and addressed the whole Jennings family on their behalf. As though he was speaking for Emmy too. When in reality he did not even have ownership of the words, never mind her or the baby.

The baby. Emmy's baby. He had not even been mentioned. Yet he had fronted up and accepted responsibility. Why? It could have been out of guilt, knowing he had done the wrong thing by her and the family, taking advantage of their close bond for one hot night with Emmy. Perhaps it was his natural instinct to protect her when the twins had ganged up on her. A pattern which had repeated itself over time. It could have been self-preservation, knowing if David found out they had slept together he would have killed him, save for the idea of marriage. Judging by the reaction of the majority around the table, he had made the right decision. Bar the supposed newly engaged couple who must look miserable as sin. Marriage was a long way from the 'just sex' he and Emmy had agreed upon. Sam did not even know if the baby was his, simply assuming she had not been with anyone since because he hadn't.

For all he knew she could have been in a relationship with the father or been artificially inseminated because she did not want any male interference in her life. He had gone steamrollering over her news without a thought to anyone, including himself. Marriage and children were not things he had ever wanted. Something he should have given more consideration to before getting carried away with Emmy at the hotel.

If the baby was his, Sam did not want her castigated for something he had been a part of. She did not deserve to take the flak on her own after fighting so hard to be accepted into this family. When it came to Emmy, someone he had been close to for a long time, he was willing to sacrifice his independence if it meant making her feel secure in some small way. He could not in good conscience have sat back and let her be vilified for what had been a very special time to him. In standing up like that, he had been defending that time they had shared together, as well as giving her some support. Even if she had not asked him for it.

'You're actually going to be my real bro now.' David gave Sam another slap on the back when he walked past.

At this rate he would be stooped over, his skin red raw, at the end of the night with all of the physical congratulations.

'I guess so,' Sam replied uneasily, his conscience beginning to bother him.

All of this could come crashing down around him at any point if Emmy decided to call him out on his deception. So far she had not contradicted his story and gone along with the news. Most likely because she was either in shock, or it was easier to simply play along for now.

They had a lot to discuss. Apart from his spontaneous engagement and parenting announcement, there was the small matter of paternity. This could very well be his baby and that was going to change his life for ever.

He thought of his father and the neglected children he had spawned over the years along with the heartbroken women left behind. Sam swore never to be that person, yet he had acted with Emmy in the same selfish, reckless way. Thinking only of his own pleasure and conveniently forgetting the possible consequences. Even if Emmy appeared to have experienced high levels of pleasure at the time too.

There was not much opportunity for him to speak to her alone over the course of the afternoon. Although the dark looks she shot him every now and then said perhaps that was not such a bad thing. He knew he was in serious trouble when she actually accepted his offer of a lift home.

'Why? Why would you do that?' she asked, waving goodbye to the family as he drove away from the house.

'I don't know. I suppose it seemed like the right thing to do in the moment.' He could not explain what had happened to her when he hadn't figured it out completely himself.

'*Congratulations* or *Are you stupid?* seem to be the other available options. "We're getting married" was a more extreme reaction than I'd expected.' Emmy's hands were clasped tightly in her lap and he wondered how hard she was trying not to slap him.

'I didn't appreciate the way they were speaking to you.' A pathetic excuse, but the truth, nonetheless. He hated the way the twins ganged up on her and wished the rest stuck up for her more. Their ignorance of the pain their jibes caused Emmy only widened the distance between them all. It was not Sam's place to tell them how to behave, and even if he did, he doubted it would make any difference other than to alienate him from the family. Emmy would argue it was not his place to lie on her behalf either, but the deed was done now. The family of his best friend believed they were getting married and starting a family. The thought alone was enough to bring him out in a cold sweat.

'I was merely trying to keep you respectable.' Even as he said it, Sam knew the joke would fall flat. As confirmed by the sharp intake of Emmy's breath next to him.

'Pardon me? Do you really think I need a fake fiancé, or a man of any description, to give my life meaning?'

'I didn't mean—' His attempt to apologise was drowned out by her justified indignation at his ill-judged comment.

'I am a qualified nurse. An independent woman. I can raise this baby on my own. It won't make me any less of a mother or a human if I don't have a man at my side.'

It had not crossed Sam's mind that she would happily go it alone with the baby. He could walk away with a clear conscience if that was what he chose to do. Except Emmy was the last person he would bail on.

'You're all of those things and I'm sure you'll be a fantastic mum. I was merely saying I could help provide more stability for the child. We both know how important that is for a good start in life.' The more he talked about it, the more his proposition made sense. It might have started out as an impulsive reaction to her news and the Jenningses' attitude to it but he was beginning to think it was the answer.

He never planned on becoming a father, but would stand by Emmy and the baby, no matter what. It was his fault for not being careful and he had no intention of following in his father's footsteps. This baby needed a dad and needed to know it was loved and wanted. Not a mistake he regretted or could ignore.

'Yes, well, we can't change the past. Nor can we pretend we have a future together. The best I can hope for is that the excitement dies down after a few weeks and I'll come clean or tell them we broke up. Anything to stop them planning the wedding of the year.'

Clearly Emmy needed more time to get on board with the idea.

'It is my baby, then? Obviously I'll be there for you no matter what. It's just...good to know. Wow. I'm gonna be a dad.' Having the paternity confirmed made it all too real and only convinced him that he had been just in his actions, if impulsive.

Emmy rolled her eyes at him. 'Of course you're the father. I don't make a habit of one-night stands. Wait... you did all that without being one hundred percent sure this was your child I'm carrying?'

He nodded, having difficulty in forming words when there was so much for him to process. 'So you're…'

Emmy stared at him, waiting for him to complete the sentence, until they eventually did so together.

'Three months pregnant.'

Sam paused again. That was a quarter of a year. All that time Emmy had known she was pregnant with his baby and had not told him. Why? Would she ever have sought him out to tell him he was going to be a father if he had not shown up at the hospital?

He fought to maintain his concentration on the road as his thoughts and feelings were running at maximum power trying to make sense of Emmy's actions. Most of which were veering towards him being purposely left out of the loop and how much that pained him.

'Didn't you trust me, Emmy?'

'Hmm?'

'I'm just trying to figure out why you didn't tell me you were pregnant. You've had three months for goodness' sake.' He was trying and failing to keep himself in check. His raised voice giving away something of his hurt that she had not contacted him at all during that time.

Emmy sighed. 'It's complicated. Obviously neither of us expected this to happen and, well, we've both got our own lives to lead.'

'That's an excuse. We're both going to be parents. You should have involved me.' He did not know what difference it would have made to Emmy or the baby, if any, had she told him from the moment she had a positive test result. Hell, he would have been there for her as soon as she had thought a pregnancy was a possibility. What he did know was that he would have felt better knowing she could confide her fears in him. As it was, this secret meant she had not trusted him.

'I had a lot to figure out for myself. We've both had messed-up families and it worries me about the sort of parents we'll make.'

'You'll be an amazing mum, and though I understand your reservations about me on the parenting score, it doesn't change the fact that I am going to be the baby's dad. Don't shut me out any more than you already have. I know what it's like to have an absentee father and it's not fair to inflict that on an innocent child simply because you think I'm going to suck as much as my own parents.' Although he had never seen himself taking on the traditional role of a husband and father, the potential for Emmy to deny him now made his heart ache more than he thought it would for the life he could have with her and their baby.

He and Emmy made a good team, and could learn from their parents' mistakes. Sam wanted the chance to prove himself now that fate had decided fatherhood was in his future after all.

'It wasn't that… I felt guilty about keeping the news to myself but I also couldn't bear the thought of ruining your life. You've always been honest about not wanting to be tied down by family life, yet here we are…a baby on the way and a marriage proposal all in one afternoon.' She attempted a smile, but Sam could see through it to the sadness Emmy was trying to mask.

He could only hope he would do better by their baby when he had already upended Emmy's world with his selfish, reckless behaviour with his rampant libido.

'Look, we're in this together. We'll work something out.' Although he was saying all the right things,

Sam was not jumping up and down with glee about the situation.

Sure, he was hurt and rightly so, but a bruised ego was not the same as an excited father-to-be.

Emmy needed to lie down in a dark room somewhere. Today had been too much. An overwhelming display of emotions from those around her.

'Why did you tell everyone we were getting married anyway? It seemed a little drastic. Especially for you.'

When Sam had first jumped up to defend her honour, she had been stunned into silence by the gesture. No one had ever stood up for her like that, but she had also known it was an act for her family's sake. By the time she realised what Sam was up to, everyone was already celebrating and accepting them as a couple. Something she had been striving for her whole life and only achieved with Sam on board. She wished it were true.

The only real part of this was the little one growing inside her. Everything else had been made up to impress her parents.

In an ideal world she would happily marry Sam and raise their baby together. However, this seemed like a sick joke. Teasing her with something she had dreamed about as a love-infatuated teen, when it was nothing more than a knee-jerk reaction to her news.

At least he had offered to do the right thing by her, regardless of the baby's parentage. It left an ember of hope burning that there was something more than chivalry behind the suggestion.

'It was a heat-of-the-moment thing. Expected.' Just like that, Sam poured a bucket of cold water over the flicker of hope, making it spit and hiss until there was nothing left but the muddy ashes of her dreams. She was done being a charity case, or the consolation prize for the real thing.

Despite Sam's hurt about the secret she had kept from him for so long, by the time they pulled up outside her house she knew she would have to do this alone. Forcing him to be in her life, or him thinking he had to be involved through some sense of duty, would not be fair on either of them. Not least for her when she would always be hoping there was something more behind Sam accepting responsibility for their 'mistake.' She was facing a lifetime of unrequited love and longing if he ended up being in his child's life for the long haul.

'Once you've slept on it, you'll realise what a mistake this whole thing was between us. You don't need to marry me or help raise a child you never wanted simply because you would feel guilty otherwise. I see no point in prolonging our agony for ever, Sam. I don't want or expect anything from you or anyone else. I never have.' She got out of the car, slamming the door on his plea for her to wait. The sobs started before he had driven away.

So much for her being stronger on her own.

Sam had slept on it. At least, he had lain in his bed, his mind whirring, trying to process everything. The frightening prospect of becoming a father and any urge to bolt from the responsibility was overridden by his sense of loyalty to Emmy and the innocent child they were about to bring into the world.

They had both had unhappy childhoods and it had affected all of their future relationships. He did not want to inflict that pain onto another generation.

She had given him an out, but now Emmy had had time to calm down and reflect on his suggestion, he was hoping to talk her round to his way of thinking.

They used to have a good relationship and if they could get that back it would be a good basis for a marriage, as well as providing security for their unborn child. Whatever she thought of him, he was not going to leave her to deal with this on her own. After the Jenningses' performance around the dinner table when she had broken the news, he was not sure they would be there for her at all. It would not be fair to walk away and leave Emmy to cope on her own simply because he had not planned for this. Neither of them had but it was happening, nonetheless. He might have to work hard at it, but Sam was not his father. He was not going to walk out when the mood took him or because he did not want to face up to his actions.

Once he had finished his ward rounds, he sought Emmy out, intending to discuss the matter with her again. He was not going to let her shut him out because she was trying to be a martyr and save him the hassle of a surprise pregnancy. Marriage was extreme but it would also be a symbol of his commitment to her and the baby.

As he was walking towards her department, he caught sight of her leaving, coat on, with her handbag over her shoulder. He rushed over, keen to catch her before she exited the building altogether.

'Hey, Emmy, I didn't realise you were finishing early today. I was hoping to catch you for a chat.'

'I...er...have an appointment.' She would not quite meet his eye and a swell of concern suddenly rose from the pit of Sam's stomach into his throat.

'Is everything all right, with you and the baby?' He was only coming to terms with the prospect of impending fatherhood and anything threatening that now would be too cruel.

She sighed. 'I have my first scan this afternoon.'

The unease subsided, only to be replaced with that now familiar hurt that she had either purposely kept the appointment from him or had not thought he would like to have been included in this important event.

'Can I come with you?' He would not impose where he was not wanted, but at the same time he had a right to be there to see his baby.

Emmy shrugged. 'If you want but I'm happy to go on my own.'

It was not the effusive 'Yes' he wanted. His intention had only been to support her, but when she was treating him as an inconvenience, Sam wondered if he was needed at all.

'I'd like to. If that's okay with you?' The idea of seeing their baby on the screen for the first time was something he could not pass up. Even if she had failed to mention it to him before now. It was a once-in-a-lifetime experience which would never be repeated and he should be there to witness it.

'You are the father, I suppose.' She started walking away, leaving it to him to follow her to the maternity wing.

Once she gave her name at reception, they both took their seats in the waiting room with more expectant couples. Sam saw a clear distinction between them and the other prospective parents in the room. Those dads-to-be were very tactile, holding hands or rubbing their partners' bellies with a reassurance they were in this together.

He had a feeling if he tried that with Emmy it would earn him a punch on the nose for daring to as much as touch her again. It was natural to want to give her the same comfort and say that everything would be all right, but Emmy clearly regretted being with him in the first place. He had a lot of work to do to convince her to have him around, never mind persuade her that marriage was a good idea.

'Emma-Louise Jennings?' The nurse called her through, and Sam refrained from any comments over the use of her full name. There was a way to go before they would get back to that level of teasing each other again.

No one really knew him at the hospital yet in a professional capacity so he should not embarrass her too much by being here. How their work and personal relationships were going to play out in the future he did not know. All he could do was stand in the corner whilst Emmy got settled onto the bed, knowing she would not appreciate his help or a reminder he was here.

'If you could just lift your top up, I'll put some gel on your tummy.' The sonographer tucked some protective paper down the waistband of her trousers before squeezing the gloopy liquid generously onto Emmy's stomach. Sam was sure he could see a little more rounding in that area, although he would never say it or he might be in danger of losing vital parts of his anatomy.

Emmy was watching the screen as the sonographer ran the scanner over her belly. Sam could tell she was anxious by the way she was clenching her fists, tense, waiting for proof the baby was okay. He felt the same.

'Do you hear that?' With a turn of some knobs and some technical wizardry, the room filled with a fast, rhythmic beat.

'Yes.' Emmy sounded breathless, transfixed by the images on the monitor.

'That's baby's heart, strong and clear.'

Emmy let out an excited gasp and turned to look at him, the love for the baby shining brightly in her eyes. He smiled back at her, his heart racing as fast as the baby's. An exhilarating but terrifying time. He had not expected to be anxious but here he was, holding his breath waiting for confirmation their baby was fine.

'And this is your baby. Why don't you come closer, Dad?' As more buttons were pressed, a steady black-and-white image was captured on the screen and Sam was beckoned to be part of the event.

When he moved closer to Emmy he could see the tears of happiness glinting in her eyes. Then she reached out for his hand and gave it a squeeze.

Perhaps she might just let him be part of her life after all.

Emmy had been caught up in the moment. Overwhelmed with love for the little grey splodge on the screen. Otherwise she would have stopped herself reaching out for Sam. He was only holding her hand and sitting in on the scan because he knew it was expected of him. She did not see the point in forcing him to do these things. It would not take long for him to realise it was not the life he wanted, raising an unplanned child with a woman he did not love. She would not make the mistake of thinking he would be in this for ever.

'Can I get a copy of the picture?' She dropped his hand and turned her attention back to the one thing that was real.

'Of course.' The sonographer printed out a strip of still photos and handed them to Emmy.

'I'd like one of those too.' Sam leaned in close to put in his request.

Emmy wanted to believe he was genuinely interested in his future role as a father, but she remained sceptical, unwilling to get dragged any further into this fantasy when she was the one who would end up getting hurt.

'Is everything all right with the baby?' That was the most important thing and why she resented Sam distracting her.

'All is as it should be,' she was reassured. 'So, Mum, what are your plans for the rest of the day?'

'Nothing too energetic. I think I'll put my feet up and enjoy the peace and quiet while I can.' It was going to be a major life change when she had a crying baby interrupting the usual silence in her apartment. She was looking forward to it.

Now she knew everything was all right, she could enjoy her pregnancy and look forward to the baby's arrival.

'I thought maybe we could get a cuppa somewhere and have a chat.' Sam wedged himself into the conversation and her plans for the afternoon. It was something she would have to get used to, unless she set some ground rules, or he got bored playing supportive partner. Whichever came first.

* * *

Instead of going to the noisy canteen, Sam decided to get takeaway drinks from the small coffee shop by the hospital entrance.

'Why don't we take these outside?' He wanted a little more privacy for their deeply personal conversation and thought they could get a vitamin D fix at the same time.

'It would be nice to get a break from fluorescent lights into the sunshine.'

He was grateful for Emmy's co-operation when he knew she simply wanted to go home. She had not tried to hide her exasperation at him tagging along to the scan. It was understandable for her to be defensive or suspicious of his motives when he had made it clear in the past he would not entertain the idea of having a family. Now it was happening he would do everything he could to make her believe he had their baby's interests at heart. Even if he had lost his chance with Emmy after his reckless behaviour.

They took a seat on the bench in the children's play park adjacent to the hospital. It was the perfect sunny day and, in different circumstances, they would have been sitting here celebrating, fawning over the pictures of their baby, instead of acting like strangers, sitting as far apart as they could.

'Thank you for letting me be a part of today.'

'You're the father, Sam. I'm not going to stop you but neither am I forcing you to be involved.' A guarded Emmy was not giving him an inch when it came to trusting him and he could see why. As well as his issues with his parents, Sam's reputation did not exactly scream commitment or that he was father material. His string of love interests had given her cause to tease him in the old days and now it was coming back to haunt him. The ghosts of girlfriends past had suddenly become an obstacle to the mother of his baby believing his sincerity in wanting to raise his own child.

He took a sip of his dark roast coffee, hoping the caffeine injection would also give his persuasive skills a boost. 'Have you thought any more about my proposal?'

'Yeah. You could have done it somewhere romantic like the top of the Eiffel Tower and preferably not in the presence of my family.' Emmy continued sipping from her bottle of water, leaving Sam snorting his coffee at the comment. At least she was keeping her sense of humour, even if she no longer felt the same way about him as she once did.

'I meant about us getting married and giving the baby the best start in life.' He wasn't fooled, Emmy knew exactly what he was referring to. She was simply trying to avoid the question. Something he was no longer going to accept when they had so much to sort out over the next six months before the birth.

She sighed and leaned back in her seat, watching the children play in the park. Sam wished he could read her mind. Before fooling around in that hotel room together, she had been an open book to him. While he did not regret a single second of their time together, he longed for the closeness they once shared.

'We don't have to get married because I'm pregnant. My father and brother aren't going to come after you with a shotgun until you make me a respectable married woman.'

'I know that, but think of the benefits of us getting

married. You and the baby will be financially stable, entitled to half of my assets. Not to mention having two parents at home sharing the responsibilities.'

If they were not going to be a couple in any other sense, with Emmy hating the sight of him now, Sam thought it more provident to go down the practical route.

'You're talking about a business transaction?'

Sam saw her interest piqued and jumped on it. 'Yes. That's exactly what our marriage would be. One of convenience.'

If that was the only way he could sell it to her he was willing to sign the contract right now.

CHAPTER FIVE

EMMY WAS BEAMING as she walked onto the ward praying that the kids could not see the puffiness around her eyes from where she had been crying.

Her overactive hormones were making her more sensitive than usual, but it was Sam who had caused her latest bout of self-pity. A marriage proposal was supposed to be romantic, the special moment in a relationship to be cherished for ever. Instead, the only circumstances Sam would consider making her his wife was because she was having his baby. Love and romance did not come into it. At least, not on his part. For Sam it was merely a contract to cement his place in his child's life. A noble gesture, if it were not for the fact Emmy wanted more. There was nothing for her to gain in this arrangement, unless she counted extra heartache. That would be guaranteed, going into a marriage of convenience with a groom she had given her heart to a long time ago.

'Hey, you. How are you feeling today, Liam?' She started with her young epileptic patient who had had a rough night according to the staff at this morning's handover.

Despite his pale colour and half-closed eyes, he still

managed to give her a great big smile. Emmy's heart broke for him, as it did for every child here who should have been outside enjoying their childhood.

'Tired,' he said, fighting to keep his eyes open.

'You get your rest when you can. You need it.' She pulled the curtains around his bed to give him a sense of privacy so he could sleep better. Not easy amidst the hustle and bustle of a children's hospital, with people coming and going, and the noise of the machines monitoring the well-being of those in residence.

Emmy liked to check in with each of the patients when she started her shifts to see for herself how they were doing. Plus, it was good for them to get to know her face when there were so many health professionals tending to them. Getting acquainted with her gave them some sense of security and she knew how vital that was to a child who was scared and vulnerable. The Jenningses had been her lifeline during her tumultuous childhood, and if it had not been for their steady, calm presence in her life, she might still be floundering around, in danger of drowning.

Not that everything in her life was plain sailing now, but that was as a result of her dubious adult decisions.

Her thoughts drifted to the other life she was about to bring into the world and let her hand rest on her belly, attempting to let him or her know she would do her very best to make them feel safe. That was the promise she was making above all else.

'Emmy, can I talk to you? In private?' Sam was hovering nearby, as he always seemed to be these days. Giving her no space to breathe or to think about anything other than him. At a time when she had plenty of other things to be concerned about.

He had no right to stand there looking so devastatingly handsome in his white coat, when her waistline had all but disappeared already. By the end of her third trimester she was going to be the size of a house.

Unfortunately, there was no way out but past the attractive human drape in the doorway. In another few months she would literally have to squeeze by him and that would drive her even more nuts.

'I'm working, Sam. Can't this wait until later?' She wanted some time away from the constant overthinking which resulted from their every conversation. His suggestion that they should get married for the baby's sake was something she could not get out of her head. It was a ridiculous notion which could never work, yet once upon a time she had considered that scenario as her ultimate happy-ever-after.

Whether he intended to rescind the offer of making her his wife, or wanted to try and persuade her again it was the way forward, this was not the time or place to have that discussion.

None of her colleagues knew their history and she would have preferred to keep it that way for now. Goodness knew how long Sam would stick around, so there seemed little point in making herself the subject of hospital gossip in the interim. Getting pregnant by the new consultant was not something she was keen to discuss with her colleagues. It would not do either of their reputations any favours.

'I actually wanted to talk to you about Marcus Moseley. We should probably go somewhere more private to chat.'

'Yes. Of course.' She rushed past him then, running from her own *faux pas*. Just because she was obsessed with him and her current situation did not mean he was too. They were at work, and unlike her today, he could separate their personal lives from their professional duties.

Sam placed his hand in the small of her back as they walked towards one of the empty consultation rooms. It was a small but intimate gesture, which she hoped no one else noticed. To her mind there was an element of possession there in his touch, maybe even protectiveness, and not something she imagined he would do to another colleague without consent. If any other male member of staff had put his hands on her, Emmy would have been quick to point out it was unwanted and inappropriate. In Sam's case, she knew it was instinctive because she was carrying his baby. What was more, she liked the subconscious gesture and the feel of him pressed against her even for a short while. It was a connection they had not made since the wedding and something she missed.

Sam had always been a very tactile person, hugging her when he visited, and she loved that warm, solid security of his body wrapped around her. His hand on her back was the most she could hope for after their last encounter had got too physical and caused all the trouble.

She was content to stand to talk but Sam pulled over a chair and insisted she sat down, whilst he leaned his body back against the desk.

'What do you know about him?' he asked.

'Same as you. Presenting with arm pain, and X-rays show past untreated fracture which hasn't healed properly. Why?'

'Do you know anything about his home life?' Sam was frowning and Emmy wondered if his thoughts had gone to the same place as hers. Something did not sit right about Marcus's story. He was a quiet boy, yet his mother acted as though he was the bane of her life. It was not the typical behaviour of a mother at the bedside of her poorly son. She was not a parent herself yet, but Emmy liked to think she would have more concern for her offspring if they were in pain to the point of being hospitalised.

'Not really. His mother always appears to be distracted, in a hurry to get back to work. I've never met the father and I don't think he has any siblings. Do you think there's something going on that social services need to know about?'

'Perhaps. I don't have proof of anything untoward. I know there were no other missed injuries picked up… Call it a hunch but something feels off.'

Emmy nodded. 'I know what you mean, and neither were able to give valid reasons for him not coming in when he first injured himself…if that's what happened.'

Sam shifted his position slightly, as though uneasy about the subject they could be dealing with. 'Do you think there's any physical abuse going on with Marcus at home?'

A shudder reverberated through Emmy's body at the thought of someone hurting their own child. It was bad enough her parents had wounded her emotionally, but it must be devastating to have someone who is supposed to love and protect you being the one inflicting pain. It happened, of course, and Emmy had dealt with domestic violence cases before. However, now she was expecting a child of her own it seemed all the more harrowing. Despite the circumstances and timing of her pregnancy, she had nothing but love for her little one already.

Her hand went protectively to her belly, her eyes filling with tears for those babies who were not as lucky as this one who had a mother who would do anything to protect it.

'I didn't see any other unusual activity on his file.' She had made a point of checking in case there was any evidence of historic abuse which they might have missed.

'Well, given that he wasn't brought in for treatment with this last broken bone, I don't think we can rely on his records being an accurate depiction of his medical background.'

'You're right. I guess I was just praying that my own suspicions weren't justified.' Her eyes were burning with the threat of tears, and though she fought making a scene, Sam was already moving towards her.

'Hey. I know this is a tough one. If you want, I can take it from here?' He was holding both of her hands in his, doing his best to reassure her everything was going to be okay.

Emmy would have given anything for one of his hugs in that moment, but she knew it would be inappropriate on so many levels. Instead, she sniffed away the tears and straightened her back.

'No. I want to probe a bit deeper and see what's going on for myself. I still have a duty of care to the patients here.' It was not going to be easy but her emotions should not interfere with her work.

There was a way to go before the baby arrived, months of being emotional and dealing with sick children, but she could not turn her back simply because it was upsetting. Those children, her patients, needed her. Being a good mother was all about putting her child first and she saw her job at the hospital as good training. Her birth parents had not stuck by her when things got tough and that made her all the more determined to stay strong for others. Dealing with vulnerable children was part of her job and her conscience would not let her back away simply because it was a difficult situation. Children like Marcus needed people like her and Sam who were willing to go the extra mile for their patients. 'That's all well and good, Emmy, but I don't want you stressing yourself out unnecessarily.'

If she believed Sam's concern was for her she might have found it endearing, but she was sure he was thinking only of his baby. Yes, that was a good thing that he cared at all when she had expected him to run as soon as he found out he was going to be a dad. However, she was more than just an incubator for his offspring, and she was not going to be dictated to or lose her identity simply because she was becoming a mother. They were not together, so he had no say over anything she did.

'I may be pregnant, but I'm still capable of doing my job. It's going to be a long six months if you scrutinise my every move for the duration. The baby is yours but I'm not.' And that was the crux of the problem and her outburst. She wanted to be his, longed for that protective side of Sam's to be for her. It wasn't jealousy—goodness knew she was happy her baby had two parents who adored it—but for the rest of her life she was going to be on the outside of Sam's deepest affections, and that hurt. With her history, she should have been used to that feeling, but it never got any easier.

She attempted a dramatic flounce out of the room but could not see the handle clearly through her blurred vision.

'Hey,' Sam said softly, and closed his hand over hers. 'I'm only looking out for you. I don't mean to come across as domineering. Of course you do whatever you're happy with. All I'm saying is I'm here to share the load with you.'

That was what was making everything so much harder for Emmy. If he had washed his hands of her and the baby and disappeared out of their lives for good, she would not have to see him every day, or be reminded that he did not want her. In time she might even have got over him. Impossible now when he was part of her life, showing her every day what a good man he was deep down. It was not Sam's fault he did not feel for her what she had always felt for him.

Emmy sighed. Pushing him away was not going to do anyone any good.

'Why don't you have a chat with Marcus, and I'll see if I can get any information from the mother? I don't want to take things any further unless we have to or unless there is any proof he is being deliberately hurt.'

'If you're sure—' Sam's tone and the look of concern were indication he did not think it was a good idea, but she thought it made sense for them to continue their investigation separately. Not to mention safer for her peace of mind.

It only took one glare for him to hold his hands up. 'Okay, okay. You know best.' He was smirking at her now and that was not any easier to deal with than the pity eyes.

Unless she poked her own eyeballs out, or wore a blindfold around him, she was going to be in trouble for a long time to come.

Emmy's palms were sweating, her heart galloping, and Sam was not anywhere in sight for her to blame it all on. It was seeing Mrs Moseley coming down the corridor which had her in a tizz. Confronting a parent with such a serious accusation was going to be tough and she had no way of knowing how the woman would react. She wondered if Sam was right and she was putting herself and the baby in harm's way if she chose to lash out.

Unfortunately, violent outbursts towards staff were commonplace these days and it was more than her pride at stake today. Except, if Emmy decided to make things official at this stage, before she knew the facts, she could be making things worse for the boy. She did not want to see him taken into care on her say-so; she would never forgive herself if she got things wrong.

She would have an informal chat, more of a fact-finding mission than pointing an accusing finger straight away. According to Sam, Marcus had closed up when he had tried talking to him, giving nothing away, so this was their last attempt to get to the truth before they would be forced to go to the authorities.

'Mrs Moseley, I wondered if I could have a word with you in here?' Emmy opened the door to the family room in an attempt to herd her inside.

'I suppose...' Although she looked wary, she let Emmy lead her into the room. 'Is Marcus all right?'

She did not sit in any of the armchairs provided for the comfort of the families visiting seriously ill relatives, clearly worried about the reason behind being sequestered into a side room.

Emmy took a seat and gestured for her to do the same, the reassuring smile she was projecting covering her own anxiety caused by the situation.

'Yes, he's fine. I just wanted to have a chat with you about anything which might be going on at home.' Emmy tried to keep her tone light and casual to avoid any unpleasantness but was aware that she was encroaching on the woman's private life.

'There's nothing going on at home that concerns you.' Any conviviality evaporated with the thinning of Mrs Moseley's lips and defensive folding of her arms.

Emmy sat forward in her chair in an attempt to close the distance between them. 'I'm not here to judge you. My job is to make Marcus better and sometimes things at home can impact on a child's health.'

'What exactly are you accusing me of?' Narrowing eyes matched the thin lips.

Emmy swallowed hard, feeling as though she was the one under scrutiny here. 'I'm not accusing you of anything, Mrs Moseley. There are just a few things we're concerned about and hoped you could clarify some matters for us. I…we…wondered how a fracture like that could have been missed for so long. Marcus must have been in pain at the time. Is there a reason you didn't bring him into hospital before now?'

Silence.

Emmy tried again. 'I'm trying to help you but if I suspect Marcus is being physically harmed, I have a duty to report it. So far, you're giving me nothing to dissuade me of that notion.' There was part of Emmy wishing she had allowed Sam to be involved in this with her so he could have been the one playing bad cop. Not that he would have been convincing as anything other than a concerned member of staff either, but she could have used the backup.

Sam was good at giving her a boost and support when he thought she needed it. Emmy was sure she was on the verge of hitting a nerve or being on the receiving end of a right hook for questioning another woman's parenting.

Mrs Moseley suddenly burst into tears, leaving Emmy scrabbling to find the box of tissues usually kept here for such emotionally charged occasions. It turned out she was correct in her assumption, just not in the way she had expected.

'I didn't hurt him, despite what you think,' Marcus's mother sniffed in between sobs.

As Emmy passed over the hankies, she could see now how tired the woman looked close up with unwashed hair, bags under her eyes and no attempt to cover them with make-up. This outburst was a sign she had reached her emotional limit.

'Take all the time you need,' Emmy coached, softly, encouraging her to continue with her story. She knew better than anyone how cathartic it was to share one's worries. Despite how the news of her pregnancy had come to light, and Sam's chivalrous but misjudged proposal, it was a weight off her mind not having to keep the secret any longer.

Mrs Moseley dabbed at her eyes with the tissue and sniffed back further tears. 'Sorry. It hasn't been easy.'

Without any further information Emmy could not be sure if she was talking about parenting in general or if there was a more sinister context. She had to push for more.

'With Marcus?'

The woman nodded and Emmy's heart sank into her comfortable shoes. Was this confirmation that the child had borne the brunt of his mother's frustrations with him? She hoped not. The emotionally charged silence seemed to stretch for ever before Mrs Moseley cleared her throat to speak again.

'He's not a bad child…just difficult to manage sometimes.'

'And you…you discipline him when he acts out?' It was the logical conclusion for Emmy to come to, if not the most palatable one.

'No! I told you, I would never hurt him, but I can't watch him twenty-four hours a day.'

'He hurt himself?' Though it came as something of a relief, it still did not explain why the mother had not sought adequate treatment for her son at the time of injury.

She nodded. 'He's always getting into scrapes but I have two jobs. I can't take time off every time he falls over or gets into mischief.'

'Isn't there someone who can help out? Family or friends?'

She gave an emphatic 'No.'

'Is his father around?' Normally, Emmy would not pry into people's personal lives but she was trying to ascertain what sort of support system was in place for the family, if any.

'Only when it suits him. That doesn't stop him from threatening to take custody of Marcus though, just to spite me. He's no father to Marcus, but if he thought he could use an accident against me, he would.'

'That's why you didn't bring Marcus in earlier?'

'I didn't realise he'd actually broken the bone or I swear I would have brought him before now. He seemed fine after a day or two, so I thought he'd pulled a muscle or something. You've got to understand, my ex-husband walked out and left us with nothing. I'm working two jobs just to make ends meet. I know the break-up has affected Marcus too, and with me working so much, he's been playing up for attention. I'm run ragged. Being a parent isn't easy.' The tears began to fall again in earnest and Emmy reached out a hand to comfort her, her own eyes welling up in sympathy. She could very well find herself in the same situation at some point: overworked, overtired, guilty about leaving a child at home and struggling to find adequate childcare, as well as managing to pay all of the bills. At least Sam wanted to be in the picture. Emotions aside, having him involved could make a big difference to her on the practical side.

His business proposal to get married was beginning to make sense now she could see where things could lead if she insisted on doing everything herself. Mrs Moseley didn't have a choice, but she did.

Sam was offering a partnership, sharing time and financial responsibilities so they could give their baby the best start in life. It was selfish to turn that down for the sake of her own pride. She was sure Mrs Moseley would have jumped at the chance if an attractive, successful man had given her the same deal. Okay, so love was not part of the contract but that did not pay the bills or give a person peace of mind. This woman and her son were deeply unhappy and that was not a future Emmy wanted for herself and her child.

'Listen, I'll go and get you a cup of tea and you can take a few minutes to compose yourself. If it's all right with you, I'd like to make a few calls and see if I can get you some help.'

'I don't want social services to think I'm not coping.' There was panic in her eyes, along with the determination to carry on regardless of the cost to her emotionally and physically. Emmy knew she would be the same if there was a threat of someone trying to take her child away hanging over her. It was about time someone gave her a break.

'Social services will have to get involved, but I do want to see if there is any other help available to you. Perhaps there's a charitable organisation with after-school clubs. Somewhere for Marcus to go and run off some of his excess energy and meet new friends. I'll see what I can do.'

'Thank you.'

By the time Emmy left the room Mrs Moseley was smiling again and looking years younger at the prospect of getting some help.

Emmy's new task was hitting close to home. She had dealt with single-parent groups in the past in relation to her patients and their families, but this time was different. She knew she could be availing of their services herself in time, depending on how well she managed to juggle work, childcare and the cost of raising a child on her own. There was one person who could save her from that uncertain future. At least Sam wanted to be a dad, to contribute to his baby's upbringing. If only she could learn to live with her husband not loving her, marriage could be the perfect solution to avoiding a similar situation to Mrs Moseley.

CHAPTER SIX

As soon as Sam was finished with his patients, he went in search of Emmy. His attempt to get some information from Marcus had proved fruitless and he had spent most of the afternoon worried about how Emmy's chat with the mother had gone. He had always been protective towards her but now she was carrying his baby he wanted to wrap her up and keep them both safe from the outside world. Although she had made it pretty clear that was not an option available to him.

Emmy had always been headstrong and independent, qualities he admired but which were now driving him crazy. It was those helping her to push him away, Emmy believing him too unreliable to be a father or a husband. He was a chip off the old block after all. Regardless of the vow he had made never to get into this situation, he still believed himself to be a better human being than his father. Something he was now having to take a second look at. He did not blame Emmy for not trusting him, but he wanted to give her reason to start. Proposing marriage had been his way of showing her that commitment. She knew he had never wanted to be tied down, but he was willing to do that for her and the baby. Even if the marriage would be in name only.

It was a big undertaking on his part and after his chat with Marcus he was more aware of that than ever. Having a child was a huge responsibility, fraught with all kinds of worry and sacrifice. Only time would tell if he was up to the job or if Emmy would even let him try.

He saw her emerge from one of the cubicles and the tension ebbed from his bones to see she was physically unharmed after her confrontation with Mrs Moseley.

'Emmy! Did everything go all right with Marcus's mother?'

'Yes. She was very emotional and apologetic. Nothing sinister, but she is struggling. It appears Marcus's father has left, and things are acrimonious between the couple.'

It was a relief to discover Marcus was not in any immediate danger at home. Sam did not like having families split up if it was preventable. Yet there was something about the tale which made him uneasy on a more personal level. Another family had been torn apart and left bleeding, the mother the one dealing with the fallout, and the son suffering as a result. The children were never to blame for their parents' actions but always the ones impacted most. It was Sam's worst fear to cause such pain to others, but he might not get much say in what happened.

If Emmy continued to keep him at arm's length, would he ever be involved in his child's life at all? He did not relish the idea of being kept out of the picture. It would still leave Emmy to do the majority of the parenting and deal with all the highs and lows which came with it.

'Is there anything we can do to help?'

'I've contacted social services and put her in touch

with a few local groups who support single-parent families. Hopefully Marcus can get back to being a kid again and forget everything going on with his parents.'

'I'm sure they'll appreciate that. The whole matter is making me re-evaluate our situation too, Emmy. Perhaps we should get something in writing about custody arrangements.'

'Isn't that a tad premature? The baby isn't here yet, but when it is, your name will be on the birth certificate.'

Although that was reassuring, Sam was concerned in case any future bad feeling would affect that and leave him without any parental rights.

'It's not that I don't trust you, Emmy, but we know family matters can get complicated. We should seek some legal advice on the subject just in case.'

She frowned at the idea. 'Do you really think that's necessary, Sam? We've known each other for practically our whole lives. This is a baby, not a car or a house you can just claim ownership over.'

'What else do you suggest? How are we going to move forward, both of us confident and secure about where we stand?' Naturally they both had reservations when this was not the ideal basis for bringing a new life into the world. If he had been sensible and done things properly, he would have wooed Emmy, given her reason to trust him and maybe even love him. Ideally they would have been in a proper relationship before even thinking about starting a family but now it was about damage control.

'Dealing with Marcus has made me think about things too. It's made me see the practical benefits of having two parents working together instead of each pretending the other doesn't exist. If the offer is still there on the table to be your wife, I'd like to close the deal.'

The sudden turnaround left Sam's head spinning. He had been hoping to at least get paternity rights down on paper but now it seemed as though Emmy was prepared to give him so much more.

'Are you saying—?'

'Yes, Sam. If the offer is still there, I'd like to marry you. That should give us both some security over the arrangements, shouldn't it?' Emmy was smiling but there was a brightness missing from her eyes to convince him she was truly on board with the decision.

This should have been the happiest moment of their lives, entering into a lifelong commitment to one another. Instead, he knew it was more out of necessity, a convenient way of sharing responsibility for their mistake. As if getting someone pregnant and having to marry had ever been on his agenda. Sam knew he had already ruined Emmy's life and all he could do was try to make amends now she thought there was no better future for her than to marry someone she did not love.

'I think we should do it as soon as possible.' Before either of them changed their minds. It was not the most romantic engagement but if this was purely a business transaction, there should be no misunderstanding. No one would get fooled into thinking this was a real relationship or run the risk of anyone getting hurt. Then he could stop fretting over why she did not truly want him.

Sam faced himself in the mirror as he pinned the white carnation to his buttonhole. Something perhaps his best man or mother should have done for him on his wedding day, but he had neither. This was not a conventional marriage after all.

It was going to appear odd to the outside world who were unaware of his arrangement with Emmy that there would be no traditional 'groom's side' but it did not seem right in the circumstances. Not least because he had minimal contact with his mother. Having her present simply for appearances' sake would not have made the day any easier. He was already a bag of nerves at the prospect of marrying Emmy without the added worry of his mother's presence. Seeing her there—a bitter, broken woman who was the result of his father's behaviour—would only impress on him the importance of not messing up the marriage or being a father. He was under enough pressure to make things work since he had talked Emmy into this crazy scheme.

Strangely, getting ready today felt very much like preparing for the real thing. He was nervous about getting the vows right and making this commitment. In putting himself forward as a suitable husband to Emmy, he was saying he would be there for her and the baby. That she could rely on him. In reality, he was praying that to be true when he had no practical experience of being a husband or a father. Roles he thought he would never have to prepare for, yet now he was taking on both, he would admit to some sense of excitement along with the anxiety.

A future with Emmy was not something completely abhorrent to him or he would never have proposed it. In fact, he was looking forward to having more than snatched moments with her without interruption from her family. A big part of him was secretly hoping they might develop a relationship beyond the façade when their partnership was so good in all other areas.

They were going to be spending a lot of time together for the foreseeable future, raising the child Sam never thought he would have. Now that fatherhood was a certainty there were aspects of that which appealed to him too. A chance to create the family neither he nor Emmy had been afforded growing up. Pride in his child's achievements, being there for every milestone no matter how small and enjoying days out at the seaside or the zoo were all simple things he had been denied by his father but were things he was now looking forward to participating in.

As Sam pondered the happy occasions soon available to him if he chose to embrace his new path as a husband and father, today did not seem as frightening as it once had. Hopefully his future wife would come to the same conclusion.

'Are you ready to do this?' Sam was standing at the open car door smiling and waiting for Emmy to take his arm.

She said, 'Yes,' when really, she wanted to scream, 'No, not like this!'

From here on in, she doubted she would ever say what she was really thinking or feeling to Sam. It was not in the contract.

Today she was going to become Mrs Goodwin. In name at least. It had been a whirlwind few weeks since they had managed to secure a spot at the register office. Neither had wanted a big wedding, not when this was nothing more than an arrangement between them. It meant keeping it a secret from her family, who would have insisted on the whole extravagance of a white church wedding, and all the expense and headaches which came with it. It did not seem fair or necessary when they weren't some loved-up couple having the day of their lives.

Now, however, walking up the steps to the town hall, she wondered if they had done the right thing in keeping it quiet. The family would be so disappointed to have missed out, and if she was honest, she was a little emotional that they were not here for her wedding day, even if it was just for show.

'Well, don't you scrub up well, sis? Going somewhere?'

When David stepped out into the marble hallway to greet them, Emmy nearly passed out from shock.

'David? What are you doing here?'

'Did you really think I was going to let my little sister and best friend get married without me?'

Emmy let go of Sam's arm and threw herself at David, so pleased to have his support on a day when she knew her nerves would be tested to the limit.

Sam cleared his throat. 'I know we agreed to keep things low key, but I couldn't let you go through this without your family.'

It was then she noticed the others hovering nearby, clearly worried about being unwanted.

'I'm so glad you all came.' She transferred her affections to her parents, hugging them hard, and even stopped for a brief embrace with the twins.

'We don't want to intrude if you'd rather we weren't here,' her father mumbled, and Emmy immediately wished she had included them from the start.

'Of course I want you here. We just didn't want a

big fuss. I would love for you to give me away, Dad.' At least that part would be genuine and filled with real emotion even if the rest of the ceremony was not.

'You look so beautiful.' Her mother was already dabbing her eyes with a handkerchief and Emmy was glad she had loved ones here supporting her, rather than some stranger they had roped in to witness proceedings.

'Thank you.' In keeping with the low-key nature of the day, she had avoided a big flouncy gown in favour of a white lace shift dress and some flowers in her hair. Sam had presented her with a posy of wildflowers he had picked himself that morning as a bouquet to add to her Bohemian look and she loved it.

He was the perfect, handsome groom in his navy three-piece suit and her family had come dressed for the occasion in outfits she knew had been bought specially for the last-minute occasion. If anyone had any misgivings about the venue or the timing, they had the decency not to say anything for now. Emmy was appreciative when the doubts had been creeping in over these past days anyway.

She had moved her belongings into Sam's house the previous weekend, setting up in a separate bedroom to his, of course. Not how most women began their married life, but this was what she had agreed to—a loveless arrangement. Who would not have had second thoughts about that? But here she was, ready to do it, and now her family were here there was no going back.

'Are we ready to go through?' The registrar ushered them into the small side room, the guests barely taking up the front row of seats.

Despite the informality, her father walked her down

the short aisle and very seriously answered, 'I do,' when asked who was giving Emmy away.

At that moment, she had a sudden urge to cling to him all the tighter, when he had been her source of stability for so long. Now she was being handed over to Sam, she was trusting him to do as good a job.

He looked as anxious as she felt when they met at the end of the aisle and she realised the enormity of this to him too. A man who had always said marriage and babies were not for him was marrying her simply out of a sense of duty. This was not a fairy-tale ending for him either. Judging by his pallid colour, it was more like the stuff of nightmares.

They said the traditional vows as they exchanged plain gold bands, though Emmy's voice had trembled as she did so. She almost broke completely when saying, 'I do.'

This was not how marriage was supposed to be and, looking into Sam's eyes, she could see her own sadness reflected in them.

They were both trapped, making the best of a bad situation. The worst of it was her family watching, believing this was real and that they had found love together. If only.

'You may kiss the bride.' The registrar confirmed they were now husband and wife before dropping that surprise on them.

'Is that really a thing? We don't have to,' she whispered to her groom.

'We may as well give the people what they want,' he replied with a grin before moving in for their first kiss as a married couple.

She was poised, ready for a peck on the lips to satisfy her family they were together for all the right reasons. What she got was hot enough to make her forget this was fake. Somewhere in the distance she heard David cheering and her father discreetly coughing. Her sisters were likely sniggering somewhere too, but she did not care because Sam's lips were on hers again for the first time in months.

There was still that same urgency that she remembered in his kiss, as though he had been starved of her for too long. Exactly how she felt about him.

He had to spoil the illusion when he broke away and winked at her. 'That should do the trick.'

Emmy had to hand it to him, he was a very good actor. For a moment he had fooled her into thinking he was actually sealing their future together with a heartfelt kiss. Every time she was in danger of getting caught up in the supposed romance, Sam was there bringing her back down to earth and reminding her that he personally was not part of the deal.

It took a lot of effort to force her trembling mouth into a smile when she turned to face her family.

'Congratulations!'

Every good wish and kiss on the cheek brought Emmy closer to tears. Confetti rained on her like the colourful, tattered remnants of her romantic hopes and dreams. Sam stopped at the top of the steps and turned her face to his. There was no hiding her pain from him now.

'Hey,' he said softly, tilting her chin up. 'It's over now.'

He dropped a quick kiss on her mouth, grounding her and reassuring her he was there with her.

That was when she heard the click of a camera and

began to question the real motive behind the kiss. Would she ever believe anything he said again if she was always convinced it was only for appearances' sake?

Sam might think the worst was over, but Emmy was worried it was just the beginning.

'A toast to the happy couple.'

Mr Jennings raised his glass and encouraged the others to do the same. He received a muted response, but they could not expect a rapturous celebration with only half a dozen guests present. They fitted into one corner of the local bar they had gone to for the impromptu wedding reception.

Sam knew every second was killing Emmy inside and his fake smile was making his jaw ache. This was not what they had planned for their wedding day in any shape or form but at the last minute he had decided Emmy should have her family around her.

A decision he was sure she appreciated and which also meant he would keep on Dave's good side. What he had not counted on was the day carrying on after the ceremony and signing of the register. Poor Emmy could not even drink to get her through the enforced reception.

She deserved so much more than she was getting today but she had not wanted a whole palaver and he understood why. There was not a whole lot to celebrate, at least not in the traditional sense. This wasn't an occasion to mark the start of their new life together, it signified the end of their independent lives. From here on in they were together for selfless reasons, not because they could not imagine an existence without one another. He would go as far as to say, given the choice, Emmy could live without ever seeing him again. One night and he had destroyed the future she might have envisioned for herself. Whatever she thought of him she could not hate him any more than he hated himself.

'So, when are you going on honeymoon? I guess with the money you saved on feeding guests and a band, you have something amazing planned?' Lisa had that smug look on her face she always wore when she stirred up trouble. Sam did not know how Emmy had endured the endless mocking for so long without slapping it off her face.

He supposed it came from a lifetime of listening to the constant digs and put-downs which had somehow become acceptable to the family. Even now she had her head bowed taking everything that was being thrown at her in that subservient pose. The others excused or ignored the twins' behaviour and Sam knew he was guilty of that too. Now she was his wife he was entitled to defend her if he deemed it necessary.

On this occasion he realised he was at fault for not organising something, or at least coming up with a reason for not booking a trip away to throw everyone off the scent of their arranged marriage.

'I…er…' Mr and Mrs Jennings were waiting to hear their exciting plans and Dave was listening intently too. How was Sam going to explain away not giving his little sister the trip of her dreams without getting a good pasting?

'With work, and the pregnancy, we thought we'd wait. We'll make it a family holiday when the baby arrives. Right, hon?' Emmy batted her eyelashes and linked her arm through his as she got him off the hook.

'Right. We'll have plenty of time for holidays. For now, we're content simply spending time with each other.' He patted her hand with the sickly sweet sentiment, knowing it could not be further from the truth. They had nothing planned beyond the legal ceremony but there would be expectations from everyone else. Things had happened so fast they had not really thought things through properly. Going back to work would be fun trying to explain. As far as anyone there knew they had only met, and this would seem like a whirlwind romance. Not a lifelong bond which had somehow morphed into a marriage of inconvenience for both of them.

Emmy stamped on his foot under the table, a reminder not to overdo it. Dave was already eyeing them with some suspicion. Maybe if Sam got them drunk they would forget how strange this all was.

CHAPTER SEVEN

EMMY'S WEDDING NIGHT turned out to be anticlimactic on so many levels. There was no romantic getaway to look forward to, far from work, family and any other stresses. Perhaps she should have booked herself a solo trip somewhere and put some distance between her and Sam one last time before they entered into their forced proximity.

As it was, they were heading home together, alone, to start their new life of domestic indifference. They walked through the door of his house and she wondered if they were supposed to go their separate ways and do their own thing now that the show was over.

'I wanted to say thank you again for inviting my family. I appreciate it made things more difficult in some ways but I'm glad they were there.' Emmy kicked off her shoes in the hall and popped her posy of flowers into a vase on the side table.

'No problem. I'm sorry I couldn't give you the day you deserved but I thought having them there would help.' Sam hung up his jacket and it seemed absurd to be returning to the mundane, still dressed in their wedding finery.

'It did but I have to say I was relieved when we finally poured them into taxis.' Emmy had sat with her soft drinks watching the others celebrate their nuptials with copious amounts of alcohol. Sam hadn't indulged as much as her family but did not take the risk of driving anyway. Their wedding dinner had consisted of pub snacks and crisps but she had been the one against a grand 'do.' It would have weighed even heavier on her conscience if they had paid a fortune for the ruse.

Yet, she had a feeling Sam would have given her anything she had asked for to make her happy. He was trying to make this bearable but only time would tell how long that would last. He might come to resent the commitment he had made in the heat of the moment. Especially if he went on to meet someone else.

The thought of him bringing another woman home with him made her sick but her claim to him was in name only. That was part of the marriage they had not discussed. It was all very well entering into a convenient partnership but she could not expect him to remain celibate.

They turned to each other in a 'What now?' moment now the hard part was over. Emmy's thoughts slipped back to the kiss they had shared during the ceremony and she would have been happy to carry on from where they had left off. They both had needs and she would not be averse to maintaining the physical aspect of the marriage. It might prevent Sam from seeking sexual gratification elsewhere and provide her with some of the intimacy she craved with him. Even if the relationship still lacked the emotional side of a relationship.

'I guess I'll be heading to bed. It's been a long day.' It appeared Sam, however, had had enough already. That did not bode well for a long-lasting marriage if he was desperate to get away from her on what was supposed to be their wedding night.

'Oh. Okay.'

'Unless you had something else in mind? Feel free to watch the TV in the lounge and make yourself a cup of tea. Maybe you would like a bath? This is your house now too so you're welcome to do as you please.' Regardless of his generosity, Sam was giving her the warmth of a bed-and-breakfast owner letting her use a room for the night.

'I'm sure I can find something to amuse myself. Thanks.' What Emmy wanted now was to strip off this layer of pretence and wash away all traces of the day. Thankfully, she had a shower in her en suite bathroom to do that without fear of running into Sam. He might have just married the mother of his child but she wondered if they would see much of each other at all.

'Goodnight, then, Emmy.' He gave her a swift peck on the cheek.

Her eyes fluttered shut, replaying the kiss he had given her earlier in front of their audience. She supposed he did not have anyone to convince any more and this was as good as it was getting.

'Night.'

She waited for him to retire to his room first, thinking it too tragic for them to split off into their separate rooms at the same time on their wedding night. Her breath hitched in her throat when she heard the door slam, sounding the death knell on her love life for good.

Sam had barely slept. How could he, hearing his new wife cry herself to sleep in the next room? As a result he had been up since dawn in an attempt to make amends for the disappointment he had caused her.

Although the marriage was not a conventional one, he should have made more of an effort. Emmy still needed, and deserved, to be treated like a cherished wife. He had made the mistake of thinking she would want her space but Emmy had been through too much to be taken for granted and he should not have expected her to resume life as though nothing had happened. A wedding day was a big deal to anyone and he was lucky she had agreed to marry him at all after everything. If he was going to hang on to her he had to remember his life was about looking after more than number one now.

He let himself in through the front door and heard her moving about upstairs. This was the first day of the rest of their lives together and he was starting as he meant to go on. This morning, he was hoping to put a smile back on her face with breakfast.

She wandered into the kitchen, looking weary and beautiful, before he had time to plate anything up for her. He was standing at the breakfast bar and she pulled up a chair to watch him.

'Morning, Mrs Goodwin. I was going to bring this to you in bed.'

Her smile turned into a yawn. 'Sorry. I didn't sleep very well.'

His heart lurched, as he replayed the sound of her sobs in his head. 'Nor me. We should have both come downstairs and made some hot cocoa.'

Okay, so that would not have been an earth-shattering wedding night either but at least they could have been miserable in company. He hated to think of her crying in her room, believing she was alone, when they had gone into this together.

'It was a strange day for both of us.' Emmy was being generous to include him when this had affected her so much more. He longed to have her back to the carefree young woman she had been before he had screwed everything up.

'Hopefully things will settle into some sort of normalcy for us soon. Starting with breakfast.' Sam pushed the takeaway cups and bag of warm pastries towards her. She took the lid off one cup and inhaled a deep breath.

'Mmm… Coffee?'

'Decaf.' He knew how much she loved her coffee but had sacrificed it for the baby. He figured one cup of decaffeinated brew was allowed now and then if it made her happy.

'And a *pain au chocolat*?' She opened the bag and helped herself to one of the flaky pastries. 'You're spoiling me.'

Sam was glad to see her enjoying the breakfast but something so simple should not be such a special thing to her. It proved how infrequently anyone did something nice for her. It made him more convinced that he had done the right thing with the surprise he had in store for her next. It was about time someone treated her with the kindness she doled out to everyone else. As her husband, it was his job now to show her she was appreciated.

He produced the folded computer printout from his back pocket and placed it on the counter.

'What's this?' she asked, after finishing her first bite of breakfast.

There was a small spot of melted chocolate clinging to her bottom lip and Sam had the urge to lick it off. His body was wide awake now as memories of that kiss yesterday came to mind. Again, he had got carried away and was lucky she had not slapped him in front of their wedding guests. Thankfully, he had managed to convince her it was a show he had put on to further the lie, rather than his libido beginning to rage out of control again. This torture of seeing her being so close and not being able to do anything about it was his punishment for his self-centred behaviour to date. He was going to have to learn to live with it and keep his urges at bay or run the risk of losing his wife and child in one more wrong move.

'Let's call it a wedding present.' Or a belated apology, he thought, after treating her feelings as an afterthought amongst all the wedding shenanigans.

He watched her scan the page, her eyes widening and her hand moving towards her mouth as she gasped. 'Paris?'

'I know you always wanted to go, and we have a few days off work. I thought a mini-break might do us the world of good.'

'Yes, but…I'm not ready to go. The flight is this afternoon.'

'You look good to me.' Make-up free, with bed-head and wearing a royal blue silk chemise, Emmy was gorgeous.

If they had been a real married couple he would have taken her back to bed and happily spent the weekend there.

'That's sweet of you to lie but I really need to go

shower and pack.' She bounced up out of her chair, full of energy and looking more like the old Emmy.

Her bare feet squeaked on the tiled floor as she did a one-hundred-and-eighty-degree turn and came running back towards him. Leaning over the counter, she planted a kiss on his cheek with a 'Mwah! Thank you, Sam, for everything.'

Then she took another bite of her pastry and skipped off. Sam had been up since the early hours of the morning trying to come up with something to make her smile and he had succeeded. In a flash of inspiration as the birds began to chirp their dawn chorus, he had remembered a conversation they had had a long time ago. One where they had talked about their hopes and dreams, at an age where anything seemed possible without real-life obstacles ever getting in the way.

Back then he was sure his had revolved around money, flash cars and beautiful women. All of which he had had in the past and none of which had ever made him truly content.

Emmy's aspirations had been simpler and more palatable than his materialistic wants. A good job, a family of her own and a visit to Paris. As one of life's true romantics, Emmy's current situation was all the more tragic.

Obsessed with those slushy movies where the couple always got their happy-ever-after, she had told him of her Paris dream. The city of love in her childhood fantasies was the ultimate destination. She had probably imagined her engagement beginning with a proposal atop the Eiffel Tower and a wedding to outshine those she had sobbed over in the movies.

Instead, all he had given her was a shotgun ceremony at a register office and a staycation. Sam would never make the romantic lead in her dreams, but he could give her the best holiday possible. Maybe then she could begin to forgive him for getting them into this mess.

'Oh, Sam. It's stunning.'

The view from the hotel was something Emmy thought only existed in the movies. They were opposite the Eiffel Tower, the bustling city traffic directly below their balcony, and she could not have been happier.

She had woken up this morning resigned to her new life with Sam, which, after last night, she thought meant living separate lives. He had apparently found it a depressing enough future too, to have splurged on this extravagant venture.

Never mind the cost of the last-minute flights, he had also booked the honeymoon suite in this bijou hotel in its prime location.

'I'm so glad you like it.' He carried their luggage into the room after refusing to let her lift anything heavier than her handbag.

She took a glance around the spacious room and marvelled at the sweet vintage furniture and the soft blue-and-white floral decor. There was even a trail of rose petals leading from the claw-foot bathtub to the four-poster bed. She did a double take. One bed.

Sam must have been thinking along the same lines. 'Don't worry, I can take the sofa. I just thought you deserved something magical and this was the nicest room they had available.'

'I'm sure we can sort the sleeping arrangements out later. We are both adults.' Married ones, at that.

Sharing a bed at this stage—married and expecting a baby—should not have been a problem but it was in this instance. It likely always would be for her but Emmy had agreed to this life so she would simply have to get used to it. Sam had gone to a lot of trouble to make this part of her dream come true at least.

'This is your trip so what would you like to do first?'

There were so many landmarks—l'Arc de Triomphe, the Louvre, the Eiffel Tower—to name a few. All of which she had imagined visiting with Sam at her side in her wildest dreams. Somehow this was not quite the same, but she would make the most of the situation.

'The nearest restaurant. Baby's hungry and so am I. If I can't partake in the glorious wines and cheeses available, I'm going to sample the finest cuisine this country has to offer.'

'You won't get an argument from me on that score. We can unpack later.'

Emmy supposed that was the most action this room would see tonight. Sam had covered all the romantic clichés with this surprise, except the most crucial one. Him. Still, she was lucky he had gone to so much trouble on her behalf and she would not be ungrateful. He was doing everything within his power to make her happy. At this moment in time he had succeeded.

'Have a lovely evening, Mr and Mrs Goodwin.' The receptionist beamed at them as they left the hotel.

Despite the rocky start and the unconventional arrangements, being called Mrs Goodwin did give her a buzz of satisfaction. As far as the outside world knew, Sam was hers and vice versa. Walking out into the bustling Parisian streets, they were simply another newly-wed couple on honeymoon. Only she and Sam knew the truth.

'Hey, watch out!'

Before Emmy knew what was happening, Sam grabbed her hand and pulled her away from the edge of the footpath. Just in time, as someone on an electric scooter zoomed by, too close for comfort.

Sam switched places so she was on the inside, and he was walking closer to the traffic, though he did not let go of her hand. It felt right, natural, and so good to have him want to protect her.

Walking hand in hand with her new husband in Paris was everything she could have asked for as they passed the aromatic *boulangeries* and *chocolatiers*.

'You know I'm making a note of these places to revisit before we go home.'

'I don't doubt it. That's why I paid for extra baggage allowance.' Sam laughed, but unlike some family members, she knew it was not his way to make fun of her weight. That had never been an issue to him, and he had always accepted her for who she was. He might not be madly in love with her, but Emmy knew he was fond of her. Comfortable enough to let people think they were a couple without embarrassment. She had the urge to hug him close but settled for leaning her head on his shoulder. When he kissed the top of her head she almost cried with happiness, or despair. The two were so inextricably linked now it was difficult to tell. He was doing and saying all the right things, but no amount of good intentions could make any of this real.

'Why don't we stop here for a bite to eat? There's a good view of everything going on and we'll catch the last of the sun on the terrace.' Sam spied a chic bistro on the corner, the tables outside packed with chatty diners, whose various accents represented how cosmopolitan the area had become. He insisted on seating her as far away from any smokers as possible as he pulled out a chair for her.

'Such a gentleman,' she teased, only for his 'Not always' to knock her completely off her feet.

It was comments such as that and his rakish grin which made her wonder if he would be interested in a replay of what happened during her brother's evening reception or if it was simply his flirty nature. The idea of having him in her bed again sent delectable quivers of arousal whispering across her skin but the physical act could never replace the emotion, the feelings, she longed for him to have towards her.

Thankfully the waiter's arrival interrupted Emmy's yearning so she could live in the moment and enjoy the surroundings instead of moping over things Sam could not give her.

He ordered a cassoulet between them, with some fresh bread and two glasses of mineral water, impressing her with his perfect French as he did so.

'You don't have to forego the alcohol because of me,' she told him, encouraging him to enjoy one passion. It was a shame to deny him the opportunity to taste some of the finest wines in the world on her account.

'It's fine. I don't need to be drunk to enjoy myself when I'm here with you.' The warmth of his smile was a clear sign of his sincerity and helped her believe he was getting something out of this trip too.

She had been so focused on what she had lost by entering into a fake marriage with him that she never stopped to think about what Sam was feeling about it all. He was giving up more than alcohol for her and the baby. His freedom and the lifestyle he was used to before their one night of madness had gone for ever. Yet he had concentrated all of his effort into making this transition into married life as easy as possible for her. She did not know what was in it for him.

'Why are you doing all of this, Sam? We're already married and we both know it's only because of the baby.' Their food and drinks arrived, and she had to wait until they were alone again for his reply.

Sam took a forkful of his meal, prolonging his answer. Emmy rested her head on both hands, waiting. Eventually he stopped chewing and swallowed.

'We rushed into this situation for the baby, but it doesn't mean we should be miserable for the rest of our lives. We've always enjoyed each other's company and it would be a shame if that was no longer the case. I don't want you to feel trapped or sad about the way things have played out. If we're set on making a safe and secure environment for our child, that starts with us. We owe it to ourselves to make this work and I'll take whatever steps necessary for you to forgive me. We wouldn't be in this situation if it wasn't for my selfishness and I'm sorry I ruined everything.'

Emmy could not even think of eating when she was trying to digest everything Sam said. Yes, she was unhappy, but it was not because of anything he had done. Rather, because of what he could not do. Love her. That was not his fault.

'I think we both played a part in what happened and how we're dealing with it. There's no need to play the martyr, Sam. We're in this together.' They both had to accept where they were now. She reached her hand across the table and he sandwiched it between both of his.

Emmy looked up and caught Sam's gaze. A current passed between them, something she thought she recognised from their last infamous night together. A hunger, a need for something more satisfying than a simple stew. That zap of electricity shot through her whole being, starting where her fingers were entwined with his. Sam was not backing away from the crazy sexual energy zinging between them either.

Emmy's heart was hammering at the implication he might want more than a platonic relationship after all and wondered if that would heal or fracture her poor heart even more.

CHAPTER EIGHT

SAM LONGED TO kiss his wife. No one would blink an eye if he leaned across the table and captured her mouth with his. Especially when Emmy was looking at him like that was exactly what she wanted too. Except he was not going to repeat the mistake of rushing things without thinking them through first.

It seemed absurd that a little thing such as kissing Emmy should cause such overthinking when they were already married and expecting a family, but this was not any ordinary relationship. There was too much history on the line if he got things wrong again. They could not afford an ill-judged fling they could not walk away from when, back in the real world, Emmy would remember why she'd never wanted a relationship with him. In the city of romance it was understandable they might get caught up in the fantasy, but he was not going to be the one to encourage or initiate another flirtation with disaster.

'Emmy, I—' Sam sat back, getting ready to explain why this was not a good idea, and saw the shame washing over her features. Given the choice she would not want a relationship with him. The only reason she was leaning towards it now was because she was trapped with him. Perhaps in time he could show her he had left his old ways behind and she might learn to love him. For now though, this was mere fantasy they could not simply wish into existence.

As they sat staring at their still-full plates, a piercing scream cut through the pained silence. He looked up to see the other diners rushing from their tables, chairs overturning in their haste to get somewhere else.

'What's going on?' Emmy's hands went to her belly, her concern and instinct for her child blazing brightly in the face of any trouble.

Sam got to his feet to check what was causing the commotion, ready to get Emmy to safety if necessary.

He could see that blasted scooter, which had nearly clipped Emmy earlier, lying halfway across the road, the traffic stalled in both directions as a result. 'It looks like there's been a road accident. I'll go and see if anyone's been injured or if I can help.'

'I'll come with you.' Emmy pushed her chair out from the table and followed him through the maze of tables and people now spilling out onto the road.

Sam did not waste time on a futile attempt to talk her out of it when it was ingrained into both of them to provide medical assistance where it was needed. There were a lot of raised French voices mixed in with faint cries and groaning coming from the concentrated circle of people standing around.

'Excusez-moi. Je suis un medecin.' He eased his way through the crowd, reaching a hand back for Emmy to grab so he could lead her safely to the scene.

The long-haired teenager who had been riding the scooter was sitting on the ground, apparently in shock, with his head in his hands. Sam heard Emmy gasp when he saw why. A little girl, no more than five or six, was lying splayed on the road near the scooter with whom he assumed was the mother weeping at her child's side.

'Que s'est-il passé?' He asked the father, who was shouting for help, what had happened.

Although Sam had a good grasp of the French language, he had to ask the man to slow down so he could better understand him. After confirming he had phoned for an ambulance, he was able to tell Sam that the guy had been riding the scooter on the pavement. Going at some considerable speed he had lost control, and had clipped the little girl, knocking her into on-coming traffic.

Sam knelt down on the tarmac to take her pulse. A difficult task when she was wedged under the bumper of the car which had hit her.

'Comment t'appelles-tu?'

When there was no response from the girl, her father said, *'Elle s'appelle Amelie.'*

'Amelie? Je m'appelle Sam.'

He was not sure if she could hear him but he did not want to frighten her as he tried to scoot under the vehicle on his back, to reach her and carry out a primary survey of her condition. Her head was millimetres away from the front wheel and luckily the driver had stopped abruptly, narrowly avoiding crushing her skull.

As she was unresponsive, he moved quickly to check her airways were clear and tilt her head back. It was an uneasy scramble to get close enough to hear if she was breathing but somehow he managed it. Listening intently and watching the slight rise and fall of her chest, Sam established she was thankfully still breathing.

His next check was to look for signs of bleeding and it was then he noticed her blond hair stained crimson. If she had a head injury of some sort they could not move her without running the risk of causing further damage. They would have to wait until the paramedics arrived to stabilise her neck and spine before attempting to get her out. The fire brigade might have to be involved too, depending on how difficult that would prove to be. All he could do in the meantime was try to prevent her from going into shock from loss of blood and make sure she was breathing.

Sam lifted her legs and set them on top of his, elevating them above the level of her heart to keep the blood circulating and prevent organ failure. He tore off one sleeve of his shirt and used it to apply pressure to her head wound and stem the bleeding as best he could.

The gravel on the road was scratching at his back, the underbelly of the car so close to his face it was making him claustrophobic, but his discomfort came second to saving a child's life.

'Emmy, are you there?' He could not lift his head to see anything and was relying on her being nearby to hear him.

'Yes.' The flash of bright pink in his peripheral vision made him believe she was crouching down beside him, awaiting instruction.

'She's unconscious but she's got a pulse. Can you pass that on to the parents?' While he made sure the child's clothing was loose around her neck and there was nothing blocking her airways, he could hear a muffled, stilted conversation as Emmy tried to relay the information to the couple.

'Sam? I've got a blanket to put over her to keep her warm.' Emmy stretched under the car and covered the little girl with a tartan picnic rug she must have commandeered from someone to do the job.

'That's great.' It was also important to keep the child's body temperature up in case she went into shock. He was glad to have Emmy's reassuring presence so close to him too, reminding him he was not alone in the dark with this girl's life in his hands.

'The boy on the scooter was wearing a helmet so he's relatively unscathed save for his skinned knees and hands. A little shaken but he's not badly hurt.' Emmy had clearly gone to the rider's assistance as he tended to Amelie. Whilst Sam was glad they were not dealing with two seriously injured adolescents, he was angered by the reckless behaviour which had caused the accident. It could have been Emmy if he had not pulled her to safety. The thought of her and the baby lying under the wheels of a car was enough to make a grown man weep and he was thankful he was not going through what Amelie's parents were right now.

'Let's hope it makes him think twice about racing around the streets in future. I'm going to stay here with Amelie until the emergency services get here to make sure there is no change to her breathing.' This was someone's baby, and though he was not yet a father, he would be devastated if anything should happen to his child. It made him wonder why his father had such a lack of interest in his own offspring. He had been able to float between families, somehow managing to neglect both. Hopefully the fact that Sam already cared about the welfare of his unborn child meant that he had not inherited all of his father's caddish, selfish ways after all.

He brushed the bloody strands of hair away from Amelie's face, imagining if this was Emmy or their baby lying here hovering between life or death. 'I'm here for you, sweetheart. I'm not going anywhere until I know you are safe.'

He reached out, took her tiny hand in his and squeezed. The closest he could get to giving her some comfort in the dark. When he felt the faintest twitch of her fingers against his palm it was like winning the lottery. Whatever the future held for him and Emmy as parents, he knew it was going to be one hell of an emotional carnival ride. He just hoped he remained strapped in until the music stopped playing.

It was getting dark by the time the drama had ended. Emmy let Sam do the talking with the French paramedics as they carefully lifted little Amelie into the ambulance. The bistro insisted on waiving their payment for all the medical assistance they had provided but neither of them had any appetite after what they had seen.

They had walked away from the scene to get a little breathing space, but Emmy stopped to look at him closer under one of the streetlights.

'You are covered in oil and dirt.' The evidence of the trouble he had gone to in aiding the little girl was there in his torn shirt and the scrapes on his face too.

Sam shrugged. 'It's not important. All that matters is that she pulls through.'

'Of course, but you look like you were in a car accident too. Let me get you cleaned up a bit.' She led him over to the beautifully lit fountain in the square they'd wandered into and forced him to sit on the wall surrounding the pool of water.

He had been subdued since the paramedics had taken Amelie to the hospital, and she was worried about him. Although it was natural to be upset over an injured child, they dealt with that sort of incident every day during the course of their work. She wondered what made this one different.

'She was so still…' Sam was staring off somewhere into the distance and Emmy had to consider the possibility he was experiencing some sort of emotional shock.

'But she was breathing, and you did everything you could to comfort her.' She had seen the way he had held her hand and heard him whisper encouraging words to the child. It was a softer side to Sam she had never seen before. Yes, he had always treated her with kindness, but she had never been able to picture him getting soppy over children. For someone who had never wanted to be burdened with a family, he clearly had some paternal instincts, different from those in his paediatrician role. There was an emotional attachment there which was affecting him deeply. It had not been a pleasant scene, but it did give Emmy some confirmation that he had it in him to be a caring father, despite his own experiences growing up.

'Let's hope it was enough. All I could think about was that it could have been you, or our child, lying there. I don't know what I would do if I lost either of you.'

'Same.' Emmy exchanged a lopsided smile with him,

overwhelmed by both his sudden outpouring of emotion and her own, having to imagine the worst happening.

She took a handkerchief from her handbag and dipped it into the rippling water behind them. After tilting Sam's face towards her, she began cleaning the evidence of his heroism away as best she could.

'I'm more invested in this little family of ours than I thought,' he said, his eyes locked onto hers, watching her intently.

Emmy's heart did a backflip, but she tried not to get her hopes up too much in case it was simply the emotional aftershock of the accident talking.

'I know it's probably too late to ask this but why have you been so against a family up until now?' When he had no choice but to get on board with the idea.

He dropped his gaze then. 'You know about my dad and his other family, how much it affected me and my mum. It wasn't only the cheating and lying, he treated all the people he was supposed to love with apathy. He gave no thought to our feelings or how we were surviving when he wasn't there. I never wanted to do that, to inflict so much pain on my own flesh and blood, no matter how unintentional.'

Emmy had no idea his thoughts on the subject ran so deep. She had always assumed his preference for a single life was based solely on having the freedom to behave as badly or wildly as he wished. Not that he was trying to avoid hurting people simply by living life. It was both endearing and tragic that he had been willing to sacrifice so much.

'You know that belief alone means you're nothing like him. That was a selfless decision you made, unnecessarily in my opinion, because you were considerate of other people's feelings. From everything I've heard about your father, and know about you, Sam, you're the antithesis of him.' This insight into Sam's psyche explained so much about his personal life and why he had never entered into a serious relationship. If he had not been so traumatised by his childhood, he might have settled down with someone else by now. It was only that legacy of guilt and fear left to him by his father which had led him here, with her.

'I'd like to think so but there are no guarantees.'

'You mean I don't get an exchange or a refund if you're defective?' Emmy employed some humour to deflect from her own burden of guilt that she had in some way benefitted from Sam's hang-ups.

''Fraid not. Sold as seen. So, there you go, that's a peek inside my messed-up world. Too late as it turns out, now we're already married.'

'We all have our issues. Why else would two otherwise sane individuals enter into a marriage without even going on a proper date?' Emmy knew to anyone else this set-up was beyond bizarre, and if her family had a hint about what was going on, they would have talked them out of this crazy scheme. Perhaps that was why she had not let them in on the wedding plans beforehand. In case they tried to reason with her, when logic had little to do with her choosing to marry Sam.

'At least we know we're both insane. Aren't you angry about what happened? This was my idea, but you didn't have to go along with it. Surely you dreamed about being madly in love with the man you married. You could have waited for him to come and sweep you off your feet.'

Emmy could not tell him he was the man of her

dreams and spoil his version of events where they were both tragic characters miscast in this relationship. It would alter this fragile one they already had if he thought she might have orchestrated this whole thing to get him to marry her.

'With my dating history, a dream is all it ever could have been. As far as my exes were concerned, I wasn't marriage material. Just good for a laugh and a casual fling.'

'Then you were clearly dating the wrong men if they didn't value you for who you are.'

'Yeah, well, I'm used to it. I'm the family joke, as well you know.' Her hackles were up now, as she was reminded of all the times she'd been the butt of people's jokes or used and tossed aside when she was no longer deemed useful. It was no wonder she had decided that a marriage based on convenience was better than getting into another doomed love affair. At least what she had with Sam was honest, apart from her hiding the fact she had been madly in love with him for years.

'Why do you put up with that? You are far from the doormat you let your sisters walk all over, and if that's how you let men treat you, it's no surprise you haven't found anyone suitable. You're not that subservient person who kowtows to everyone else's whim.'

'Aren't I?' When it came to relationships with family and boyfriends, that was exactly who she became. Afraid if she did not act the way they wanted her to, that they would cast her aside the way her birth parents had done.

'Not with me.'

It was only when Sam said it, she realised the truth in those words. With him she had never been afraid that he would abandon her for simply being herself. Until now. Ironically, if she did open up about how she truly felt about him it would make him think twice about being with her. Especially after he had shared his own fears. He would be worried more than ever about hurting her if he was incapable of returning those feelings.

'Well, you're like part of the furniture. I don't have to worry about impressing you.'

'Nice,' he said, rolling his eyes at her.

'You know what I mean. It doesn't matter what I say or do, you've never been mean to me. There was no need to change who I was around you.' As she said it, the reason she had harboured a crush on him all this time was there, shining bright. Sam accepted her unconditionally.

'I never had reason to be mean to you and neither does anyone else. Why don't you see that?' He reached up and stopped her tending his wounds so she would focus on what he was saying.

It was too much for her to simply accept his word as the truth. There had to be something about her which made everyone in her life turn their backs on her at some point. Even with him, now, she was waiting for the inevitable rejection once he got bored of her too.

'Clearly there's something wrong with me. My own parents gave me away once they were sick of me. They raised me for three years. If there had been any sort of bond there it should have broken their hearts to do that. No, it seems to have been a relief since they never made any attempt to reconnect or get me back. As for the Jenningses, as good as they were to take me in, I wasn't enough for them, and they went on to have the twins. I'm sure if they'd known that would happen they would never have considered adopting someone else's discarded child. I must be really hard work or plain irritating.' All of the feelings she had been holding back for years came tumbling out of her mouth in the wake of Sam's honesty. She did not know if it was going to make him see her any differently other than to think she was more of a basket case than ever. By telling him all of this she was highlighting all the inadequacies which had caused people in her life to abandon her, providing Sam with reasons to do the same.

'Well, you are pretty annoying at times…' Sam was grinning at her and not taking her concerns about her personal defects seriously at all.

Emmy scooped some water from the fountain and flicked it at him. 'I'm pouring my heart out to you here. At least pretend you're interested.'

'Sorry, but you know this is completely neurotic, right? You were a child. All kids are a pain at times, but their parents don't simply sign them away. It's your parents who were the waste of skin, not you, and the Jenningses absolutely adore you. Your mum, dad and Dave would lay down their lives for you. The twins, probably not so much, but they're spoiled and immature. Again, their problem, not yours. Someday they'll grow up and see what an amazing sister they have in you.'

'If I'm such a great person, then why couldn't I find someone who wanted to marry me for real? It took a family friend getting me knocked up at a wedding reception to warrant even a half-baked proposal.'

Sam flinched at her caustic take on their situation but on the surface that was all it had been.

'You've sold yourself too short for too long, Emmy. I don't know who else didn't treat you the way you deserved but perhaps you were following the pattern your birth parents set. You got involved with men who thought you weren't worth a commitment but, in reality, it was the other way around. They never deserved you. Neither do I.' He took the hand which she had been tending to his injuries with and kissed it. It was all very romantic, everything she could have dreamed of, but that was the problem.

'You never would have married me if it wasn't for the baby.' That was what it came down to in the end for Emmy. They were only here because of a mistake and nothing else.

'Maybe not but I wouldn't have married anyone else, I can guarantee you that. You are the only woman I could ever have imagined spending the rest of my life with because we know each other so well. Okay, so we kept a few of our personal neuroses quiet until now, but I'm sure we can work our way around that along with everything else.'

Emmy was in danger of sliding off the wall and drowning in the fountain as Sam completely melted her defences. 'What are you saying?'

'That maybe we should give this marriage thing a try for real.' He dropped her hand, only to caress her cheek instead.

Emmy leaned into the palm of his hand, her eyes closed, as she let herself believe they had a chance together, when he was telling her the next best thing to 'I love you.'

CHAPTER NINE

SAM WAS SAILING close to the wind. If he got this wrong in any way, this relationship would be over before it properly began. Marriage had been pushing them apart and tonight, opening up, and listening to Emmy's fears in return, made him realise he could not lose her or what they had together. He had been trying to keep his feelings for her in check but tonight had been his undoing. The emotional fallout from the accident and realising how lost he would be without Emmy had made Sam face up to what was happening.

There was a chemistry between them they could no longer ignore, and the way Emmy was responding to him now, burrowing into his palm like a pussycat, said she felt the same way. By denying it he was afraid they were hurting each other more. They had not discussed physical intimacy within their marriage, but they were only human. Recent history had proven that in the bedroom they could set the sheets on fire. This time they did not have to worry about the consequences. Other than him falling any deeper for Emmy than he already had.

With her eyes still closed, pressed into him, she looked more content and happier than he had seen her in a while. Like a moth to a flame he was drawn to her smiling mouth, brushing his lips softly across hers. She accepted him quickly, kissing him back, and beginning that tugging sensation within him, begging for more.

With both hands now cradling her face and pulling her closer, he deepened the kiss. This was not the way either of them had pictured their lives turning out, but she was his and he was hers now. They did not have to hold back, and after everything she had told him about her past lovers, there was no reason to. Tonight, he would show her how perfect she was to him.

'Mrs Goodwin, would you like to take this back to the honeymoon suite?' His voice was ragged with the raw lust pumping in his veins for her. If she had any doubt about how much he wanted her she only had to listen.

Her eyes popped open, her pupils dark with the same need. She bit her bottom lip as she nodded her head, that urgency for intimacy overriding any bashfulness. That coy exterior did not last for long when Emmy was in the throes of passion and Sam was keen to get her there soon.

He stood up, bowed and held out his hand *à la* a Regency suitor expressing his interest in a twirl around the ballroom floor. Emmy giggled, kicked up her heels with a squeal and accepted his invitation with a curtsey. This was exactly why they were so good together. They were both incorrigible dorks.

The childish behaviour was soon replaced with that of a more mature nature. As they strolled back to the hotel, their path illuminated by the lights of the Eiffel Tower, they finally let the romantic mood consume them. Hand in hand, lips on lips, they stumbled towards the consummation of their marriage. Stopping every now and then, disappearing down a cobbled alleyway when Sam could not contain his need for her a second longer. The passionate interludes—mouths meshing, tongues clashing, hands searching under clothes for that skin-on-skin contact—made their journey twice as long. It also hiked up the expectation of what was to come in that honeymoon suite. Foreplay without either of them being naked.

'Bonsoir,' he said to the evening receptionist when they finally reached the hotel, before they rushed up the flight of stairs to their room. His heart was racing, breathing rapid, as the blood pumped furiously to all parts of his body in anticipation.

The last time he and Emmy had shared a bed they had not had the luxury of time or spending a night together. Although their tryst then had been a frenzied feast of fun, tonight he was going to slow the pace so they could properly enjoy one another. After making love for the first time as husband and wife, he hoped it would prove enjoyable enough for Emmy to want to continue a real relationship with him for a long time to come.

Emmy was breathless with excitement as they fell into their room in between a flurry of kisses. This was not their first time together, but it had all the build-up of a new relationship when they had so much to prove to each other in bed. That their last foray into a hotel bedroom had not been a fluke in its explosive display of fiery passion. If they were going to entertain the idea of a physical arrangement in the marriage, it was necessary that they could maintain that level of chemistry and enjoy a healthy sex life. After a lifetime of lusting after Sam, she was sure she would not have a problem keeping her side of the bargain, but she could not say the same for him.

It was one thing having an exciting, illicit hook-up, during someone else's wedding reception, praying no one noticed their absence. Quite another sleeping with the same person for the rest of their lives. If tonight was a flop and did not meet expectations, it could jeopardise everything. It might make Sam think twice about this addendum to the contract. The pressure alone of making him think she was worth sacrificing all other women was making her doubt the validity of that.

'Hey. Stop thinking. I can see those cogs whirring.' Sam called her out, knowing her well enough to understand what was going on in her head.

'I just...' She could not find the words to tell him she was afraid their next move could be the wrong one, even when it felt so right.

'Shh.' He put his finger on her lips. 'There's no need to overanalyse this or worry about what happens next. We're married. We shouldn't have to concern ourselves with the morning after the night before, only feel, enjoy, be together.'

It was a convincing argument. Especially when he was dotting kisses across her neck and her mind could only focus on the butterfly sensation of his lips flitting over her skin.

'What if—?' She attempted to ask what would happen if he could never learn to love her and the sex was just that, an act without emotion—could they survive on that alone? But he cut her off with a kiss, stealing the words from her lips with his, and reminding her to live in the moment. All her concerns about the future could wait until she could think straight again, when she was not distracted by Sam stroking her bare skin under her clothes, making her want to get naked right now.

'What if we simply enjoy our honeymoon and leave everything else until we get back home?' He lifted her top over her head and stripped off what was left of his shirt.

'Sounds good to me,' she said, breathlessly, with Sam busy undoing the buttons on her skirt, leaving her standing in nothing but her underwear. Thank goodness for the rush of blood to the head she had in the airport when she had splashed out on an expensive navy lace and silk set in place of her comfortable favourites. She had not predicted him seeing her in them but figured having something sexy close to her skin would make her feel better. How right she had been.

'You look amazing.' Sam confirmed she had made the right choice, kissing her shoulders as he slid the straps of her bra down her arms.

Emmy shivered, felt her nipples harden against their silky confines, then gasped when Sam bit gently on one puckered nub. She braced herself on his shoulders to remain upright as he peeled her underwear away so he could take her fully in his mouth. With her breast in his hand he licked and sucked her pink tip until she thought she would orgasm from that sensation of his rolling tongue and grazing teeth alone. There was an impatient second when he took time to release the clasp on her bra but only for a short time as he resumed his attention on her other breast. Her legs were quivering, her body aching with need for him, but she did not want this to end.

She let her hands do the talking, deftly unbuttoning his trousers and pushing them and his boxer shorts down his legs. Sam kicked them off so he was gloriously naked in front of her, as big and proud as she remembered. Eager to please him the same way he had done for her, Emmy kneeled before him. She saw that flare of desire in his eyes and smiled, knowing she put it there. With the flat of her tongue, she licked the full length of his shaft, the muscles of his thighs tensing under her hands as she did so.

She moved one hand to take hold of his erection, slipping up and down the smooth ridged skin to make him groan. Full of confidence and bravado, she stared up at him as she took him into her mouth. His eyes almost rolling back in his head as she swirled her tongue around his engorged member.

'Emmy—' His ragged warning only emboldened her, taking him deeper into her mouth, her throat, to enjoy him fully.

He thrust his hips with his next groan, and she tasted the salty evidence of his arousal. Sam's hands were tugging her hair, urging her up on to her feet again.

'Do you know what you're doing to me, Emmy?'

'Probably the same as you're doing to me.' She took his hand and slid it onto her panties so he could feel the wetness there for himself.

With a guttural groan he whipped them off and hoisted her leg up onto his hip. One breath-stealing thrust, and he was inside her, filling her, completing her. His sigh of satisfaction matched her own now they were finally joined together.

Emmy wound her arms around his neck and Sam hitched her other leg around his waist. He carried her over to the bed without breaking the connection between their bodies. The rose petals on the covers were cool against her skin, their perfume adding to the romance of the moment. It was easy to believe this was their honeymoon and forget the disaster of their actual wedding night. How she longed for everything they had in Paris to fly back home with them.

'I'm not hurting you, am I?' Sam asked as he lowered his body on top of hers.

'No.' That weight of him was wanted. She revelled in that feel of him pressing down on her, cocooning her. Being his.

He moved slowly at first, letting her get accustomed to having him fill her again after such a long time. Emmy closed her eyes and luxuriated in that most intimate of acts. The sensation of Sam's hot breath on her neck, his thighs brushing against hers, was almost enough for her to completely unravel. Then he was kissing her again, kneading her tender breast in his large palm and sending her into more raptures.

Emmy was a banquet stretched out before him. So many delicious tastes to savour. Every sample he took making him yearn for more. The kiss on her neck, the lick of a taut nipple, brought soft content moans to her lips. A sound which he wanted to hear again and again, knowing this was one area he could please her.

Sam slowly withdrew from her slick core and slid down the bed until his head was buried between her soft thighs. He filled her again, this time with his tongue. Using it to reach deep inside, swirling around that most sensitive spot, until she was calling out his name and arching off the bed.

Before she came back to earth, Sam thrust his hips and slid his straining erection into her wetness. That evidence of her orgasm strengthening his arousal, driving him faster towards his own satisfaction. Emmy too was urging his pace with her panting breaths at his ear and her nails raking over his back. She wanted him to reach that pinnacle with her and he was only too pleased to play catch-up. That pressure building inside him was allowed to break free, his climax taking everything in him and leaving him collapsed on top of Emmy, unable to move.

'That was…can't catch my breath…you're amazing.' His head was nestled against her breast so he could feel her chest rising and falling as she fought to get her breathing under control.

'So are you.' She kissed the top of his head, making him smile.

Given the choice right now he would happily make love to this one woman for the rest of his life. As someone who had let her down from the start he couldn't say for sure if he alone would ever be enough for her. All he could do was hope this feeling of euphoria they had created in each other would last.

At least for this weekend they were living as a couple, far from the everyday worries they would have to face back home with the reality of their arrangement. Combining work and raising a child together could test the strongest of relationships. Their now not-so-convenient marriage might not survive the strain when one of the party had feelings for the other.

* * *

It took a few moments for Emmy to realise where she was when she woke up, wondering if she was imagining the over-the-top boudoir. Then she remembered she was on honeymoon with Sam and rolled over with a lascivious grin on her face. It quickly disappeared when she found his side of the bed empty. She sat up, clutching the silk sheets to her naked body, looking to see if his things had gone too. The only clothes strewn recklessly across the floor were hers.

All at once, her fears came rushing in, shoving away her happy thoughts. Perhaps in the morning light he had regretted crossing that line with her and wanted to put some space between them. She did not think he would have gone home without her but even going for a walk without telling her was a warning sign that all was not well.

Last night she had been on top of the world, feeling loved in every way possible. She should have known it was too good to be true. Today she was right back down to earth, scrabbling to get back on her feet and face the world again. She hoped whatever problem had developed while she had been sleeping, Sam would have the decency not to share it. They were supposed to be putting on a united front and she would be humiliated if he had left a message at reception ultimately rejecting her.

She was deciding whether to get dressed and packed right away or take a shower first when the door opened. When Sam walked into the room carrying two takeaway cups in his hands and a paper bag in his mouth, she burst into noisy tears.

He dropped the bag on the bed and set the drinks on the bedside table. 'What? What's happened?'

She was trying to smile through the relieved sobbing and was sure she looked grotesque in the process. 'I thought you'd gone.'

He frowned at her as he came to sit on the bed. 'Why on earth would I do that?'

'I thought you regretted last night.' She was afraid to look at him in case there was any element of truth in her fear.

'Er, why would I do that when I had the time of my life? You really need to start trusting I'm not going to run out on you. I'm not your parents or one of your ex-boyfriends. I'm your husband.' He caught her chin between his finger and thumb and forced her to look at him, to believe in what he was telling her.

As well as his sincerity, she swore she could see disappointment in those big eyes that she should think so badly of him after everything he had done to make her comfortable in this relationship.

'I'm sorry. It's just going to take some time for me to get used to that.' To trusting someone.

'You were sleeping. I only left the bed to get breakfast from that bakery we saw yesterday. I thought you deserved the real deal this morning. Freshly made croissants from the *boulangerie*. I would never go anywhere without you. Especially when you're here lying naked in bed.' He tugged his shirt over his head and scrambled in beside her. Emmy let out a squeal of delight as he caught hold of her for a kiss. He tasted of minty toothpaste and promises, and she relaxed into his embrace once more.

'What about breakfast?' she asked with a pout.

'Sod breakfast. There's only one thing I'm hungry for this morning and that's you.' Sam pretended to nibble on her neck, making her laugh and forget all her insecurities in the process.

'I could get used to this,' Emmy sighed, leaning back against Sam's solid chest. He squeezed the sponge over her shoulders and let the soapy hot water cascade over her breasts.

'Don't get too used to it. Our flight is first thing in the morning.' He kissed the side of her neck and wrapped his arms around her.

'Nah-nah-nah. I'm not listening.' She stuck her fingers in her ears so she would not hear things she did not want to.

'Idiot,' he said, somewhere outside of the white noise in her head.

She turned and stuck out her tongue at him, only for Sam to grab her legs and twist the rest of her body around so she was effectively straddling him.

'That's better.' His voice had already changed from teasing her to wanting her.

'Again?' She could barely believe it when they had spent most of the day already making love. Not that she was complaining. She had been content lying here in the bath with him, looking out at the spectacular view and listening to the busy world outside. To some it might have seemed like a wasted opportunity not leaving the hotel room to visit the city she had longed to see for so long but spending this time with Sam had been so much more important to her. She might never have this again with him. Despite everything he had said, neither of them could promise this marriage would last for ever.

'It's our honeymoon. If you are able to walk by the end of it, we're doing something wrong.' Sam's casual tease took her breath away again before he carried her back to bed. They did not bother to dry off first.

This time making love was a long, leisurely affair. Lying on their sides, looking into one another's eyes, Sam took her body with his once more. Each time felt like the first, every thrust of him inside her a surprise and delight. With her limbs wrapped around his body, Emmy knew she was exactly where she wanted to be.

CHAPTER TEN

'STOP KICKING THE man's chair, Stevie.'

'No.'

'Do as you're told, or I'll confiscate your games console.'

'You're too hard on him, Dan.'

'Well, one of us has to discipline him and you let him get away with murder.'

Sam listened to the family argue in the row behind them, his head banging off his chair with every thump of their child's foot against his seat. He did his best to grit his teeth and ignore it but the family dynamic going on was making him more uncomfortable in more ways than one.

Emmy was sleeping against the plane window, with little wonder. They had worn each other out in bed over the weekend. Although he wished they'd had longer to get to know each other before returning to normal life. Despite being in each other's lives for so long, there was still a lot about each other they apparently did not know. He would never have known Emmy was dealing with such deep-rooted issues around feelings of abandonment if she had not shared that information over the course of the trip.

That was obviously something that still affected her in her adult life, just as his hang-ups about his father continued to dominate his life decisions. If he had been aware that it was an ongoing problem with Emmy, he might have thought twice about the wedding. He ran the risk of hurting her even more if he could not give her everything she needed from him. Now he was worried more than ever about repeating his father's mistakes.

He had every intention of taking care of his family and being there for Emmy and his child, but as he had found, life did not always go to plan. What if work took up more time than he could devote to school plays or sports days? What if he and Emmy discovered down the line that a physical relationship was not enough to sustain their marriage? The fallout from any breakdown in their relationship was going to affect them and their child, however hard they tried to avoid it. Sam wondered if he was courting even more trouble by sparking a sexual relationship with Emmy. Once they were home she would expect them to move into one bedroom, intensifying their bond, and putting more pressure on him to be the perfect husband. There was a reason he had never wanted to get married and this was it. Too much expectation for him to possibly ever live up to, and after the euphoria of this mini-break, it felt as though he could only go down in Emmy's estimation from now.

'I need the toilet.'

'Dan, you take him.'

'I always have to take him.'

'I'm so sorry it's too much to ask for you to take

your son to the toilet. I'll do it, shall I? Like everything else.'

'I work, Sharon.'

'And I don't? At least you get paid and have time away from the house…'

The family who had probably spent an enjoyable break at a theme park or the beach began to descend into a domestic row as they faced their imminent return home.

Suddenly the plane felt very claustrophobic with Sam trapped, listening to his worst fears play out in real time.

'I'll see you later, then,' Emmy called as she got out of the car. There was no fond farewell or goodbye kiss from her husband before he drove on to find a parking space. She was left standing there in the dust watching him leave, trying to figure out what she had done wrong.

It had been this way since their return from honeymoon. That period of their marriage apparently well and truly over. She had tried to ask him about it and why things had changed so dramatically between them but the only answer he could give her was that he was busy and tired. Except the distance had been there since the moment they had stepped off the plane, back on home soil.

Her idea, or the one he had led her to believe was true, that they would continue their loved-up relationship from where they had left off in that Parisian hotel room, could not have been further from the truth. There were no more shared baths or nights cuddled up together in bed. If anything, Sam seemed to be avoiding her. His shifts usually conflicting with hers, and on evenings where they were alone together, he always had paperwork to catch up on in another room away from her.

She went to bed at night wanting to cry herself to sleep but found herself too empty inside to summon the tears. This was her life from now on and though she had seen it coming, she had tried to pretend they were making it work. She did not even have friends or family to confide in with the truth. Her colleagues believed her life with Sam was something out of a romance novel, and if the truth came out to her parents or David, they would be devastated by the betrayal. They were invested in the relationship between her and one of their trusted friends. If it came down to it she could not be sure they would take her side in the break-up. She could imagine the conversations would remind her Sam was a dishy doctor, a catch way too good for the likes of her, and she should consider herself lucky he had 'taken her on.' In their eyes she would be the one in the wrong. She always had been when it came down to taking sides between her and anyone close.

Rows over stolen make-up or clothes ruined with the twins when they were growing up had all been ruled in Lorna's and Lisa's favour when their parents got involved.

'You should be pleased they want to be like you…'

'They don't know any better…'

'I'm sure they didn't mean to do it…'

An argument with Sam would no doubt have the same result with her being the one urged to work harder to make things right, to make life easier for everyone else. Her feelings never seemed to be taken into consideration against anyone else's. As though she was acceptable collateral damage in the scheme of things. Easier to hurt her than real family.

Sometimes she thought they considered Sam more a part of that than she was when they went out of their way to make him feel comfortable. Usually she simply put up and shut up. Yet as her pregnancy progressed and her marriage stalled, Emmy knew she could not continue this way for much longer. Living like this was making her more miserable than if she had been left alone to raise the baby. At least then she would not have been under any illusion that something was there between her and Sam.

In hindsight, it seemed the honeymoon had been to appease her after her post-wedding blues. It certainly had not been to develop any emotional ties when they were more distant than ever. She simply had to face the fact Sam had physical needs and she had satisfied them for a short while. It was difficult not to think about who might have taken her place since.

During their romantic getaway he had told her she was the only one he could have imagined marrying but not that she was the only woman he would sleep with. They did not have anything written on paper, nor had they discussed being monogamous, but she had hoped that would be part of the deal. Sam knew she did not sleep around but that was where they differed. She had become one of those women who had thought she could change her man with marriage and ended up disappointed to find out otherwise.

There was no proof he had embarked on an extramarital affair, but she had intimate knowledge of his rampant sexual appetite. Given they had not slept together since their return from Paris it was only a matter of time before he sought relief from another quarter. Sam would have the pick of more attractive, slimmer women than his pregnant wife, so he would have no reason to go without affection or intimacy. It was Emmy who would suffer, wondering every night he worked late who he was with and why it was not her.

When she started her shift, it was with a feeling of dread, knowing their marriage was over before it really began. Unless she could persuade her husband she was the only woman he needed in his life, her future was looking bleaker than ever. She did not want to bring a baby into their home with them living separate lives, its mother miserable and pining after someone who could not give her what she wanted. Sam had tried to warn her, explained why marriage was not for him, but she had gone willingly into his bed and there was no one but herself to blame for falling even deeper in love with him.

Tonight, she was going to tackle some big decisions. If she was going to make changes in her life, she had to do it now lest she left it too late. Prior to the baby's arrival and before there was nothing left of her shattered heart to piece together. She would seduce him, beg him to talk to her, do whatever it took to find out where they stood as a couple once and for all. If she didn't hear what she wanted, their marriage could be over before they hit their one-month anniversary. Confirmation she remained unloved and unwanted, that everyone left her in the end, and foolish to believe that Sam could see past her physical imperfections to a woman he could see a future with.

It would, however, make the twins' year.

* * *

This was killing him. Emmy had left a brief voice message on his phone asking him to make time for her tonight if possible. That said everything about the state of their so-called marriage. Yes, he had been avoiding her, for her own good. Now it seemed as though everything was about to come to a head, and he was going to lose her for ever. He could not expect her to carry on as they were when she was so unhappy, but there did not seem to be any other way to avoid hurting her except by keeping his distance. It was not fair to lead her on and pretend this was a proper marriage, or one in name only. They had fallen somewhere in between with messy emotions getting in the way of the hot sex and confusing everything. If they were splitting up it needed to be her decision, so she felt in control and not a victim. He did not want to be someone else to let her down and make her believe it was her fault. By bedding her he had simply hastened the end, knowing they were in deeper than they had intended but still pretending this was a marriage of convenience.

'Are you coming for drinks?' Ben, one of the nurses on the ward, asked as he gathered his stuff to go home.

'No. Emmy has something planned.'

Ben whistled.

'Lucky you. Make the most of it. As soon as the babies start coming you won't get the chance to plan any sexy time together.' He waggled his eyebrows suggestively, making Sam laugh at a time when it was the last thing he felt like doing.

'I will,' he said, already trying to find excuses to avoid *the talk*. They had not told anyone about the baby, so he knew Ben was only kidding around. Even if his words were hitting close to home.

Once sleep was scarce and tempers frayed, Emmy would resent being trapped in this marriage. He was worried he would too. Perhaps that was why his father had moved from house to house, family to family, never settling long enough to contribute anything valuable to any of them. If they could not admit this had been a mistake, they risked dragging this discontent through their child's life too, making them all unhappy in the long run.

'Dr Goodwin! I'm glad you're still here. Can you give us a hand with a young patient in A & E?' A visibly stressed nurse from paediatric A & E rushed into the staff room looking relieved she had got to him before he had left for the night.

Sam thought of Emmy waiting for him at home, anticipating his arrival and expecting an explanation for his recent behaviour. He wasn't a coward, but he knew what would always take priority and it was time they both realised it.

'Sure.' He did not even ask about the patient's condition first, sure it was where he had to be. They needed him, Emmy did not. He was never going to make the difference in her life he could make to his patients. Tonight, she would see that for herself.

'I waited up.'

'You didn't have to.' Sam took off his coat and slumped into the nearest armchair. Emmy was sitting in the dark by the window, presumably watching for his car to pull up into the driveway. He had thought, hoped, she would have gone to bed by now, the case keeping him at the hospital until well past midnight.

'I was worried about you.' She had not even changed into her comfy pyjamas. Sam looked around to see if there were packed bags anywhere but saw nothing to indicate she had finally had enough of him.

'I told you I got caught up at work.' He was tired and irritable after a difficult night in the emergency room. It was the worst possible time to be having this conversation. Yes, he thought she would be better off without him but he did not want her to hate him. At the end of the day he was still the baby's father and it was important they could at least remain amicable. Things like sharing childcare or putting on a united front for special events in their baby's life would be difficult if she could not bear the sight of him.

'Yes, but I haven't heard anything from you since.' There was a steeliness to her voice in the shadows.

Although she could not see him, he shrugged like it was no big deal. Making it clear he was not going to account for his whereabouts every minute of the day. Even wearing his father's attitude made his stomach roll but he reminded himself he was doing this for the better good. 'In case you've forgotten, we're not *really* married.'

'Oh.' Her simple exclamation sounded as though he'd punched her in the gut.

He had to steady himself on the arms of his chair so he would not rush to her and apologise on bended knee. Instead, he swallowed the bile in his throat and doubled down on the onslaught of blows. 'You had your little romantic trip but we're back in the real world now.

I have other responsibilities and priorities. I thought you understood that, Emmy.'

'I thought… I thought after Paris we were going to make a go of this relationship and try to be a real couple.'

'Emmy, Emmy, Emmy. That was never on the cards. The very nature of our marriage is its convenience. That to me means continuing to live our separate lives whilst raising our child together.'

'For you that means sleeping with other people?'

He wanted to yell, 'No!' Instead, he said quietly, 'You knew who I was when you married me.'

The fact was she knew better now who he was but that was why he was doing this. She needed that nudge to realise sympathy was not a reason to excuse anything he did to cause her pain.

There was a pause. He thought he heard her sniffing and imagined her trying not to cry. Everything he had hoped to avoid with this stupid marriage contract in the first place. 'Then I'm afraid I can't do this, Sam. I can't stay married to you when it is making me so unhappy. It's not fair on anyone.'

The chair creaked as she stood but he did not get up. Neither did he attempt to convince her to stay. As her shadow crossed the room and out the door all he could say was, 'I'm sorry things turned out this way.'

The only true statement he had made since coming home.

Emmy could not bring herself to tell anyone about the break-up. Not anyone at work and certainly not family. There would be too many questions, and how could she explain what had happened without admitting that the whole marriage had been a sham? The only thing worse than everyone knowing her relationship with Sam had been fake was the realisation that she could not even make that work. There was surely nothing more pathetic than a woman who had married for security and it not lasting the month.

As a result of being unwilling to share her woes with anyone close, she had nowhere to go after walking out on Sam. It had been a necessary step, pre-empting the toxic atmosphere which would surely develop when things were already so fractured between them. She was at a loss to explain what had happened to them between the passionate kisses in Paris and the cold shoulder back home. Why he had changed so suddenly from a loving husband to someone she simply shared a house with. A virtual stranger to her but the person he had always told her he was when it came to women. She should never have convinced herself he was anything but that womaniser with no intention of settling down. At least she could protect their child from growing up in that environment which would inevitably have an impact, even if it was too late for her.

'Thank you for coming out at such short notice, Mr Sutherland. I really appreciate it.' After a few nights spent in a cheap hotel room, Emmy knew she had to find somewhere to live before her money ran out. She did not want to end up homeless and penniless before the baby arrived. Her parents' place would have been her absolute last resort. Thankfully, she had the brainwave of contacting her old landlord, who had yet to rent out her old flat to anyone else. Goodness knew what he thought about her returning so quickly and with a wedding ring on her finger, but he said nothing. Mr Sutherland did not say much as a rule.

'I ain't carrying anything for you. Here's the key. Rent's due at the end of the month,' he grunted, before shuffling off down the street.

'It's okay, I don't have much with me,' Emmy called after him. Despite his gruffness she was tempted to run after him and give him a hug. Getting her old place back was the one bright spot in the dark days which had followed her so-called honeymoon.

She twirled her Eiffel Tower key ring around her finger. Mr Sutherland had not bothered to take it off the flat key and she was happy to be reunited with it. A gift to herself long before babies and marriage had been on her radar. However, now she would associate it with bittersweet memories of seeing it for real.

She yawned. It was getting late and she was standing on the pavement with all of her worldly possessions packed into bags when all she wanted to do was climb into bed. With her rucksack and handbag over her shoulders, she extended the handle on her trolley bag and began dragging it up the steps. It was packed so full she had to walk backwards, hauling it with both hands. Next time she walked out on a marriage she would make sure to book a removal van first.

Once she was inside, she dropped everything on the floor, her muscles aching, and her lungs fit to burst as she flopped onto the couch. Her phone vibrated in her pocket, on silent so she would not have to deal with anyone. The endless vibration forced her to look at it. It was Sam calling.

'Ugh.' Emmy let her phone fall onto her chest. There was no way she was answering that one after the way he had behaved. It was not as if he was going to apologise or beg for forgiveness. More than likely he was calling to have their marriage annulled, beg her not to tell David or to assert his rights over custody of their unborn baby. Given his sudden change from adoring spouse to wannabe bachelor, she remained sceptical that the responsible father act would last. For days she had wept over him, and did not owe him a conversation now.

The fact that he was working at the same hospital was going to make things awkward and difficult to avoid him for too long. With the personal leave she had taken now over, there were decisions to make, and actions to take before her pregnancy was too advanced to do anything. If he was not going anywhere, she might have to. Everything would come out eventually so she might have to bite the bullet and tell her family.

Perhaps it was time for a completely new start, transferring to another hospital while she juggled working with motherhood. As much as she wanted her mother and father to be hands-on grandparents, only too willing to babysit when needed, she could not rely on it.

How could she expect them to support her and love her baby when she had grown up doubting they felt that way about her? She was not going to subject her child to that sense of being the outsider in the family. If it came to it, Emmy would go it alone with her baby. After all, she was the only person she could truly rely on.

The phone buzzed again with a notification. Curiosity got the better of her when she saw her soon-to-be ex-husband had left her a voice message.

'It's Sam. I was hoping we could talk… I want to

make sure you are all right. No one seems to know where you are and, well, I'm still the father of this baby. You know where I am.'

That was the crux of it all and she could not change the past, or biology, as much as she wished she could. Sam was the father, she was the mother, and whatever their relationship, she still wanted the best for her child. Whether that meant staying where she was and giving Sam a second chance to prove his worth, or moving away to start over on her own, remained to be seen.

Exhausted from her step backwards into singledom, she was too tired to make any more life changes tonight. She had waited a lifetime for Sam, now it was his turn to do the hanging around. As she drifted off to sleep, still on the sofa wearing her coat and shoes, a smile crossed her lips. Something she had feared she might never do again since leaving her husband.

CHAPTER ELEVEN

IT WOULD NOT be overdramatic for Sam to say he had become a shell of a man recently. Since driving Emmy away his conscience refused to let him sleep or eat properly. As a professional, he had managed to keep his private life separate from work and continued doing his job to the best of his abilities. That did not mean he was not worried sick about Emmy and the baby or that he did not regret how stupid he had been.

'Emmy, please talk to me…' He made another desperate plea to the voicemail on her phone. It had come as no surprise that she would not want contact with him after everything. In order to protect her from an unhappy life spent with him, he had pushed her away, but the scheme had proved too successful. She seemed to have vanished into thin air.

If he had not been so wrapped up in his own loss, he might have realised there was something serious going on beyond his empty house and broken heart. It had taken him a few days of licking his wounds and feeling sorry for himself before trying to reach out to her. The continued silence had frightened him enough to swallow his pride and ask others if they had news of his wife's whereabouts.

'You've lost her already?' Shelley, one of the paediatric nurses who worked with Emmy, had quipped when he had begun searching for her in earnest.

'Yeah. Uh, we're taking some time out but I wanted to make sure she's okay.'

It came as a surprise to her colleagues to find out they had separated already, and Emmy would not be happy he had shared such personal information, but he was getting desperate by that stage. As it was, they could only tell him she had taken some personal leave.

The next logical place to try and locate her was at her parents' house. Whether she was there or not, he was not looking forward to the confrontation which would inevitably occur with his arrival. He was either already persona non grata, if the family had heard Emmy's side of the story, or he was going to have to break it himself and land himself in the messy stuff.

This house had been a refuge to them both during their tumultuous childhoods. Today he was as anxious as though he was about to face a firing squad on the other side of that door. One deep breath in and he pushed the doorbell, reminding himself this was about his missing wife and unborn child. Not his popularity.

'Sam? What are you doing here? Is Emmy in the car?' It was Dave who opened the door, peering over his shoulder looking for his sister. That answered some questions. No, she was not here, and she had not told them about the break-up or the reasons behind it. It filled Sam with dread and his blood ran cold to discover Emmy really was missing.

'No. I'm afraid not. Can I come in?'

'Sure.' Dave stood aside to let him in, the frown burrowed into his forehead a sign he knew already there was something serious going on. Sam was not looking forward to confessing his darkest deeds to his oldest friend, but if that was what it took to keep Emmy safe, he would take the consequences on the chin. Literally, if he knew Dave as well as he thought he did.

'I wasn't expecting you to be here, mate, but I'm glad you are.' He needed some moral support as he faced his in-laws with the news that he had been so unkind to their daughter she had either run away or got into trouble. Either way, Sam was to blame. Although Dave would be mad at him, he was sure he would put that aside to concentrate on finding his little sister.

'I just called in to see the folks. What's up?' Dave led him into the living room, where Mr and Mrs Jennings were sitting enjoying a cup of tea.

'Hi, Sam. What brings you here?'

'Sit down. Is Emmy with you?'

Sam took a seat, sagging under the weight of guilt of ruining yet more lives. 'Um, I don't know how to put this to you, but Emmy's missing.'

'What do you mean she's missing?' Dave flopped down beside him on the sofa, making Sam aware of his bulk and concern at the same time.

Sam cleared his throat. 'She, uh, we, uh, agreed to part.'

He was tempted to close his eyes to shut out the pain and confusion he could see on all three faces peering at him.

Eventually it was Mrs Jennings who threw her hands up and laughed. 'All couples fight. You'll kiss and make up soon enough. How many times have we argued and threatened to walk out?'

No one in the room returned her too bright smile.

'I get the feeling this isn't the same thing Sam's talking about.' Mr Jennings looked a lot sterner about the news.

'You've only been married five minutes. What did you do?' Dave's hard stare would have been intimidating enough without the clenched fists and Sam was already bracing himself for the inevitable hit.

'Things would never have worked out between us. We just figured that out too late. Anyway, that's not the point. I haven't heard from her since and it's been days. I'm worried something might have happened to her. Especially if she hasn't been in touch with you guys.' The family had been his last stop. With them in the dark as much as he was, he might have to make things official and report her disappearance to the police.

'Woah. Hold up. You can't simply drop that on us and expect us not to have questions. Emmy idolises you, bro, she always has, so I'm assuming you did something to upset her?'

Sam was too busy processing Dave's revelation to defend himself.

'Emmy *idolises* me? Since when?' It was news to him, but he was not simply going to take her brother's word on that score when he was completely unaware of the true nature of their relationship.

'Are you serious? You're married, for goodness' sake. If you don't know she's been in love with you since she was a kid, then it's no wonder things aren't working out. You're an idiot.' With that, Dave got up and crossed the room away from him, his phone to his ear. Presumably trying to get hold of Emmy himself.

Sam looked to her parents for confirmation that this was not simply some wild theory Dave had conjured up to make him feel even worse than he already did. They did not put his fears to rest.

Instead, Mr Jennings shook his head. 'Why do you think we were all so overjoyed when you two got together? We've been waiting years for you to admit how you felt about each other.'

'But—but—' Sam had always had a soft spot for Emmy but had kept his distance out of respect for her and the family, until Dave's wedding night. His feelings for her had developed a lot more since then. He never considered hers might have too. Paris had been magical but falling in love with her had not been in his plans. That was why he had forced her hand into leaving him. He had been afraid of hurting her, the baby and himself, somewhere further down the line. These last days without her had showed him how futile that whole exercise had been when they were both hurting. Now he was finding out she might have loved him all along, he knew how much pain she was in being apart when he had been torn in two without her.

'Why is it coming as a surprise to you that she's in love with you? Surely you two talk. Why else would you have married?' It was Mrs Jennings who took a softer approach, sitting on the edge of her chair and making him think about their recent actions.

'We, uh, decided to get married for the baby's sake. A marriage of convenience to raise the baby together. Except, well, you know my family history. I didn't want to end up like my dad, never at home and oblivious to any pain I might cause. When I realised we were getting in too deep, I thought we should live different lives to avoid any misunderstanding or hurt.'

'And that's when she disappeared?'

Sam nodded, though he ought to be hanging his head in shame as he sat explaining to Mr Jennings and the others about the crazy set-up he had engineered. If they had ever thought him worthy of Emmy, that would all change after today. He could never look either of them in the eye again after this.

'David's right, you are an idiot.' Mrs Jennings verbally slapped him across the face with the insult as she stood and cleared the tea dishes away. Sam supposed it could have been worse. He certainly deserved everything they threw at him.

'Emmy's at work. Clearly, it's only you she's avoiding.' Dave hung up before Sam had the opportunity to speak to her for himself.

'She's okay?' It was such a relief to have finally tracked her down, though he wished her colleagues might have given a heads-up and prevented him from making a show of himself here this morning.

'I told you, she's working and not very happy with me for phoning, or you for worrying everyone.'

'I'm glad you did. At least now I can tell them to call off search and rescue.' Sam attempted to rebuild some hastily destroyed bridges with some humour, now they knew everything was okay with Emmy and the baby.

'So, what are you going to do about all of this, Sam?'

'You have to go and sort things out with Emmy.'

'Stop being a moron or I'll be forced to hit you.'

Mr and Mrs Jennings, and Dave, each took a turn at trying to talk some sense into him, but Sam had already made his mind up to go and see her. It was time they were honest with each other about their feelings. Perhaps then they might actually have a chance at making things work and being a family once and for all.

* * *

'It's just a misunderstanding. Sam forgot I was staying with my parents for a few days, that's all.'

'Hmm, well, he seemed pretty concerned. You might want to give him a call.' Shelley did not look convinced by Emmy's explanation, but the state of her marriage was not gossip fodder. She wished Sam had not given people cause to question their relationship, but she supposed that was partly her fault for ignoring him this long.

In all honesty she never expected him to come looking for her when he had seemed so keen to return to his single life as soon as possible. There might also have been an element of wanting him to suffer a tiny bit, the way she had. It was backfiring on her now with her curious co-workers and her brother now involved.

'That's what happens when you're both working two different timetables. We might need to invest in a weekly planner to see what the other is doing.' She brushed off any concerns with a light laugh before resuming her duties. Until recently, lying was not something which came easily to her. Now she seemed to do it at the drop of a hat. All to cover up the fake relationship with Sam. Something which had caused no end of problems and was now redundant anyway. The only partnership they would have in the future would be in raising their child and she remained unconvinced that would even happen. Sam had proved to be as unreliable as he had always told her he was.

Now she had more trouble in store with her family if David's phone call was anything to go by. He had told her he was checking in with her after Sam had showed up on their parents' doorstep claiming she had vanished into thin air. Finding out she was still in the land of the living had satisfied him for now, but David would realise there was more going on behind the scenes than a mere tiff.

It was all such a mess, and if Sam had involved her family, she was going to have to explain the whole deal surrounding her pregnancy. Confirmation that even as an adult she was still a failure whom nobody really wanted.

Emmy rubbed her temples trying to massage away the throbbing pain lurking in her head. She had been a bit light-headed this morning and her skin was clammy in the cloying heat of the hospital. It would be no surprise if she was coming down with some sort of bug when she was so exhausted, her immune system probably too run down to fight off infection. The stress of the whole situation with Sam was something which would only continue to mar her pregnancy if she did not tackle it head-on soon. There was no more hiding. Once she was settled properly back into her flat again she would talk to Sam to sort things out as amicably as possible, but she was also going to have to tell her family everything and get it all off her chest.

Maybe then she could properly start looking forward to impending motherhood and focus her energy on the only thing that really mattered in this mess. Her baby.

'Good morning, Liam. How are you today?' Emmy set aside her own personal issues as soon as she was back on the ward.

'Good. Mum brought me some art supplies to keep me busy.' One of the tables on wheels they used at mealtimes had been commandeered as a makeshift craft table, sitting over the bed, laden with paints, paper and pencils.

'That should keep you busy. Try not to get it everywhere or you will have Sister in telling you off.' She bent down to pick up an errant scrap of paper from the floor and the dizzy sensation which overtook her almost caused Emmy to black out. It took a moment for her to regain her composure, holding on to the bedside table until everything stopped spinning.

'Are you okay, Emmy?' Liam sat up and peered over at her.

'I think I just stood up too quickly. No need to worry. I'll look forward to seeing your masterpieces later,' she reassured him before making a hasty exit.

Once out of Liam's eyeline, Emmy gave in to the need to rest against the wall outside. Her body suddenly felt as though it was on fire and she was beginning to fade out from consciousness again.

'Help.' She did not know who she was calling out to. All she could think was that something was wrong and she could be losing her baby. The chaos she and Sam had created in trying to do the right thing had been so destructive their baby was already suffering because of them.

'Emmy? What's happened? Can someone get a trolley, please?' It was Sam's voice she heard pleading for assistance, his hand which reached for hers, as she concentrated on breathing so she would not pass out.

Inhale. Exhale. Hang on, little one.

She did not know she was crying until she saw her tears making a puddle on the shiny floor.

'Stay with me, Emmy.' Sam put his arm around her

shoulders and helped her remain upright until extra hands were there, urging her onto a stretcher.

'Sam? Are we losing the baby?' She was flying down the corridor at speed, the fluorescent lights above her head becoming a bright blur. All the while she could feel Sam's hand clenching hers.

'Not if we can help it. I'm so sorry for everything. I came to tell you that. No matter what happens, I am here for you. Your family are right, I am a prize idiot.'

Even in her fugue state, the odd comment managed to filter through her consciousness.

'Why would you say that? They love you.' *So do I*, she said to herself as she began to drift out.

'I'll explain everything later. Just you make sure you come back to me, Emmy Goodwin. I need you. I love you.'

As blackness swirled around her, she decided her mind was playing tricks on her. Sam did not love her. Nobody did. That was why she had to keep this baby safe inside. So for the first and probably only time in her life she would have someone who loved her unconditionally. Without Sam's baby she would have nothing left to live for. She needed that ray of light to have something worth leaving this quiet darkness for and bring her back to life. Sam's voice at her ear, calling her name, was the last thing she remembered before she was lost in the abyss.

'I don't know what I'll do if anything happens to Em or the baby.' Sam was sitting in a chair in the hospital corridor, head in his hands, and feeling more powerless than he had ever felt in his life. Even when his father had gone and his mother had been at her lowest, he had been able to work and contribute something, albeit only financially. Here, now, there was literally nothing he could do to help his wife and child.

Worse than that was the knowledge that it was likely because of him their lives were in the balance.

'I hope you're not still going to try and tell me you don't love her after this.' Dave gave him a friendly pat on the back, more than Sam thought he deserved in the circumstances.

As soon as Emmy had been taken for blood tests, he had phoned the family to let them know what had happened and they had all driven down to the hospital to provide him with moral support and be closer to Emmy. If she could only see them now, faces streaked with tears, nerves shredded waiting to hear she was going to be okay, she would realise how much she was loved. Despite what she might think, she was a very much cherished member of the family and an important part of everyone's lives. Even the twins were in attendance, clearly upset that their big sister, along with their baby nephew or niece, were fighting for their lives.

His breath hitched in his throat with the reminder of what they were all going through, Emmy in particular. He was trying to be strong for her, and the baby, but that could not stop the tears forming in his eyes. The love he had denied too long was there for everyone to see.

'Only an idiot would do that,' he said, trying to smile through the pain.

'Our Emmy won't give up without a fight,' Mr Jennings insisted, holding his wife's hand and trying to convince everyone that she would survive anything.

Except she had not survived marrying Sam. It was his fault she was here, hovering between life and death.

All he had thought of was himself when he had driven her away. He had not wanted to force her into a life with him, but never stopped to think about what it was she might need. The future had seemed so scary to him, under pressure to be a good husband and father, but those were the roles he had accepted, and he should have done better. If he had not been so wrapped up in his own feelings, he might have seen what the rest of the family could. That they loved each other, and both were afraid to admit to it. One open, honest conversation, instead of dodging around their fears about the consequences, could have prevented all of this.

It was understandable that she hadn't confided in him, if everything her family said was true, when emotional attachment was not something he had encouraged. Looking back, it made sense about why she had agreed to marry him in the first place. Emmy was a romantic; she would never have dreamed of going through with a wedding simply because it was the logical thing to do. Everything she did was filled with love and commitment, although he had apparently been blind to it until now when it could be too late to do something about it.

Sam did not regret marrying Emmy or getting her pregnant, and he should never have let her think that he did. The upset and stress so early in the pregnancy was not good for her or the baby but he had neglected to consider any of that. He did not even know where she had been living since moving out when it clearly was not with her family. Who knew what conditions she had had to put up with in the interim because she had been too embarrassed by the situation he had put her in to go to her parents?

'Emmy is also more fragile than any of us realise. We are all guilty of ignoring her feelings because it's more convenient. Without meaning to upset anyone more, she has been suffering for a long time. I totally hold my hands up and say I'm the most recent cause of her heartache and take full responsibility for that. As soon as she is through this, I am going to be the best husband and father I can be.' His voice broke, his very soul calling out for her to be well enough to give him a chance to prove his sincerity on that score.

'What do you mean she's been suffering for a long time? Did you know she was ill?' Mrs Jennings's hand was on her heart, that same pain Sam was feeling obviously causing her distress too.

'I mean emotionally. Emmy is very sensitive and sometimes, well, she doesn't feel as though she fits in, or at least that she isn't wanted.' He looked pointedly at the twins, who had the decency to hang their heads.

Mrs Jennings gasped but it was Mr Jennings who strongly refuted Sam's comment. 'Emmy was always wanted. She is very much part of the family.'

'Sam's right, Dad. We don't always stick up for her when these two can't keep their snide remarks to themselves. The rest of us don't take it personally but for Emmy I guess there is always going to be an issue about being a real member of the family.' Dave jumped in to echo Sam's thoughts, and though he was grateful for the backup, he wished they weren't having this conversation at all.

'We don't mean anything by it.'

'We'll never do it again. I promise we'll try to do better.'

The twins sniffed and genuinely looked upset enough Sam wanted to believe them.

'We might not be blood, but Emmy is our daughter, and nothing is going to change that. I had no idea she felt that way, but we are all going to do better for her.' A determined-sounding Mrs Jennings spoke for the whole of the family, with all nodding their heads in agreement. As a group of people who were supposed to love Emmy enough for her to feel secure, Sam included, they had failed her. He could only hope along with everyone else that they got to make amends and could look forward to welcoming the next generation of the family.

CHAPTER TWELVE

EMMY TRIED TO lick her lips, they were so dry, but even that seemed a task too far in her current state. She was hovering in the dark somewhere between sleep and consciousness, trying to find her way back to the light.

'Emmy? Are you awake? I think she's trying to come to. I can see her eyes moving.' A familiar voice was out there somewhere. One she really wanted to hear.

'Sam?' Her voice was little more than a croak, but it seemed to get his attention as she felt a hand grip onto hers.

'I'm here, Emmy. Open your eyes and you'll see.' Regardless of everything that had passed between them, Sam was here, and she wanted to see him again. It had been too long without him.

There were other voices and sounds going on around her, but she blocked them out to focus on the one she wanted to hear most in that moment. With every ounce of strength she could muster she forced her eyes to open. It took a few seconds for her to focus, everything seemed so bright.

'Sam?' she said again, searching for him.

He squeezed her hand. 'I'm right here by your bed.'

Emmy turned her head a fraction and watched as his handsome face came into view. 'You haven't shaved,' she noted, trying to lift her hand to stroke the dark stubble lining his taut jaw.

He smiled and rubbed her fingers across the bristles. 'I've been a bit preoccupied worrying about you.'

'Me?' She was delving into her brain trying to remember what had happened and where she was. Everything was so jumbled, and nothing made sense. Why was she in bed feeling so rough and why was Sam here after they had split up?

It all came rushing back to her in one overwhelming wave of emotion. Sam's harsh words…leaving their home…working…then the blackness… She dropped his hand and placed hers on her stomach. The tears came even though she was too tired to cry.

'The baby… I'm so sorry.' For her, him and the child who would never get to take its first breath. She should have reached out and asked someone to help instead of trying to do everything herself. It was her fear of not fitting in, of having to admit she had failed, which had cost their baby its life. Her fault.

'Shh.' Sam brushed away her tears and kissed her gently on the cheek. His soft touch, so loving and gentle, only made her cry for what they could have had together if things had been different. 'Everything's going to be okay. Our little one is every bit as stubborn and strong as its mother.'

Still woozy, his words did not register straight away. Then she saw the grin on his face. 'You mean—?'

'Our baby is hanging in there. An infection led to maternal sepsis. That's what caused you to pass out. You were running a high temperature, and you gave us quite a scare, but they gave you fluids and antibiotics. As long as you take care from now on, hopefully there won't be any more drama for the rest of the pregnancy.'

'Hey, honey. We're so glad you're both doing okay.' It was then she noticed her father in the room and her heart swelled a bit more. He walked over and gave her a peck on the cheek, followed by her weeping mother.

'I'm so sorry, Emmy, if we ever made you feel left out. We just took it for granted you knew how much we loved you. You're our daughter, no matter what biology says.'

Emmy managed to sit up and give her mother a half-hug because she looked as though she needed it. Just as she was dealing with her parents' unusual display of emotion, Lorna and Lisa rallied on both sides of the bed to hug her in tandem.

'We are so sorry for every mean thing we ever did or said to you.'

'Can you ever forgive us? We will be the best aunties ever. Promise.'

Emmy glanced at Sam, who did not fool her with his attempt to look innocent. She was sure it was not only the life or death experience which had prompted this sudden outburst from her family; he had a hand in this somewhere and she was grateful.

Even David was there with a kiss and hug, apparently too choked to say more than 'It's good to have you back, sis.'

'Do you think Emmy and I could have a moment in private together?' Sam asked the others. Emmy wondered how they had all managed to get in here with visitors usually limited to one or two. Again, something Sam had probably arranged but she could not figure out why he would have gone to so much trouble, when he had made it clear he did not want her the last time they had seen each other.

'Sure. Let's go, folks, and let these two sort things out.' Her father herded the others out of the hospital side room, his words indicating she had missed a lot while asleep.

'Sam? What's going on? I mean, I'm grateful you are all here but if I'm okay there is no need for you to stick around. Don't feel as though you have to pretend any more. We agreed to the split.' Even though that particular memory was breaking her heart all over again.

'I'm done pretending, Emmy. I'm here with you because I want to be.'

'What does that mean, Sam? I'm too tired to keep guessing what it is you really want.' Her head was still fuzzy; bits and pieces of memories, or dreams, were slowly coming back to her and she was trying to decipher which were real or in her mind. Like hearing him tell her he loved her.

That had to be her mind playing tricks on her, letting her believe she had something worth living for before she had lost consciousness. Sam had made it clear to her that the honeymoon was over and, with it, his desire to be a real husband to her. She had been getting ready to start her life over again, learning to live without him, when disaster had struck. Now the danger had passed, she did not want to take two steps back, with Sam thinking he had to take responsibility for her. They had been there, done that, and it had not worked out first time around. Next time she settled down it would be with someone who loved her as much as she loved him. She and the baby deserved nothing less.

'I want you to come home with me.'

Emmy sighed. As much as she wanted that, she had learned not to accept Sam into her life at any cost. It hurt too much. She could not afford to be selfish any more if it meant putting her baby at risk again as well as her heart.

'Sam…I'm not a problem you have to keep fixing. We tried to do the right thing, but it didn't work out. You have no reason to feel guilty or as though you're obligated to take me back simply because I ended up in here. I'm fine. I've got my old flat back for now, and if it comes to it, I'll transfer out near my folks.'

'Why would you do that when you have a job here, a home with me to come back to and our baby on the way?'

It sounded so straightforward put like that, but the reality had been somewhat different. Emmy knew dreams did not always work out exactly the way she wanted. She was married to Sam and expecting his baby but that was where the fantasy ended because he did not love her. This was her wake-up call, as well as closure on her marriage.

'Sam…I know I said I could co-habit and co-parent with you, that marriage would be in name only, no strings attached. The truth is…' She gulped in a deep breath. 'The truth is I have feelings for you and that complicates things.'

'What sort of feelings?'

'Pardon me?'

'I can understand if it's disappointment you feel towards me, maybe even a very strong dislike, after the way I behaved. If it's something more than that, I would like to know.'

'Why? So I can be humiliated even more? Why does it matter now? It doesn't make any difference to our situation.' Except to put more pressure on him to do the 'right thing' when it was not necessary. Emmy had her family and soon she would have her baby. There would be plenty of love in her life.

'Because I don't want to be the one to say, "I love you," and not hear it back.' Sam looked at her sheepishly, reminding her of the teen who used to visit her brother but probably spent more time with her. Could it really be true that he loved her? Her heart gave an optimistic extra beat which registered on the monitor by the bed.

'Do you mean it? I don't want you to say it simply to get me to agree to go home with you and salve your conscience.'

Sam shook his head. 'I was coming to tell you before you took ill. I've been going out of my mind without you. I'm sorry I drove you away. With everything that went on with my dad, I was afraid of repeating history. That's no excuse, I know. I hurt you and that was the one thing I was trying not to do. By admitting that I had fallen for you, I thought it would only make things harder. I didn't want to fail you but that's exactly what I've done.'

'You haven't failed anyone. Although I'm still waiting for those three little words…' Emmy would not believe this was happening until she heard them and could be confident she was not having some sort of pain-induced hallucination.

Sam cupped her face in his hands and leaned in, so he was only a breath away. 'I love you, Emmy. I probably always have, though I was too stupid to realise it. I'm here for you, if you want me?'

They were the words that Emmy always wanted to hear but for her sake and the baby's she had to be sure there was something more behind them to ensure a different outcome if she went back to Sam.

'I love you too but is that enough, Sam? It wasn't before.' This might all be new to him but to her it was familiar ground. She loved him but he had practically thrown her out of the house, told her he did not want a 'real' marriage. What had changed over these past few days other than him realising he missed her?

'I wasn't being honest with you or myself because I was afraid of the consequences. All I can offer you now is my love and a promise I will do better by you in the future.'

He pushed his chair back and got down on one knee by the bed. 'I love you, Mrs Goodwin, and hope that you will do me the honour of becoming my wife again.'

Emmy smiled through her happy tears. He got extra points for the proposal this time. 'Yes. Yes, I will, Mr Goodwin.'

If Sam was facing his fears and going all in with the relationship, desperately trying to exorcise the ghosts of his past, Emmy too needed to leave her insecurities behind in the name of love. Sam had been a constant in her life for a very long time, loving her for exactly who she was. It had simply taken them this long to realise it.

EPILOGUE

Fifteen months later

'YOU MAY NOW kiss the bride.'

Emmy grinned at her husband, waiting for him to repeat that passionate kiss along with their wedding vows. Instead, Sam reached for the baby, who she had been holding throughout the ceremony.

'I think Abigail would like to spend some time with her adoring aunties.' He passed their daughter to Lorna and Lisa to fuss over her.

Despite their history, Emmy had asked them to be godparents to the baby. She wanted them to be part of her family, and since the scare early on in her pregnancy, they had been nothing but kind to Emmy. They had turned out to be amazing aunts who absolutely doted on their little niece. The whole family did.

Once Emmy's arms were free, Sam wrapped his around her and gave her a kiss to rival the leading man in any romantic movie. They were more in love now than ever and making up for lost time. Even with a young baby to look after, they made time for each other. Their relationship took priority over everything and Emmy could not have been happier.

Today was a double celebration. Abigail's christening followed by a renewal of their wedding vows. Something they both wanted to do over, so they got it right this time. Marrying for love and being honest about it.

Sam was a wonderful husband, as well as being a hands-on dad, and had finally put to rest his fears about becoming a carbon copy of his own father.

'I have a surprise for you, Mrs Goodwin,' he said, whispering into her ear.

'Another one?' Emmy had to be the luckiest woman in the world when he was constantly showing her how much he loved her with thoughtful gifts and sweet gestures, in case she ever forgot.

'Your parents have agreed to babysit so we can go on honeymoon.'

'Where?' Emmy gasped. As much as she loved her baby and would miss her, the thought of a few days alone with Sam sounded like heaven.

'Where else? Paris.' He grinned at her, knowing he deserved a gold star for pulling this one out of the bag.

Emmy let out a squeal before hugging him tightly. 'I love you, Sam Goodwin.'

'Good. This marriage lark is supposed to work out better when both parties can admit that. I love you too, Emmy Goodwin.'

Emmy's husband kissed her long and hard, and she did not care who was watching. After all, they were among family.

* * * * *

THEIR MARRIAGE MEANT TO BE

LOUISA HEATON

MILLS & BOON

To the staff and horses at Fort Widley,
who all gave my daughter, as well as many others,
hours of joy and happiness. x

PROLOGUE

Five years ago

A WISP OF her son's golden hair fell across his forehead as the fan at the side of his hospital bed blew air around the small room. Bex reached out to smooth it back, her touch light, delicate. Tender.

It was easy to pretend he was just sleeping, after a hard day playing outside in the garden. His little face was so relaxed in repose. The lovely, long eyelashes that he'd inherited from his father rested still and inert upon his soft pink cheeks.

If only he *was* sleeping.

If only he didn't have half his face obscured by the tube that was breathing for him.

If only he'd not had a stroke.

The nurses had turned him onto his left side, and he had one hand gently curled into a relaxed fist. He still had dimples where his knuckles should be. How she loved his little hands. They were so expressive. The way he'd clap them when he was happy. The way he'd raise them above his head, begging to be picked up. There was nothing Charlie loved more than to be held by her, so he could play with her hair as he rested his head against her chest.

The doctors said that he wouldn't be doing that any more.

He wouldn't be doing *anything* any more.

Was it her fault? Could she have prevented this? If she'd only got him to hospital sooner…

The burn of tears scorched her eyes, filling them with salty tears that ran freely down her face as she leaned over him, adjusting his blanket and trying to sing him his favourite lullaby.

Although the words got stuck in her throat halfway through, she eventually succeeded in getting to the end.

This wasn't how the fairy tale was meant to end.

If she ignored the machines in the room she could pretend that he was breathing on his own. She could pretend that she'd just put him to bed for an afternoon nap having read him a story.

At the side of the bed was his favourite book. His favourite grey teddy. She picked up the bear and tucked it in beside her son, stroking his hair once again, unwilling to stop touching him, because it meant that he was here, still vital, still alive.

She was unwilling to acknowledge that in reality Charlie was already gone.

The nurses had told her to take as long as she liked, before they'd slipped quietly from the room.

She had to wait for Ethan. He needed to be here for this. He should be here already. She didn't know why he wasn't. She needed his support. Needed to feel his arms around her when they came in and switched off the machines.

She bent low and gently dropped a kiss to her son's forehead. His skin was warm and soft, as it always was.

'I love you. I love you so much! You are my *everything*.'

The lump in her throat almost stopped the words and she had to wipe her eyes, unable to see for tears. Sniffing, she continued to stroke his face, his hair. Trying to imprint upon her memory how he felt. The shape of him. The scent of him. The curves of his face, his soft cheeks, his perfect, perfect sweetheart lips.

Never again would she hear his wonderful laugh.

Never again would she hear Charlie say *'Mummy!'* and see his beaming smile as he raised his arms, wanting to be picked up.

What she wouldn't give to feel his little body clamped onto hers, the weight of him on her hip, his little sticky face and hands…

Life was much too cruel. To do something like this to an innocent little boy.

'Sleep tight, Charlie. Sleep tight. Mummy will love you always.'

And she allowed her grief to consume her as the sound of her desperate cries filled the room.

CHAPTER ONE

Present day

SUNLIGHT FLICKERED THROUGH the trees as Bex drove to the farm. It was such a beautiful day, warm and bright, with a gentle breeze to help cool the intense summer temperatures they'd been experiencing lately.

Bex wished she could enjoy it. Normally, she loved summer…the longer days, the brighter nights. It gave her more time with the horses. Gave her time to actually ride them herself. And there was nothing she liked more than an evening walk along the bridle path that ran through Ruddington village.

But today she'd received a call about some animals that had been found abandoned and neglected on an old farm. The owner had died a couple of months ago, from what they could tell, and the animals had been left to fend for themselves. The cows had already been taken, the chickens rounded up and redistributed amongst rescuers and fosterers, but Bex had been called because apparently there were two horses there, and she ran a rescue and rehabilitation centre that mainly focused on equine animals—though there were a few rabbits, ducks, geese and three pygmy goats, too.

Days like today saddened her. They reminded her that bad things happened. She hated to see suffering. And although the sun shone bright in a perfectly azure sky, with not even a single wisp of white cloud, she knew she might have to call out a vet to put an animal to sleep if these horses were in terrible shape.

She had veterinary training herself. She was a qualified veterinary nurse. But the final decision would fall to a vet, and for that she was grateful. It had been her main reasoning for choosing a nursing course over becoming a full veterinary surgeon—she didn't think she'd be able to put an animal to sleep, even if she knew it would ease their suffering.

It would break her heart. And her heart had been broken enough times in life already.

Losing Charlie the way she had meant that she'd turned away from veterinary nursing, too. Watching owners lose their beloved fur babies... Watching them hold them as they fell to sleep...

It would bring back too many bad memories.

She hoped fervently that when she got to this farm she would find the horses in not too bad a condition. Hoped that they'd had access to fresh water in the intense heat of these last few weeks and that they'd had a paddock to graze in...maybe a tree to provide shade?

She indicated and turned down a track through some trees, wishing she could enjoy the drive as she went through a beautifully green tree tunnel, but she knew what might await her at the end.

Jenna's car was already there, with the double horse trailer hitched to the back, ready to go. Her assistant at the centre had called her about twenty minutes ago.

Parking alongside, she got out, locked up her vehicle

and looked for her. In the distance she saw Jenna standing by a fence, feeding hay to a tall, dark Clydesdale that, from this distance, looked to be a good eighteen or nineteen hands high. It had dark chestnut fur, with a white blaze to its legs as if it was wearing flares.

Bex waved and began to walk over.

'Hey, so, what do we have here?' She kept her voice soft and gentle, noting how nervous the horse seemed. His ears kept flicking back and occasionally he stamped his hooves as if wanting to flee, but his hunger and need for the hay that Jenna held overrode such instincts.

'A very hungry boy. But he doesn't look in too bad a state.'

Bex gave him a quick primary survey. His eyes were bright and full of life, although his coat needed a good brush and trim. His ribs could be clearly seen, and no doubt felt, and he had a nasty cut on his back leg that looked as if it had happened maybe a couple of days ago.

She gazed around the paddock to see if she could see what might have caused the cut, and saw part of the fencing had broken and pieces stuck out. He must have caught himself on one of those.

'Hey, boy…' She slowly reached out to let the horse smell her, before seeing if he would let her stroke him. He flinched a little, his nostrils flaring, but he let her do it. 'Okay.' She smiled. She could work with this. Get him fed. Make him better. Provide him with a safe space. 'I thought the report said there were two horses?'

Jenna shrugged. 'I've only found this one. Though, to be fair, once he realised I had food he kind of didn't want me to leave. Want to take over and I'll look around?'

'No, you carry on. He seems to like you. I'll go and take a look.'

Bex bypassed the old farmhouse, taking a dry, stony path around the side of it towards some outbuildings at the back. The heat bore down hard and heavy on her back, and she was glad she'd put her long brown hair up in a ponytail.

She found a large barn, an equipment shed and then, round the back of that, a small two-horse stable, painted in black and in a state of disrepair. Both the stable doors were open. One of the stalls was empty, but the other contained an almost skeletal horse, lying on dirty hay, breathing heavily, unable to get up.

'Oh, you poor thing…' Bex let out a sad sigh, feeling her heart ache at the misery this animal must be going through.

It was in a terrible state, from its hooves all the way to its ears. It didn't even have the energy to be alarmed at her approach.

She moved slowly and then crouched to get closer. She reached into her back pocket and pulled out her mobile and called the veterinary practice she used. 'Hi, it's Bex Clarke.'

'Oh, hi, Bex! How are you?' answered Chloe.

Bex recognised her voice easily. They spoke to each other often when she had to rescue animals, and she treated all the staff there as if they were great friends.

'I'm out at an old farm on Loughborough Road. I think it's called Five Acres. I was called out to rescue these two horses and I really need a vet out as quickly as possible to help me assess them. I think one's in pretty good shape, but I'm worried about the second one.'

As she spoke, she looked around for a container in

which she could put some fresh water, or at least find some fresh hay, but nothing seemed available. How long had this animal been without water? Would it die of heatstroke? Or thirst? Neither way was a good way to go, and this poor forgotten and neglected animal deserved a chance.

'Okay. Well, Patrick's got a full schedule, and he's in clinic all day, so is Hannah... But we've just recently taken on a new vet who's free. He's a horse specialist and I can send him out to you now, as he's just got back from another visit.'

'Okay. Sounds great. When can he get here?'

'I'll tell him to go straight away. He should be with you in about...fifteen minutes?'

'Perfect. Thanks, Chloe. Hope to see you soon.'

'You, too.'

Bex slipped her phone back into her pocket and stroked the horse's face. 'I'm going to do my best for you, honey. You hold on, okay?'

She stood up and looked about her, saw a broken bucket outside and walked with it over to an outside tap, rinsing it out and making it as clean as she could, before filling it with water and taking it back to the horse.

The bay sniffed the water with interest and took a small drink. It was as if it didn't have enough energy to drink, so Bex scooped the water up herself and tried to get it into the horse's mouth.

'That's it. Come on. Just a few sips...that's all I need you to take.'

It was hot in the stables, despite being in the shade, and as she sat there, willing the horse to drink, she felt sweat begin to prickle under her armpits and down her back.

Soon she heard voices—Jenna's and a deeper voice—and then footsteps crunching over stone.

'You hear that? Help's coming. We're going to get you through this, one way or another. I just need you to want to live.'

In the time it had taken the vet to get here she had tried to assess the animal. Apart from neglect and starvation, she couldn't see anything physically wrong with the horse. Of course, they'd need blood tests to confirm there was nothing internal going on, and she had no idea how strong this horse's heart was, or its will to live.

The footsteps got closer and she continued to murmur softly to the horse—until the footsteps behind her came to a stop and a shadow fell across her.

'Bex.'

She knew that voice. That deep tone. Hearing it once again, she felt it resonate through her body like a clanging bell and her heart began to pound.

She turned, frowning, and there in the doorway, silhouetted by the bright sunlight behind him, was Ethan. Her ex-husband.

Though technically they were still married. Neither of them had filed for divorce. They had simply let their relationship die and drifted apart, and they hadn't spoken to each other for what…? It had to be at least five years…

He looked good. But he always had. She hated it that she'd noticed. And the old anger, an ire that she'd thought she'd put behind her, rose in an instant.

'Chloe said it was you. I had to check twice,' he said, as if he still couldn't believe it.

'You've grown a beard.'

She hadn't imagined that this would be the first thing she would say to Ethan if they ever ran into each other again. She'd always thought that if that happened she'd be calm and put-together and she'd just say hello and act as if it was nothing—maybe even ignore him? But seeing him in the flesh had somehow disconnected her brain from her mouth and it had just come out.

Mind you, the beard looked good. And she felt a sudden ache for him that surprised her with its intensity. This man *knew* her. Physically, mentally, emotionally. They'd gone through hell together, and that kind of experience connected two people in a way that good times didn't.

But she knew she had to push that ache for him to one side.

Stick with the anger. That's easier.

'I've had it a while. Is this the fella?'

Ethan stepped forward, past her, clearly focused on his work, then set down his bag and pulled out a stethoscope to listen to the horse's heart.

As he'd stepped forward, she'd stepped back, almost as if she couldn't trust herself to be in such close proximity to him. She had so many questions for him. So many things she wanted to say, but suddenly couldn't. She stood in the doorway, watching him, trying to remain calm and trying to push down the lid on her feelings towards her ex-husband.

It was a box that she didn't want to reopen.

Their relationship was in the past and it needed to stay there. She'd moved on, and she had to remind herself that this man had hurt her more than she'd ever thought possible. She had stood in front of her family and friends with this man and promised to be with him and love him through sickness and in health and for better and for worse.

And that last vow was the one they'd both broken.

The vow was so simple. People made it thinking that they knew what the 'worse' part would be. When they thought of the 'worse', they imagined arguments—maybe even an affair. They never imagined that the 'worse' could mean the death of your child. And abandonment. They never imagined that.

He wasn't there for me.

Looking at him now, she saw the man Ethan had once been and the man he now was. In his face and in his body she saw some similarities.

But it would seem that in the last few years Ethan had been looking after himself. Clearly he'd been going to the gym. The sleeves of his shirt were wrapped around clearly defined muscles in his arms that had never been there before. His waist was flatter. Neater. And that led her to wondering if he had a six-pack under that blue-and-white-checked fabric. He'd caught the sun. Been out in it too much, maybe. The tip of his nose red, as it had always used to get when he'd been outside too long.

She was annoyed that she remembered that. Remembered the first time she'd ever noticed.

They'd been on their honeymoon in the Seychelles. Two whole weeks spent frolicking beneath the sun and in the sea. They'd sunbathed and scuba dived and swum in the cooling waves, and then at night they'd dined on beautiful seafood and clinked glasses of champagne over candlelight before going back to their room and making love, over and over again. Lying in each other's arms and noticing silly things, like how the sun had brought out the freckles on her face and a red glow to the tip of Ethan's nose…

She'd applied some after-sun to his nose, touching the tip of it with a drop of white cream and slowly rubbing it in, and then he'd pulled her close, smiling, staring deeply into her eyes. And then they'd been kissing and touching… And then the rest of the world had been forgotten as they'd lost themselves in each other and—

'Bex?'

His voice brought her back to the present and she realised that he'd been speaking to her whilst she'd been lost in a once much-loved daydream.

'I'm sorry?'

'I said it doesn't look good. I'm not sure it's fair to persevere and put this animal through unnecessary suffering.'

'Oh.'

She looked at the horse…looked at its eyes. She saw suffering there, but she also saw something else. A plea. A chance. *Just give me some time. I'll be okay.* That was what she seemed to think it said. This horse still had life in him. He wasn't lost like Charlie was. He deserved every chance.

'Is his heart weak?'

'It's on the fast side, but I don't hear any murmurs.'

'And you think we should give up?'

She didn't want to. None of this was the horse's fault. It might once have been a fine animal. He had just been forgotten about. Abandoned. And she knew how that felt. What it could do to you when you felt alone. It made you feel like giving up. But she felt, in her heart, that this horse did not *want* to give up. It was just tired. Tired of fighting. If someone helped him…

'I don't know. I think he deserves a chance.'

Ethan sat back on his haunches and sighed as he looked the animal over.

She waited, wondering what was going on in his mind—something she was used to doing. She'd often thought of Ethan as being like the sea. He could look calm and still on the surface, but underneath there were riptides and currents and eddies, perhaps a veritable storm of something that he refused to allow anyone to see or experience.

He'd always hidden parts of himself.

That had been half their problem.

'If you can get him standing…if you can get him eating…then maybe…maybe there's a chance.' Ethan shrugged, then looked at the horse's teeth. 'He's young. He might have enough fight.'

She nodded. She'd take it. 'Okay.'

They'd need hay. Food. A reason to try and make this horse get up. *If* he could get up. She hoped he would. His life depended upon it. Otherwise he'd end up as yet another sad statistic.

'I've tried to give him water, but he seems too exhausted to drink.'

'I'll load him up with some fluids—see if that helps. Why don't you look for some straps and ropes to help him stand?'

Ethan wasn't looking at her much. Was that because he still felt guilty?

'Okay.'

She stayed briefly, stroking the horse, whispering

calming words to him as Ethan found a vein and installed a bag of IV fluids which he hung from a hook on the wall. Then she went to the trailer behind Jenna's car to fetch the straps and ropes.

She saw Jenna with the other horse. 'Want to get that one loaded into the trailer? Then you can come help us with this other one.'

'You found it? How is it?'

'The vet says if we can get him standing and eating then he won't put him down.'

It felt strange to be talking to Jenna about Ethan. Ever since establishing her horse rescue and rehabilitation centre she had made sure not to give any details about her past to those she worked with. She didn't want their pity but, more than that, telling the story of Charlie was upsetting even now, five years later. If he'd lived, her little boy would be seven now. The perfect age for riding horses, and he would have loved her centre.

Jenna and the others only knew that she'd been married before and that it hadn't worked out. That she was separated. She felt that was enough detail.

But now Ethan was back. Here in Ruddington. What had made him move jobs? What had he been doing with himself these last few years while they'd been apart?

All *her* energy had been put into creating the centre. Her parents had helped fund it, but it was all in her name and she'd been working hard. She'd not been going to the gym, like Ethan, but she had new muscles, too, and she was ready to flex them. If he was back in her life, then she knew at some point he would get to see that. She wasn't the woman he knew from before her. The loss of Charlie, and the years after, had moulded her into someone new. Someone fierce.

'Oh, that's brilliant. Let's hope, then, eh?'

Bex passed Jenna a lead rope and then took the others back around to where Ethan and the other horse were. As she neared the dilapidated stable she heard Ethan talking to the horse, trying to get him to stand on his own.

The horse remained where it was.

'I've squeezed through half a litre already, but he's going to need much more.'

'That's okay. He's got people willing to fight for him now. Here, take these.'

She passed him the straps and ropes and they began to loop and fasten them around the horse's body. It was difficult getting the straps under the horse's prone body, but they did it, with much sweating and huffing and puffing and sweat pouring down their faces.

Bex stood, feeling sweat sticking her shirt to her back. She held the horse's reins in one hand and a load of hay in the other. 'Up! Come on—up!' she commanded.

The horse's nose twitched at the hay, and he stretched out his neck for it, but made no move to stand.

'Up! Come on—you can do it!' She let the horse get a mouthful of hay, which he munched on contentedly. 'Well, that's fifty percent of the deal…'

'We need him to stand,' Ethan repeated.

'I know!' she answered impatiently, angry that he was telling her what needed to happen. She was trying. 'What if…?' She paused, thinking. 'We need to get him out of this stable. What if I call Roland to come over with his digger? We could use the machine to drag the horse out of the stable and help lift him to his feet. I very much feel that he wants to do it—he's just not got the strength to. Heaven only knows how long he's been lying here.'

Ethan looked uncertain.

'It's worth a try!' She glared at her husband. 'To *save a life*.'

He met her gaze, and she was once again reminded of what it felt like to look deeply into his eyes. They were a soft pale blue. He had gentle eyes. Come-to-bed eyes. And when they'd looked at her intently Bex had always used to feel as if she could stare into them for ever. Yet now she could see uncertainty in them. Doubt. And she hated that. She wanted this animal to have a chance to live.

'All right. Call Roland. Whoever he is.'

Ethan grabbed a bottle of water from his bag and took a long drink as he stepped out of the stable.

Bex nodded and grabbed her mobile once again, calling Roland. He was the maintenance man at the centre, and his digger would be perfect for this if they could get it here.

Once she'd made the call she gave the horse a pile of hay to eat whilst they waited, putting it alongside the bucket of water, in case it wanted it.

Ethan leaned against a paddock fence, waiting. Bex watched him for a moment, then walked over to stand beside him. 'It's been a long time,' she ventured.

Five years, to be exact. Five years without a word. Five years of not knowing whether he was alive or not.

He nodded, looking out across the farm. 'Yeah. You been okay?'

Since when did he care how she felt? 'I've been

busy,' she answered tersely. And despite her anger she couldn't help but ask, curious, 'You?'

'Same.'

It was horrible that this was so awkward—but, then again, how could it be anything else? They'd once been so close! Able to finish each other's sentences. Sometimes they'd not even had to speak at all, and had been completely comfortable in each other's company. Distance, grief, time…they were all powerful grenades that had blown them apart. Now that they were no longer talking about the horse, no longer focused on business, they both seemed tense. Abrupt.

'So, you run a…er…rescue centre now?' he asked, finally risking a quick glance at her.

She nodded. 'Yes. The Grange Horse Rescue and Rehabilitation Centre.'

'Snappy title.' He sipped his water.

Bex said nothing. Not sure what to say. The Grange had become her life these last few years. It had saved her. Kept her going. Given her a reason to get out of bed every morning.

'You rescue horses and rehabilitate them? Try to find them new homes?'

'Kind of. I also have a therapy centre. So the horses that have recovered are able to help children and adults with learning and communication difficulties. It helps both humans and horses, really.'

'That's amazing…' he said softly.

She appreciated the compliment. 'What about you?' she asked. 'I thought you were going to Abu Dhabi.'

'I did. I got a post as resident vet for a prince who owns a racing stable.'

That sounded impressive. 'What made you come back to boring old England?'

'There's only so much scorching sun an Englishman with fair skin can take.' He looked at her, took another swig of water.

'I'm sure...'

He'd asked her to go with him. After Charlie died. Despite all their difficulties, he'd asked her to go. Said it might help her. That, staying where they were, they'd find all their memories of Charlie would be too much. But his invitation had been half-hearted. As if he was only doing it out of duty. And she'd not seen it that way. All those memories and reminders of Charlie that he'd been so desperate to get away from had been the exact reason she'd wanted to stay.

She'd lost her child and she needed to feel close to him still. She'd wanted to stay in the family home. Wanted to walk past the park where Charlie had enjoyed going on the swings. Wanted to be able to be near his grave, so she could take flowers and talk to him.

She'd never understood her husband's desire to get away from all of that and flee. She'd not understood it and not understood *him*. It had been the final nail in the coffin of their marriage when he'd left.

'The change was good, but I felt the time was right to come home,' he said now. 'I'd been out there long enough. Felt like I'd made a difference. But I needed to come back home. Be with family.'

She plucked a strand of grass and toyed with it. There'd always been problems with his parents.

'Are your mum and dad okay?' she asked.

The last time she'd seen his parents had been at Charlie's funeral. Sylvia and Gregory Clarke had been shadows of their former selves. Sylvia, thin and pale, exhausted, and for some reason unable to look her in the eye. And Gregory had looked unkempt. His shirt unpressed, his tie askew, his face flushed with alcohol.

Although she'd not blamed her father-in-law for needing a flask of Scotch to get through the funeral. In fact, she'd kind of wished she'd had one herself. No one needed to see a coffin that tiny.

'It's been a difficult few years,' he said, turning around at the sound of an engine.

Bex turned, too, and there was Roland, coming down the driveway in his off-roader, pulling behind him a small digger on a trailer. 'Great. He's here.'

'I'll go and check on the patient. See how that IV is doing.'

She watched him go and then indicated to Roland where he should park. It wasn't long before he'd driven the digger off the trailer and brought the vehicle round to the broken stable.

Their patient was munching on hay still, and Ethan was fixing another IV bag to its tubing.

Bex and Roland attached the straps and ropes to the digger, and then Roland got back into the driving seat.

'We need to pull him out of that stable first…so, reverse. Nice and slowly,' she instructed.

The straps that had been lying across the ground lifted as Roland reversed and began to pull the horse forward. Bex had been hoping that the horse might try to stand on its own at the movement, but it didn't. It simply allowed itself to be pulled out of the stable and into the bright sunshine.

Bex held up her hand to tell Roland to stop. He got

out, adjusted the straps, and then got back into his little cockpit.

'Now lift…nice and slow.'

Bex stood by the horse's head, holding its reins, speaking soothingly as the digger slowly began to lift upwards.

The horse struggled a little, unfamiliar with such a situation, its hooves desperately trying to find ground, until finally it was able to stand and Roland paused the digger.

Bex turned to look at Ethan and beamed. 'We did it! He's standing *and* eating. So, what do you say? He gets the chance to live, right?'

Ethan nodded. 'He certainly does.'

When Chloe had told him that he'd got a callout to a horse rescue, Ethan had been pleased. But when she'd told him it was for Bex Clarke, he'd wondered if he was ready.

He'd been telling the truth when he'd told her he'd needed to come home for family—what he hadn't told her was that he'd come home for *her*. It was time to put things right. It was time that they began speaking again. He'd not needed his dying mother to tell him that—his mind had already been made up—but she had.

He didn't have any aspirations that they would suddenly fall back in love with one another and return to the marital bed, but he did hope for friendship. For the ability to be in the same room as one another and feel comfortable. For the opportunity to show her that he was still the man she'd once loved and that he would be there for her now in whatever form she needed…in a way he'd not been there for her before.

It had been a small matter of simply looking her up on the internet to find out where she was. When he'd discovered that she was no longer in East Leake, but had set up her own rescue centre just outside Ruddington village, he'd simply waited for a job opportunity to present itself. His credentials after working for the Arab prince at his prestigious racing stables had certainly helped swing the offer his way. The experience he'd gained there, looking after race horses, was unmatchable.

But seeing Bex today had been scary in so many ways, and he realised that it was not going to be as simple as he'd hoped. People were complicated. Their situation was more complicated still, and he didn't want to rush things. Didn't want to say something rash and ruin whatever it was that he was trying to build.

And Bex clearly still held anger. He could tell in the way she'd spoken to him. Her tone.

He had hurt this woman, and even to try to get close to her once again would be like trying to approach a skittish horse. It would take time and patience and an understanding that she might not be as ready as he was to get close. That she might not trust him. That she might need to call the shots for a while, until she was ready. Maybe even lash out a bit.

And he would let her.

They had all the time in the world, and if she felt any warmness towards him for helping her get that horse on its feet today, then he would take that small smidgeon of gratitude and hope that it could be built into something more.

As he looked at her now, smiling and happy as she helped settle the weak horse into the trailer for the trip back to the rescue centre, he knew that their recovery had to go the same way. One step at a time.

When the horse was secure, Bex closed the trailer and came over to him. 'Thank you.'

He nodded. 'No problem. He deserved the chance, just like you said.'

'He did.'

She kept on looking at him, as if she was waiting for him to say something, and although he had plenty he wanted to say, now was not the time.

His mind scrambled for something else. 'Does he have a name?'

She shrugged. 'We don't have any documentation and there's no one to ask. I guess I'm going to have to name him myself.'

He smiled. 'Well, if you want any suggestions I'm happy to help.'

She nodded.

'I'll pop by tomorrow. See how he's settled in. Maybe take some blood, run some tests—just to be on the safe side.'

'Okay.'

He was happy that their first encounter after so many years apart had actually gone quite well. It showed how much they'd matured. Or it showed how time took the edge off the sting of pain, anger and hurt. Either way, he'd take it. He was hoping he could show Bex by being back in her life that she could begin to see him as a good thing. A friend. Someone she could trust.

Someone who had vowed never to hurt or abandon her ever again.

CHAPTER TWO

As PROMISED, Ethan drove over to The Grange Horse Rescue and Rehabilitation Centre the next morning. He'd not been sure what to expect, but once he'd made it through the village and reached the outskirts he found Bex's centre at the end of a long and twisting driveway that had taken him through trees until the world opened up again.

There were a couple of paddocks filled with horses and ponies, what looked like a large education centre and, behind it, a few rows of stables. Off to one side was a large indoor paddock—no doubt for taking classes when the weather was bad. But today that was not a problem. Like yesterday, the sun blasted him with a heat so thick it was almost as if he could grab it.

He parked his off-roader next to some other vehicles and walked up to a fence where a couple stood, watching Bex lead a horse by its reins around the interior. The horse was a dappled grey, with a thick white mane, and atop its back was a young boy, maybe seven or eight years of age, wearing a thick horse rider's helmet and a huge smile.

'Is that your son?' he asked the couple.

They turned, smiled and nodded. The mother answered. 'It is.'

'He looks happy.'

'Oh, he loves it here. It's the highlight of his week.'

It was clear on the little boy's face. He was simply beaming—as was Bex. But as she led them past she noticed Ethan and her smile faltered, before she pasted it back on and turned to check on the boy.

'You okay up there, Jake?' she asked.

'Yes.'

'One more lap, okay?'

Jake bent low and draped his arms around the grey's neck, and began talking to the horse in a babble of sound.

His mother turned to Ethan. 'Jake's autistic and he used to be non-verbal. We did everything we could to get him to talk but nothing worked. And then one day, when we were out at the park, this dog ran over to us and Jake was clearly mesmerised by the animal. I'd never seen him light up like that. So we did a bit of research and found this place. If Bex had never set it up we would never have heard our son tell us that he loves us.'

What a precious gift.

Ethan stared out across the paddock as Bex continued to lead the horse over to a three-step mounting block. Jake was still draped around the horse's neck, and he could just hear the little boy telling the horse how much he loved him and that he would come back next week to see him again.

Bex stood watching, smiling, and then she helped the boy dismount. Jake gave her a high five, and then she was leading him through the gate and back to his parents.

Jake ran into their arms, yelling, 'Thanks, Bex!'

'My pleasure. I thought next week maybe Jake might like to try a little bit of trotting. What do you think, Jake? Would you like to go a little faster on Dobby?'

Jake nodded enthusiastically as his mother removed his helmet and passed it back to Bex.

'We'll see you next week, Bex. Take care!' said the mother, and the little family walked away.

Ethan watched them go, aware that the boy—Jake—was about the same age as Charlie would have been, had he lived. Was Bex aware of that, too? Stupid question. Of course she was.

'Good morning,' he said.

She finished waving goodbye to the family, then turned to face him, her smile disappearing. 'Here to check on the patient?'

'I am.'

'I'll take you to him. I just need to drop this off first,' she said, brandishing the helmet.

He let her lead the way, taking the time to have a really good look around. Everything looked newly constructed and in excellent condition. The education centre was adorned with a row of beautiful hanging baskets, all heavily filled with pansies and trailing lobelia. In the window he saw adoption packs, and posters for different classes Bex ran here. Inside he could see a small shop, next to a reception desk, and beyond it an office.

They went in and down a corridor marked 'Staff Only', and there he was met by the scent of leather and rope. He saw reins, lead ropes, riding boots, helmets. They adorned the walls like trophies.

Bex replaced the helmet and led him back outside

without a word. The tension between them was palpable, and the air was thick with a heady mix of horse manure, wood shavings, hay and pollen. It was a veritable assault on the senses.

'Have you given him a name yet?' he asked, trying to break the silence.

She turned. 'Spirit.'

That was a good name, and it was just like Bex to pick something so positive. She had always been optimistic. He could imagine her spending hours staring at the horse, talking to him, trying out different names until she found one that she thought was perfect.

'I like it.'

'It suited him.'

Ethan said nothing. He'd woken this morning feeling worried about seeing her again, but also keen. There was so much he needed to put right with this woman, but when he was with her she made him so nervous. He wasn't sure what was the right way to tackle the vast mountain of hurt that lay between them.

There were helpful analogies. How do you eat an elephant? One bite at a time. How do you climb a mountain? One step at a time.

Did they help him?

The hardest part of this—engineering a meeting between them—had already been taken care of, but though he'd imagined plenty of conversations between the two of them, and how they might go, those imaginings went right out of the window whenever he was with her.

Bex was important to him. Getting his apology right was important to him—and would no doubt be important to her, too. He didn't want to screw it up.

She looked good, wearing a pale blue short-sleeved tee shirt, cream jodhpurs and black riding boots. Her long brown hair was in a high ponytail, and loose bits of it had freed themselves and hung either side of her face. He suddenly felt an ache for her, wishing he was free to reach out and tuck those strands of hair back into place, or to cradle her face in his hands and just look deeply into her eyes the way he'd used to.

There weren't enough words in the world to explain just how much he'd missed her and how much he regretted his past behaviour. But there were things she didn't know. Things he'd never told her. Because he'd kept them a secret…always waiting for the time to be right. Only it never had been. Now, if they were going to have any kind of a friendly relationship, he needed to be honest with her.

He'd done some research online, but nothing had told him about who she was now. She could have moved on. She could be with someone. He had no right to assume she'd still be single, like him.

They bypassed the main stable block and went to a separate building, built to contain at least four horses. He saw two horses, poking their heads out, but they didn't look like the ones they'd rescued yesterday.

Bex led him to a stable door at the far end. 'He's in here. This is our quarantine block, but I put him at the end because we can get the digger to this one if we need to, to help him stand again.'

Ethan peered inside to take a look at Spirit before he went in. As before, the horse lay on the ground, munching on hay, but this time the ground was clean, the stall in excellent condition, and from somewhere classical music played. He looked up and saw speakers, high in the rafters. He turned to look at her, an eyebrow raised.

'French research has shown that playing classical music to horses reduces acute stress,' she said defensively. 'It regulates their heartbeat and limits stress-related behaviours.'

He nodded, remembering reading something along those lines. And who was he to argue? Bex had been running this centre for nearly three years. He knew, because he'd looked it up on the internet. And they played classical music at the vets he now worked at. In the area out at the back, where they kept all the animals that had had surgery, they played classical music.

He didn't know why he was surprised. Of course Bex would know about it. She had always been about trying to reduce stress. Trying to help people *and* animals feel at ease. It was one of the things he loved about her. One of the things he missed.

'He doesn't seem any the worse for wear after being transported yesterday. But I'd like to go in and take a blood sample, and give him a more thorough check-over.'

'All right. But I ought to go in first. He's got used to me and he gets a little unnerved by others.'

'You slept here in the stall with him, didn't you?' he asked. He just knew it. She wouldn't have transported him to somewhere new and then just left him alone overnight.

'Of course I did!' she said, staring back as if challenging him to argue with her about it.

But he didn't want to argue. In fact, it warmed his heart. She hadn't changed. Bex was still the woman he'd fallen in love with all those years ago. She was generous. Had a large heart. And even though that heart had been torn into two she was still able to embrace those who needed it and would benefit from her comfort.

Bex opened the stall and went inside. 'Hey, Spirit.' She knelt down and stretched out her hand so the horse could smell her.

Spirit's nose twitched and Ethan saw the alarm leave its eyes. Clearly these two had bonded in the short time they'd been together.

Bex turned and beckoned him in.

He moved slowly, and made no sudden moves that might startle the horse. It might not be on its feet, but it was still an incredibly strong animal and might easily knock the two of them over with a swipe of its head if it panicked. Yesterday, Spirit hadn't had much fight, but since then he'd been loaded with fluids, rehydrated and fed. Strength would slowly be returning, and they still knew nothing about the character of this horse.

Bex seemed to trust him, and Ethan trusted her judgement, so he let her continue to soothe the horse whilst he opened his bag and got the equipment he'd need to take a blood sample.

It was the same equipment as was used on humans. A Vacutainer tube and needle-holder…an eighteen-gauge needle. Once he'd got everything ready, he knelt beside the horse as Bex held its head, and palpated for the jugular vein in the throat latch area. He found it easily enough, and drew off some blood for the tests.

He wanted to do whole blood testing. Examine the red blood cells and the white for infection. He also wanted to do a CK and AST to check for any muscle damage, liver enzymes, urea and creatinine as well as electrolytes. The results would give him an overall picture of Spirit's general health.

'All done.' He stood slowly and moved away, noticing how Spirit kept nudging Bex with his nose. 'He likes you.'

'It's only because I've spent so much time with him.'

'You have that effect on people, too.'

The words were out before he realised what he was saying, and Ethan left the stall and placed the blood samples into a pathology bag, trying not to meet Bex's gaze. It was true. Bex had that effect on everyone. She had such an easy-going nature that people felt they could trust her quite quickly. He couldn't remember anyone not getting on with her, or anyone who disliked her.

When he heard her put down the latch on the stall, he gave her a quick glance. 'I'll have the results back to you as soon as I can.'

'Thanks. You know, if you're not in a rush, I'd like you to take a look at the other horse we brought here with Spirit. He's got a bad cut on his leg. It looks okay to me, but I wouldn't mind a professional opinion.'

Was this her olive branch? Was this her way of showing that she was prepared to work with him? Not that he would ever turn her down.

'Sure. I'll take a look.'

He smiled, sweating in the heat, part him longing to be in his vehicle where there was some lovely air conditioning.

He wasn't sure if he was sweating because of the heat, or because of being near Bex.

This felt so strange. Chatting and conversing with Ethan. They were both good at pretending their relationship hadn't happened and only talking about the horses, considering there was still a lot they needed to talk about and weren't doing so. Chatting about the horses, keeping the conversation on safe topics, was easier.

Are we never going to speak about what happened ever again? she wondered.

Bex didn't talk to anyone about Charlie except her parents. But there was one person who'd gone through that experience with her and they should be able to talk about it—especially now that it wasn't so raw—but Ethan seemed as if he wanted to keep their exchanges on safe topics, and part of that was frustrating. All her hurt over Charlie she'd kept inside, burning inside her like a stoked furnace, and the one person she should be able to release it to, who would help smother the flames, wasn't talking about it!

Part of her wanted to wake him up. Smack him on the shoulder and say, *Hey! We need to talk about this!* Only she didn't. Why? Was it because for all these years she'd been waiting for him to reappear in her life and now that he was here all those questions, all those words, that pain and anger, suddenly seemed hemmed in, like water behind a dam?

She watched him check over the second horse they'd rescued. He was in a much better condition than Spirit. He could stand on his own, for a start, and didn't seem so flighty.

Ethan checked the cut, noticed the granulation of tissue forming at the edges and told her it was healing. She'd known that. Her veterinary nursing training had told her that. But something about Ethan being here had made her not want him to leave. She was angry at him, wanted to rage at him, and yet she didn't want him to go. It was puzzling.

Seeing him yesterday had surprised her, but she'd spent a surprisingly good night in the stall with Spirit, lying there, thinking about all the good times they'd had. Good times were much better to remember. They didn't hurt. And she felt she needed to remind herself of those good times, because at some point she and Ethan were going to have to talk about what had happened. And that was scary.

Sometimes she wasn't sure if she even wanted to, because last time they'd tried talking about it, it had torn them apart.

Not having Ethan by her side each day had become an awful new reality. One she had tried really hard to cope with until it became normal. A numb normal, but normal just the same. And now a miracle had occurred and he was back, and he was here, and they were talking, and it was perfectly adequate. Why would she want to ruin it all before they could begin?

'It's fine. Healing well. I could prescribe some antibiotic cream, just in case?' he said.

She nodded. 'Thank you.' She didn't need it. She already had a supply and had been using it.

'I'll write a script. You'll have to collect it from the surgery or have someone drop by for it.'

'I'll do that.'

She walked with him back to his car. Was it her imagination or did he seem as if he didn't want to leave either? It would be all too easy for her to read things into his actions—especially because she wanted him to stay and talk. She ached for him. In a way she'd not expected. He'd hurt her so badly, walking away the way he had all those years ago, and she'd pined for the marriage they'd once had. It had been so good between them. They'd had the fairy tale before it had all gone wrong. She missed those times.

A memory emerged, unbidden, and suddenly she was talking. 'Do you remember that time we were in the New Forest?'

He stopped, paused, turned to face her with a slight smile upon his lips. 'That horse that wouldn't leave us alone?' He gave a small laugh. 'I do.'

She'd expected him to say much more. Expected him to reminisce about how that horse had kept interrupting their picnic, determined to reach past Ethan to get to the carrot sticks Bex had brought to dip into hummus. How they'd had to give it an apple, even though they'd known you weren't meant to feed the New Forest ponies. How it had stood over them snickering until it had got everything it wanted.

Only he didn't say anything else, and that left the silence awkward.

'What made you think about that?' he asked.

She wasn't sure. 'I don't know. The heat of the day? It was hot back then, too.'

'We had some good times together,' he said.

And he was right. But they'd been outweighed by all the bad ones at the end, and if she was trying to brainwash herself into thinking they'd only had good times then she was failing, because memories of the bad ones would wash over her, too.

'Maybe, we should...' he shrugged '...I don't know...meet for coffee one day. Have a chat. About... everything.'

She stared at him, surprised. She'd thought this conversation wasn't going very well, and now he'd asked her out for coffee. To talk about 'everything'. Was that even wise? Perhaps if they met on neutral ground…in public. Then she wouldn't lose control and start yelling. Because she wouldn't want to embarrass herself.

'Maybe.'

'Well, I know where you are now. I'll call you soon with those blood test results, and I'll be back to check on Spirit, too.'

He'd reached his car and unlocked it, was throwing his bag into the boot.

Bex simply nodded, trying not to look disappointed or upset. Truth was, she didn't know *how* to feel right now. Murky waters lay ahead, she just knew it, and she wasn't sure she wanted to wade in.

'I guess I'll see you soon, then?'

'You can count on it.'

He smiled and closed the door, before reversing and driving away.

Ethan sat in the car outside the surgery with his head in his hands. Had he been too impulsive, asking her out for coffee? She'd not seemed thrilled to take up his offer. Perhaps he'd misread everything?

Only, they really needed to talk. He wanted to fully explain, and he wanted to clear the air between them. Make her see why he'd acted the way he had…why he'd abandoned her. But now he felt he'd made a mistake.

Perhaps he should have just stuck to talking about Spirit. Perhaps he should have kept things professional. Maintained the distance that was between them and let Bex live the rest of her life without him unburdening himself upon her. Did she really need that? She was doing well without his presence in her life. Was it fair of him to drag her back down into those dark days?

No. It wasn't. It might make *him* feel better to do so, but would it help *her*? She seemed happy. Successful. More like the Bex he'd fallen in love with. He didn't want to ruin her life again. Perhaps the best thing to do would be to maintain the status quo. Talk only about work, chat to her as if they were old friends and nothing more. If he met her for coffee, they'd only talk about what life was like for them both now—what they were doing, what they hoped to achieve, where they saw themselves in five years' time.

In other words—stick to safe topics only.

Before he could chicken out, he picked up his mobile and dialled the rescue centre. A woman answered. Not Bex. So he left a garbled message asking if Bex could call him on his mobile when she had a minute and left his number.

There. The ball was in her court. If she wanted to spend more time with him then she could decide that. Before he put his phone away he let his gaze linger on his screensaver. Charlie. Their little boy. He was standing in the back garden of their old home, wearing just a pair of orange shorts as he stood under a lawn sprinkler, his face full of laughter, his eyes closed with mirth, hands held up to the sky as the water sprinkled down around him.

He could recall that day so clearly: Charlie's endless chuckling, the way he'd squealed, running through the water. Bex had been standing off to one side, hands on her hips in mock sternness, after she'd come home from work to find them like that. Then she'd gone inside to get their son a towel. He remembered how it had felt to wrap his little boy in that huge soft towel and lift him up, smiling, laughing still. The weight of him. The feel of him. He'd been a solid little boy. Real.

And yet sometimes it felt as if he'd imagined him.

A little boy so full of life…

With so little of it left ahead of him.

Bex stared at the message in her hands. At the phone number written there. Ethan was asking her to call him when she had a free moment.

She wanted to. Wanted to pick up the phone there and then to arrange something, to see him again. But another part of her was scared.

Had there been too much water under the bridge for them? Were they being fools in thinking they could talk? Were they just going to reopen old wounds? Because she wasn't sure who that would help. It might feel good to get out some of her old upsets and frustrations, but would that change the past?

No.

Annoyed with her yo-yoing thoughts, she picked up her mobile and dialled the number before she could change her mind. Maybe she was being foolish, and maybe she would get hurt again, but her connection to Ethan was something stronger than either of them could imagine.

The phone rang and rang, and she was just about to hang up when it was finally answered and she heard Ethan's breathless voice on the other end.

'Hello?'

She sucked in a breath. Considered cutting the call, not speaking. But she realised he'd know it was her and what was the point of that?

'It's me. Bex,' she added, feeling silly for saying her name. Surely he recognised her voice? 'I got the message you left with Jenna. Just thought I'd return your call.'

'Great. I'm glad you did.'

'Have you got Spirit's blood results?'

'Erm…some of them. They're all good so far. He seems to be in quite good health, considering the condition we found him in.'

'That's great news!'

Why did she feel so nervous? Why did she sound like a teenage girl again, talking to her crush? She was clutching the phone as if it might slip away if she relaxed her grip. Was she waiting for him to ask her out on a date? It was ridiculous!

'Also…'

She heard him pause. Was he in just as much doubt as she was?

'I wondered if you were busy this weekend. Might be good to have that catch-up? Nothing heavy…just a chat.'

Her stomach dropped to the floor. *Nothing heavy.* Could anything be light between them?

'Yeah, sounds great. I've got a couple of sessions booked this Saturday, but I'm free on Sunday,' she said, knowing that he never liked to plan work on Sundays. Ethan wasn't religious, but he saw Sundays as days of complete rest. He'd never used to arrange any work for Sundays.

'Okay. Er…the afternoon? About two?'

'Perfect.'

Why was her heart thudding in her chest? Why did it

feel as if she had a galloping horse inside her ribcage? Why did she suddenly feel nauseated?

'Where should I pick you up from?' he asked.

She gave him her address in Ruddington village. 'You know it?'

'No. But I'm sure my phone will get me there.'

When he rang off, she let out a heavy breath and tried to steady her breathing. It was just a chat. Probably coffee. 'Nothing heavy,' he'd said. But she knew that there was so much that needed to be said.

He almost cancelled. Spent ages in his bedroom, carefully selecting clothes. He settled for some jeans and a white shirt, even though it was still hot. It seemed disrespectful to turn up in a tee shirt and shorts. This was his wife. The mother of his child. And they hadn't seen each other properly for years. This meeting would set the tone for the rest of their relationship and he wanted it to go well.

He didn't want to argue with Bex. They'd done enough of that. Nor did he want to upset her in any way. They both needed to look ahead now—not back.

The GPS on his phone directed him to her home on St Mary's Crescent. It was a narrow road, and her house was on a corner plot. He saw a garden full of roses out at the front, and down the side of the house, alongside the driveway, there were runner beans growing up canes, as well as a trellis full of sweet peas in full multi-coloured bloom.

It was just like Bex to fill her life with colour. She always had.

He knocked on her front door and patiently waited, his heart hammering and his mouth so dry he wasn't sure he'd even be able to get words out. But when she swung open the door and he saw her, wearing a beautiful white short-sleeved summer dress with tiny roses on it, he forgot all about his dry mouth and his hammering heart and the queasiness he'd begun to feel in his stomach.

Bex looked simply breathtaking.

Her hair was down today, and he realised how much she'd let it grow since they were together. It fell in thick chestnut waves over her shoulders and down her back. Her lips were slicked with some type of lip-gloss and she'd put on make-up, giving her eyes a smoky look.

'Wow. You look great.'

She smiled at his compliment. 'Thanks. So do you.' She pulled the door closed behind her, slipping her keys into her bag, and then asked him where they were going.

'There's a nice little café in Clifton Village. I thought we could grab a drink and then go for a walk in Clifton Grove?'

She looked down at her flat shoes. 'Will these be all right, do you think?'

'Sure.'

Actually, he had no idea. But he didn't want to cause her the trouble of having to change her outfit.

He escorted her out to his car, opening her door for her and then getting in on the other side himself. He started the engine to get the air conditioning going. It was another hot day. The perfect English summer. But today there was a nice soft breeze, so the heat itself didn't seem so stifling.

He drove them through Ruddington and over the two hills that took them to Clifton Estate. They moved through the estate until they reached the village and then passed an old brick-built dovecote. Soon they came to the tiny café that had outdoor seating. There was a table free outside, so they sat down and picked up the menus.

'This is nice. I've never been here before. How did you find out about it?' she asked.

He could hear the nerves in her voice. 'Oh, I just searched online for cafés that were open, and thought this one sounded nice.' He didn't want to tell her that he'd put a few hours into making his choice. Searching for a café that had Bex's favourite dessert on the menu.

'Oh, look—they do a Knickerbocker Glory!' she exclaimed.

Inwardly, he felt rewarded. His research had paid off. He'd known she'd like that. When they'd been together she'd used to tell him about how her parents would take her to the seaside each summer, and how, on the last night of their break, she and her parents would have Knickerbocker Glories. They reminded her of simpler times. Happy times. Of summer sun and joy and delight.

'You should get one,' he told her.

'I don't think so. Too many calories.'

Her body was perfect. It would always be, no matter what. 'Treat yourself. I'll have one, too, if you want.'

She looked at him as if they were in on a naughty secret together and he liked that.

'All right. I will.'

The waitress came out at that moment. A Goth-looking girl, with so many piercings in her ears it was difficult to count how many she actually had. 'What can I get you?' she asked.

He ordered, also asking for a couple of coffees afterwards.

The waitress smiled. 'It'll be right out.'

And then she disappeared towards another table, where an old man had settled with his West Highland Terrier. The dog lay on the floor beneath the table, thankfully in the shade, panting in the heat, and Ethan heard the waitress offer to bring the dog a bowl of water.

He looked back at Bex and smiled. 'So, this is weird, huh?'

She nodded. 'Just a bit.'

'I'm so glad we ran into each other again. It's really good to see you doing so well. Your rescue centre is amazing—all the work you do there.'

'Thanks. Well, a lot of hard work went into it. A lot of planning. Finding the right site… Working with the builders during construction… Dad helped a lot.'

He knew Bex's father was an architect. 'Did he run up the design for it?' he asked.

She nodded. 'He did. I told him what I wanted, though, and he added things that I hadn't thought of.'

'Like what?'

'We have a sensory room for some of my human patients.' She smiled. 'Being with the horses soothes them, and calms them down, but sometimes they arrive at the centre and they've been having a bad day. They need some time to settle for a bit, before they go out to the animals.'

'That's a great idea.'

'We consulted with a SEN group when we designed

it. Spoke to a few special needs schools…asked them what they had in their rooms—that kind of thing.'

'Animal therapy is really something…'

He'd read many studies about the research that was going into animal therapy. Whether those animals were dogs or cats or horses, there was something special about the relationship between an animal and a human who struggled to communicate or settle. Just being in an animal's presence produced serotonin—the happy drug. It reduced the production of cortisol production, the stress hormone, and slowed a racing heart…lowered blood pressure. It was incredibly powerful and soothing.

'You must find that really rewarding,' he said.

'I do. Sometimes I can be out in the paddock with a child on a horse and no one has to even say anything. That child and that horse somehow communicate with each other through touch, through smell, through the look in their eyes. The horses know that these are special kids…they know they need nurturing. It's like they know they need the calm that an animal can create with them. Sometimes I forget to breathe, because watching it happen is just so magical.'

He could hear the wonder and awe in her voice and wished he could experience a moment like that with her. Share something as wonderful as that.

The waitress reappeared then with a tray, breaking the moment and stopping him from staring into Bex's eyes as she served them their order. He looked down in wonder at the tall glass filled with lashings of ice cream, whipped cream, fruit, meringue and jelly, topped with sprinkles and chopped pistachios. He wasn't sure he'd be able to eat all of it.

'Wow…'

Bex's face had lit up at the sight of it.

'These are huge. Maybe we should have shared one?'

He picked up his long spoon, knowing that sharing a dessert might have seemed more intimate than he needed this moment to be. They weren't in that place. They were still struggling to identify just what they were to each other right now. She was most definitely his client. Still his wife, technically. But were they friends? Colleagues? Something more?

Bex spooned in a mouthful of cream and fruit. 'Oh, my God, I think I've died and gone to heaven.'

It was a simple statement. A cliché, even. But it was one that—for them, at least—called up a touchy subject.

The atmosphere changed immediately.

They both looked down at their desserts, appetites suddenly waning as her words hung in the silence that followed.

Bex dropped her spoon, looked down at her lap, then up at Ethan. 'Do you think of him?' she asked.

He met her gaze, held it. 'Of course I do. All the time.'

She nodded. 'It happens when I'm doing things… silly things. Like putting away laundry, or feeding the horses, or being out for a drive. Then I'll think about him. About how I could be folding *his* laundry. Little pairs of trousers. Little tee shirts. Sorting endless pairs of superhero socks. I'd be getting him to help me feed the horses. Taking him out for a ride on them. He'd be old enough now. Old enough to enjoy things. To tell us what he likes and doesn't like. Playing… Filling the house with laughter…' Bex looked away, sniffing and wiping at her eyes. 'Sorry. I'm babbling.'

Ethan reached for one of the napkins that the waitress had brought out with their order and passed it to her. She accepted it and dabbed under her eyes.

'You don't ever have to apologise for talking about our son.'

She nodded, forced a smile and picked up her spoon again, playing with the ice cream in her glass. 'I always dreamed of taking him riding, you know? And now I have this centre—this centre that helps kids with learning difficulties, or brain injuries—and I see what those animals do and I sometimes wish…' Her voice trailed away.

He knew what she wished for. He wished for it, too.

For Charlie to be here still.

They took a walk down into Clifton Grove afterwards, and followed a path that took them alongside the River Trent.

Bex loved walks like these. They reminded her of when she was a child and she and her brothers had played in a Green Belt area that had a brook running through it. There was a lovely nature walk you could follow there, surrounded by trees and high grass, with a path of compacted, sun-cracked earth. Bumblebees flew, dragonflies zipped about, and there was the sound of trickling water all the time, and the sun shining down upon their backs.

This was the same—except that instead of a narrow brook there was the river, with fishermen casting their lines into the water. And instead of the easy nature walk she'd taken with her brothers she was walking with Ethan. They hadn't argued—which was good, she supposed—but they had talked of Charlie. They'd needed that, to break the ice, and she knew that if she were to get any real answers from him about what had happened she had to tread slowly.

'Tell me about Abu Dhabi,' she said.

He'd wanted her to go with him. She'd refused, effectively ending everything. She needed to know that he'd learned something out there.

Ethan smiled. 'It was hot. Incredibly so. But the work was rewarding. Prince Abdullah has a racing stable and he also breeds horses, mostly putting his prize stallions out to stud. Believe you me, that privilege costs people thousands. And—you'll find this funny—I was included in the price.'

She raised an eyebrow. 'You? How?'

'Any horse sired by one of his stallions came with vet care during the gestation, plus the services of the Prince's personal vet—me—to attend each delivery.'

'Wow.'

'I know. I think whilst I was out there I got to deliver four highly prized foals. Each successfully, thankfully, and without problems.'

She was glad he'd had that experience. It sounded intriguing. A whole new world—which was what he'd been chasing. But was that all? Was that all he'd learned out there?

'I've been informed of another rescue horse and I'm going to be taking her in on Monday,' she said. 'By all accounts, she's pregnant. Maybe you could take a look at her?'

'Okay. Not a problem. Just give the surgery a call

and let them know when she arrives, and they'll book a time slot.'

They walked a bit further along in silence. But Bex had so many questions for him. 'Are you enjoying your new job in Ruddington?'

He nodded. 'I am.'

'And…do you live in Ruddington?' She wanted to know if she'd be running into him in the village whenever she went there to get some shopping.

'No. I'm in Keyworth.'

Just a few miles away. 'Not far, then?'

'Not at all—and I get to enjoy a nice drive through the countryside to work each day. No sitting in snarling traffic on a motorway.'

They came across the weir, the sound of rushing water getting loud. They stopped to look at it.

'That's good,' she said. 'It's been nice to just…shoot the breeze. Break the tension between us.'

'Yeah…'

'You think we can do this?' she asked. 'Be friends? Move forward?'

He shrugged. 'I don't see why not. We're both adults, and we both want this to be…easy. Better than it used to be.'

She turned to face him and the breeze whipped her hair into her face. She had to tuck it behind her ear. 'I do want that. I want that very much. I hated it when we were at each other's throats. I lost my friend, my husband, my son. I…I have so much I need to ask you, and I'd like to be mature about it.'

'Me, too.'

And suddenly, surprisingly, he pulled her close, the way he'd used to. He hugged her, and initially she froze, panicking. But soon she was breathing him in, relaxing in his arms, and she sank into the hug, enjoying the comfort and familiarity of him around her once more. He smelt great. He felt even better.

His hugs had always made her feel safe and secure. Protected. As if he was her shield. But it was more than that. In his arms she felt a connection with him. Felt that she was special. That he cared for her and refused to let anything harm her because that would break his heart, too.

It had been way too long since he'd hugged her. The last time had been just after Charlie had been rushed to hospital. They'd watched the doctors swarm around him, heard the medics' voices calm, steady, certain in their processes and procedures for matters such as this. She and Ethan had stood there together, clutched tightly in each other's arms, terrified.

His arms around her had tried to shield her from the view of the doctors poking needles into their son, drawing blood, putting tubes into him. Acts that at the time had seemed invasive and aggressive and painful, even though they'd known that the doctors needed to do it if they were going to have any chance of bringing Charlie back.

Ethan had held her close, stroking her hair, gently making a *shh* noise, turning her away from the worst of it whilst he watched with a determined eye, the ever-watchful and protective father.

Back then she'd wanted to break free from his arms. To place her hands on his chest and push hard, race to her son's bedside and hold his hand, let him know that he wasn't alone, that he had to fight whatever it was that was happening to him.

But Ethan had held her tight, knowing that they had to stay out of the doctors' way.

She didn't want to break free this time. Right now she was happy to be held by him here. Beside the river. In the sunshine.

His embrace was a comforting one.

Whatever she needed to say could wait.

CHAPTER THREE

THE TRAILER BACKED up slowly towards the quarantine stables and the paddock. Bex directed Roland, holding up her hand when he was positioned perfectly, his brakes squeaking.

Roland got out of the driving seat and smiled. 'We had a nice uneventful journey.'

'That's great. How's our mummy-to-be?'

He laughed. 'Not quite as described, but easily bribed by food.'

'Let's see her.'

Roland opened up the back of the trailer and Bex was treated to her first view of the mare she'd been told was simply being rehomed with her because the current owner couldn't afford to look after another horse.

The owner had sworn blind that there was nothing physically wrong with her, that it was simply a matter of finances. But as Bex looked at the pregnant mare she began to suspect that Darcy had not seen a vet or a farrier for some time. Her hooves were overgrown, her coat was matted, as was her tail, which was thick with seeds and sticky bobs. Her left eye looked fine, but her right was swollen and closed, and she had tear stains running down her face.

She sighed. 'You poor thing…'

Why weren't people just honest? If Darcy's owner had informed her from the outset that there was an eye problem she could have had Ethan here for her arrival, to get her prompt treatment. Instead, the poor mare would have to wait until this afternoon, when he would arrive at three.

She gave Darcy a primary survey and couldn't see anything else, but clearly this horse had not been as meticulously cared for as the owner had made out. Bex was tempted to ring her up and give her a piece of her mind, but knew that she wouldn't. She didn't like confrontation—and what would such a phone call do except to make Bex even more frustrated and angry?

Look at me, I've grown up.

Darcy was here now. And life could only get better for her from now on.

'Can you get her into a quarantine stable, Ro? I'm going to check on Spirit.'

He nodded.

Bex washed her hands in the sink, dried them on paper towel, and then headed towards the end bay of the quarantine stable.

Suddenly she stopped in surprise.

Spirit was standing! All by himself! Without the need for being lifted by heavy machinery.

A smile broke across her face and she walked towards him, her hand out for him to smell her. Spirit nuzzled her hand and snickered, shaking his head and mane, and then tried to nudge her.

'Hey, look at you. You getting better? You getting stronger? Good boy!' She stroked his face and gave him some love as quiet tears welled in her eyes.

These were the moments she loved. These first signs of recovery. These first signs that showed her a horse wanted to survive. To try to get better. Every time she saw them they made her cry. Every. Single. Time. There might still be a difficult road ahead—there might be potholes and dips and breakdowns—but these moments showed her that it was all going to be worth it. She wasn't the only one fighting for a horse's survival. The animal wanted to live, too.

She'd sat by her son's bedside for many long, tortured hours, waiting for him to show signs of recovery. To show that he was going to get better, despite what the doctors had said. She had been certain that he would recover from the stroke that had cut him down at the tender age of just two. Only he hadn't.

One minute he'd been playing in the back garden, kicking a football around, trying to get it past her as she'd stood in goal. The next minute he'd faltered. Slowed. A strange look upon his face.

Bex had straightened, her smile disappearing, instantly knowing something was wrong, and then his face had gone slack, empty, his eyes unseeing. He'd crumpled to the ground, unable to hear her shouts, unaware of her holding him, calling his name, shouting for help before pulling her phone from her back pocket and calling for an ambulance.

Afterwards, she'd tried to comfort herself by telling herself that Charlie had died doing something he loved. Playing with his ball…playing with his mum. He'd been *happy*.

To begin with, that thought had meant nothing at all. It hadn't soothed her, and it hadn't comforted her. In fact, she'd treated it with disdain in her grief, anger and denial. But then, as time had passed, the knowledge had begun to provide some comfort. The thing that didn't was the fact that she couldn't remember her last words to him.

Had she been cheering him on? Had she encouraged him? Joked with him? What had those last words been? It was as if her brain had shut down, refusing access to that file—which was weird, because she would have thought that her brain would have shut down the image of Charlie collapsing. Not her last words.

If only Charlie had opened his eyes.

If only Charlie had been able to breathe on his own.

If only Charlie had showed *any* signs of recovery…

Needing to stop her spiralling thoughts, Bex grabbed a brush for Spirit's coat and opened his stall, going in slowly, always careful not to startle him until she knew his character better. Spirit had not reacted well to the other grooms trying to look after him or clear out his stall—he only seemed to be relaxed with her. That was fine to begin with, but she knew she would have to prepare him to get used to other people at some point.

She let him sniff the brush, then used it gently along the side of his face. It was softly bristled. Not the kind of brush that would get out barbs or sticks or seeds—just something to get the horse used to being touched. Lots of animals—especially horses—could be quite fickle with parts of their bodies that they hated being touched, so this brush was perfect. Feather-light. Not aggressive. But it allowed the groom to earn the animal's trust. Allowed a person to get close. Create a bond.

She thought of the bond she had with Ethan. They were talking now—that was something. The forum was open for them to talk some more. They'd do it in baby steps.

She'd tried not to show how much their hug had impacted her, but she'd never been one to hide her emotions and her face had broken out into a broad smile as she'd hugged him back, and just for a moment she'd felt a sense of déjà vu. Remembering those early days when his hugs had felt so wonderful.

She remembered being at their school prom, in a lipstick-pink dress that someone had ruined by spilling a drink down it. She'd cried, thinking the evening spoiled, but Ethan had simply taken her hand and pulled her into his embrace and held her, telling her that it would all be okay.

They'd swayed together, and being in his arms had taken away all the hurt and the upset of thinking her evening was ruined. Because it hadn't been. They'd had a fabulous night together. And it hadn't been because of the music or the food or their friends or dressing up. It had been because being in Ethan's arms had felt magical. Somehow his presence, his arms, the security and love she'd felt there, had made all the problems of the world go away.

As she brushed Spirit's body, noting when his back quivered, when he seemed uncomfortable, she wondered if she and Ethan would ever return to the comfortable intimacy they'd once had. She still found him attractive. Of course she did. Maybe even more so after all this time apart. Absence had certainly made her heart grow fonder. She'd not dated anyone else. Hadn't kissed anyone else. Hadn't slept with anyone else.

She'd been asked out—a couple of single dads had asked, and she'd been flattered, but just not ready.

It was almost as if she'd pressed 'pause' on having any close, physical intimacy with someone. And now Ethan was back, and it was confusing, because her body wanted the ecstasy and happiness that she knew Ethan could give her. She *knew* him. Had felt comfortable with him.

But her mind? Her heart? Well, they were both still apprehensive—if not downright scared of opening themselves up to hurt again. Ethan had hurt her. Had not been there for her when she'd needed him at the worst time of their lives. He'd let her down and she didn't know if she'd ever be able to put that behind her. Not unless they talked about it. Worked through it.

Spirit suddenly bucked and neighed and Bex stood back, turning to grab his head reins. She noticed Roland stood outside the stall.

'How's he going?' he enquired.

'Stand back for me, will you?' she asked him. 'He's still nervous of other people.'

Bex understood completely. She was, too.

Nervous of Ethan. And of thinking about that kiss on the cheek he'd left her with when he went home.

Ethan had been looking forward to going back to The Grange, and when he arrived and saw Bex coming out of her office with a sheaf of papers, a broad smile stretched across his face instantly.

Since their talk yesterday he'd felt more optimistic. Bex seemed to be in exactly the same place mentally as he was. Wanting to move forward. Not intent on beating themselves up about the past, and most importantly wanting to be friends.

That was a good start for them. It could have gone so

differently. So badly. They could have clashed with one another and broken each other's hearts all over again, leaving them both awkward and angry and stuck with having to deal with each other every time he visited her horses.

Since driving her home he'd felt on cloud nine, and had often found himself looking at the clock today, wishing time away, knowing that he would get to see her again this afternoon.

He'd left her yesterday with a polite kiss on the cheek, but when he'd leaned in and inhaled her scent and her soap it had been such a familiar aroma to him he'd felt a punch of lust deep and low, like a surge of lava, rushing through him, hot and demanding to be fed.

He'd stepped back to his car after waving her goodbye on shaky legs, still reeling from the shock of his reaction. Now he was wondering if the same thing would happen today.

He raised his hand in a wave, and when they got close he leaned in to peck her on the cheek.

The same thing happened. Instead of a muscle memory, it was as if his body had a scent memory. It knew what this woman could make him feel and it was hungry for more. Like an addict, long separated from his drug of choice, he was suddenly being tempted once again and having to fight the cravings.

But he could not take her in his arms. He could not pick out the strand of straw he saw stuck in her ponytail. He could not press his lips down onto hers and pull her close against him and make the rest of the world go away.

They weren't there yet.

But he hoped to be.

So instead he settled for a smile, and asked her where the new patient was.

'In the quarantine stable with Spirit.'

'How have you been? It was good to see you yesterday…have a chat.'

She turned to him and smiled—a large, genuine smile that was warm and welcoming. 'I'm good! And I agree…it was great to catch up with you as well.'

It certainly was great to see Bex here, thriving in this environment. It did wonders for his heart and soul and it gave him some peace—because before, after Charlie died, all he'd seen in his wife was anguish and distress. A terrible depression. She had been pale-faced, red-eyed, prone to outbursts. Withdrawn. Accusative. Her anger at losing Charlie had transplanted itself onto him, for not being there when it had happened, and soon they'd simply not been able to be in the same room as one another.

To see the woman he loved change from being a happy, bubbly person into someone he didn't recognise had been incredibly painful for him, and the worst of it had been that he hadn't been able to stop it from happening. He'd wanted to be close to her, to give her what she needed, but she'd wanted more from him than just a reassuring arm around her shoulders. More than just his presence.

She'd wanted to see that Charlie's death had torn him in two the way it had her, and she'd questioned why he wasn't wailing and screaming into the void with hatred at the world the way she had been.

She'd thought that losing Charlie hadn't upset him. That he hadn't been stricken with grief.

Only he had been. And she would never know the struggle he'd had keeping it all inside, refusing to let it out, never letting her know that he secretly worried that he was to blame for their son's death.

At the quarantine stable, Bex led her over to Darcy, the pregnant mare. 'I'm really worried about her right eye,' she said.

'Let me take a look.'

He rubbed some antibacterial gel over his hands and then put on some gloves. Darcy didn't seem that nervous a horse, for which he was grateful, because some skittish horses could be really hard to examine if all they wanted to do was gallop away.

He spoke to the mare in a soft, soothing voice, not really using any words, just the soft sounds of his voice, and soon got her used to him touching her. He could see the eye was swollen and sealed shut, her face tear-stained and crusted with something. He moved past it, running his hands over her body, gently smoothing, stroking, examining her as he did so, so that she didn't startle.

He reached into his bag for the fluorescein dye and added some drops to the eye. Then he got out his ophthalmoscope. He'd strongly suspected a corneal ulceration and saw he was right—the dye was staining the ulcer bright green.

'It's not too bad,' he said. 'I don't think it's in danger of rupturing the orbit.'

'Oh, that's good news. I was really worried about that.'

'It's quite superficial at this stage. It's been caught early. They usually look worse than they are.'

'Can you treat it?'

'I'll prescribe some gentamicin, which should be safe for her to take whilst pregnant. You'll need to apply it every six to eight hours.'

'All right. How far along in her pregnancy is she, do you think? The owner said she thought she was about eight months, but I think she might be more.'

Ethan palpated the horse's abdomen and examined her teats. 'I'd say more like ten—she's pretty big, and she's starting to produce milk. The foal is moving well… I can hear a strong heartbeat. We can only assume everything is going well in there.'

'I'll keep an eye on her.'

'Plenty of treats for the mum-to-be.'

'Absolutely.'

'Anything else you're concerned about?'

Bex shook her head. 'Nope. Do you want to see Spirit? He stood on his own today. I think he's making excellent progress, considering how we found him.'

He could hear the pride in her voice. He recognised it from the days when he would come home from work and Bex would meet him at the front door, thrumming with joy and happiness, practically bouncing up and down in excitement, pleased as punch, and say, 'Charlie smiled for the first time today!' Or, 'He clapped his hands!' Or, 'He said Dada!'

She'd always been so pleased with each milestone—and why shouldn't she have been? He'd been proud, too, and keen to see their son repeating the event just for him. And when Charlie had… There was no feeling in the world that could equal that. That joy. That pride. His son had taken another step towards growing up, towards becoming the wonderful human being he was meant to be.

If they'd known that Charlie's time would stop at the age of two, would they have taken even more pride in each developmental stage? Or would they have dreaded the slow, inexorable march towards his terrible destiny?

'That's great, Bex.'

He let her lead the way and, sure enough, when they reached Spirit's stall he was standing there, his long face hanging over the stall door, watching for Bex.

As Ethan drew close, too, Spirit seemed to startle, and then he reared his head back and tried to hide.

'He's not good with other people at the moment, but he's fine with me. Why don't you stand back over there, and I'll see if I can lead him out past you?'

'Okay.'

Ethan trusted Bex implicitly, but he felt his heart begin to race slightly. Spirit was clearly a highly strung horse, and frightened horses could be dangerous. They could kick, buck, knock you over, squash you…or cause serious damage with their hooves. The fact that Bex was going into his stall, confident that none of those things would happen to her, was slightly worrying for him. He could see they shared a bond, but how strong was it? Would Spirit run her down to get away from perceived danger?

He just had to stand there, fighting the urge to protect her, while Bex opened the stall door and gently led Spirit out, using soothing tones.

Ethan could see the animal looked brighter. Clearly a few days of good nutrition and nourishment and plenty of clean water had had a beneficial effect. He was still all skin and bones, his spine, ribs and pelvis simply draped with skin, not yet having a layer of fat and muscle to pad him out and give him the usual soft and supple equine shape.

'He's looking good, but he's going to need the farrier. Those hooves need some work,' he said.

Bex nodded, and got Spirit to take a couple of steps towards Ethan, but then the horse began to worry and pull back on the reins, not wanting to come any closer.

'I think he's had enough,' Ethan said, standing straighter, standing his ground, and then suggested Bex take him back into his stall.

Bex led Spirit back, congratulating him and telling him he was a good horse, a clever horse.

Ethan relaxed somewhat once Bex came out of the stall once again, grinning happily as she came towards him.

'He's made huge progress in such a short amount of time,' she said. 'I want to thank you for agreeing to give him a chance.'

'Well, the rest of his blood results came back and he's all clear. Just needs feeding up and a bit of socialisation.'

'He's not ready yet. Maybe when the quarantine is over I can start putting him with some other horses. Maybe Mouse…'

He did not know who Mouse was. 'Who's that?'

She laughed. 'A stocky little Shetland pony who is so sedate and calm around people we almost called him Zen.'

'He sounds perfect.'

Ethan liked this. Being close to Bex again. Standing beside her just chatting. As if nothing had happened… as if everything was normal. Though of course if everything was normal he'd be able to drape his arm around her. Pull her close. Kiss her. Maybe get playful and take her into that empty stall…lay her down against the straw bales and begin undoing buttons…

When had their last kiss been? Their last proper kiss?

He couldn't remember.

I wonder if she can.

But he could hardly turn and ask her. Or could he…?

Ethan turned and looked at her as she smiled, and for a moment they were both briefly caught by the other's gaze. The rest of the world faded away—the scent of horse, of hay, of grass, the background classical music, a horse snorting, the stamp of hooves on solid ground. All faded to nothing, and all he was aware of was her eyes. Normally hazel, out in the sunshine, right now, in the shade of the stable, they looked like pools of melted chocolate. Dark. Mysterious. Flecked with gold.

She was looking at him with questions in her gaze. *What is this? What's happening? Do you want to kiss me?*

He very much wanted to kiss her. He very much wanted to just stare into her eyes for ever and rediscover this woman who had been away from his life for so long.

He wished that everything could be normal again. For the past not to have happened. He could not kiss her whilst they still had pain unresolved, no matter how much he wanted to. Because if he did kiss her they might pretend for a while that everything was fine, but the real world would come crashing down upon their heads at some point.

And yet…

She was so close! Right there. Gazing into his eyes, her lips parting…

He felt pulled towards her like a magnet, unable to resist her, his body yearning, aching, for the familiarity of her touch. Tentatively, he leaned towards her. Slowly. Imperceptibly. Waiting to see if she would stop him. If she would say, *No, this is a bad idea.* Only she didn't. So he got closer. Closer. Staring deeply into her eyes. Looking. Searching. Checking to see if this was okay…if she would take flight.

The gap between them was mere inches. Her pupils were widening, darkening. His own heart was thrumming, his blood pulsing, adrenaline rushing through him…

And then doubt assailed him. What if this was a bad choice? A bad decision?

Regretfully, painfully, he stopped, pulled back, hating himself for doing so, and pushed away from the wall that he'd been leaning on.

'Sorry. I ought to get back.' He picked up his medical bag.

She seemed flustered, but agreed, nodding quickly, looking anywhere but at him. 'Of course. You're a busy man. We can't hog you to ourselves.'

'I'll call in a couple of days to see how Darcy's eye is doing, but if you have any concerns before then…'

They'd stopped by his car. Bex had her hands in her back pockets. 'Don't worry. I'll keep in touch.'

He smiled, opened up his car, feeling awkward.

That moment in the stable played in his mind, over and over. What would have happened if he had kissed her? Would they still be in that stable now?

'See you soon.'
'You can count on it.'
It was incredibly difficult to drive away.

CHAPTER FOUR

SHE'D NEARLY KISSED HIM. The temptation to do so had been overwhelming. Standing there, staring into each other's eyes. It had been as if time had stopped. As if the past hadn't happened.

He'd been about to do it. She'd seen the intention in his gaze. The questioning. *Is this okay? Is this all right? May I?*

And her answer had been...*Yes! Do it!*

Because, no matter what had happened in the past, you couldn't fight biology—and she and Ethan were still clearly highly attracted to one another. Always had been...always would be. And sometimes logic went out of the window and you just had to give your body what it wanted. Take what the heart wanted.

And she'd wanted to kiss him. To let herself be lost in the moment, to forget all that had happened between them and just enjoy and remember the delight she'd always felt when he pressed his lips to hers. To pretend that everything was all right and that the world was giving back their happiness after stealing it away so brutally.

But, as always, Ethan had pulled away. The walls had come up and he'd said sorry, and then he'd left.

Watching him drive away, she'd felt a mixture of relief, disappointment and anger. Relief because she didn't know what would have happened after the kiss. How it would have changed things. Disappointment because she'd wanted that kiss very much indeed. And anger because… Why couldn't he stay and face the situation? Why did he always run? He might have changed his body and his looks, but he was abandoning her again! Leaving her wanting!

She tried not to feel angry as she led Spirit out to the paddock to try and do some exercise with him. He needed to move now. Not just be standing there in that stall, eating and drinking. He had to start building muscle. Getting strong. Building trust with her and others. Getting him out in the sunshine would help.

A couple of days had passed. It was a little less hot today. Still about twenty-five degrees, though, and Bex could feel the warmth of the sun upon her arms and face. Spirit had a halter on today, and a long training lead, so that she could stand in the centre of the paddock and get Spirit moving in a circle around her. A walk would do to begin with. He didn't need to trot, or gallop. But he at least needed to take baby steps and try.

He'd walked quite slowly from his stall, still feeling his way on his newly trimmed hooves.

They'd had such a palaver getting him used to the farrier. It had taken Graham three visits even to get Spirit to let him lift a leg and examine a hoof. But eventually he'd given him new shoes and trimmed his hooves, working on Spirit in five-minute stints here and there, until all four hooves were done, and hopefully now, Spirit would be able to stand easier and move better.

'Okay, baby, show me what you can do.'

She made a sound in her throat—a sort of *tsk, tsk*—to encourage him to begin walking. At first he seemed uncertain, and she'd needed to go over to him and gently pull on his halter to get him moving. Then she backed away to the centre of the paddock and kept on speaking to him, encouraging him, pleased when he made one full lap, then two. On the third, he began to tire, but she was already pleased with his progress.

'Bex!' Jenna called from the fence by the education centre.

She turned, smiled at her assistant. 'What is it?'

'It's Darcy. She's in first stage labour.'

Bex felt a rush of adrenaline and excitement. This was always a precious and wonderful moment. 'Have her waters broken?'

'No, she's pacing. There's some patchy sweating. She keeps getting up and down. Want me to call Ethan? Let him know he needs to be on standby?'

At the sound of her husband's name, she faltered. The last time she'd seen Ethan she'd been left feeling upset. He'd called and spoken to Jenna on the phone about Darcy's eye, and Bex had got the feeling that he was avoiding her. But Darcy's well-being needed to come first.

'Yes, please. I'll get Spirit settled, then join you.'

'Okay.' Jenna gave her a big grin and two thumbs up, before racing back inside.

Bex gently led Spirit back to his stall. She checked his water, gave him a bit of a fuss for doing so well in the paddock, and let him chomp on a carrot that she had in her back pocket. Then she closed his stall, washed her hands, dried them, and headed over to Darcy's stall.

As Jenna had stated, the mare was clearly in the first stage of labour. Pacing. Occasionally stamping her hooves. Lying down, shifting, shuffling, neighing, then getting back up again. She certainly seemed agitated, but all were good signs.

Jenna arrived back in the quarantine stable. 'I left a message with the surgery. They said Ethan's out, tending to a horse with colic, but they'll call him and ask him to pop in on his way back.'

'Right.' Bex tried to smile.

'He's nice. Don't you think?' said Jenna. 'Handsome. Rugged. Shame he's got a wedding ring on.'

Was now the moment to mention to her assistant that she, Bex, had slid that ring onto Ethan's finger in front of all their family and friends? 'Yeah…'

'He's such a refreshing change from the last vet we had. That locum… It was like he'd always got out of the wrong side of bed. Could barely say two words to you. Ethan's kind of—'

'My husband.' Bex looked at Jenna, who had become a friend, and gave her an apologetic smile. 'We've been married for ten years.'

Jenna simply stared at her, open-mouthed, in complete disbelief. 'What?'

Bex sighed. 'Remember I mentioned that we were separated? Have been for five years. He's been off in Abu Dhabi, working over there, and now he's back.'

Jenna looked stunned. 'Is he back for you?'

Bex shrugged. 'I don't know.'

'Haven't you asked him *why* he's back?'

'It's complicated…'

'I bet it is! Wow, I mean…I can't believe it! Why didn't you say anything before?'

'Because I wasn't sure what was happening. A few days ago we went for a coffee and a walk and had a really nice time together. And then, when he came to see Darcy's eye, we nearly kissed, and—'

'Whoa, there, missy! Hold your horses. You *nearly kissed*?'

'Just heat-of-the-moment stuff. Don't worry. Nothing happened. It passed.'

'But he's not been here since then, has he?'

'No.'

'And we've just asked him to stop by?'

'Yes.'

'Huh.' Jenna smiled. 'Want me to leave you guys alone when he gets here?' She winked at Bex. 'Allow you two to bond again over the romance of bringing new life into the world?'

Bex looked at Darcy. She and Ethan had already brought new life into the world. And then they'd lost it. She hoped desperately that the same thing wouldn't happen with Darcy and her foal. Everything seemed great, but these things could change in an instant. Perhaps they did need this as a bonding experience? Perhaps it would bring them closer if everything went well? Plus, it would be wonderful for Darcy to be a mother, to finally have a good home, a safe place to have her baby.

'You can stay,' she told Jenna. 'Don't you want to see the foal?'

'Well, of course I do! But I don't want to get in the way of true love if you two need some privacy.'

Bex smiled. 'It's not like that any more. We'll be fine.'

She reached out and stroked Darcy's face and mane. She was at the stall door currently, moving the wood shavings around as if she were trying to make a perfect nest. As Bex stroked her, she heard a splash. Darcy's waters had broken. They looked clear. No sign of meconium. It was a great sign that labour was progressing well.

In the distance she heard the rumble of a diesel engine coming up their long driveway, and then footsteps.

Jenna looked over her shoulder, and then back at Bex. 'Your beloved has arrived.' She picked up a couple of bits and pieces that needed putting away. 'I'll go take your afternoon sessions.'

Bex tried to grab her arm to keep her there, suddenly alarmed at the idea of being alone with her husband after what had happened last time. She didn't need any more evidence that her husband was going to keep leaving her.

'You don't have to go.'

Jenna grinned. 'Oh, I do. You two need to talk.'

And, infuriatingly, she walked away with practically a skip in her step.

'Hello, Ethan!' Bex heard her call as she went.

Bex turned to see Ethan drawing close and felt her cheeks colour. 'Hey. Her waters just broke.'

'When?'

'About two minutes ago.'

'Okay. How's she looking?'

'She's coping well.'

They stood at the stall door, observing the mare for a moment. They could see her contracting, her abdominal wall squeezing in.

Bex risked a sideways glance at Ethan. Dammit.

Still as handsome as ever. Still able to give her butterflies in her tummy. Still able to make her heart pound. Or was she only feeling those things because they hadn't spoken since that aborted kiss?

'It's good to see you again,' she ventured.

He was checking his watch, timing the contractions, but then he looked at her and nodded. 'You, too. Look, about last time—'

'It's fine. Best left unmentioned.'

'No. No, it's not. I…I want to apologise. Properly. I should never have tried to…' He sighed. 'I'm sorry. I'm not very good at this. Knowing the right thing to say. Or do. You might have already noticed that.'

She smiled, kind of enjoying his awkwardness. 'Maybe…'

'It's always been hard for me to express what I feel.'

Bex raised her eyebrows, impressed at his insight. More than that, impressed at him admitting it. She'd always been frustrated by his inability to just tell her how he felt. Was his heart breaking? Was he grief stricken? Was he hurting just as much as her? Before, she'd only ever got the brick walls around his heart. Watched as he shut down or walked away. She was enjoying this new side of her husband, hearing him admitting things.

'I've been having therapy.'

She turned to look at him. Stunned. 'Really?'

'It started when I was abroad. I decided it was time. I knew I needed to look at myself and my behaviour before I could face you ever again.'

'You started therapy for me?' She didn't know whether to feel honoured or afraid.

'In a way. But I mostly did it for me. I didn't handle things with Charlie all that well, and I didn't want to walk back into your life the same person who walked away from you.'

Bex was reeling. This was such big news—that he'd done this…was admitting it to her. What did it all mean?

'I can see hooves,' he said suddenly.

He was right. The foal was beginning to show. Two little hooves were emerging. Darcy was doing it all on her own. Without help. This was amazing!

Bex didn't know how she was feeling. There was the wonder of new life, and now Ethan's admission that he had been in therapy to make himself a better person before he met up with her again.

What did that mean? That he wanted to try again? Or was she racing ahead? Perhaps it just meant that he'd thought that if he went into therapy he would discover why he shut down all the time, so that he could then explain his past actions to her? Did the fact that he didn't understand why he'd acted the way he did absolve him from blame?

Probably not, but…

Bex let out a long breath as the foal's nose began to emerge between its two long, gangly front legs.

Darcy strained and pushed, strained and pushed, her long neck stretching out and forward as she contracted to give birth to her foal. It had white hooves and a white blaze that they could see. And then came the hard part: the passing of the foal's chest and shoulders. If Darcy could get past that, she'd be free and clear.

As she rested between pushes, the foal seemed to slip back into the birth canal, re-emerging with each push.

'It's a big foal…' Ethan muttered.

'Do you think she needs help?'

'Let's give her a few more minutes. I'm sure she can do it.'

They both knew the importance of trying to let the mare give birth by herself. And now Darcy was lying down on her side, grunting as she passed the shoulders and chest of her baby.

Bex felt a sigh of relief. Just the foal's hips and hind-quarters to go. 'Come on, Darcy, you can do it.'

With one final push Darcy delivered her baby and it slipped out, hot and wet, still half in its sac.

'Yes!' Bex beamed at Ethan, and she had thrown her arms around him to give him a celebratory hug before she realised who she was hugging and let go.

Ethan stared at her for a moment.

Darcy turned to look at her baby and sniffed it, before standing up. The cord and the sac still hung from her, but she was doing what all new horse mamas should—she was washing and licking her baby. Bonding with it. Getting to know her.

'She's gorgeous,' Bex said, staring at the foal, taking in her colour, her markings, her long, gangly legs.

'Any idea what you're going to call her?' Ethan asked.

She nodded. 'I thought Liberty would be a good name.'

'I love it.'

He turned to smile at her and she smiled back at him, not quite believing that a minute ago she'd given him a hug, and in that brief instant, sharing such a moment with him, it had been special.

He'd helped her. They'd saved Darcy's eye, helped her deliver her baby, and now here they both were, happy and well, with no complications. This was how life was meant to be. And Ethan was opening up. Admitting he'd done wrong by her. And she'd needed to hear that. Was there going to be more?

Bex felt tears burning the backs of her eyes, and before she knew it she was wiping them away.

Beside her, she saw Ethan produce a handkerchief and she took it, laughing and sniffing and dabbing at her eyes. 'It's a happy day.'

It was. Ethan was smiling broadly, and now he draped an arm around her shoulders and hugged her from the side.

Sometimes she wished she could be all stoic, like him, and not wear her heart on her sleeve, but things like this just got to her. She took happiness where it could be found and she relished it—because she'd already had the worst thing happen to her, and she'd been in the depths of despair, and she knew what that felt like. She'd told herself long ago that if she wanted happiness then she had to look for it and find it in the tiniest things.

But days like today…when her horses had babies of their own and it all went well…when she stood there and watched as a foal tried to work out how to use those long limbs beneath it and coordinate them to stand… These were amazing days.

She appreciated Ethan offering her a hankie, and she loved it that he'd felt able to put his arm around her and share her joy as she happy-cried, despite what had happened between them. That he was still there for her meant a lot.

'You should celebrate,' Ethan said. 'A successful

delivery and a brand-new life calls for a glass or two of champagne.'

She nodded and looked up at him. '*We* should celebrate.'

She meant it. She wanted to spend time with him. Talk. Get closer.

He smiled down at her before turning his attention back to the foal, almost as if he couldn't look down at her for too long, because if he did then he would try to kiss her again.

Would she welcome such a kiss?

Yes, I would. Right now, I would.

This was such a great moment. She didn't want to spoil it by dwelling on the past. What had happened, had happened—it was gone. Darcy was safe, and Liberty was here, and Ethan was in therapy and addressing the actions of his past. Today they'd watched this new life enter into the world and his arm was around her.

Right now she felt so close to him. Emotionally. As if it was somehow right that he was the person who had witnessed this with her. She was sad that Jenna hadn't seen it, but there was a camera in each stall—she could watch the replay.

Liberty almost got to her feet, but then fell down again. Bex laughed, falling in love with the new baby already, and watching as the foal tried to stand once again, this time making it and standing there, lurching and wobbling like a drunkard.

Her proud mother stood by and nuzzled her, knocking her down onto her bottom, her legs splaying.

'We don't have any champagne here, but the least I can do is make you a cup of tea,' she said. 'And I think there's chocolate digestives in the biscuit tin.' She knew they were his favourites.

'How could I resist?' He looked down at her once again and she looked up, smiling, laughing. And this time when their gazes locked with one another they were caught.

Bex's smile faltered even as her heart leapt, and this time they couldn't fight it. They'd been united by watching this new life come into the world, they'd shared a unique and wonderful event, and they'd both needed something happy, something unifying. It connected them, bonded them, and now they were both helpless against their own biological drives in that moment as his head dipped towards her, her eyes closed, and she waited to welcome his kiss…

'How's it going in here?'

Jenna's voice broke sharply into their reverie and Ethan released her, stepping away. Bex blinked, as if needing to orientate herself after her friend's interruption, her cheeks bursting into heat.

She glanced at Ethan, but he was suddenly pretending to check his phone. 'Oh, it's gone great. Baby's here. It's a girl.'

Jenna looked between them. 'Sorry…did I interrupt something?'

Ethan shook his head, smiling. 'No.'

Bex looked at Jenna. 'No. Nothing. Come and say hi to Liberty.'

Bex walked Ethan back to his car, feeling pretty frustrated and annoyed that their moment had been interrupted by Jenna's arrival. Although how was she to have known they were about to kiss? She'd literally only just told Jenna that they'd been separated for five years. But she was getting irritated with how they weren't moving forward with their relationship and felt that they needed to. One of them needed to take control of the reins and push in the direction it needed to go.

They could dance around each other as much as they wanted and nothing would get solved, but if Ethan could go into therapy and try to move forward, then didn't that signal to her that he wanted the same thing as her? He'd been going to kiss her and, dammit, she'd wanted that, too.

'Darcy's eye is looking great,' he told her. 'You've done a fantastic job.'

'Thank goodness it wasn't a serious ulceration.'

'Do you need me to see Spirit at all?'

'No. He's doing well. I've started him on lead training and he's building up strength. I thought I might get him to do some hydrotherapy when he trusts others a bit more. Otherwise I'll never get him in the pool on my own.'

'Jenna told me you have a pool here. That's amazing. You've really got quite a place here, you know?'

They reached his vehicle and he loaded his kit bag into the back, closing the boot with a slam. He looked at her.

'About earlier… I—'

She didn't wait. She didn't give herself time to second-guess what she was doing. She didn't want to hear a bumbling explanation of why he had tried to kiss her, and maybe it was a good thing they'd been interrupted, because she didn't think it was. She'd wanted him to kiss her. Wanted to feel that way again. So she stepped forward, held his face with both hands and planted a kiss upon his lips.

It almost felt as if they'd never been apart. As if the last five years hadn't happened. Her body responded to him in the way it always had. It came alive with his touch, her nerve-endings singing when she felt his hands settle about her waist, when she felt him respond to the kiss, deepening it as if he was hungry for her, too, and holding back from her had been painful.

She didn't care if anyone saw. She didn't care if anyone wanted to interrupt them. All that mattered was kissing him. Showing him that he still mattered, that she still had feelings for him, complicated as they were, and that she wanted to move forward. To sort through them and then hopefully have the happy ending she'd always dreamed of with him.

Life had done its absolute best to derail them. To destroy them. And for a while it had totally succeeded. But time did strange things to wounds and to scars. They stopped hurting as badly…the pain faded. You still knew that they were there, and you saw them, cast your gaze over them occasionally and remembered the mechanism of the injury, but they became easier to deal with. Time and distance gave you the ability to reassess them, to think of how you might have avoided the hurt and the pain and how things might have been if life had worked out differently.

The scar on her heart caused by the loss of Charlie, and then Ethan, was still there, and although Ethan was the cause of some of that pain, she also knew that he was the cause of her being so happy for so long. Of bringing joy into her life, bringing delight and laughter and belonging and warmth. He had changed her life for the better, too, and that wasn't something she could forget. And it was this aspect she still yearned for. This was what she looked for now, wanted, needed, as she got up on tiptoe and kissed him.

This man had helped her choose her university course. Sitting up with her late in the night discussing all her options, supporting her when she'd chosen a different university from him and they'd had to be apart for a while. This man had driven for miles each weekend to come and see her, turning up at her student flat late at night with pizza and ice cream and the promise of his body. This man had held her hand when she'd stood at the graveside during her grandparents' funerals. This man had held her many a night when she hadn't felt well. This man had helped her study for her exams. Had travelled with her to so many places just because she'd wanted to see them. He had spent hours in the Louvre with her, and never told her that he was bored. He had nursed every scrape and wound she'd ever suffered.

This man had given her Charlie.

This man deserved a chance to explain to her what had gone wrong for them.

This man deserved an opportunity to apologise.

He deserved this second chance, and she was willing to give it to him. She hadn't been capable of it before, because she'd been hurting so much, but now she was able. His coming back, his being here, had made her think more calmly.

When the kiss ended, she was breathless, and she looked into his eyes, uncertain of what to say, uncertain of what to do.

Their foreheads still touched as they gazed into each other's eyes, and his thumbs were stroking her cheeks.

'I wasn't expecting that.' He smiled.

'It felt right.'

'Let me take you out somewhere special.'

She smiled. 'I'd like that. I'd like that very much.'

The hydrotherapy pool was one of Bex's favourite places at the centre. There was something about it… Maybe it was the mural on the wall that she'd had a local artist create—white horses in the foaming crests of waves—or maybe it was the way the horses responded when they were placed in the water and how, week after week, she would see their confidence grow.

The pool itself was rectangular, and just over twenty-five metres in length. It had rubber slip-resistant matting at the entry and exit ramps on both ends, and three pump filtration systems to keep the water clean, clear and chlorinated. And afterwards, when they were done, there was a solarium that helped dry the horses off.

Today she led a horse called Monty with Jenna. They each held a lunge rein on either side of the pool and gently encouraged him to swim through the water. He'd been having hydrotherapy sessions for a few weeks now, ever since he'd contracted laminitis—an inflammation of the soft tissue in his hooves.

'So how are things going with you and Ethan?' Jenna asked.

'It's going okay.'

'Looked more than okay to me.' Jenna smiled.

Bex gave her a look across the pool. 'You mean the kiss?'

'Yes! Did he kiss you or did you kiss him? Details like that are important.'

'He was going to kiss me—but then you turned up, so it didn't happen.'

'Oh. Sorry about that.'

'So I kissed him at his car.'

'So, are you…like…getting back together?'

'I think you're getting ahead of yourself, Jen.'

'Right. Of course. You said it was complicated.'

'That's right.'

There was a pause, then, 'Just what *are* the complications, exactly? Because you look like you want to be together. I mean, what did he do? Did he sleep with someone else? Did you?'

Bex wasn't sure how comfortable she was with saying any of this to Jenna. Not because she didn't trust her. She did. Implicitly. It was just that she'd got used to not talking about it. Ruddington and The Grange Centre had been her fresh start. She hadn't wanted to bring her past here.

'Neither of us slept with someone else.'

'Then what happened? He insulted your cooking? Called you names? What? Oh, please don't tell me the *sex* was awful!' Jenna whispered the word 'sex'.

Bex laughed, keeping an eye on Monty as he swam easily through the water. 'He loved my cooking and, no, he didn't call me names. And the sex was as wonderful as sex can be. Mind-blowing, even.'

'So, what, then?'

Bex sighed as Monty's hooves sought purchase on the rubber matting and he began walking up the exit ramp. Once fully out, he gave himself a bit of a shake and they turned him around, let him have a little bit of a breather, and then led him back into the water again.

'He let me down. He wasn't there for me when I needed him, and I couldn't get past that.'

'That can't be all. There's something you're not telling me.'

Nothing got past Jenna.

'Yes, well…it's something I find difficult to talk about.'

Jenna nodded. 'Okay. I understand. Just know that I'm always here if you do ever feel the need to talk about it.'

They guided Monty to the other end of the pool, and when he was out led him into the solarium so that he could dry off. The heat in there really helped with horses' circulation, and helped rid their muscles of any acids that had built up during their exercise in the pool. It stopped them from being cold and helped speed up the healing process.

Bex smiled at her friend. 'I know. I guess I should have told you about Charlie.'

Jenna frowned. 'Who's he?'

'He was our son.'

CHAPTER FIVE

How did you get ready to take out the wife you'd been separated from for five years? The coffee date had been easier. It had just been coffee…they had just been clearing the air after having met up again. But this time he'd asked her out because she'd kissed him. And that kiss…

Well, that kiss had been something.

Unexpected. Fiery. Passionate. Hot.

A culmination of every emotion he'd felt for the last five years. Maybe even longer than that.

That kiss had said something. Had communicated something. The fact that she still cared. That she'd kept her feelings for him tightly bound up inside and now they had burst forth. That she still wanted him.

At least, he hoped so. If that were true, and he'd read it right—and he really didn't think he was wrong—then he really needed this night to go well. Because he wanted her back, too.

He missed her. But saying he missed her was too simple a phrase to fully explain how he felt without Bex at his side each day. She was his better half. She was the person he had loved to turn to at the end of every day, the person he'd saved his jokes for, his stories. The person he'd liked to see first thing when he woke and last thing before he closed his eyes at night.

He needed to tell her that.

Needed to tell her everything so they could move forward.

These last five years he had felt as if he was living in a wilderness without her. He'd felt incomplete. He'd believed that feeling had come from losing Charlie only—but, no, it had been the loss of his wife, too.

He'd lost them both. And although he couldn't ever get Charlie back, he could get Bex—and he really didn't want to screw this up.

When they felt a loss like losing a child, most people clung to those around them, seeking the safety and security of the familiar. They imbued their possessions with sentimentality and kept them close. But Ethan had done none of those things. He'd isolated himself, become withdrawn.

Every reminder of Charlie had been too painful to bear, with his own guilt thrown into the mix, too. Had he been to blame? Was there something in his family genetics? He should have been honest with her from the start. Told her about Elodie…

He'd known that what he'd done had hurt Bex, but he hadn't been able to stop himself. He'd needed to distance himself because his own pain had been too overwhelming. He'd needed to get away. From all reminders.

He knew he'd done wrong. He knew he should have been her soft place to fall. The strong arms to support her. But losing his son…his precious firstborn and only child…?

He'd been overjoyed to see him come into the world.

He'd watched him being born. Had cut his cord. That sweet boy with his golden hair and his cheeky smile and that wonderful, gorgeous, infectious laugh. His loss had torn Ethan in two, and he had not known how to take care of Bex when he was doing his absolute damnedest himself not to collapse into a bawling mess in the foetal position on the floor.

It had been all he could do to drag himself out of bed each day and keep on breathing. To put one foot in front of the other and just *be*.

To somehow find the energy within him to be there for his wife… He just hadn't been able to do it.

He'd not wanted to end up like his own mother, who'd also lost a child. But he had understood his mother. Understood what had made her the person he saw each day. It wasn't just her illness that had taken her from him, but all her grief and all her sorrow.

And so now, as he got ready, sorting through his clothes to find the perfect shirt, the perfect trousers, he knew how much rested on tonight.

It wasn't a simple date. This wasn't a coffee and a knickerbocker glory, or a walk by the river. This was something more.

She'd kissed him. Not a friendly peck on the cheek, or a quick kiss goodbye on the lips. It had been passionate. It had had meaning and intent. It had told him that she wanted something more than friendship—and, by God, he wanted the same thing.

He wanted her back. He wanted to prove to her that he could be the man she'd once fallen in love with and she could love him again.

It was silly even to think that picking a blue shirt over a white one might somehow win him his wife.

They were only clothes. Did they really matter? All he needed to do was show her that he'd made an effort and wanted to look good for her. So he picked a shirt and a pair of lightweight trousers, because it was still so warm in the evenings, and laid them on his bed before going to take a shower.

Maybe she was just as nervous as he was…?

The ticking of the kitchen clock was making Bex nervous. Each tick was another second that brought closer the moment there would be a knock on her door from Ethan.

Occasionally she'd check her hair and make-up in the hall mirror. Fiddle with her earrings, tweak a curl or two, straighten the spaghetti straps of her dress… Everything needed to be perfect. Or as damn near perfect as it could be.

Tonight was going to be a big night. She could feel it in her bones and in her blood, which was whooshing around her system with a healthy dose of adrenaline, making her legs feel shaky and her stomach filled with butterflies.

She couldn't wait to be with Ethan again. To see him. To touch him. Hold his hand. Maybe draw him close and gaze into those gorgeous blue eyes of his… She knew logically that she was only putting a pin in their issues and pushing them to one side, but the thought of being with him again…

She'd bought special underwear. She wasn't sure why—it wasn't as if they were going to fall into bed with one another—but she wanted to feel as special as this night was going to be, and she'd seen the beautiful matching set in dark red silk in a shop window, on a mannequin. She'd been unable to resist and had splurged, telling herself it was a treat she deserved.

The silk felt good against her skin. And it couldn't be seen under the blue summer dress she was wearing.

Bex checked the clock again, biting her lip to see that only a minute had passed since her last check, when it felt more like ten or fifteen.

He'd said he would pick her up at eight. It was now seven fifty-nine p.m.

She peered out from behind her curtains into the street, to see if she could spot his car, but it wasn't there. She let out a breath and tried to slow her racing heart. She had no idea where they were going, or what they were going to do, but that just added to the excitement.

She was just checking her small clutch bag one more time to make sure she had everything—keys, mobile, tissues, lip balm—when she heard a car engine. She looked out and saw his car pull up in front of her property.

'Okay, Bex. This is it,' she said aloud. 'It's just Ethan. Just your husband.'

She smiled to herself, wondering if she'd ever been this nervous when they'd been dating. Honestly, she couldn't remember. There'd been excitement, but nerves...? Maybe on their wedding day, but after that...

She watched him get out of his vehicle and smiled without realising she was doing it. He looked great. But then again, he was one of those guys who looked effortlessly amazing in anything, whether he was in board shorts at the beach, or dressed in the finest tuxedo. Tonight, he was wearing a plain white shirt and dark trousers. He had unbuttoned the top two buttons of his shirt as if he'd just finished a day at work and wanted to relax and kick back.

It took quite a bit of restraint not to just race to the front door and open it, but she waited, biting her bottom lip, listening for the gentle rap of his knuckles against the door. Then she went to open it.

Pulling the door wide, she smiled at him, suddenly feeling shy. 'Hi…' She felt heat bloom in her cheeks.

'Hi. You look gorgeous.'

She beamed at the compliment. 'You, too.'

He smiled and stepped back. 'Ready to go?'

Bex closed the door and he walked her to the car, one hand in the small of her back, before reaching to open the door for her, making sure she was safely in before closing it.

What am I doing? Is this crazy? Are we fools to think we can ignore everything?

She watched him walk around the front of the vehicle before getting in at the driver's side. 'Where are we going?' she asked.

'Well, I remember that you like Thai food, so I thought we could go and eat at this place called Malee's that's just opened up. It's got some great reviews and it looks quite quirky inside. I think you'll like it.'

He was right. She loved Thai food. 'Sounds great,' she said. She loved it that he remembered that fact about her, and she hadn't been out for a meal in ages.

All her time was taken in building up the centre, creating a business and finding staff that she trusted. Either that or she was on long drives to go and rescue horses from anywhere in the UK and bringing them back to be rehabilitated. Her days involved long hours, but she needed that—because if she filled her time with the needs of her animals then she didn't spend too long thinking about her own.

When they got to Malee's, Bex was amazed. On the outside it looked like a normal restaurant, but inside it was like a Thai market. Booths and tables were set as if under individual stalls, each with a brightly covered canopy. There were multi-coloured lanterns and there were even some tables set up inside tuk-tuks! The kitchen was open-plan, and in the centre of the restaurant, so diners could see their food being prepared amongst the baskets of fresh produce, rich greens and a veritable rainbow of ingredients. The aroma was of spice and mouth-watering flavours.

A waitress met them at the door.

'Table for two under the name Clarke,' Ethan said.

They were taken to one of the tuk-tuks, painted bright lime-green with a blue canopy, and invited to sit down.

'Ethan. This place is amazing! How did you find it?'

'I looked online after one of the vets at the practice mentioned coming here.'

'It's fabulous! I've never seen anything like it.'

'Me neither.'

They were presented with menus whilst the waitress poured them both water with ice and lime wedges and took their drinks order.

Bex let her gaze trawl the menu and simply couldn't make up her mind what she wanted to eat. It all sounded wonderful, and with the delicious aromas of cumin, ginger and garlic she could smell, her stomach rumbled in anticipation.

Eventually she settled on sharing a starter with Ethan, scallops in a black pepper sauce, and a Massaman curry. Whilst Ethan ordered roast duck with a honeyed soy sauce.

'I can't wait. I'm starving!'

'You must work up quite an appetite at work sometimes?' he said.

'Oh, yes.' She nodded. 'It can be quite physical.'

'How's Liberty doing?'

'Feeding well. She and Darcy are doing great.'

'That's good to hear. I'm glad.'

'You never can tell what first-time mothers are going to be like, can you?'

Ethan smiled. 'I guess not. We did okay as parents, though, don't you think?'

Bex nodded. 'We did. Considering.'

'We did read a lot of books,' he said, trying to lighten the mood.

'We did. And ignored them all!' She laughed.

'Do you remember that first night home from the hospital? How Charlie wouldn't stop crying? And how he sucked on his arm so badly that by the morning he had a blister?'

'Oh, my gosh, yes! I can remember being terrified that the midwife would think we'd done it!'

'She was good, though. Didn't make us feel guilty.'

'Well, we did that all on our own,' Bex said.

'I remember being terrified for the first six months or so.'

She smiled. 'Me, too. It got better when he started sleeping through the night.'

She played with her locket. The one that contained a small curl of Charlie's hair. Ethan's gaze dropped to it.

'I'm glad we brought him into our bed when he couldn't sleep, though,' he said. 'I cherish those nights snuggled into him. Sometimes even now, when I'm in bed, I remember what he felt like…all hot and toasty.'

'Me, too.'

She could feel a lump forming in her throat. Those nights with Charlie had been precious. The way he would curl on his side, his little fists tucked under his chin, sleeping with them on either side of him, protecting him. She could remember many hours of just lying there, staring at his beautiful face as he slept and occasionally reaching out and stroking his soft, downy cheek. Amazed at this wonderful, perfect little human they had created.

The waitress arrived with their scallops.

'Wow, these look great.' She brightened, afraid they had taken the evening in too maudlin a direction.

'We should be able to talk about him freely, Bex,' said Ethan. 'Don't feel guilty.'

'I don't. Just sad.'

'I know.'

He reached out and placed his hand on hers. She looked down at their hands entwined and smiled, trying to ignore the tears welling in her eyes. Eventually she had to pull her hand free, so she could use a napkin to dab at her eyes.

'Let's hope everyone thinks I'm crying because of the spicy food.' She laughed.

'No one's watching us. And who cares what anyone else thinks?'

The scallops were amazing. Thick, juicy and perfectly tender, served in a tasty black pepper sauce, the heat of which hit nicely on the backs of their throats.

All around them conversation bubbled. The noise level was quite high as the restaurant bustled with staff, in the kitchen food was fried and tossed in pans, pots clanged, spoons scraped, and glasses clinked as people made toasts.

But in their little lime-green tuk-tuk Bex and Ethan only had eyes for each other.

It was good to sit across from him again and eat a meal, she thought. When they'd been married, they'd tried to eat their evening meal together as often as they could. It hadn't always been an option. Sometimes Ethan would get called out to an emergency, or Bex would be doing a night shift at her own surgery, looking after the animals that were staying over after surgeries. But when they'd been able to eat together they'd made sure that they had.

She'd forgotten this. What it felt like to share a meal with him. The sense of déjà vu was strong. But she liked it. Had missed it.

When their main courses arrived, the conversation changed again.

'So...you surprised me with that kiss...' Ethan began.

Bex blushed and dabbed at her mouth with her napkin. 'It felt right at the time.'

'And now?'

She paused for time. Took a sip of her drink. Smiled. 'We still have things to sort out, but...I'm glad that I did.'

He smiled broadly. 'Me, too. You know, I wanted to kiss you before, but I wasn't sure how you'd react. We ended so badly... I wasn't sure what sort of reception I'd get.'

'I wanted you to kiss me. Even if it was only going to be once. Just to be kissed again by you would have been enough. I couldn't remember the last time we had kissed.'

'I couldn't remember either.'

'But I didn't just kiss you because I couldn't remember the last one. I kissed you because…' she laughed, blushing '…I wanted to.'

He stared so intently into her eyes then that she almost regretted they were in a public space. Because if he'd looked at her like that and they'd been at home she'd have been reaching for him. Undoing those shirt buttons, unbuckling his belt.

It had been so long since she had been physically intimate with him—and she'd been with nobody else since their split either. Sex was something she'd hidden under the rug. Forgotten about. Not needing it any more. Isolating herself had seemed like a fitting punishment for not being able to save her son. Why should she have any gratification? She'd failed as a mother.

But now, sitting opposite her husband, staring deeply into his eyes, feeling the heat and attraction that was between them… Her body had woken up and it wanted what it wanted. From Ethan. Because it knew—and *she* knew, damn well—just how he could make her body sing. They'd always been such a good match—mentally, emotionally and physically. Whether it had been the tender kind of lovemaking they'd enjoyed, or the quick, frantic, I-must-have-you-now sessions that would leave them laughing and breathless and in a state of half-undress.

All the fun she'd had with him was coming back, making her feel hot and uncomfortable and itching for physical touch.

'Do you want to get out of here?' he asked.

She knew what he was implying—and, yes. She did. So she nodded, and he reached out to take her hand and pulled her along. They paid for their starter quickly and rushed outside. And then they were hurrying, holding hands, hearts pounding, blood whooshing until they reached the Old Market Square.

There weren't too many people there, and most of them were on their way to another place. Ethan pulled her up the steps towards the Town Hall, past the stone lions and through the arches, and stopped. There they were hidden. There they had privacy.

She stared at him, breathing heavily, looking into his eyes again, making that connection, telling him with her gaze that she needed him here in the dark.

He took a step towards her, stroked her face, and then he pressed her against the cool stone wall and began to kiss her.

It was like lighting a fuse on a firework.

The hard stone at her back was forgotten as he pressed himself against her and her whole body came alight. Her hands were everywhere. As if they were trying to touch everything, trying to remember him, to remind herself of the contours of his body, the way he felt.

He was everything and more. She could feel the work he'd done at the gym, could feel the well-defined muscles in his abs, the broadness of his chest. And when she reached for him and took him in her hand the noise he made in his throat was enough to make her feel as if she would explode.

This was everything. The world, the past—that very painful past they shared—all was forgotten in this moment. All that mattered was each other. And she was so terribly hungry for him. She ached for him in a way that she had never done before.

She felt his hands lifting her dress so that he could reach for her underwear, move it so that he could enter her, and when he did she held on to him, one leg up around his waist, and tried to stay as quiet as she could—even though all she wanted to do was gasp and groan and urge him on.

For a few moments they lost themselves in each other. Coming together in a union that had been forged in fire.

Oh, how she had missed this! And even though a small part of her was screaming at her, telling her this wasn't the solution, that she still needed answers from him, that they were in a public place, that they could get caught—none of it stopped her.

Because she needed him. Needed him to salve her wounds. He had caused some of the scars upon her heart, so he was the only one who could soothe them. He was the only person on this planet who knew the pain in her heart as intimately as she did. He was the only one who understood.

He was the *only* one.

His movements became more frantic and he suddenly shuddered against her and slowed, his breath warm on her neck, his fingers digging deep into her thigh.

She became aware of how the stone rubbed against her back and shoulders and she blinked and laughed softly. She looked around them, glad to see that they were still alone, still unnoticed, and aware that both of them had taken an incredible risk in doing what they had done.

Bex lowered her leg, adjusted her underwear and dress, and then helped Ethan buckle up. She looked at him uncertainly.

'Well! That was…' She had no word for what that had been. *Exhilarating* came close. *Thrilling?*

Ethan seemed to be taking some time to catch his breath, but he pulled her towards him and just hugged her, sinking his face into her hair. For a moment they just stood there, swaying as if to some silent music. Ethan was stroking her hair. She was holding him. It was as if they were saying, *Yes, I've found you again. I lost you, but now you're back.*

Bex had no idea what this meant.

Had it simply been the two of them needing to lose themselves in a physical release? Had it been a reconnection? The start of a new chapter for them?

They'd not used protection, but she wasn't worried about getting pregnant. They'd needed IVF to conceive Charlie. Nothing like that was going to happen, even though there'd been no clear reason as to why she'd been unable to get pregnant before. And she trusted that Ethan hadn't slept around. He wasn't that kind of guy. Never had been.

No. That wasn't a worry.

The worry was what would happen next.

Ethan walked Bex to her door. The night had not gone the way he'd expected—though it had moved in a very surprising and delightful direction.

He almost couldn't believe what they had done! They'd taken quite a risk. But fortunately they hadn't been seen and at the time it had been one that hadn't seemed like a risk at all.

It had been an instinctual driving need. Something primal. Something that he couldn't fully explain to himself. He'd just needed to lose himself in her—to find that connection they'd once had before which had been lost for far too long. And in that moment he had lost himself. Lost everything. All the pain, all the hurt, all the grief… For just a moment he'd been able to cast it all to one side and allow himself to revel in the glory of her body, of the way she felt, the way she tasted, the way they'd come together to make the outside world go away.

It was addictive, and already he craved more. But he knew, sensibly, that they were in danger of allowing their physical need for each other to hide the difficult past that they needed to overcome if they truly were to have any future together.

His head was clear now, and he knew that they needed to face their demons. And yet…

It was such a seductive feeling to know that they could delay that just by being with each other physically. Putting a sticking plaster on an old hurt. Pretending it wasn't there when it was, still waiting to heal.

'I had a great time tonight,' he said, smiling.

'Me, too,' she replied.

'It went a little crazy there for a while.'

She gave a gentle laugh. 'Yeah. It did. But it was the good kind of crazy.'

He nodded, knowing he ought to just kiss her goodnight and walk away. Knowing that that would be the right thing to do.

'Do you…do you want to come in for a coffee before you go?'

He thought about saying no. He really did. For maybe a microsecond.

'That'd be great.'

And so he followed her indoors, silencing the voice that told him to walk away and encouraging the voice that said this night should never end.

She had a nice place. Homely. Comforting. Large squishy sofas with a creamy white throw over one of them. Leafy plants. A fireplace stacked with logs. And walking towards them came an elegant Siamese cat, chocolate point with large blue eyes, miaowing loudly.

'Hey, Salem.' Bex reached down to pick up the cat and gave him a hug.

'You always did want a Siamese,' he said.

'I got him from a rescue centre when he was eighteen months old. It took us some time to get used to each other, but now we're great.'

He smiled and gave the cat a stroke. Salem sniffed at Ethan, then allowed him to scratch at his ears and under his chin.

'He'll want his night-time feed. I'll just be a minute. Make yourself at home.' And she disappeared into the kitchen.

Ethan sat down on one of the sofas by the fireplace and looked at the small table next to it. There was a photo frame with a picture of Charlie in it. A picture he'd never seen before. In it, Charlie was fast asleep in bed, face down, bum high in the air, his knees tucked under him. His little cheeks were rosy-red and his face was soft in repose.

Ethan picked up the picture, marvelling at this new image of his son.

'I took that picture the morning of his stroke.'

Bex stood in the doorway to her living room, watching him.

'I've never seen it.'

'I took it on my phone. Forgot it was there until… much later. He looked so perfect. So healthy. So normal. It's hard to imagine that—' Her voice got caught in her throat and she stopped talking.

Ethan looked up at her and felt a painful twist in his chest. 'He looks gorgeous.'

She nodded, still unable to speak.

Ethan put the photo down and got up, going over to her and taking her in his arms. This was what he should have done before. He had, hadn't he? Once or twice, he had. He could remember… When he'd met her at the hospital and they hadn't known what was going on. At that point he had held her. Told her it would be all right. That kids often got sick but they bounced back.

That was what he'd kept telling himself. That Charlie would be fine. It wasn't serious. It couldn't be. He was only two years old. Serious things didn't happen to two-year-olds. Maybe other two-year-olds, but not theirs.

And then the doctor had taken them into that family room. His face grave, his voice low, he had delivered the death sentence. Charlie would not wake up. His brain was irreparably damaged, and he could not, would not, come back from this.

That was when Ethan had let her down.

Up until that point they'd held each other. Touch providing the comfort and security that the other person gave them. But the second those words had entered his ears, had reached his brain and sunk in with their dread definitive purpose, he had dropped Bex's hand and retreated into himself.

He hadn't even been aware of it back then. Hadn't realised he'd let go. Pulled away. Abandoned her in her time of need. *Their* time of need. It was just something that had happened. Retreating into himself.

But when he'd explored that moment in therapy his therapist had pointed it out, asking him, 'How do you think your wife felt in that moment? Hearing about her son and having you leave her as well?'

'I let you go,' he whispered into her hair.

Bex stiffened in his arms. 'Yes.'

'I let you go when you needed me most.'

Quietly… 'Yes.'

He tightened his hold on her, squeezing her tight. It was almost an apology, a physical sign that he knew what he had done and this time he would not let her go.

'I didn't realise at the time that I'd withdrawn from you. That I'd abandoned you. I'm *so sorry*, Bex. They're just words, I know, and probably too late, but…I *am* sorry for what I did. You needed me. You needed me to be there. And I—'

She pulled out of his arms, looked up at him. 'What happened back then?'

He could see the hurt in her eyes. Even now, after all this time. But of course it would be there. It had never been resolved. She'd been left wondering. Left angry. Bereft. With no answers that made any sense.

'I just couldn't deal with it. Losing Charlie was so unexpected…so awful…that I…' He swallowed hard. 'It was too big. Too much. It was like I couldn't breathe. Like the words the doctor was saying were being said someplace else, to someone else. And when I looked at you, you were just…'

He closed his eyes with the pain of that day. Of that moment. The way Bex had crumpled in the chair, her cries of anguish tearing his heart from his chest so savagely it had been as if he couldn't get any air.

'I left the room so I could breathe. I needed to be outside. I needed…'

'Needed what?'

He looked at her again, opened his mouth to form words, but nothing was coming. His gaze dropped back to Charlie's photo, taken hours before the fatal stroke that had taken him from them.

'I needed to put some space between me and what the doctor had said. Some space between us. Because your pain was so raw and so real. I felt disbelief. This couldn't be happening to us. It was somehow this terrible dream, and if I allowed it to be real—if I acknowledged it, saw you cry, heard you cry—then I would have to face the reality of my own pain. My own guilt at not being there.'

Bex frowned. 'That's why you kept yourself apart?'

'I know it was wrong. I do. But it was self-preservation. I was protecting myself.'

'And what about me?'

'I couldn't help you. I knew that I couldn't. I'd already failed you both.'

'But *why*?'

He knew he owed her the real answer, but it was something that no one in his family had ever addressed. Not really. His therapist had told him that was why it had been so easy for him to isolate himself and not talk about his pain. It was something he was used to.

It was something he'd been taught to do. But now was the time. He knew he had to tell her.

'When I was six years old, my parents lost a child.'

Bex sank onto a sofa and he did the same, sitting opposite her.

'A child? Why did you never say anything?'

'My parents refused to talk about her.'

'Her?'

'Elodie.'

'Elodie…' Bex sounded out the name as if she was trying it out for the first time. Which she was. 'What happened to her?'

'She died in utero. She was delivered stillborn by Caesarean section, during emergency surgery to save my mother's life. She'd begun to bleed. Placenta praevia.'

Bex's eyes filled up. 'Oh, my God…'

'My father was just so thrilled my mother had survived that Elodie's loss got pushed to the back burner, and when my mother came round after a few days she had to focus on her own recovery, rather than on the loss of her daughter. When my mother came home from the hospital my father was already drinking, to cope with everything, and when the loss fully set in drinking became a way for them both to escape. My mother told us to never speak of Elodie again as it caused her too much pain.'

'I'm so sorry I never knew. Why did you never tell me?'

'When we first met it didn't seem right. Then we got married, and I meant to tell you, but after all the trouble we'd had conceiving, when you got pregnant through the IVF I was scared to tell you. I didn't want you worrying in case something happened to you or the baby, so I kept it inside. Then when Charlie was born we were so happy, and he was so healthy, and I thought there would be no point in telling you.' He paused. 'Then Charlie died, and I felt like maybe it was my fault. Maybe there was something in my family that—'

His voice broke. He'd never got to know his sister, so he didn't miss her exactly, but he did often dream about what she would have been like.

'I couldn't bear to see your pain. I felt guilty.'

'The autopsy showed nothing genetic,' she said numbly.

'I know that now, but at that time I didn't know, and I just wanted to run away. Not to be reminded. My therapist has made me see that I do the same thing as my parents. Not the drinking! I don't drink because I've never wanted to become like them. But I use the same coping mechanism of dealing with a horrific event by pushing it to one side. I don't talk about it. I create a distance between myself and it. And because your pain was so raw, right there in front of me, I took myself away from you so that I didn't have to confront it and end up like them. Broken and bitter.'

For a moment there was silence. Ethan wasn't sure if he could even look up and see her face in case he saw judgement there. A judgement that he would never be able to bear, because Bex's reaction to all this was so important.

Maybe it was wrong of him to expect her to support him now, when he'd not been able to do the same for her in the past, but he hoped she would. She'd always been stronger than him, even when torn apart by grief. She'd had the strength to face it head-on, when all he'd done was hide from it and pretend it didn't exist until it was easier to deal with.

When she moved from the sofa opposite to sit beside him and reach for his hand, he risked a look. Tears were burning the backs of his eyes and they burst forth when he saw that she was smiling encouragingly at him.

'Thank you for telling me, Ethan. Thank you for being vulnerable with me.'

She reached up to stroke his face, and then she leaned in to place a kiss upon his lips. He could taste his own tears upon their lips, but that didn't matter. What mattered was that she hadn't rejected him, or berated him for his handling of this all-important matter between them.

He'd known he needed to tell her the truth, no matter how late it was in coming. She'd needed to hear all this, and now it was out in the open.

'Can you ever forgive me?' he whispered, staring into her eyes.

She nodded and pulled him in, wrapping her arms around him, resting her chin on his shoulder. 'I wish you had told me before.'

'Me, too. I'm so sorry.'

'It's okay. It's okay now.' She took his face in her hands once again and made him look at her. 'I know now. I *know*.'

And she kissed him. Just once, at first. And then again. And again. And then it became something more, and he was responding, feeling his body fill with a need and a hunger that he'd thought already sated just hours before.

Losing himself in her this time was different. He'd been laid bare, and although it had been uncomfortable at first, he'd discovered a strength in it. A strength in the truth. In the honesty of tearing down the walls and brushing away the cobwebs, bringing his grief out into the open to finally reveal everything to his wife.

He'd always thought of his grief as a weakness. A fault in his character that, left to run free, would result in him becoming like his parents. Rather too fond of alcohol and dependent on it.

But his grief had never been a weakness. It had been nothing but strength. Strength of the love he had felt for his son. And instead of allowing it free rein, so that he could deal with it, he had been afraid of it. Afraid of its devastating power.

Not any more.

And now, as he kissed his wife, feeling the glory of her curves, the softness of her body beneath him, he realised that instead of fighting to keep his equilibrium, all he'd ever needed to do was surrender himself. Trust that Bex had his back as much as he had hers. They could have faced the loss of Charlie together, with her soft edges blunting the sharp edges of his pain, but instead he'd left Bex alone. Left her vulnerable and alone and frightened.

He vowed never to do such a thing again.

Vowed that he would always be there to protect his wife.

The woman he loved.

CHAPTER SIX

BEX WOKE THE next morning and just lay in bed for a moment, her body completely sated and her mind brimming and overflowing with thoughts, feelings and emotions, like water escaping a full bathtub.

Last night had been…

She sighed with a slight smile. A satisfied smile.

Last night had been amazing. Eye-opening. Confessional.

She'd experienced so much with Ethan last night—had learned so much. Ethan had had a younger sister. Or should have had one. Now she understood his parents' natures. Why they'd never got too excited over her being pregnant with Charlie. Almost as if they'd been afraid to. The poor things… She understood, too, why on occasion his parents numbed their pain with alcohol. But she'd never known their full devastation, and now that she did she felt some empathy with them.

They had also lost a child.

Elodie.

What would she have been like? She'd be a grown-up now. Bex would have a sister-in-law. Elodie would most probably have been a bridesmaid at their wedding…

And Ethan had never mentioned her.

She understood why. Children got raised with their parents' habits. With their wishes and desires. And if they never spoke about Elodie, why would he?

And yet…she wished that he had. Wished that he'd felt able to confide in her, his wife. Wished that he'd been able to tell her before she got pregnant with Charlie. But clearly—as she'd learned last night—Ethan dealt with trauma and upset by distancing himself from it, just as his parents did. By not talking about or acknowledging their loss.

Ethan had done the same.

And who was she to judge how someone dealt with grief?

Even after the loss of Charlie she had not really blamed Ethan for walking away, for never talking about him or being there for her. It had never been about blame. It had been about the loneliness. The abandonment. About not having her husband by her side when she'd needed him the most, in her weakest moments.

Her own response to grief was to submit to it. To allow the waves of pain to completely subsume her. But there was no wrong or right way to deal with it. Only the way of each individual. Methods might clash. Reactions might cause confusion, and in their case arguments, but their ways had never been *wrong*.

She understood him a little more today.

And it was wonderful to have him back in her bed. She had missed him so much, and on both occasions when they'd made love last night she had felt completely different things.

The first time, in the shadow of the Town Hall in Old Market Square, had been exhilarating and passionate, full of need and angst and a raw, lustful yearning for each other. It was as if they'd been on a diet for five years and had suddenly been presented with a buffet table and told to go wild. To stuff their faces. Grab anything and consume it as quickly as possible! Feeding a hunger that had run unabated for years with no time to stop and relish anything.

The second time had been here in her home. Starting in the living room and then she'd taken him by the hand and led him upstairs to her bed. That second time she had had time to enjoy the flavours as she'd fed her hunger. The nuances. The spice, the sweet kisses, the warm, heated licks, the pleasurable shivers as she'd arched her back and his mouth and hands had found places that only Ethan knew to bring her pleasure.

Last night made her wish that they had never lost those five years. Five long, lonely years of wandering in the wilderness alone. Life was so short. They both knew that more than most people did. They couldn't afford to waste any more.

Ethan had told her what had happened. He had opened up. Shared his vulnerabilities, broken his heart in two and showed her everything. For that she was eternally grateful, but what they needed to do now was move on from the pain of their past.

Was there a future for them?

Was there a future for them together? As man and wife?

She felt hopeful that there was, because before all this they had been wonderful partners to one another. Yes, they might have lost their way for a little while, but surely now they could get back on track?

Even to think that they could, to think that they could salvage what they had and maybe somehow bring it back stronger than before… Better than before… Well, that thought brought a huge smile to her face.

Bex got out of bed and got ready for work, and all the time as she showered and ate breakfast, drove to the centre, the smile never left her face.

Ethan's first appointment of the day was a four-month-old filly with a growing umbilical hernia. Normally he wouldn't operate on them in a horse at this age. He liked to leave them, to see if they repaired themselves between six months to a year, but this hernia was getting bigger every day, so he was heading out to Apple Tree Farm to perform surgery.

He liked the thrill of what he called field surgery. You could never be too sure when the anaesthesia would wear off, so you had to work quickly and carefully and it could be a difficult balance at times. But there was something wonderful about operating on a horse in its own stable, rather than bringing it into the surgery—which was a whole other process. There was less stress on the animal if it was anaesthetised in a place it knew, surrounded by people it knew, and when the animal woke up it wasn't in a strange place with weird smells, so it recovered better.

The farm's owner Greta met him with him a wave, and they walked around to the stable where little Jessie waited. She was a beautiful white filly, with an off-white greyish mane, and he knew she would be a stunning horse when full-grown.

'How is she today?' he asked.

'Good! Her mum is keeping a watchful eye.'

He smiled. 'As mothers do. Will she be a problem, do you think?'

'No. And I've got Bill and Annie here to keep her distracted whilst you work on her little one.'

'Great.' This was another reason why field surgery was much better. Babies and their mothers didn't get taken from each other. 'I'll just need to get her weight, so I can give her the right amount of anaesthesia.'

He measured her heart girth by wrapping the measuring tape from the highest point of her wither to just behind her elbows. Then he multiplied that by itself, and then by her body length, and divided it by three hundred and thirty to give him the weight in pounds. Then, just to be sure, he assessed the horse on its body score, looking for a healthy layer of fat.

Jessie bucked a little, still unsure of human touch. 'Steady, girl, steady…' he cooed.

Once Jessie had settled a bit, he organised the anaesthesia and, as it took effect, got Greta to help him lay the horse down gently.

Behind them, her mother neighed and snorted, and he heard the farm workers trying to soothe her. He stopped to make sure she was all right. The workers' safety was paramount. But she seemed okay so he decided to carry on, rolling Jessie onto her back and shaving away some of the fur from around the hernia.

It wasn't huge. Only two fingers wide. But there were definitely more intestinal loops in it than before, so this surgery was definitely the best call.

He used lidocaine to numb the area, and then quickly and effectively cut away the hernial sac, exposing the linear alba—a tendinous, fibrous material that ran vertically down the midline of the abdomen.

'Here it is.'

Ethan grabbed sutures and began stitching up the

hole, working fast, his face a mask of concentration, until the hernia was repaired.

'There we go.' He snipped the last stitch and wiped down the area so that it was all clean.

'Will she be all right like that?' asked Greta.

'I'll put a belly band on her and leave it for a few days, but we need to get her up first.'

He placed a cloth over Jessie's eyes and rolled her back onto her side, so that they would be able to help her stand when she woke up.

For a while, it seemed Jessie was taking full advantage of the drugs, and having a nice little sleep, but pretty soon her head lifted—and then dropped again.

Greta laughed. 'Come on, Jessie!'

The cloth came off her eyes and this time they were able to help her get up onto her feet, wobbly as she was.

Ethan put some silver cream onto a gauze pad and held it against her wound before he wrapped the belly band around her waist. 'Keep that on her for three to four days, then you can take it off. We'll start her on antibiotics, but I'll need you to keep an eye on her temperature and check her each day for any signs of infection. She should be fine now.'

'Thanks, Ethan. That's great. A job well done.'

'I try.'

He watched Jessie and her mum reunite, and as always it brought a smile to his face. The bond between a mother and her child was the strongest, and it was amazing to see that bond in his animal patients.

'I'll get going, then. Give me a call if you have any concerns.'

'Will do. Thanks, Ethan.'

He was looking forward to his next call. He was

going to drop in on Bex at the centre on the way back to his surgery. He didn't have any patients to see, but he thought it would be nice to pop in and see her. He missed her.

Being with her the other night had proved to him just how strong their bond was. It was a bond that had endured even during those five lost years. In Abu Dhabi he'd often found himself thinking about her. Missing her. Wondering what she was up to. Whether she was looking up at the same moon and stars as he. If she missed him, too.

And now they were back together, reunited, and their need for one another was just as strong. He felt freer now than he ever had before, because he'd told her everything. Turned out that revealing your weaknesses to another person was actually a strength, because it brought you closer. It had created an intimacy between them that he'd not noticed was missing. He could be himself now—without having to watch what he said, without having to protect her or himself from the difficulties of the past.

They'd talked about Charlie. They'd talked about Elodie. They'd talked about how he'd reacted after their son's death. And lying there in her arms, talking about those things, had been just as important, just as invigorating, as it had been to make love to her again.

The hardest thing about that night had been getting out of her bed and going home. The temptation to stay had been intense, but if he had then he wasn't sure he'd ever have gone home again. And then what? They'd have been living together. He couldn't presume that that was what she wanted, and besides, he wanted to prove to her that he could woo her…show her once again just how special she was to him.

It would be good for them both to do that. To reaffirm what they had.

As he drove up the long driveway towards the centre he could feel the butterflies in his stomach as he anticipated seeing her again, holding her in his arms and kissing her.

In the paddocks a variety of horses stood in the sunshine, heads down, munching on grass. It was always such a wonderful sight, and he had a sudden yearning to go out riding. He'd not sat on a horse since Abu Dhabi, and he missed it.

He parked near the education centre and Jenna waved to him from inside. 'Are you looking for Bex?' she asked.

'Yes.'

'She's round the back with Spirit.'

'Okay, thanks.'

He headed to the quarantine stables and found Bex in the paddock there, trying to work with the rescued horse on a lead line.

She'd seen him approach and he was pleased to see a big smile break across her face.

'Hi!' she said.

'Hi. How's he doing?'

'Building strength. He's getting there. He's just not letting people near him, except me, at the moment. Want to come in and see if you can help socialise him a bit?'

'I'd love to.'

He opened the paddock gate, and as soon as he took a few steps towards Spirit the horse reared a little and whinnied. Ethan took a step back, then headed over to Bex. She had her hair up in a ponytail and she turned to smile at him again as he got close. He pulled her in for a long kiss, feeling his body stir in response.

'Good morning…'

'Good morning to you. How are you?'

'Good. I've just come from doing a surgery.'

'You always did like to start your day cutting.'

'There's nothing quite like it—though I *can* think of another way to start my day well.'

He smiled at her, and she laughed.

'Yes, that's wonderful, too.'

'I missed you when I left.'

Bex began trying to get Spirit trotting in a circle around them again, as they stood in the middle of the paddock.

'I missed you, too.'

He was pleased to hear it. It would have been devastating if he'd got here to find out that Bex had had second thoughts about their relationship and the direction it seemed to be heading.

His gaze fell upon the horse. He certainly seemed upset that he was in the paddock. His earlier easy gait, when it had just been Bex with him, now seemed off. It would be easy to leave. To walk away and let the horse return to its previous behaviour. But Bex was right. Spirit needed to get used to having someone else around.

'Want me to take the lead? See how he does?'

'Sure. Have at it.'

She passed him the guide rope and he tried to take control. Almost immediately Spirit stopped moving forward and tried to pull back, stamping his hooves uncertainly, clearly feeling off-guard and uncomfortable.

'He's not sure of you,' said Bex.

'No, he isn't…' Ethan made a couple of noises to try and encourage the horse to move forward, even at a walk, but Spirit just tried to pull away.

'Maybe it's still too soon. Here—let me.'

Bex took the guide rope once again, and Spirit began to walk in his circles.

'Maybe it's men in general. We don't know his history, or how he was treated. Have you tried him with Jenna?'

'He doesn't like her either.'

'So he's bonded with you?'

'Looks like it.'

'It won't do him any good in the long run if he doesn't let others near him.'

'I know. Maybe I should find a horse whisperer?' She turned to look at him and smiled. 'Know any?'

He smiled. 'Around here? No. Maybe you should just keep trying. Persistence is key.'

'Don't I know it?'

'I could pop in most days, if you like. Get him used to me visiting.'

She turned to face him. 'Are you saying that because you want to see Spirit every day, or me?'

'Can it be both?'

Bex laughed. 'I don't have a problem with that.'

'Good. Look. I ought to be getting back. Can I call round this evening? It would be good to see you.'

'Sure. I'll make us dinner.'

'You don't have to go to any trouble.'

'It's no trouble. About seven?'

'I'll be there.'

He took a step towards her and planted a kiss upon her lips. Then, with a growl of reluctance, he made himself walk away and go back to his car.

He felt that his little visit had gone well—and, even better, he had a date to see Bex again, later that evening. It was going better than he'd ever thought possible—whatever it was that they were creating here. He didn't want to hope too much, but was it possible that they could end up back together? That would be a wonderful resolution, and he thought Charlie would have approved.

That was something that had always haunted him after he'd split with Bex. What would Charlie have thought about the way he'd handled everything? And he'd known, deep in his heart, that his son would have been upset.

To get back together with Bex would be the icing on the most perfect cake in the world. It was where he was meant to be. By her side. These last few weeks he'd spent with her had simply reminded him of that fact, and he couldn't believe that he had allowed their relationship to get so bad that he'd felt the only thing he could do was walk away.

But he was confronting that now. His therapist would be proud when he saw her next. He would tell her that he had bared his soul to Bex and that she had forgiven him. It had been gracious of Bex to do that, he knew—especially because he'd caused her so much pain. To give him the opportunity to reveal all, to listen to him… Well, that just showed how gracious she was.

He couldn't screw it up now. They'd got past the

hard part. They'd done it. Now their relationship was all about moving forward. Forging new connections and building on the strong foundations that they'd had before. Ethan couldn't imagine his life without her in it any more.

He got into his vehicle and began the drive back to the surgery. He had another case coming in about half an hour and he wanted to be prepped and ready.

But knowing he had a date with his wife that evening kept the smile on his face all day.

'And do you remember that time when the heel broke on your shoe, when you were bridesmaid for your friend Ellie?'

Bex laughed, remembering. Of course she did! She'd not known what to do! Carry on walking and pretend that everything was fine? Or stop and slip off her shoes and go barefoot? She'd decided on the latter, and had been known as the Barefoot Bridesmaid for months afterwards by all their friends.

'How *is* Ellie? Have you seen her lately?'

'I speak to her on the phone. She and Jack moved away to Bristol when he got a job there. They've got two little ones now. A boy and a girl. Four and two.'

Ethan smiled. 'That's great.'

'In fact, I spoke to Ellie just a few days ago. I told her you were back.'

'What did she say?'

'She asked me what I was going to do. I told her I was going to play it by ear…see how things went.'

'And now?'

Bex smiled and took a sip of her wine. 'And now I can tell her it's going well.'

He seemed pleased by that, and that in turn pleased her.

Their relationship *was* going well. Better than she could ever have imagined. Since he'd opened up to her they'd spent a lot of time together. Dinners. Suppers. Meeting for coffee. Meeting at the rehabilitation centre.

Sleepovers…

These past two weeks it had felt almost as if they were back at the beginning of their relationship. When everything had been exciting and thrilling. Ethan was *dating* her, and she was enjoying being the centre of his attention and knowing that he was working hard to show her just how much she meant to him.

It went both ways. He meant a great deal to her, too. The love she had for him had never truly gone away. It had been an ember for a long time, and now it was being coaxed back into a flame that was beginning to burn bright. It both delighted and terrified her at the same time—simply because everything was going so well, and they were both trying so hard. They were putting in the effort. Giving each other time to be heard. Giving each other time to listen. Giving each other comfort.

It was great right now, and she wanted it to stay that way, but she was worried about what would happen when the rush of all this wore away. Would they take each other for granted? Would old resentments rear their ugly heads? What did their future look like?

She hoped they could move forward and keep their

relationship as it was right now. Fun and exciting and filled with passion and desire.

'I've missed our old friends,' he said now. 'You must give me their details so I can give them a call. It would be good to chat to Jack again.'

Bex nodded. 'I'm sure he'd love to hear from you. Remind me, before you go, to give you his number.' She took another sip of her wine and grimaced. 'What do you think of this? It tastes a bit…odd.'

Ethan took a small sip from the glass she held out to him. 'It tastes fine to me—although as a non-drinker I'm no expert.'

'Hmm…' She put the glass down on the coffee table. 'I'm not convinced.'

'Want me to get you something else?'

She raised an eyebrow. 'Maybe.'

He moved closer, then leaned in and kissed her. 'How about this?'

She laughed.

'Or this?' His lips trailed away from her mouth and found the side of her neck.

Bex closed her eyes in bliss, revelling in the feel of his warm lips, the deliciousness of his tongue as he licked her throat before kissing it again.

'Or perhaps this?' he whispered, undoing the buttons of her blouse and exposing her shoulder, trailing his mouth across her sensitive shoulder and clavicle.

'I'll take it all…' she breathed, leaning back against the cushions and moaning softly as Ethan nibbled, licked and kissed his way around her body.

His fingers were deftly dealing with buttons and her skirt's zip, with bra hooks and lace underwear, and before she knew it she was naked beneath him on the sofa and he was doing things to her body that sent her soaring.

The physical side of their relationship had always been good and time apart had simply made it better. She wasn't sure how. Absence making the heart and the body grow fonder? She didn't consider it too deeply. Didn't worry about it. Right now, all she cared about was the sensations and the feelings and arching her body against his mouth and his tongue.

When he slid himself inside her she gasped with delight and need, clutching him to her as if she never wanted to let him go. She rode the wave, a tsunami of arousal, feeling it build from deep within her core with a fiery heat that burned, feeling him move above her rhythmically, urging him on, needing him to go faster and faster. Harder. Deeper. Until she felt herself explode into a thousand stars, her breath coming in short gasps, her hands grasping him tightly to her, as he climaxed shortly after.

His movements slowed, his breathing became less laboured, matching hers, and she slowly became aware of the other details that she'd missed in her frenzy. The softness of his touch. The warmth of him. The solidity of him. His gentle, adoring kisses. His smile of satisfaction.

She was sated, too. Perfectly happy to stay where she was for evermore. 'Let's never move from here,' she said.

'Never move from this sofa?' Ethan gave a gentle laugh.

'Why not? We could stay entwined for ever.'

He smiled. 'Sounds perfect.'

And he kissed her gently on the lips, rolling off her

and lying behind her, spooning her and pulling the throw over them both.

She felt his arm around her, his body at her back. Felt the exquisite sense of happiness that currently filled her soul. She entwined her fingers with his and held his hand between her breasts and closed her eyes.

Yes. She wished it could be like this for ever.

But she could feel the uncertainty of the future looming over them.

Bex led Spirit out into the main paddock. For him, quarantine was over. He was doing well, there were no signs of any infection or disease, and it was safe for him to be put in the normal stables. But before she could do that she needed to get him used to some of the other animals. So she went to fetch the Shetland pony—Mouse.

Mouse was a good little boy. Short, stocky and incredibly gentle. But more than anything Mouse was incredibly relaxed about humans. He sought them out. Would prefer to stand by the fence being stroked and adored. Bex hoped some of his behaviours, once observed, might help Spirit calm down around other people. It was all part of his rehabilitation.

She also had a very special visit to do this morning. She was taking two of the donkeys she had—Billy and Trigger—to a care home for people with dementia, so they could stroke and pet the animals.

Animal therapy was highly satisfying, and Bex loved these visits. Some of the residents could be quite unresponsive until the donkeys showed up, and then suddenly their faces would come alive, smiles would appear, and everyone benefited. The residents. The donkeys. And the staff who took care of the patients even got to relax and smile, and forget briefly about all the work they had to do that day.

Bex was looking forward to it—she just wished she didn't feel so tired today.

As she led Mouse out to the main paddock to join Spirit, she smiled at the reason she was so tired. She and Ethan had stayed up late! Wrapped in each other's arms, making love in the bedroom, and even in the shower—though that had been awkward. But they had certainly laughed a lot as they struggled for room.

In fact, they'd been having a lot of late nights, lately. And who could blame them? They were rediscovering each other. Having the kind of fun they'd had when they'd first met. It was as if they were dating all over again—and why shouldn't they? They'd created a lovely bubble for themselves, and whilst they were in that bubble everything was sparkles and rainbows.

She'd forgotten how much fun they'd used to have. Forgotten how when Ethan laughed hard his head would go back and his smile would become so broad and his eyes would gleam…

For five years she'd forgotten that Ethan. Her memories had only showed her the Ethan she remembered after losing Charlie. Sullen Ethan. Brooding Ethan. Ethan with dark circles under his eyes. A man unable to be in the same room as her, making her feel that there was something wrong with her. Making the secret guilt she felt over Charlie's death loom larger.

But he wasn't like that! And neither was she!

Bex opened the gate and unclipped the lead rope from Mouse's head harness, then released him into the paddock. On the far side, Spirit lifted his head from munching grass and watched as Mouse ambled towards him.

Bex saw Spirit's nostrils flare briefly, but then curiosity got the better of him and he slowly came over to give Mouse a once-over.

Mouse did what he always did. He stood there patiently as the larger horse sniffed him over, and once Spirit had decided that actually Mouse was all right he went back to eating grass.

'Well done, Mouse. Teach him who to trust.'

She closed the gate and watched them for a while, then headed over to see if Roland had got the donkeys loaded up into the trailer.

Roland gave her the thumbs-up and passed her the keys. 'All ready for you.'

'Great. Can you tell Jenna to keep an eye on Spirit and Mouse before we go? And remind her that the Canton family are coming at ten for their lesson.'

'Will do.'

She got into the four-wheel drive and waited for Roland to return, and then they slowly began the drive towards Blossom House, the care home. Yet again, they had a beautiful summer's day for it. The sun was shining and the sky was a clear blue. It would certainly be a lovely day for sitting out in the garden with the residents.

When they arrived, they got the donkeys offloaded and waited for the staff to bring the residents into the garden. Some were able to walk by themselves, others had frames, or sticks, or leaned on the arm of a staff member.

Once all the residents were sitting down on the outdoor benches and garden seats, Bex and Roland were able to bring the donkeys over.

'This is Trigger,' said Bex, introducing the off-white donkey to a little old lady with a shock of pure white hair.

'What do you think, Marjory? Isn't he lovely?' asked a care assistant, whose name tag said Joe.

Marjory lifted a shaky hand to stroke Trigger's fur, and when her hand connected with the docile donkey a huge smile broke across her face. 'I like to ride the donkeys at Skegness beach,' she said.

'You do?' asked Bex.

'Me and my brother Reggie. I love donkeys.'

Bex smiled at both Marjory and Joe. It was amazing how the donkeys dredged up memories.

'Mum and Dad always pay. A shilling, it costs.' Marjory leaned in to sniff the donkey's fur. 'They all smell the same.'

'They do.' Bex smiled.

'We stopped going after Reggie died.'

Bex's smile faltered and she looked up in question at Joe.

'We think her brother died of a brain injury,' he said.

She looked down at Marjory, who was still smiling, still stroking the donkey. 'I'm so sorry, Marjory.'

'I like to ride the donkeys at Skegness beach,' she repeated.

Bex blinked rapidly, aware that conversations could be repeated often with dementia patients and how they could cycle back quite quickly in their brains. Clearly the donkey had provoked two memories. The joy of riding donkeys at the beach and the sadness of the death of her brother.

Marjory was smiling still. Stroking Trigger's fur.

Bex wondered what it must be like to lose a memory. To have something painful disappear. Would life be easier if she could forget about what had happened to Charlie?

These last weeks with Ethan she had enjoyed their time together so much. But was it because the bliss she felt allowed her to forget the pain of the past, if only for a brief time? Maybe not *forget*. That was the wrong word. But push it away. Shove it into the dark recesses of her mind simply so that she could enjoy the joy she felt in the present.

Was Ethan a sticking plaster?

Was she using what they had to pretend that a wound wasn't there?

Because eventually the bubble would burst. It always did. And reality could be as sharp as a knife.

She'd always feared the awfulness of dementia, but was it perhaps a blessing to someone who had terrible memories of a past filled with tragedy?

No. No, dementia was never a blessing. You lost the good as well as the bad. It wasn't selective. It didn't only melt away the bad times, did it? It took too much of who a person was.

Marjory still knew she'd lost her brother even as she smiled and stroked the donkey, her face serene and blissful.

Bex smiled at the older woman and pulled a carrot from the pouch around her waist. 'Do you want to feed him, Marjory?'

Marjory took the small carrot stick and held it out for Trigger, who munched on it quite happily. The sound of crunching was quite audible in the care home's back garden, amongst the sound of birds and bumblebees.

Bex knew she had to find a way to move on with Ethan, but she wasn't sure of the best way to do it.

'It looks like a case of sweet itch.'

Ethan was examining the skin of her mare Lily, after Bex had noticed Lily almost rubbing herself raw, using a fence post.

Sweet itch was an inflammation of the skin, much like an allergic reaction, and it was caused by the bite of a midge. In particular a female midge. Horses could react to something in the midge's saliva.

'I thought so. She's had it before—just never this bad.'

Bex hated seeing something so painful-looking on one of her animals. She took great care of them, but in the summer there was an abundance of biting insects, and midges couldn't be kept away.

'I can give you an insect repellent to use, but you'll need to keep a close eye on her—make sure she doesn't react to it. Horses who suffer from sweet itch tend to have sensitive skins.'

'She was fine with one before, but I'll keep a look-out.'

'And try and only graze her in dry areas, away from any decomposing vegetation or sources of stagnant water.'

'I will. I've got a rug I can put on her to stop her rubbing, but I'm worried she'll overheat.'

'Try her with the repellent and maybe just use the rug at dawn and dusk, when the midges are most active. She can go without during the day, when the sun's at its hottest.'

She smiled. 'Good idea. Thanks. And thanks for coming out at such short notice.'

'I'd just finished my lunch, so it was no problem.'

Ethan walked with her out of the horse's stall, and waited for her to lock it before staring at her.

She felt nervous. 'What is it?'

He shrugged. 'I've just been thinking. About you and me.'

'Oh? Was it good?'

He laughed. 'Course it was. I was just…' He sighed. 'We've been spending a lot of time together lately, and it's been great. I think it's really good between us… I just wondered if you'd like to…' He swallowed hard. 'If you'd like to leave a few things at my place.'

'How do you mean?'

'Some toiletries. Some clothes. We're practically living with each other as it is, and I thought it would be nice if, after staying the night, we don't have to rush off in the morning to change clothes before work.'

Bex smiled and looked down at the floor. She was afraid of this. Of rushing ahead. Of bursting the bubble. 'I like what we have right now, Ethan. It's perfect.'

'Don't get me wrong—there's nothing I like more than waking up with you in my arms. But you always leave because you need to go and change. I'm just saying it might make sense for you to have a drawer for your things at mine and maybe a toothbrush in the bathroom.' He smiled.

'A drawer?'

'A drawer. Or two drawers. Whatever you need.'

She began walking towards his car. 'I have what I need right now.'

'You *like* dragging yourself out of my bed to race across to Ruddington to shower and change before work? When I have a perfectly workable shower in my home? I'm just trying to make it easier for you.'

'No, Ethan.'

He stopped. 'I don't get why not.'

She turned, exasperated. 'Because what we have is amazing right now!' She glanced around, aware that she had raised her voice and instantly calming herself down so that the centre workers didn't get to learn all the ins and outs of her personal life. 'Why rush it? Why take the risk of destroying something amazing?'

He stared into her eyes, his face serious. 'Because I've already lost five years with you. Five long years. Why on earth would I want to lose any more?'

'It's only been a few weeks for us, Ethan. I'm not sure a few great weeks is enough to build a future upon.'

'It's not just a few weeks, Bex. It's been years for us. We're not new. We're not strangers. We were paused. I don't want to be paused any more. I want to press Play.'

'And I want that, too!' she said.

'Then let's do it!'

'I can't!'

She hated this conversation. Here it was. Reality butting in and ruining everything, just as she'd imagined.

'Why? I don't understand.'

'Because I had you once!' she blurted out, feeling tears burning the backs of her eyes and hating herself for crying. 'I had you. I had a husband, and I had a son, and I was happy. And then I wasn't. There was a stroke, and I lost my child. And then I lost my husband. I don't want to be in the same position of losing anyone again.'

He stepped towards her, took her hands in his. He lifted one, kissed the back of it. 'You won't lose me.'

'I don't know that. You walked away once.'

'And I'm sorry. I've tried to explain why, and you know I've been working on that. But I'm asking you to have faith. Take one tiny step into the future with me. Acknowledge that it's there. Or that it could be there. You don't have to have a drawer if you don't want to. If that's too big a step we can start smaller.'

She looked into his imploring eyes and knew that he was right. If they were to have any kind of future that actually sat in reality and the real world, then she needed to have faith and trust that this time he wouldn't walk away.

'I can probably manage a toothbrush,' she said grudgingly, but with a smile.

He leaned in, kissed her. 'That's all I ask.'

The weekend after Ethan had pushed for more, he found himself out on another date with Bex.

'Now, this is the life!' she said.

He continued to slowly row the boat across the lake as Bex sat back, her fingertips trailing in the water.

They'd come to Highfields Park boating lake and taken out a sun-bleached blue boat. Ethan sat powering the oars, whilst Bex reclined in a beautiful white broderie anglaise dress.

She looked stunning, with her sun-browned skin glowing against the bright whiteness of her dress, her face shaded by a broad brimmed floppy straw hat. He loved seeing her like this—relaxed. At peace. Too many of his memories were of her looking defeated by grief, with an epic sadness in her eyes, so to see her like this was magical, and it made him feel good to think that he'd had a part in it.

'Remember when we came here before the wedding?'

She laughed. 'I do. That swan really didn't like you, did it?'

He smiled at the memory. They'd not hired a boat back then, but had been walking around the lake, feeding peas to the birds, when a huge white swan had come waddling along, ambling through the thick throng of mallards and geese and coming practically right up to them, demanding the green treats. When Ethan hadn't fed him quickly enough, the swan had hissed and flapped its wings at him and Bex had run away, laughing so hard she'd almost bent double.

'It did not. I wonder if it's still here?' He looked around him but couldn't see any swans.

'I'll protect you—don't worry.'

'Like you did last time?'

She smiled at him. 'Absolutely.'

Today was a good day. Bex had driven to his home this morning and on the doorstep presented him with a small gift bag.

'What's this? It's not my birthday.'

She'd come in, kissed him. 'Open it.'

Intrigued, he'd opened up the bag, taken out the tissue paper and then laughed when he'd seen the pink toothbrush at the bottom of the bag.

He'd reached in and pulled it out. 'Thank you.' He'd

leaned in towards her and given her a soft, gentle, but heat-inducing kiss, and for a brief moment he'd thought that maybe they wouldn't make it to the boating lake at all.

His body had responded to his wife's as it always did. With heat and longing and need. And he would have happily stayed in if she hadn't taken the toothbrush out of his hand and trotted up the stairs to place it in his bathroom.

The fact that she had brought the toothbrush showed that she was willing to take a step towards them being together again, and he'd watched her go up those stairs in his home and felt his heart swell with love for her even more. He knew she was nervous. Knew that she was anxious about what their relationship was. And, yes, he had let her down in the past. But there had been a special set of devastating circumstances, and now he knew he'd been in the wrong and he knew better.

He was willing to show her as much as he could that he was here for her and always would be. All he needed from her was a show of trust. A show of faith. And, although the toothbrush was only a simple piece of plastic, a tiny thing, to him it meant so much more. To *them*, it meant so much more. She was saying, *I want to trust you. Show me that I'm right to do so.*

He'd been tempted to follow her up the stairs. Maybe take hold of her hand and lead her into the bedroom. But he'd had the whole day planned for them and it would have been a shame to waste it.

Now they were out on the water, relaxing in the summer sun, with just the sound of the water lapping at the hull of the boat and the creak of the oars. There was the occasional quack of a duck and the soft, gentle murmur of conversation or laughter from people on other boats.

They were having a great time together, and when that was done, he had another plan up his sleeve.

'A picnic?'

Bex was astounded. Ethan had really pulled out all the stops to make today special for her. First the boating lake, then a swim in the open air at the local lido, and now he'd brought her back to his home, into the back garden, and there, laid out in the middle of the grass, was a picnic fit for a queen.

'You always enjoy them.'

'I do. Thank you.' She took his hand in hers and kissed him, before going over to the large, soft blanket and sitting down upon it.

Ethan's back garden was beautiful, lush and green, with a variety of shrubs, mainly pink and blue flowering hydrangea, a red camellia, multitudes of purple and pink fuchsias, and behind them all, standing proud, lupins and hollyhocks and one or two sunflowers, their faces turned up to the sun.

'Did you plant all of these?'

'No! They were already in situ when I rented the property.'

'It's gorgeous.'

'Perfect for a picnic.'

Her ears picked up the sound of running water, and behind them she noticed a water feature that looked like a series of stone mushrooms, with water trickling slowly from one to the other, and opposite it an old-fashioned sundial, grey with age and moss.

Trees like willow and birch towered overhead, and

Bex lay back in the sun, propped up on her elbows. 'I could get used to this.'

He smiled at her, opening the picnic basket. 'Good. I want you to.'

She laughed, removing her floppy sun hat and laying it down on the ground, and running her fingers through her hair. 'The simple pleasures in life are always the best, don't you think?'

'Absolutely. Good food, amazing company, brilliant sunshine and the beauty of a summer's day.'

'You're getting poetic.'

He laughed. 'Being with you makes me appreciate everything all the more.'

She enjoyed the compliment. It reminded her of times before, when Ethan would stare into her eyes and tell her how his life was so much fuller with her in it. How the world had made more sense once he'd met her. How he'd finally felt complete.

Did he still feel that way? She hoped so.

The question was, did she feel the same about him? Their relationship had taken a step forward since they'd become intimate. She slept over at his place a lot now. Her toothbrush had moved in, even if she hadn't, and she often found herself counting down the hours of the day, knowing that they were going to be together again.

Something felt right about being back with him. It was comfortable. Familiar. It was home. And she was incredibly lucky to be given a second chance with him. She could only hope these wondrous summer days would continue. These days of being made to feel special. Of being courted. Wooed.

He was seeing her again. Noticing her. And that meant something after the way they'd parted—because back then, with the grief of losing Charlie, Ethan had stopped seeing her. Had stopped noticing what she needed. Had made her feel she was all alone in the world.

Having him be this attentive to her now was a balm to her soul.

'I've got all your favourites—sandwiches cut into tiny triangles, red grapes, carrot and cucumber sticks, hummus, strawberries, cheese, freshly made cheese straws that I made myself, sausage rolls, mozzarella salad and—oh, olives. But they're for me. I know you don't like them.'

'This is perfect, Ethan! And I'm starving.'

'Tuck in.'

She grabbed a plate and helped herself to a selection of food, loading her plate and munching on fresh strawberries as she did so. She took a couple of his cheese straws, and they were delicious. Flaky, crumbly and wonderfully cheesy. She dipped the carrot sticks into huge dollops of hummus and then, without really thinking, grabbed an olive and ate one of those, too.

'Hey! I thought you didn't like olives?'

'I don't.'

'You just ate one.' He looked at her, smiling, confused.

She shrugged. 'I just felt like trying one. They're okay, actually. Are they different to what I've had before? Can I have another?'

Before he could answer, she popped another one into her mouth and he laughed. 'What's mine, is yours.'

'Excellent.' So she ate another. It was weird, but suddenly she wanted the olives more than she wanted anything else. 'I guess we all change with time.'

'I guess… Have I changed?' he asked, dabbing at his mouth with a napkin.

She tilted her head and looked at him, assessing him. 'You've been working out. Those muscles of yours are quite…' *Hot. Sexy.* 'Impressive.'

'I meant in character. Personality.'

Bex let out a breath as she contemplated him. 'You're who you've always been, but you're…I don't know…more aware now, I think.'

'Aware?'

'Of what you do. Of how you make people feel. Of how you want them to feel. I feel as if I know you better now.'

He laughed. 'Another victory chalked up to therapy.'

'Do you still go?'

'To therapy?' He nodded. 'Once a month.'

'And you get a lot from it?'

'I do. I think it's something I'll always do now. Did you never think of doing it?'

She sighed. 'I saw a grief counsellor after Charlie. Attended a bereavement group for a while. But I didn't stick with it.'

'Why not?'

'Too many sad stories in the world. I had enough sadness of my own. I suppose I just started to learn how to wade through it all by myself.'

'I'm sorry you had to do it alone,' he said, sincere, his voice low.

She smiled. 'I had my parents to talk to—but what happened, happened. We can't change it. Any of it. All we can do now is move forward, and I like where we're going.' She reached out for his hand, squeezed it.

'Me, too.'

'Do you...do you ever think of what the future might be?' she asked, almost scared to hear the answer.

'In general, or...?'

'For us.'

'Oh. I do think about it. Of course I do. I'd like to think that we'll be able to get back what we once had.'

'How do you mean, exactly? Like...living together?'

He met her gaze, smiled. 'I'd like to think so. One day. When we're both ready. It took a lot for you to decide you wanted to move your toothbrush in, so...' He smiled. 'We'll go at whatever pace you need.'

So he wanted them to be back together. He'd said so. Quite clearly. That was both exhilarating and terrifying and... She didn't know what. She felt a mass of emotions right then. It was quite overwhelming. Of course she wanted that, too...but it was scary. She'd lost him once before and she wasn't sure she could go through that again.

Whilst they kept things like this—hot, exciting, passionate—she felt she would always have him. But what if they did move in together and life became horribly normal and filled with everyday nothingness? Both of them slipping into bad habits and not making an effort for one another?

The effort he was putting in right now fed her soul. She yearned for their time together, because she knew she would have his full attention every minute. Knew that he was trying to court her, that he was giving her his best. And in return she was doing the same for him. But if they moved in together and the excitement wore off...

It didn't bear thinking about. She couldn't bear not to be seen by him again. To be taken for granted or ignored. They were both such busy people. He worked full time. She had the centre. Right now they made time for each other. Would they still do that if they moved in together?

He lifted her chin with his finger and leaned over to press his lips to hers. There was something wonderful about kissing in the sunshine, out in the open, surrounded by nature. It was secluded here. Private. No one to see them.

As Ethan deepened the kiss she felt heat roar into life, and she knew without a shadow of a doubt that she wanted him. Wanted to lie back on this blanket and have him make love to her beneath the baking sun. Only they couldn't. There was all the food…the plates. It would get messy—though, that might be fun, too! And then they could wash it all off in the shower…

Bex reached for his belt, began undoing it as their kissing became more frantic. Her hunger for him was primal. She didn't know what had happened to her, but it was as if she was different lately. Acting differently, not thinking things through thoroughly, just reacting to her needs and wants. It was powerful, feeding a drive that she hadn't yet learned to control.

Maybe I don't need to control it? I just need to go with it.

Her quick, searching hands found his flesh and pulled him in close. Maybe she was just trying to absorb as much of him as she possibly could before she had to make a difficult decision…

* * *

Bex and Jenna were in the kit room, assessing the saddles. The room was thick with the scent of leather and horse.

'You want something light to begin with. He's not used to having things on his back, as far as we know.'

Bex nodded. 'Agreed. Maybe I should just start him off with a saddle pad? See how he gets on with that?'

'Sounds good.'

They headed out to the paddock that contained Spirit and Mouse. The two animals stood in the shade on the far side, quietly munching on grass.

Bex moved into the paddock, carrying the saddle pad, and made a couple of clicking noises in her throat that she knew would bring Mouse over with Spirit following. It seemed just lately that they stuck to each other like glue.

She stroked Mouse's face and patted his neck, and then she reached out her hand to Spirit and smiled when he came in close and nudged her gently with his head. She was still the only person who could get close to him, but he was slowly getting used to other people being about. He'd stand and watch Roland or Jenna as they worked in the paddocks with other horses and ponies as if intrigued, and once he had allowed Jenna to get within about ten feet of him before running away, which was a kind of progress.

Bex stood at Spirit's left side and began stroking and touching his back. When he seemed totally relaxed, she brushed him with the saddle pad. As there was no reaction to that, she draped the pad over his back, ever so briefly, before removing it again.

He lifted his head, as if checking to see what she was doing, before returning his attention to the grass. Bex did it again. And again. And on the fourth try, she left the pad upon Spirit's back.

'Good boy! You are a good boy, aren't you?' She

stroked his neck and fed him some apple quarters she had in her treat bag.

She had a good feeling that he would be okay with a full saddle on him, too. Spirit might have been mistreated by his previous owner, but they had clearly put kit on him and he wasn't frightened by it. Even so, she didn't want to rush him.

From the fence, she grabbed a couple of ropes, and began draping them around him, tying them under his chest, his stomach, seeing how he reacted. Apart from a couple of muscle shivers he seemed fine. It would probably be a different story if Jenna tried it with him, but for now she was satisfied that tomorrow she could try putting a saddle on him.

At that moment, up the long drive came a minibus filled with children from a special needs school, who had come to learn about how to look after horses. She'd got the day ready for them, filled with the basics—from mucking out to brushing and bathing the horses, and feeding them—and then, right at the end of the day, they would each get half an hour riding a pony. That would be the highlight for them.

She loved these days very much. But she missed not having Charlie around terribly, and on days like today, when she was surrounded by children and their bright, happy, smiling faces, she missed him even more.

CHAPTER SEVEN

RIPLEY WAS LIMPING.

At first Bex wasn't too sure. But as she led the ponies around the large paddock with their young riders she became more certain.

Using the walkie-talkie that she habitually carried hooked onto her jodhpurs, she called through to Jenna, asking her to bring a replacement horse. It wasn't fair on Ripley to be carrying a rider, no matter how light they were, if she was in some sort of discomfort.

'Right, everyone. You see these red cones? I want you to guide your pony through them, weaving in and out. You can use your pony's reins to steer them, as we showed you earlier. Naomi, do you want to lead the group?'

Naomi, a young redheaded girl with a cheeky face full of freckles, nodded from beneath her large black riding helmet and started her pony, Luna, moving towards the cones. The young riders led their steeds through the cones like a long snake, although some of them were going quite wide and having to turn their ponies quite sharply, because they'd not got the hang of steering yet.

It took a lot for riders to become confident in leading their ponies. To a child, a horse was a big, strong animal, and plenty of kids didn't feel they were confident enough to order such a large animal around. But it would come with practice and time.

Bex smiled in the sunshine, but she was really having to force it today. Something felt off. *She* felt off.

She couldn't pinpoint it but she had a headache, and she wondered if, in this perpetual heat, maybe she was dehydrated? Standing in the middle of a paddock in the full sun, with nothing to protect her except for a layer of factor fifty, probably wasn't the best idea if she was. She needed shade and water.

So when Jenna arrived, with a replacement pony for Ripley, Bex asked her if she would continue the lesson. That way she could take Ripley to her stall, get her settled, examine her hooves and then rest for a little while with a drink.

'Sure, no problem. You all right? You look a little peaky,' Jenna said quietly, so as not to startle their young learners.

'I just need some water. All this heat and sun…'

Jenna nodded in understanding. 'Well, call me if you need anything.'

'Thanks. These guys have got about twenty minutes left of their lesson.'

Bex left the kids in Jenna's capable hands and led Ripley slowly towards her stable. Once there, she removed Ripley's saddle and saddle pad, then gave her water and hay and a quick brush-down, before she went to get some water from the staff room for herself.

Opening the bottle, she knocked back almost half of it, hoping it would help, before going back to look at Ripley and check her hooves. It could be something as simple as a stone, or a shoe that needed replacing. She hoped it wasn't going to be more than that.

But when she lifted Ripley's hoof her stomach turned at the sight of an abscess.

'Oh, hell…' Bex swallowed and allowed Ripley to place her hoof down, immediately feeling as if she might throw up. She straightened and took a few short breaths. The nausea had come so suddenly, and she wondered if she'd drunk the water too quickly?

She grabbed her radio again and asked whoever was on Reception to speak to the veterinary surgery and ask if Ethan could pop in to drain the abscess. She was perfectly capable of doing so herself, but right now, whilst her stomach was still churning, she didn't fancy seeing all that pus.

'I'm sorry, Ripley. How'd you get this, huh?' she asked, stroking the pony's neck.

There were many reasons why hoof abscesses formed. Environmental conditions going from wet to dry, horseshoe nails being placed too close together, poor hoof balance, penetrating wounds, or simply ground bruising—walking on hard, rocky ground, which she supposed was Ripley's problem. The ground was hard between the stables and the paddocks.

They were usually so careful with these animals. They had all arrived as rescue cases at one time or another. They'd all already had hard lives. Bex tried to give them a happy life—feeding them well, training them, trying to rehome those she could, providing exercise, love and comfort for those that stayed.

These horses meant the world to her. She was like their mother. And when they hurt so did she.

* * *

Ethan examined the hoof. 'Definitely a superficial abscess. I'll open it and get it drained. Gravity will help pull out the infection.'

He began his prep, getting gloves, making sure the area he would work on was clean. It was essential during this procedure, as well as after, as you didn't need extra infection getting in.

'You did well to spot it. Was she lame?' he asked.

'Limping slightly,' Bex replied.

He looked at her. 'For someone who spends a lot of time outdoors, you look a little pale. You okay?'

She didn't seem her usual perky self. He hoped it wasn't something he'd done. Last time he'd been with her she'd been smiling and happy, and somewhat out of breath after a very passionate episode of lovemaking.

'Just dehydrated. I'm fine.'

'Are you making sure you drink plenty? In this heat, you need to take care of yourself.'

'I know.'

She answered him a little more sharply than he was expecting, but if she was feeling unwell it was probably causing her to be a bit snappy.

'Maybe you should go home?' he suggested.

'I've got eight horses in a lesson and they will all need their tack taken off. I can't expect Jenna to do it by herself.'

'Get Roland to help.'

'It's his day off.'

'Then someone else.'

'They're all busy. Honestly, it won't take long and then I'll go home, okay?'

He nodded. 'Promise me?'

She smiled. 'I promise.'

And then she rubbed at her belly.

He raised an eyebrow. 'Hungry?'

She shook her head. 'I feel a bit sick.'

'It's this heat. I tell you what—you're my last call for the day. I'll treat this abscess, then you put your feet up in the office and I'll help Jenna get the horses settled. Then I'll take you home, make sure you're all right.'

She sighed and nodded. 'Okay.'

That surprised him. He'd kind of expected her to put up a fight. But he wasn't going to point that out! He was just glad she was letting him help her, and he did want to make sure she got home safely. Maybe he could stay for a while and look after her? They could watch a movie, or something. It would be nice…

Once he'd treated Ripley's abscess he gave Bex some antibiotics for the pony and told her how to take care of the hoof—how to keep it clean and how to monitor it. Then he settled her into her office at the education centre, with a desk fan blowing on her and a bottle of water, and headed out to help Jenna remove the horses' tack.

Jenna thanked him for coming to help. 'Bex was looking a little peaky,' she said.

'And she's not one for admitting she's ill.'

Jenna laughed as she removed a saddle and draped it over the paddock fence. 'Oh, tell me about it! In all the time we've been here, I don't think she's taken a single day off sick.'

'Hmm… Maybe I can persuade her to take a day off tomorrow. Just until she's better and fully rehydrated. Do you know what's on her schedule?'

'I could check. But I can always ask Annalise or Sherie to come in to cover if need be.'

'Would you mind?'

'Course not. Though should we check with Bex first? I'd hate her to think we were taking over and planning stuff without her consent.'

'I'll talk to her and text you later, when I've got her approval.'

Jenna smiled. 'You seem pretty sure of yourself.'

He laughed. 'Oh, I'm sure she'll fight me on it—don't you worry.'

They were getting to the last of the ponies. 'You two seem to be getting on really well now,' said Jenna. 'You look good together, you know?'

'Thanks.'

'Are you guys getting serious?'

He stopped to think and then nodded. 'I really hope so.'

Later, as he drove Bex home, he relayed the conversation he'd had with Jenna. 'It's just one day off. Rest up. Rehydrate. Let someone else run things.'

'No, I—'

'Do you think they can't run the place without you?' He looked at her in question as they stopped at a traffic light on the road back into Ruddington village.

'Of course not. It's just—'

'Let Jenna and the others show you that they can run the centre. It's just one day. You do trust them, right?'

'Of course I do!'

'Then let go. Hand over the reins.'

For a moment it looked as if she was going to be furiously angry. Then he heard her let out a long breath and she smiled at him, shaking her head as if she couldn't believe she was agreeing to this.

'Fine.'

He smiled. Victory! 'Good. I'll text Jenna later, if you give me her number. Or you can text her. Whatever you want to do.'

'I want to go into work tomorrow.'

'Well, you can't. You'll be resting. Doctor's orders.'

'You're not a doctor.'

'Vet's orders, then.'

He reached out to take her hand and squeezed it, glad that she had acceded to his request. Was it a sign that she was willing to show some give and take? Or was it simply that she felt more awful than she was letting on?

'Are you hungry? I thought I'd cook for you when we get in. Then maybe we could watch a movie, and I'll run you a nice cool bath before bed?'

She nodded. 'Sounds good. I think I *am* hungry. But I feel sick, too. So…'

'Food will probably help that. What have you got in? Any pasta? Sauce?'

'Yeah, but I don't fancy that.'

'What do you fancy?'

'I don't know. Something…spicier. With a bit of a tang.'

'Shall we order takeout? Chinese?'

She shook her head. 'Indian.'

'Okay.'

He parked on her driveway and she led him inside, dropping her keys into a dish and heading for the stairs so she could take off her riding boots.

She sat on the bottom step, rolling her toes to bring

them back to life. 'Maybe I should take that bath first?' She lifted up her shirt and sniffed. 'Yes. Most definitely.'

'I'll run it for you.'

'Thanks.'

He headed past her and went into her bathroom. He put the bath plug in and began to run the water, keeping the temperature of it quite cool, but adding bath salts and bubble bath to make the room smell nice. Then he headed back downstairs and found her rummaging in a kitchen cupboard for the takeout menus.

'This place is good,' she said.

He took the menu. 'The Spicy Naan?' He began looking through. 'What do you normally have from there?'

'It's all good. Maybe order a nice chicken curry? Saag aloo? Rice?'

He smiled, glad her nausea wasn't as bad as he'd thought. 'Sounds good.'

She kissed him on the cheek. 'I'll go and have a soak. You order the food. It'll be half an hour, anyway.'

He ordered the food and washed his hands and face in the kitchen. Then he noticed a few breakfast dishes on the side, so he rinsed those, too, and placed them in the dishwasher. Then he sat on the sofa, fighting the temptation to go up there and talk to her whilst she was in the bath.

There was nothing he wanted more than to see her in those bubbles, naked. But he knew if he did he'd want to join her, and she wasn't feeling well. So he ought to be respectful of that and let her have her bath in peace. Maybe later, if she was feeling better, they could have some gentle fun?

He thought of his conversation with Jenna. The way she'd asked him if he and Bex were getting serious. He'd answered plainly. Had Jenna asked Bex the same question? Would Jenna tell Bex what he'd said? He didn't mind. He didn't care who knew how serious he was about Bex. He cared about her a great deal, and his wasn't a love that had ever gone away.

It had always upset him to see her feeling unwell. She was such a force of nature, so full of life, to see her running even at eighty percent, rather than her full hundred, was disconcerting. He'd advise her to stay away from the wine tonight. Just water for her. Or tea. Or coffee. Fluids and rest…

After about twenty minutes he heard the water draining from the bath, and soon after, just as the doorbell rang with the delivery of their food, Bex padded downstairs in a silk bathrobe tied at the waist, her shapely legs on display.

He felt his body react. Was she wearing anything under that robe? It didn't look as if she was. Then he realised he was staring.

'Are you going to answer the door?' she asked with a smile.

Ethan cleared his throat. 'Yeah.'

He waited for her to disappear into the lounge and then he answered the door, paid the delivery guy and took their food through to the kitchen.

'Do you want a bit of everything?' he asked.

'Yes, please.'

He grabbed a couple of plates and served up the food, then headed into the lounge, where Bex was sitting on one of the sofas. He put a plate in front of her on the low coffee table and handed her a knife and fork.

'Thanks. I'm starving now.'

'Feeling better?'

'Mmm…' She nodded, taking a large forkful of chicken madras, widening her eyes and nodding at how good the food was.

'I'm glad. You had me worried. Make sure you drink plenty of water with this,' he told her.

'You like looking after me, don't you?'

'Of course I do.'

'I wish you were as easy a patient.' She chuckled and had a forkful of potato and spinach.

He pretended to be affronted. 'I'm a model patient.'

'A model man flu sufferer.' She smiled.

'True.' He laughed.

She had him bang to rights. He hated getting colds. He tended to get bad sinus problems, and they would make him feel miserable. And there was nothing he liked better than to lie in bed feeling sorry for himself until it passed. Every time he'd been ill Bex had dutifully cared for him, picking up the snotty tissues that he'd tried to throw into the bin, basketball-style, and failed miserably. Had she ever complained? No.

'Do you feel tired?' he asked. 'Want to watch a movie? Or do you fancy an early night?'

'A movie sounds good. But then I would like to just sleep. I feel I need to catch up.'

He nodded. He'd been feeling the effects of their many late nights himself. And, as much as he loved to make love to Bex, there was something to be said about getting a good full eight hours.

The other night they'd spent so long enjoying each other's bodies they'd only gone to sleep around three, and then they'd both been up again at six a.m. Food.

Water. Sex. All things the body thrived on. But so was sleep. They'd had plenty of the other things. He was willing to make the ultimate sacrifice.

'Want me to go home tonight?' he asked.

She looked at him sharply. 'No. No, I don't. I want you here with me. We can spoon.'

He smiled, glad she wanted him to stay. 'Sounds perfect. I guess there's only one last thing to ask you…'

She frowned. 'What's that?'

'What movie do you fancy?'

They had a look through her streaming services and chose a romantic comedy she'd never heard of, with no actors she recognised. She wasn't expecting much of it, but it was surprisingly funny and, at the end, quite emotional.

From nowhere, she found tears welling up, and after she'd sniffed three times in a row Ethan passed her a tissue from the box behind her sofa.

'Thanks.' She laughed, embarrassed.

'You okay?'

'I'm fine! It's just… She didn't think he loved her. She thought he'd left her…'

She'd realised the film was hitting a nerve, and so when he'd pulled her in close, wrapping his arms around her, she'd allowed him to comfort her. Sinking into his embrace, enjoying the feeling of being loved, of being safe and secure and seen. Heard.

'I'm sorry!' She hiccupped a laugh. 'All that water you made me drink—and now I'm crying it all out again.'

'Don't be sorry.'

Bex sniffed and dabbed at her nose with the tissue.

On screen, the hero had tracked the heroine down on the beach as she'd stood contemplating the waves and had called her name. She'd turned, seen him, and Bex had almost felt the heroine's heart open up with joy.

Why the hell was she crying over this? She didn't normally cry at movies. The only time she'd ever been emotional like this before had been just after Charlie was born, when her body had been run amok with hormones and she'd cried at adverts on the television!

'I feel so silly.'

'For having empathy? Don't. I think it's adorable.'

On screen, the hero had taken the heroine's hands in his and he was telling her how he couldn't live without her, that he loved her, and Bex felt another wave of tears threaten. They were going to get their happy-ever-after. She had known that feeling.

And lost it.

She knew she would never be able to fully explain to Ethan how that had felt. Not only to lose the love of your life, but also to lose the child you had so longed for. After all that trying, all the IVF, the drugs, the injections, the scans.

They'd both worked so hard to not let the scientific method of conception take away from the glory of being told that she was pregnant with Charlie. Tried to love every moment of her pregnancy, including the nausea, the heartburn and the stretchmarks, and then the delivery itself. Eleven hours in labour. One hour of pushing. Charlie being blue and floppy when he was born, because he'd had the cord around his neck, and the panic as they rushed him over to the Resuscitaire. Then that cry. That fabulous cry as his lungs had opened up and he'd grown pink and vital and alive.

They had swaddled him. Taken endless photos. Got him into a night-time routine, standing over his crib and watching him sleep, his podgy little body relaxed in repose.

Bex wondered if this fictional hero and heroine would have to face such a journey? Or would their lives be wonderful and perfect?

She'd often wondered why hers hadn't been.

As the credits rolled up the screen she realised she was shattered. 'I ought to go to bed, but I'm not sure I've got the energy.'

Ethan smiled at her and scooped her up in his strong arms, and she laughed out loud as he carried her up the stairs and towards her bedroom. He really did like to take care of her, and she was thrilled that he was being so attentive.

He pushed her bedroom door open with his foot and walked her over to her bed, gently laying her down upon the coverlet. 'Your Majesty…' He kissed her on the lips. 'What do you need?'

'A glass of water in case I get thirsty?'

'Coming right up.'

He disappeared back downstairs, and whilst he was away she slipped on a pyjama set of grey tee shirt and daisy-patterned shorts and then went to use the bathroom and clean her teeth.

Ethan rapped his knuckles on the bathroom door. 'I've left it at the side of your bed.'

'Thanks!' she called, through a mouthful of toothpaste.

Once done, she headed back to bed, smiling at Ethan as he lay on his side, waiting for her, his chest bare and no doubt the rest of him, too.

She clambered into bed and, as promised, he spooned her body with his and she relaxed into him, feeling right at home, safe and secure. Loved. Happy.

Was she going to be lucky enough to get some of her happy-ever-after back?

She hoped so and closed her eyes, falling asleep, almost immediately.

When she woke up the next morning, she lay in bed feeling weird. Ethan was fast asleep at her side, and they were both a few minutes away from their alarms going off.

Her stomach felt…odd. Still. She couldn't put her finger on it, but when she propped herself up on her elbow to take a drink of water she was hit by a sickening wave of nausea. Had there been something wrong with that curry?

'Holy-moly…'

She gulped hard and breathed out slowly, trying to control the sick feeling that was washing over her. This dehydration was more serious than she'd thought. Very gradually she sat up, swinging her legs out of bed, still breathing in, two, three…out, two, three…

Behind her, the alarm went off, and she heard Ethan slap the button on the top of the clock and yawn.

'Morning,' he said.

'Hey.' She didn't turn to face him. She felt that if she moved she might throw up. She just needed to breathe right now. Concentrate on that.

The mattress rocked as Ethan got out of bed. She heard him pull on his shorts and a tee shirt and then he was walking past her towards the bathroom, rubbing the sleep from his eyes. When he glanced at her, he saw something was wrong and was instantly at her side.

'What is it? What's wrong?'

'I don't feel very well. I think I might be coming down with something.'

'You're still not feeling any better?' He laid the back of his hand against her forehead. 'You don't feel like you have a fever. What are your symptoms?'

'I'm still nauseated, and I feel shattered, though I've slept really well, and I've got a bit of a headache. I think I might need to see someone. Check my bloods, or something.'

He nodded. 'Want me to call the doctors for you?'

'They don't open for another hour.'

'Okay. Well, you get back into bed and stay there. I'll bring you some coffee—'

The thought of coffee almost did her in, right there and then. She made a noise in her throat and shook her head, grimacing.

'Tea?'

'Maybe… I don't know.' She could feel tears welling. She couldn't help it. She hated feeling this way, and for some reason she felt scared.

Ethan took her hands in his, kissed them. 'Hey, I've got you. We'll get this sorted. The doctor will see you and he'll prescribe something to get your electrolytes balanced again.'

'You think that's what this is? My electrolytes?' She looked up at him hopefully.

'Well, unless you're pregnant!' he joked, then stopped smiling when she didn't smile back.

Now was not the time for his jokes. And she met his gaze with a fierceness she'd not felt in herself for some time. 'Please don't. You know I can't be.'

'I'm sorry. It's just that you said you felt sick...and it's the morning...and you've been off a bit lately...'

She looked at him fearfully. She *couldn't* be pregnant. Could she? She'd needed IVF to get pregnant before. They'd not managed it naturally. And, yes, they might have had unprotected sex, but when they'd first got married they'd had unprotected sex for years and nothing had ever happened!

'Unexplained infertility,' the doctor at the hospital had said.

Her symptoms might sound like pregnancy, but she couldn't be pregnant! No. She refused to believe it.

'I don't get pregnant, Ethan. Doctors have to help me. With needles and petri dishes or whatever they are. No. This has to be something else. Maybe it was that curry? Or just the high temperatures lately?'

He nodded. 'Okay. I'll go and get you a drink, and maybe some dry toast. See if you can eat that.'

'I don't want toast. But I think there are some ginger biscuits in the pantry. Maybe one or two of those?'

'All right. I won't be a moment.'

She watched him go, her hand clutching her stomach, desperately hoping that the nausea would pass.

He had four surgeries lined up today—an arthroscopy on a racehorse, an operation to improve a soft palate, a tooth extraction and a standing surgery to remove a keratoma—a hard tumour on the inside of the hoof.

He needed to be focused—and he would be—but he couldn't help but worry about Bex.

She'd really looked quite frightened when he'd left, but she'd texted him since to say she had a doctor's appointment at eleven that morning and would call him when she got out.

He hoped it was nothing. People got sick. But then again when Charlie had passed out playing football in the garden, they'd panicked but assumed it would be something simple. Something that children got but that neither of them had ever heard of. And in the end, it had been. Neither of them had known that children of his age could suffer strokes but, as the doctor had said, babies could suffer strokes in utero…

Babies.

Could she be pregnant?

Her symptoms suggested it as a possibility, but there were many things that could make a woman feel sick. She might just have a bug, the curry last night might have upset her stomach, even though she'd been feeling off before that…

He was leaping ahead here, trying to get his head around what else might be happening.

The chances of her being pregnant were extremely slim, but what would it mean for them if she were? Could he go through that again? They would feel fear every second of every day. But if he was prepared for it, then he would cope with it and be there for her, show her that this time he would never leave her side.

That was why he'd hated leaving her alone at her home.

'But you have to go to work,' she'd said, pushing him away.

'I don't. I can go with you to the doctors.'

'How many surgeries do you have today?'

'Four.'

'Four horses that need you, Ethan. Four worried

owners who are fretting about everything going well today. You can't let them down.'

'I don't want to let *you* down.'

'You're not. Now, go.'

As he'd left, she'd been making her way to the bathroom to freshen up. Wash and brush her teeth. Maybe she'd felt better after that?

I could be worrying about nothing...

She could have heatstroke, or still be dehydrated, or—

Suddenly he hit the horn on his steering wheel as some idiot overtook him on the country lane and then cut back in quite sharply, causing him to brake. He finally made it to the surgery, thankfully in one piece, and checked his phone before going inside. He sent Bex a text.

How are you feeling?

He waited for a response, worrying at his bottom lip until he saw the three dots indicating that she was sending him a reply.

Same. But the biscuits stayed down!

He smiled. Good. That was a good thing.

He put his phone in his pocket, grabbed his bag and headed into work. He had to focus on his patients now. Bex would let him know after eleven. There was nothing he could do until then.

The waiting room was stifling, despite the fact that they had the windows open. The sun streamed in through the large panes of glass, and although she'd initially managed to take a seat in the shade, the sunlight soon found her as the sun made its way across the sky and the doctors ran late.

When she was eventually called in, a full forty-five minutes after her appointment time, Bex shook hands with Dr Campbell, a locum, and nervously sat down.

'How can I help you today?' she asked.

Bex let out a heavy sigh. She always got nervous when she saw doctors. It had been this way since Charlie died. It was almost as if they triggered some form of PTSD in her. Making her remember trying to get an answer from them, hoping for good news. She didn't like to bother doctors unless she absolutely had to.

'I've been feeling a bit off just lately. I think I might be really dehydrated. I've had headaches, tiredness… I've felt sick. And this morning I really felt like I was going to throw up. I work outside all day—I work with horses—so it's probably that.' She smiled.

Dr Campbell smiled back at her. 'And how long would you say you've been feeling different?'

She shrugged. 'I don't know… It's got worse these last few days.'

'And you've been drinking and eating all right?'

'Yes. Though not this morning. I couldn't manage breakfast. Or coffee. I had tea and some biscuits. Ginger biscuits. Hoping they'd settle my stomach.'

'Did they?'

'A little. But after an hour or so it all came back up. Eating little and often seems to help, but I never know if I feel sick or whether I feel hungry.'

Dr Campbell glanced at her records. 'And is there any chance you could be pregnant?'

She laughed. 'No.'

'You seem very sure. You've not had any unprotected sex? Had any condoms break?'

Bex opened her mouth to answer, but nerves got the better of her. How did she explain her situation? 'I can't get pregnant. I had to have IVF to have my son.'

The doctor scrolled through her records and clicked on a document, reading it for a few moments. 'Unexplained infertility. Okay… So you've not been having any intercourse?'

Bex paused. 'Well, yes… But, like I said, I can't get pregnant, so…'

'I think we ought to test you anyway. I can take a blood sample. That's the most accurate way. And we'll also check you over in general…see if you're lacking in any vitamins.'

'Oh, okay…'

As the doctor got together the materials for a blood test, she continued to ask Bex questions. 'Any breast tenderness?'

'Erm…' *Now that she mentioned it...* 'A little.'

'And when was your last period?'

'I don't have regular periods. I have three, maybe four a year.'

'And when was your last one?'

'In the spring. April, maybe? May? I wasn't really paying attention.'

Dr Campbell leaned forward to tie a tourniquet around her arm, swabbed it with an alcohol wipe and then came at her with the needle. 'Sharp scratch.'

Bex looked away. The doctor had got her thinking. Could she really be pregnant? Was it a possibility?

'Do you think I might be…?'

'Pregnant? I don't see why not. Unexplained infertility is difficult for people to get their heads around, but at the very basis of it is the fact that there is no biological reason we can find as to why a woman isn't getting pregnant. There isn't anything wrong with you…you don't have a hostile uterus…your husband's sperm has got a lot of swimmers…you ovulate—even though it's rare—and you have no fibroids or polycystic ovaries. Everything looks great. Sometimes, after they've had a pregnancy, couples who struggled before find they can get pregnant on their own.'

She withdrew the needle and began labelling the samples.

'Don't worry about it. Wait for the results. This could just be a vitamin deficiency. We don't know yet. Whatever it is, we'll take it one step at a time. Now, I suggest you go home, relax, drink plenty of water and eat whatever your stomach will tolerate.'

'When will I get the results?'

'We'll call you tomorrow.'

CHAPTER EIGHT

THE NEXT DAY Ethan wanted to take her mind off the wait. He wanted to take his own mind off it, too.

Bex had called him after her appointment, to say that the doctor had drawn blood and told her that her being pregnant was a possibility.

The idea of becoming a father again… Terrifying.

How would he know what was safe? How could he protect his child? He'd thought Charlie was safe. He'd thought Charlie was fine. There had been no signs or symptoms to suggest that he would have a neurological event at the age of two. No reason to believe their child wouldn't live as other children did.

When Charlie had died and he and Bex had split apart, he'd never imagined having another child. He'd grieved and gone to Abu Dhabi, throwing himself into his career so that he didn't have time to think about relationships or the future, or what that future might look like. Looking after the racehorses owned by the Prince had been intense. He'd almost literally worked himself into the ground, as if in punishment for failing to protect his son. For letting him down. For walking away from the love of his life, knowing he had failed her, too.

Prince Abdullah had noticed. Thanked him for his dedication but told him he needed to talk to someone.

So he had.

He'd never assumed for one moment that Bex would take him back. He'd never thought they would get close, and he'd certainly never believed he would find himself in this position again.

'I could go and get one of those tests from the chemists?' he offered now. 'You know…seeing as you're in the bathroom anyway…you could pee on a stick, right?'

He heard the toilet flush and then the taps running as she washed her hands before coming out, still pale despite the bronzing of her skin caused by her days in the sun.

'I guess… But I think the blood test will be the most accurate. Don't those sticks sometimes give false negatives? Or false positives? I'm not sure I want to be tortured by that. Let's just wait to hear from the doctor.'

'Okay.'

He passed her a flannel that he'd rinsed in cold water, so she could wipe her face with it. It was another hot day. Scorching, in fact. And the weatherman that morning had suggested temperatures would get up into the mid to high thirties.

'Do we know when she might call?'

'No.'

'Okay. Well, we can't sit here waiting. We'll go mad. Let's go out.'

'I don't feel like being sociable. I do need to go to the centre, though. I haven't been in for nearly two days.'

'They can cope without you.'

'Well, I'm not sure I can cope without it.'

'Then let me drive you. It's my day off. That way,

I can keep an eye on you and make sure you don't do too much.'

'Fine.'

She got into the car, wearing some pink shorts and a white tee shirt, and he was glad that she hadn't put on her jodhpurs. Jodhpurs meant she was in work mode. Wearing those cute little shorts told him that she didn't plan on doing anything she shouldn't.

Once they arrived at the centre they saw Jenna in the front paddock, leading a group of four children through their paces, getting them to canter. Jenna gave them a brief wave, and he and Bex headed into the education centre and down the corridor towards Bex's office.

She sat behind her desk, then turned in her swivel chair to open the window and let in the soft, warm breeze before she picked up her post and began to go through it.

'What can I do to be helpful?'

'See if Roland needs a hand? Check on the horses?'

He nodded. 'Okay. But promise me you won't leave this room.'

'I won't.' She smiled.

'Unless you hear from the doctor.'

'Go!'

She managed a laugh and he went, a smile upon his own face, glad to have something to do.

He wasn't in the quarantine stable, but she heard male voices coming from the main stable block and saw Roland shovelling wood shavings into a wheelbarrow.

'Rollo? You seen Ethan?' she asked, her stomach churning.

'He's in with Misty. Just told me he thinks she might have an infected bite.'

She looked down the stable towards Misty's stall and let out a long breath. She had to go and tell him. Had to go and rock his world the way her own had been rocked.

When the doctor had called she'd felt as if time had stopped. Just briefly. Her heartbeat had slowed, she'd heard the thump of her pulse in her ears, and then the words she'd never thought she'd hear again.

And now? Now Ethan had to know.

This wasn't something either of them could hide from.

For a brief moment she studied him as he examined the bay mare…this man she had chosen to create a life with. A *second* life with. A life that might not make it. A life that might be doomed, like Charlie's. Or Elodie's.

How can I do this?

Adrenaline was coursing through her system, making her feel shaky, but now all her symptoms made sense.

'Ethan?'

He glanced at her. 'Come and look at this bite. I think it's—'

'I'm pregnant, Ethan.'

He stopped. Turned. Met her gaze. 'What?'

She shook her head. Shrugged. 'I'm pregnant.'

She could feel herself begin to shake. She had admitted it. Out loud.

His mouth dropped open and he stared at her. 'You're sure?'

'The doctor just called.'

His gaze dropped to her belly and her hands came to rest upon it almost without her thinking.

She realised she was waiting. Waiting for him to react. Waiting for him to say something that would make sense of all this—that would somehow make it much easier to deal with. But he seemed just as shocked as she did. Would he run? Would he abandon her again, the way he had before when life got tough?

'I thought that was impossible...'

'I know,' she said. 'So did I.'

'So, what do we do now?' he asked.

'Dr Campbell's organising a scan, because I don't know for sure when I last ovulated. And she's told me she's sent a prescription to my local pharmacist so that I can start taking folic acid.'

He nodded. 'A baby?' He came over to her and laid his hand on her belly.

'What are we going to do?' she asked, almost imploring. She was hoping he'd take control, tell her everything would be all right. Tell her that he would be there for her, no matter what.

Now it was his turn to shrug. 'I don't know. I never expected this.'

It wasn't the answer she'd hoped for.

Ethan leaned upon the paddock fence in the sunshine, his gaze drifting past the horses in the field, watching Bex as she told Jenna their news.

Jenna clapped her hands to her mouth, then beamed, before throwing her arms around Bex and hugging her tight.

He smiled. It was good she had such a good friend in Jenna. And of course Jenna would be happy for them.

He and Bex would have to tell their parents, too. How would they react? Would they be just as happy? Or would they be as terrified as he was?

Of course a new baby was wonderful news. He was

over the moon—he really was. But overriding all that joy and happiness was fear. Fear that they would lose this baby, too.

Everyone worried about the first trimester, and later about Sudden Infant Death Syndrome, but the dangers never went away once you got past the first year of life. Death stalked everyone, no matter their age, and they knew that more than most.

How could he protect Bex from being hurt like that again? How could he protect their child? There was absolutely nothing he could do! Nothing! He was powerless.

The only thing he could do was make sure she didn't take any unnecessary risks. He'd make sure she took the folic acid and ate well, and it would probably be a good idea if she didn't ride any horses whilst she was pregnant. Maybe she should even stay out of their paddocks and stalls, in case one kicked or became startled for some reason. Horses could do that. It was because they were a prey animal—they were always on the alert.

He and Bex had been too relaxed before…maybe this time, if they really focused on preventing any danger…

Bex wouldn't be happy about it, but if they were going to be sensible and take all reasonable precautions then surely she would agree to it? It wouldn't be for ever. Just for a few months…until the baby was born.

His heart thudded in his chest at the idea of holding a baby in his arms again. Watching Bex give birth, holding that precious bundle, experiencing that moment when you soaked in every detail about the baby. What it looked like. Who it resembled the most.

Whether it had any hair. A cute little button nose and plump cheeks…startlingly blue eyes. Then that first bath. The first nappy-change. Taking the baby home…

He and Bex were going to get a second chance. This wasn't just about just the two of them any more. This was about stepping forward into the future. He needed to let her know that he was committed and that he wanted to be there for her.

He wasn't playing any more. This was serious. He was going to become a father again and this time he wasn't going to screw up.

And this time he had nothing to hide.

Her doctor had suggested Bex keep a packet of biscuits by the side of her bed, so that when she woke in the morning, before she moved, she could try and eat a biscuit or two to help with the morning sickness.

And it was working.

Now that she knew what the sickness was caused by it seemed easier to deal with. She wasn't dying, she wasn't dehydrated, and she wasn't sick with some strange disease. She was *pregnant*. Carrying her second child.

Today, as she lay there, chomping on a ginger biscuit, Ethan turned over and laid his hand across her. 'Morning.'

'Hi.' She brushed some crumbs off the duvet.

'Did you get a good night's sleep?'

'I slept like a log. Now I'm eating this, so that I can make it to the bathroom to get washed and ready for work without feeling like I'm going to lose my dinner from last night.'

It was hard to eat a biscuit first thing, but she'd been told it might help, so…

He smiled and kissed her, propping himself up on his elbow. 'What have you got on your calendar for today?'

'I thought I'd try and start putting a saddle on Spirit. He did well with the saddle pad, and I think he's ready for the next step.'

She wanted to move forward again now. Now she knew she wasn't sick she could return to work, return to what she loved best, and she hadn't seen Spirit for days. She didn't want his progress to backtrack, so it was important he got worked on every day.

'You're not going to do it yourself, are you?'

She turned to face him, surprised by his sharp tone. 'Why not?'

'Because he's unpredictable and you're pregnant. What if he kicks you? Or reacts badly?'

She couldn't imagine him doing that. 'He's never reacted that way before. He's fine with me. You know that. You've seen me work with him.'

Ethan sat up. 'Well, now's the perfect time for him to get used to someone else dealing with him. You said it yourself—he needs to be socialised with other people.'

'But I don't think anyone else will get near him with the saddle.'

'So leave him for a bit. Get him used to others before someone else puts the saddle on him.'

She reached for his hand, squeezed it, happy that he was trying to protect her. 'It'll be fine.'

'What if it's not?' he retorted.

Bex frowned, unsure of his tone, but before she could say anything else Ethan threw off the bedcovers and got up, dressing himself and walking out of the bedroom. She heard him trot downstairs and then the distant noise of kitchen cupboards being opened and closed.

Spirit would be fine with her. She knew it. People who worked with animals had a sixth sense for them—those who had the training and the qualifications and the experience. Years and years of it. She'd always been around horses and, yes, there were a few unpredictable ones—but you always knew about those. Right from the beginning.

Spirit had given her no reason to believe that he would be bad with her and yet Ethan wanted her to send someone else in with the saddle? She couldn't risk anyone else getting hurt. It took time for a horse to build a bond with someone after such a tragic start as Spirit's. And that horse had bonded with *her*. He trusted *her*. She knew it. It would be fine if she went in.

But she understood his reticence. She was pregnant now. This wasn't just about her any more. They'd lost one child—of course he'd be worried about losing this one.

She was, too. Of course she was! A second chance like this… She didn't want to put it at risk.

But he more than anyone else in the world had to understand that they couldn't live their lives in fear because of it. It would drag them down. Terrify them. Make them flinch at every little thing. She knew she couldn't live that way.

This baby was a little miracle, and she wanted to celebrate it and enjoy it. And that meant living her life the way she always had. She wouldn't take any stupid risks, and he'd have to trust her enough to realise that.

Bex put on her robe and hurried downstairs. The smell of percolating coffee wafted up to meet her nostrils and turned her stomach.

She stood in the kitchen doorway, watching him. 'I can't live in a bubble, Ethan.'

He sighed and nodded. Then came to her and wrapped his arms around her, pulling her into a hug. 'I know. I'm sorry. It's just…'

'I know. You're scared. I am, too. But we've got to try and be normal. Carry on as if we're first-time parents. Full of excitement and happiness, not fear.'

'But we're not first-time parents. We've already lost our son. I nearly lost you, and now I have you back, and there's this baby, and…'

Bex saw tears in his eyes and her heart ached for him and what he must be feeling right now. She hugged him tight and then pressed her lips to his in a gentle kiss. Once, twice. Three times. She gazed into his eyes, trying not to cry, too. Trying to tell him that she heard him. That she knew.

'We're going to be all right, you know?'

'All three of us?'

'All three.' She smiled. 'And this baby, whoever it is, is going to grow big and strong and hear all about its big, brave, elder brother, Charlie.'

Ethan stared at her. 'I love you.'

Her heart almost stopped. This was the first time either of them had said it since being back together. It thrilled her. Made her ache for him.

She knew she couldn't hold back any more from telling him the same thing. 'I love you, too.'

* * *

She'd picked out the perfect saddle for Spirit, and Roland had offered to carry it for her to his stall in the stable block.

He and Jenna had been so great since hearing their news. Bringing her snacks, fetching her drinks, telling her to go and put her feet up and lifting bales of hay for her, doing whatever they could to help make her life extra easy.

She felt incredibly lucky to have such good people to work with.

Spirit had nuzzled at her when she'd called his name, and seemed genuinely happy to see her. He must have been wondering where she was. She opened up his stall door and stroked his long nose and tickled behind his ears, where she knew he liked it, taking a few minutes to get reacquainted with him.

Roland left them to it, knowing that this was something she would have to do alone. But she noticed he hovered by the stable doors, just in case, hosing down the floor with a power jet.

'Hey, boy. Want to try a saddle today?'

She placed the saddle pad on him first, and as before he did nothing, seeming quite content and happy. It was always an honour and a privilege for an animal such as this to place its trust in her. It created such a strong bond, and she knew deep in her heart that the saddle would be fine, too.

And it was.

Spirit barely reacted. He stamped his feet a little, to get used to the extra weight, but then stilled and returned to munch on his hay. She fastened the straps beneath him, making sure they fitted perfectly—not too tight, not too loose—and then she made a big fuss of him and took his reins.

She began to lead him out of the stall towards the small side paddock, where there was a three-step mounting block. She felt totally relaxed, leading him out into the sunshine, and she walked him in circles for a little while, before positioning him by the block.

She would not try to mount him completely. All she was going to do was climb the steps and lay her weight on the saddle, resting her stomach and chest on him to see how he would react.

Bex felt absolutely sure that he would be fine and so would she. Her feet would not leave the block—she just needed to see how he would react if he felt as if someone was trying to ride him.

Her nausea pushed to one side, she climbed the steps, still holding his reins. She watched his body language carefully, then gently and slowly rested her weight upon the saddle for just a brief second.

He didn't react. Just stood there. Calmly.

So she did it again. And again. Each time leaving her weight on him for longer and longer periods.

And he trusted her and let her do it.

Clearly Spirit had been ridden before. Before he got abandoned.

He was doing well. Very well. Much better than she'd hoped. She was sorely tempted to throw her leg over and mount him properly. Just sit on him.

But her instincts told her not to push it.

He'd done enough for today.

She'd try that tomorrow.

* * *

Every time the phone rang Ethan panicked, rifling through his pockets to reach it before it rang out, just in case. When he saw Bex's name, his panic would escalate. Ever since finding out she was pregnant, he saw danger everywhere, and now, when her name popped up on the screen he thought it was going to be her, or someone who worked with her, ringing to tell him something awful had happened.

'Hello?'

'He did it! He was fine!'

His palpable relief allowed him to relax back in his seat.

'Great. Who?'

'Spirit! He let me put the saddle on him and he took my weight without reacting at all! Do you know what this means?'

'I'm afraid you're going to tell me.'

'That he's ready to be ridden.'

He closed his eyes. 'Please tell me you aren't going to ride that horse.'

There was a pause. 'Why not? Didn't you hear me say he was fine?'

'Bex...please. You're pregnant. I don't want you getting on that horse and riding him. In fact, if I'm completely honest, I'm not happy about you getting on *any* horse and riding. But most especially him!'

'Ethan. I know what I'm doing. You have to trust me.'

'I do trust you. It's the horse I'm not sure of.'

'You don't know him like I do.'

'It doesn't matter. I don't want you on that horse. In fact...I forbid it.'

He didn't mean to be angry. He didn't mean to forbid anything. But it just came out. And once it was said, the words and the tone hung in the air like a dark, thunderous cloud.

'You *forbid* it?' she asked in disbelief. 'Who put you in charge? This is *my* centre, and these are *my* horses, and I will care for them and look after them the way I choose!'

'I'm not telling you otherwise. I'm just not sure you're thinking this through properly. I don't want you putting yourself and the baby at risk.'

'You think I'm stupid enough to do that?'

'No, of course not!'

'That's not what you've just implied. I need you to trust me, Ethan. *Do* you trust me?'

And then he made the greatest mistake in his life, when he paused and let the pause hang there.

'I see.'

'Bex, please—listen to me...'

'No! You don't get to tell me what to do!'

And the call was ended.

Ethan stared at the phone and dialled her number, but she didn't answer. And he couldn't go racing over there, because he was all the way past Keyworth and he had a surgery to do.

He hated the fact that they'd argued. Hated the fact that she'd hung up on him. He could only hope and pray that she would see the sense in his words and keep herself and the baby safe.

When he got home late—the surgery had overrun after there'd been complications—his house was empty. Bex wasn't there. She hadn't come over, so must have gone to hers instead.

Was she so mad at him that she didn't want to see him?

He didn't even bother to take the time to change. He drove to her place, parked outside. But when he tried to open her front door and walk in, as he had plenty of times in the last few weeks, he found the door locked.

He knocked, and then bent down to open the letterbox and call her name. 'Bex?'

She appeared in the hall, arms folded. 'Go away, Ethan!'

'We need to talk, and I'd rather not do it through a letterbox.'

'I have nothing to say to you.'

'Would you please let me explain?'

'No. You made it quite clear that you don't trust me, or my judgements. I know you blame me for Charlie. You never said it, but I know that you do. You think I should have got him to the hospital quicker. Should have realised he wasn't well sooner. You blame *me*! And now you don't trust me with this baby either.'

He couldn't believe what he was hearing. 'No! That's not true!'

Where was she getting this from? Did she really have feelings of guilt?

'Do you think I wasn't scared out of my life?' she went on. 'Do you think I didn't know what was happening? I *knew*! I knew I was losing him! Do you think I want to take that risk all over again?'

'Bex, please…'

'Go away! I don't want to see you.'

She stormed up the stairs and he heard her bedroom door slam.

Ethan stood there for a moment, his forehead resting against the front door, in absolute despair. Maybe it would be best if he left her alone? He didn't want her getting so upset that it somehow affected the baby. She needed to calm down and so did he.

Because the truth of it all was that he had to admit that he *did* think she was being reckless in her determination to ride that horse. And he'd been trying to be polite about it for so long, his fear and anger had spilled right over, and he wasn't sure he could mop any of that up now. She knew that. Had felt his worry. But she had seen it as an order, a demand, an indication that he didn't trust her instincts as a mother.

Had he ruined everything?

Ethan walked back to his car, giving her bedroom window one last look, hoping that if she was watching him she would see the sorrow on his face.

He would give her space and time. Something he didn't want to do, having vowed never to walk away from her ever again, but he knew that this time she needed it. Time and space to process everything.

Maybe it would mean she would stay away from Spirit. At least for a few more days. And then he could talk to her. Put things right.

If she let him.

He sank into his seat, feeling as if the wonderful world they'd begun to rebuild had never been on firm ground at all. It had been built on ground riven with cracks and chasms that had been temporarily filled in with loose, weak soil.

And then there'd been an earthquake.

CHAPTER NINE

SHE KNEW THAT everyone around her at the centre realised something wasn't right. She saw it in the looks that Jenna and Roland passed between them, and in the way they kept coming into the office to tentatively ask if everything was all right? Did she need anything? A cup of tea? Something to eat? For Jenna to take her lesson?

She refused them all. Just because she was pregnant, it did not mean that she was incapable! She knew what she was doing, and she didn't need anyone else trying to do the things she was meant to do.

And now, as her last lesson of the day finished, and the kids from Cherrywood School were being loaded back onto their bus, her thoughts turned to what had happened between her and Ethan.

She knew he was only trying to protect her. Of course she did. But he had to learn to trust her. Trust was important in a relationship, and that didn't just apply to fidelity. It applied to the fact that she needed Ethan to understand that she knew how to keep herself and the baby safe. That she knew not to take risks and, more importantly, as someone who had worked with horses her entire life, that she knew which ones she could trust and which ones she couldn't.

And she trusted Spirit. She couldn't explain how she knew that he would be fine with her. It was a gut feeling. It was his body language when he was with her. It was the bond that the two of them had built ever since she'd first seen him in that ramshackle old shed.

Just as their baby was growing within her, Spirit also needed to grow—and that meant helping him, schooling him to be ready for life at the centre and maybe at some for ever home, if she chose to find him one. And, like a child, he needed to be worked on every day. Bit by bit. His education was growing. His confidence was building.

Now he needed to have someone ride him. That was his next step, and she felt absolutely sure that she had to be the one to do it. He wasn't comfortable with anyone else just yet—though he was getting used to Roland or Jenna being in his stall without trying to bite them now, which was a step forward.

Subconsciously, her steps had brought her to him in the paddock. She'd put the saddle on him at lunchtime, just so he could spend an hour or two with it on him whilst she took her class in the next paddock. So he could see her working with other horses, with completely strange riders that he didn't know. To see it was safe. That he was in good hands.

Spirit instantly came to her. Their connection was stronger than any she'd had with past horses. Something inside her told her that maybe she would really struggle to say goodbye to this handsome boy. That maybe his for ever home was with her. And as she walked to the gate he trailed her, shadowing her, as if waiting for her to come in so he could nuzzle her properly.

He whinnied as she came in, and nudged her with his head waiting for her to stroke him. Bex smiled as she kissed his long nose and told him how handsome he was, and then she checked his straps and the position of the stirrups, playing with everything, touching him on his belly, his flank.

He trusted her totally.

And she him.

And she would prove it.

'We'll be fine, you and me, huh?'

Determined to prove to herself that her instincts were right, she led Spirit over to the mounting block and positioned him just so, before climbing the steps. As before, she laid her weight on him, talking soothingly to him, letting him know that everything was all right.

When he didn't react, she started swinging her leg over him, one foot still on the block, then back again. Each time she did it Spirit stood there patiently, and even turned to look at her, as if to say, *Well, are you getting on, or not?*

'Okay, okay. I'm getting on.'

She knew Ethan would be angry if he knew—but he wasn't here, and he'd never find out. But secretly she would know, and would be able to smile with satisfaction that *she was right* because she knew that she would be. And as she settled onto Spirit's back properly, for the first time ever, he just stood there and waited for her command.

Joy surged through her. She'd *known*! She'd known he would be okay! And although she knew she ought to get straight off, leave it at that for the day, her success made her nudge him forward slightly with her heels.

He began to walk.

It felt good to be on a horse. She actually hadn't ridden for a while—she was often too busy running a therapy class, or attending vet appointments, or in her office passing paperwork from one file to another and keeping up to date with her taxes on the computer. She'd never realised how much paperwork could be generated from one business, but it was a lot.

She'd always told herself, *Make sure you get on a horse every week.* Only she hadn't lately, because she'd spent all her free time with Ethan.

She wished he could see her now. So she could prove to him that her instincts were true. She briefly considered getting out her phone and making a short video to show him where she was, but decided against it, knowing that she had to focus on this first ride.

'We'll just go to the bottom of the paddock and back again, okay?' she told Spirit. 'A nice, slow walk.'

It felt wonderful to be back on a horse again. She'd missed it. In the warmth of the summer sun and the cool breeze even the rocking motion of the horse as it walked didn't have the capacity to make her feel sick. In fact, did she feel *better*? She seemed to…

Bex had her eyes closed, enjoying the heavenly feeling of her nausea lessening, the sensation of riding again, even at a walk, and the heat of the sun upon her arms. So when the first deer broke through the undergrowth and startled Spirit, sending him rearing up in fright, she screamed and fell to the ground with a thud, the back of her helmet connecting with the hard-packed earth beneath her, stunning her and making her see stars.

Bex stared blearily up at the blue sky, breathing heavily, and vaguely heard Spirit snorting some way to her left. She turned to look at him, to make sure he was okay, and watched as he came back to her and nudged her with his nose. Then she began to feel light-headed, her vision glazing, before she passed out.

Ethan was used to bad traffic. Living in the countryside, you got used to a certain amount of time being stuck behind slow-moving traffic—like tractors, for instance. They didn't bother him. He would just trundle along behind them until he got the opportunity to be free of them.

But now, knowing he had to get to the St George's Hospital in Nottingham as fast as he possibly could, whilst still sticking to legal limits and not putting himself at risk, he seemed to get stuck behind every awful driver there was. Every slow driver. Every person who didn't know which lane they wanted to be in or which turning they needed. They'd slow down and indicate to go left, perhaps, and then they'd get to that junction, see the road name, realise it wasn't the turning they needed and then start driving again. *Really slowly.* Looking for the next turn-off. Holding him up. Making him catch *every single red traffic light* there was.

He hit his horn once or twice, out of frustration. Swore. Threw his hands up in frustration. But he finally reached the main road and could get nearer to his destination.

The call, when it came, had been from Jenna.

'There's been an accident. Bex got thrown off a horse and has been taken to hospital.'

He'd literally frozen. Weirdly, he'd expected this. It was as if he'd just been waiting for something bad to happen. Because that was what happened to Ethan when he got happy. Life threw a spanner in the works. Made him hear that Bex was hurt after riding a horse, when he'd told her not to.

'How is she?'

'I don't know. She was unconscious when I got to her. I called an ambulance straight away.'

He'd tried to imagine it. And now, as he saw the Queen's Medical Centre in the distance as he came racing over Clifton Bridge, he felt himself take his foot off the accelerator.

He'd rushed to this hospital once before.

For Charlie.

Was he strong enough to go into the same A&E again? Face those same doctors? Hear the same empty reassurances?

He suddenly felt helpless. No matter what he did, it wouldn't matter anyway. He couldn't help her. He couldn't help his unborn child. The power was out of his hands and he could lose them. Lose them both!

When he began to hyperventilate, he knew he had to pull over, so he took the exit near the old cinema and parked up, trying to catch some air. He got out of his vehicle and paced, sucking in great lungsful of air, trying to calm himself.

When he had control, he got back into his car and drove the rest of the way.

Typically, there was nowhere to park at the hospital. He spent a good twenty minutes driving round and round, looking for a parking space, and eventually managed to get one when a couple came out, the woman with her arm in a sling. They pointed to their car and told him they were leaving. Did he want their space? they asked.

Yes, please!

Once the car was parked, he ran. Ran as fast as his legs would carry him to the A&E department. His eyes scanned the waiting room, looking for Reception, and then he dashed over to join the queue. He stood there impatiently as the receptionist did her job and took down the details of each new arrival, and then it was his turn.

'Bex Clarke. Brought in by ambulance. I need to see her.'

He hoped this wasn't the moment when the receptionist checked Bex's name against the list of inpatients and gave him *that look*. The one that could mean he was too late.

The receptionist scanned her screen, tapping at her keyboard. 'She's in Majors. Head down that corridor there and turn right.'

'Thank you.'

He rushed past the waiting room, filled with people with assorted injuries, and saw Jenna pacing outside a curtained cubicle. She saw him and waved.

'Thank God you're here! I thought you weren't coming!'

'I got held up. How is she?'

'The doctor's in with her now.'

'Which horse was it?'

But he knew what the answer was going to be, and

he felt rage swell inside him briefly, before a full-on wave of fear flooded his soul.

'Spirit. But it wasn't his fault, Ethan!'

Was Jenna trying to plead the horse's case?

'Of course it was! I told her not to ride him, I told her—'

'Spirit was fine. He let her ride him without flinching. He was…well, *golden.* I saw them from the centre. I was watching them. It went perfectly. More perfectly than we could have hoped to expect.'

'Then what's she doing lying here in A&E?'

He didn't mean to raise his voice. Didn't mean to shout at Jenna.

'He got spooked. A herd of deer broke through the undergrowth and leapt across the paddock fence and he reared up. No one could have predicted that. It was an accident and not Spirit's fault.'

His legs went weak then.

It must have showed on his face.

'Here, there's a chair.' Jenna guided him to a seat and he sat down upon it gratefully, feeling his legs wobble beneath him.

'Is she all right? Is the baby?'

'I don't know.'

'What injuries did you see? Did she hurt her back or her spine?'

'I just know she was unconscious.'

'And you called an ambulance?'

She nodded. 'I travelled here with her.'

'What did the paramedics say?'

'I…'

He looked at her. 'Jenna? What aren't you telling me?'

'There was a pelvic bleed…'

A pelvic bleed? Was she losing the baby?

Ethan got up and began to pace once again. 'I can't do this! I can't do this again!'

'You can. She needs you!'

'Does she? She didn't listen to a word I said. I told her not to get on the horse and she did, and now she could be losing the baby? I can't lose another child! No!'

He stared at Jenna and then began to walk towards the exit.

'Where are you going?' Jenna shouted after him.

But he couldn't answer.

He had no words.

All he knew was that he wasn't ready to be torn apart once again.

Bex was lying in the bed, wiping the tears from her eyes, when Jenna came in.

'Don't you go scaring us all like that!' Jenna said, coming forward and giving Bex a hug. 'How are you? How are you feeling? What did the doctors say?'

'I'm okay. I'm okay…' Bex looked past her. 'Where's Ethan?'

Jenna looked awkward. 'He…er…he left.'

'Why?'

'I don't know. He was here. He was angry. Shouted a bit, and then he left.'

Fresh tears welled up in Bex's eyes. He'd left her. Abandoned her like before.

Her bottom lip wobbled and trembled before she burst into more tears.

This is my fault!

Ethan had begged her not to get on Spirit and she

had ignored him and done so anyway! Why had she taken that risk? Just to prove that she was right? How stupid was that? Was it more important for her to be right than it was for her to be happy?

And now look. Ethan had left.

What had she expected? She had pushed him away. Told him to leave the last time they'd spoken.

No wonder he couldn't trust her. All these mistakes she kept making.

Again and again and again.

The guilt with which he was so familiar came flooding back. Being here, back in this place where they'd lost Charlie… It all felt so terribly familiar. A mad dash to the hospital—but this time for his wife and his unborn baby.

He'd never felt so scared in his entire life.

This was what he'd been so afraid of when he'd asked her not to ride that horse.

She'd told him he needed to trust her. Had accused him of not doing so.

And maybe she'd been right. Jenna had said it had all been fine with Spirit. What had happened with the deer had been an unforeseen accident. Not the horse's fault. Not Bex's fault. She'd judged Spirit perfectly, according to Jenna.

He couldn't protect her from all unforeseen accidents. That was the problem. But it was fear, through and through.

He couldn't protect her from a driver coming out of a junction without looking properly. He couldn't protect her from someone knocking her over on the street. He couldn't protect her from illness or injury.

From the flu, or a dodgy curry, or a loose paving slab, or a domestic accident in the home.

Everywhere in this world there were dangers, and he couldn't wrap her up in cotton wool, which was what he had tried to do.

If he tried to confine Bex, what would that do to her? What would that do to anyone? That wasn't living. You couldn't live your life in fear, afraid to go out. Afraid to do anything.

Bex loved horses. She had made them her life. And if Charlie had lived they'd be his life, too. And this new baby… No doubt they'd put her or him on a horse as soon as they could. How could they not?

If you were alive you had to live. To experience this world. Yes, it could be scary, and it could be dangerous, but it could also be wonderful, and beautiful, and only by getting out there and living did you get to see that world.

Today there had been a terrible accident. And they might have lost a second child.

He thought of the hours he'd spent in therapy, talking about what loss had done to him, and he remembered the therapist's words. *'You've come through the worst anyone can go through and you've survived.'*

Maybe they were all stronger than they realised? Stronger *together.*

How must Bex be feeling right now?

He couldn't abandon her! He'd risk anything to be with her. His life without her had been empty.

They'd been given a second chance and now she was lying in a hospital bed, terrified and alone, and no doubt upset right now…

Ethan headed back into A&E and snagged the attention of a doctor.

'Bex Clarke. How is she?'

'Are you a relative?'

'I'm her husband.'

'Ethan?'

He heard her call his name and he pushed past the doctor and saw her lying there on a bed, a little pale, but none the worse for wear.

Jenna sat on a chair beside her, and now she looked up at him and smiled. 'I'll give you some privacy.'

'Bex!' He went to her and threw his arms around her, holding her tight, then pulling back to look at her. 'Are you okay? Do you hurt?'

'I'm fine. Bit of a headache.'

The doctor stepped to the other side of the bed. 'Hi. I'm Dr Malik and I've been looking after your wife since she was brought in.'

'Ethan Clarke.' He shook the man's hand.

'She's doing very well. A little bit of concussion, so she might have a headache for a while, but the pelvic bleeding has stopped, and the ultrasound has confirmed baby is viable and happy. Heart beating as expected.'

Ethan looked at Bex and let out a sigh of relief. They weren't going to lose it. 'Thank God. And you guys… Thank you. You have no idea how much!'

'We'd like to keep her in for another couple of hours, just to monitor her, but I don't see any reason why she can't go home later on this evening, as long as she sticks to bedrest for a while.'

'Thank you. Thank you so much.'

Dr Malik nodded and left them alone.

He turned to her, took her hand in his. 'You scared me.'

She clasped his hand in hers. 'I know. I'm sorry. I guess you're going to tell me you were right?'

He shook his head, surprising her. 'No. *You* were right. I have to trust you. Trust your instincts. You know Spirit well enough.'

'But he threw me off.'

'Because of the deer. Not because he wasn't ready for you to ride him. You know him. I don't. And you asked me to trust you and I didn't. So, I'm sorry. And I'm sorry for forbidding you to ride him. I can't wrap you in cotton wool. I know that.'

She smiled and laid her head against him. 'Thank you. You must have been so scared coming here again…'

He nodded. 'And you.'

'The last time I was in an ambulance, I wasn't the one on the bed.'

'I love you, Bex. I love you both so much already… I only said what I did because I was terrified of losing you. Out of fear that history would repeat itself somehow.'

'I know.' She kissed the back of his hand and pressed her face to it. 'But we're fine and I love you.'

'You do? I thought you hated me because I'd acted like an oaf.'

She smiled. 'You did, didn't you?' Then she laughed. 'But I forgive you. Of course I do. You think you're the only one who was scared?'

'I need to say something, though.'

'What?'

'I trust you. Implicitly. And I've never blamed you for what happened to Charlie. I could never blame you.

I blame myself for not being there to protect you. To protect him.'

'You couldn't have protected him from that. No one could.'

Ethan clambered onto the bed beside her and wrapped his arm around her shoulder, so that she could rest her head upon his chest. 'Do you think we're going to be okay?'

She sighed and nodded. 'I do.'

'Do you think you're ever going to let me forget that I told you that you were right?'

She laughed. 'No. In fact, I might ask you to put it in writing. Frame it and put it on the wall. *"Ethan said I was right."*'

He kissed the top of her head and she turned to look at him. 'I love you, Ethan. Don't ever stop trying to protect us.'

He met her lips with his. 'I won't.'

EPILOGUE

'BOOTS?'

'Check!'

'Helmet?'

'Check!'

'Pony?'

Daniel chuckled. 'You're silly, Daddy.'

Ethan smiled at Bex, meeting her gaze and knowing how important this moment was for her.

They'd both waited so long to get Daniel out for his first proper ride. They'd wanted him to be old enough to be aware of it, even though technically this wasn't his first time on a horse.

As a baby, he'd had pictures taken of him with Bex holding him in place on a saddle on the back of Mouse, the Shetland pony. But he was four now. Old enough to understand that he had to be safe, and that there were rules, and how he must respect the animal.

He scooped Daniel up and helped him into the saddle. Bex adjusted the stirrups to fit his feet.

'What's his name, Mummy?' Daniel asked.

'This is Benson.'

Daniel leaned forward and whispered, 'Hello, Benson.' He giggled as his mum passed him the reins, showing him how to hold them.

'Now, remember…no kicks. Just gentle pressure, as if you're squeezing him with your feet. That will make him go forward.'

'Okay.'

'And when you want him to stop you pull back on these, all right? Now, I'm going to lead him for you, so you don't have to worry about making him change direction.'

'Giddy up, horsey!'

Bex helped lead Benson and Daniel around the paddock, with the fat little pony taking nice, tiny steps, so she didn't have to worry about Daniel losing his balance.

'Son? You're a natural!'

Ethan took some pictures with his phone, checking each one and smiling, his pride in his son shining bright in his face, his heart and his soul.

Daniel had brought so much into their lives, shining light into the dark corners. He often spoke about his big brother, Charlie, asking his mum and dad about him and if Charlie would have liked dinosaurs, like him, or if Charlie would have enjoyed peanut butter sandwiches—all the important things to a four-year-old.

And Ethan knew that Charlie would have loved being a big brother to Daniel. He saw so many similarities between the two boys. The way Daniel chuckled at something he found funny. The way he slept in his bed. And Daniel had taken a shine to Charlie's grey teddy bear, and now it had become his favourite toy, too.

His life had come full circle.

Their lives.

He turned to Jenna and asked her if she'd take a photo of all of them together.

'Sure will.'

He gave her his phone and rushed over to stand on the other side of Benson. He and Bex held hands across the saddle, with their other hands behind Daniel's back.

'Say silly sausage!' said Jenna.

Daniel chuckled again, and both he and Bex turned to each other to laugh.

Jenna took the picture.

Afterwards, it sat on the mantelpiece, under Charlie's picture.

The whole family together at last.

Exactly as they should be.

* * * * *

MILLS & BOON

Coming next month

THE VET'S UNEXPECTED FAMILY
Alison Roberts

Finn's smile faded. He was standing very close to Hazel and she was still smiling at him. Without thinking he reached up and touched her cheek with the back of his forefinger.

'It's a good thing that Michael is long gone,' he said. 'The guy was a complete jerk.'

There was something in Hazel's gaze that he'd never seen before despite it looking like something that could have been there forever. Something… lost? It made him want to take her into his arms and hug her. Instead, he just held her gaze.

'Don't let anyone think you're not beautiful just the way you are,' he added softly. 'Because it's not true.'

It felt like time had stopped. Or maybe Hazel had just frozen, shocked by what he was saying. She didn't believe him, did she? But what else could he say that might convince her?

Maybe he didn't need to say anything. The idea of showing her was a lightbulb moment, like tempting her to stay here by offering a place for Ben to recuperate. Only this flash of inspiration wasn't purely intellectual. It was more of a physical thing.

Because… because Hazel really was beautiful and… and he really did want to kiss her.

Just gently. Good grief, he wasn't trying to seduce her or anything. He just wanted her to know that he meant what he'd said. And that she deserved something a hell of lot better than someone who didn't think she was perfect just the way she was.

And… maybe it was his imagination but it looked as though Hazel wanted him to kiss her. She certainly wasn't ducking for cover as his mouth drifted slowly closer to her own. And then his lips brushed hers and it was Finn who felt like he needed to duck for cover because there was a strange sensation that came with that barely-there kiss. A tingle that felt like static electricity or something. A strangeness that was disturbing, anyway.

So Finn backed away fast. He put on his most charming smile, as if that kiss was nothing out of the ordinary for two friends and turned away to pick up the tray on the table.

'Call me,' he said. 'If you need any help in the night. With Beanie or Ben.'

JOIN US ON SOCIAL MEDIA!

Stay up to date with our latest releases, author news and gossip, special offers and discounts, and all the behind-the-scenes action from Mills & Boon...

millsandboon

millsandboonuk

millsandboon

It might just be true love...